What the critics are saying...

ಸಿ

Knights of the Ruby Order:

Torn

"Silent for the first few chapters, Torn's sexuality is at its highest level and will cause many hearts to flutter." ~ *Romance Reviews Today*

"If you want a story filled with danger, excitement and passion, KNIGHTS OF THE RUBY ORDER - TORN is the story for you." ~ *The Road to Romance*

"In KNIGHTS OF THE RUBY ORDER: TORN, Kate Hill creates a world that is brutal and colorful, weaving a story of honor and hope, deceit and triumph." ~ *The Romance Studio*

Crag

"If you're in the mood for an erotic read that is sure to tug at your heartstrings, then the second installment of Kate Hill's latest series...is a must read!" ~ *Romance Reviews Today*

"CRAG is an emotionally gripping and fascinating tale." ~ *Sensual Romance Reviews*

Kate Hill

Torn and Crag

KNIGHTS OF THE Ruby Order

ELLORA'S CAVE
ROMANTICA PUBLISHING

Paperback Trade Inn
145 East Fourteen Mile Rd
Clawson, MI 48017
(248) 307-0226

An Ellora's Cave Romantica Publication

www.ellorascave.com

Knights of the Ruby Order: Torn & Crag

ISBN #1419954148
ALL RIGHTS RESERVED.
Knights of the Ruby Order: Torn Copyright © 2003 Kate Hill
Knights of the Ruby Order: Crag Copyright © 2003 Kate Hill
Cover art by Syneca

Trade paperback Publication May 2006

Excerpt from Knights of the Ruby Order: Lock Copyright © 2004 Kate Hill

Ellora's Cavemen: Dreams of the Oasis I Copyright © 2006

With the exception of quotes used in reviews, this book may not be reproduced or used in whole or in part by any means existing without written permission from the publisher, Ellora's Cave Publishing, Inc.® 1056 Home Avenue, Akron OH 44310-3502.

This book is a work of fiction and any resemblance to persons, living or dead, or places, events or locales is purely coincidental. The characters are productions of the authors' imagination and used fictitiously.

Warning:

The following material contains graphic sexual content meant for mature readers. This story has been rated E–rotic by a minimum of three independent reviewers.

Ellora's Cave Publishing offers three levels of Romantica™ reading entertainment: S (S-ensuous), E (E-rotic), and X (X-treme).

S-*ensuous* love scenes are explicit and leave nothing to the imagination.

E-*rotic* love scenes are explicit, leave nothing to the imagination, and are high in volume per the overall word count. In addition, some E-rated titles might contain fantasy material that some readers find objectionable, such as bondage, submission, same sex encounters, forced seductions, and so forth. E-rated titles are the most graphic titles we carry; it is common, for instance, for an author to use words such as "fucking", "cock", "pussy", and such within their work of literature.

X-*treme* titles differ from E-rated titles only in plot premise and storyline execution. Unlike E-rated titles, stories designated with the letter X tend to contain controversial subject matter not for the faint of heart.

Also by Kate Hill

The Blood Doctor
By Honor Bound (*Anthology*)
Captive Stallion
Darkness Therein
Deep Red
Dream Stallion
Forever Midnight (*Anthology*)
God of the Grim
Highland Stallion
The Holiday Stalking
Immaculate
In Black
Infernal
Knights of the Ruby Order 3: Lock
Knights of the Ruby Order 4: Mica
Midnight Desires
Moonlust Privateer
Vampires at Heart (*Anthology*)

Contents

Torn

~11~

Crag

~149~

Knights of the Ruby Order:
Torn

☙

Chapter One

☙

Honey Wine hated him.

Not that she particularly liked any of the creatures she cared for. She was just a keeper in a zoo of wild, looming beasts, forced by her own master to stitch their wounds, set their broken bones and watch the weak ones die in misery. Liking any of them would be too painful, akin to befriending a pig or a chicken, all the while knowing they were only meant for slaughter.

She felt little or nothing for most of them, but she hated *him* from the first.

He didn't look like the others. His hair, a mass of dark waves, hung just below his ears. No ragged, filthy beard marred his smooth face, only bruises and fresh blood covered his oval chin and high cheekbones. Shrewd eyes, the same blue-gray color as a northern ocean, stared at her from beneath dark, heavy brows. His nose was straight, well shaped. *Most likely he won't have that long, once he goes to the Entertainment*, Honey Wine thought as she washed her hands in a basin of water. As if reading her mind, he smiled slightly, the almost imperceptible motion causing a fresh trickle of blood to moisten the dried, sanguine crust on his lower lip and chin. Rather than helpless, his smile appeared arrogant.

Like all the new ones, he'd been stripped naked, his wrists and ankles shackled together, making long strides impossible. She knew by the length of his lean, muscled legs that such a restriction must annoy him, and she nearly smiled at the thought. He hadn't even spoken to her, but she despised the lack of fear in his eyes. She loathed his cool expression and the haughty carriage he managed even when bound like a naked monkey between four guards prodding him with the handles of their leather whips. They dragged so hard on his iron manacles that blood stained his hands and feet.

"Get in there, beast." Bron, the head guard, scowled, shoving the prisoner into the small holding cell. The captive's large, long-fingered hands braced flat against the wall to keep his face from sustaining further damage.

Bron glanced at Honey Wine through his gridded metal helmet and said, "The Mistress wants this one examined so we can prepare him for the Entertainment."

She grasped her wooden box of supplies and moved toward the cell. "Step back, you bunch of stinking dogs. I need space."

Bron's eyes bulged with fury, and his hand tightened on the whip, but he knew better than to challenge Honey Wine. She was not merely a slave healer, but had been one of the guards. The Mistress was also her sister, though the spiteful monarch had banished Honey Wine to this hellish prison.

"Don't give me that mangy look." Honey Wine curled her lip at him. "I used to be your superior, remember?"

Bron cursed under his breath and turned away with his men, except for one.

Timus, the youngest of the guards, a burly man Honey Wine had known since childhood, leaned close to her and whispered, "Be careful of that one. It took eight guards to bring him down, and six of them are still being tended by healers as we speak."

She nodded, and Timus unlocked the cell to let her inside. The prisoner turned and watched her curiously. She avoided his penetrating eyes as she looked over his body. He was tall but too thin for her taste. Though his neck was strong and his shoulders broad, every bone and muscle stood out on his sinewy body, like a fanatical monk who never ate quite enough. Perhaps he was. *No, he has the power and grace of a predator, and the guards would never have chosen a man who could provide little entertainment. Also,*

Timus had just said the beast had given eight armed guards trouble.

She stepped closer, feeling the heat of the chase emanate from his body. His skin gleamed with sweat and rivulets of blood from a number of shallow wounds streaking his chest, arms and legs. His cock dangled thick yet flaccid. She swallowed her disgust.

"Sit," she stated.

He stared at her, the strong ridge of his brow shadowing his blue-gray eyes, making him look almost primitive. She repressed a shudder.

"Animals. Where do the guards find such animals?" she muttered, then raised her voice. "Timus, what language does he speak?"

Timus glanced over his shoulder. "He wouldn't speak to us at all. I'm not sure if he can."

She sighed with frustration and pointed to the worn wooden bench in the corner of the cell. Again an amused smile crept onto the prisoner's mouth. What did the fool find so damn funny? She placed her supply box beside him and opened it. As she searched for the proper tools, she asked him in five languages if he understood her. He continued watching her with interest but didn't speak.

"Have you got a tongue?" She grasped his jaw and squeezed, knowing she must have caused him discomfort since his lips were torn.

He jerked away.

Sighing with frustration, she reached for his face again, but this time he opened his mouth slightly. His teeth were large and shockingly white, except where bloody saliva stained them. She suddenly realized he didn't reek as so many of the others did, nor were there any lice in his hair or on his flesh. She thought she detected an herbal scent from his skin, but in the smoky prison, it was difficult to discern any smell except that of fire, blood and sweat.

Whoever he was, he knew how to care for himself, and yes, he did have a tongue. Perhaps he was from a good family. Perhaps he was missed. *I doubt it. Not with his haughty ways.* It didn't occur to her that she didn't know enough about him to form such an opinion. It was just a smash of conflicting personalities, Honey Wine, and the prisoner.

She cleaned his wounds none too gently and applied salve. Several faded scars marked his chest and back. So, as she'd guessed, he was no stranger to work or war. She gripped his chin in her hand and scrubbed blood from his face and lips with a piece of wet cloth while he stared tauntingly into her eyes. Quickly finishing her work, she tossed him brown leather trousers, the uniform of all beasts. As he dressed, his gaze never left her. It was as if he knew how much his look disturbed her.

For the rest of the day, Honey Wine carried out her work in the vast prison beneath her sister's palace. Once, she'd been a guard above. She'd worn a black uniform trimmed in gold. She'd carried a curved sword with a royal jewel set in its handle. Though she was only a half-sister to The Mistress, she was treated with respect and trained in the elite Royal Guard.

Then she'd spoken out against her sister's Entertainment. The cruelty and unfairness of it sickened her, so like a fool, she publicly rebelled. Stripped of her power, she was forced to serve in the zoo below. *If you feel so much for the beasts, then you should tend them.* Those had been her sister's words, that was her sentence. Honey Wine should have kept her silence. The Entertainment continued, and she was deprived of her birthright.

As she worked, she avoided the new beast's cell. The few times she glanced toward it, she noticed him pacing like a caged tiger. His long legs crossed the cell in two strides, yet his face appeared calm. There was none of the fear, panic or hatred seen in the others when they arrived.

Later, two beasts were brought from the training ground with gashes that needed stitching. The guards complained about this. The creatures weren't supposed to do serious damage to each other during training or else their blood would be wasted for the official Entertainment.

When Honey Wine finished repairing them, she drew water from the well in the center of the dirt-packed floor and washed blood from her hands and arms before slipping out for the night. With her duties finished, she was allowed outside to do as she pleased before returning to her quarters across the corridor from the holding chambers.

She stood behind the high, spiked walls of the courtyard and sighed as she looked up at the pale three-quarter moon. It felt good to breathe fresh air and look at a world not muted by smoke and shadowed by death.

Dropping her hooded cloak at her feet, she walked to the center of the courtyard and sank into a round, stone-rimmed pool. The water ran fresh through a fountain, and she let it spray her face while fat, colorful fish fluttered by her ankles.

Refreshed, she retired to her chamber to sleep until dawn when the day would begin, the same as yesterday.

* * * * *

Honey Wine stepped into the prison, shocked to find it empty of guards as well as beasts. An unsettled feeling crept into her stomach as she backed toward the door.

She bumped into what felt like a warm, hard wall and jumped, raising her fists to a defensive position. He stood naked in front of her, all long, sinewy limbs, muscled torso and rock hard cock. He gazed down at her with blue-gray eyes, his face shadowed with a night's growth of beard. His lips slid into an arrogant grin, revealing his white teeth as he reached for her.

Honey Wine punched him, but he dodged the blow and dragged her into his arms. What was wrong with her? She knew how to fight better than that! However she could scarcely remember how to defend herself, and her limbs felt leaden. Though she tried to struggle, she felt unable to move. Suddenly she realized she didn't want to. He held her gently, his big hands caressing her back down to her buttocks.

The prisoner bent, his mouth touching hers. It felt soft, and he tasted good—like herbs. He smelled of warm skin, clean sweat and masculinity.

He never spoke, but she heard his voice in her mind. It was husky and sensual, as deep as the most primitive desires of manhood. It spoke of savage lust and made her heartbeat quicken almost as much as his hand that had slipped between them, lifted her skirt, and fondled her pussy and clit.

Honey Wine felt one of his long fingers deep inside her, rubbing, circling and gathering moisture that he used to stroke her swollen clit until she shattered in a climax of pure liquid desire. She felt her legs sinking, but he caught her and pressed her against the wall. Bending his knees, he entered her with a long, slow stroke that had her moaning before his steely cock was buried to the hilt in her quivering slit. She clutched his shoulders, fingers biting into muscle as he began thrusting.

The sensations were so powerful that Honey Wine couldn't keep from moaning as another orgasm built. She heard his ragged breath mingling with hers, felt his broad chest crushing her breasts.

Orgasm struck her like a war hammer, and she shook and throbbed as he growled his own climax close to her ear.

* * * * *

Honey Wine awoke panting, her body still throbbing in the aftermath of a dream more erotic than any real sexual experience she'd ever had. She tossed off her sheet and lay still for a moment, allowing the cool night air to dry the sweat from her body.

What was wrong with her that even in her dreams she couldn't stop thinking of the beast? For the thousandth time, she wished he'd never been brought to the prison.

* * * * *

"You have absolutely no idea what's going to happen to you, do you?" Honey Wine said from where she stood outside the bars of his cage. She'd spent last night telling herself that no beast would intimidate her. She was not going to avoid an animal under her care, not that she had a choice.

He rose from the bench and grasped the iron bars in his fists, watching her with those blue-gray eyes.

Lips twisting in a cruel smile, she shook her head as four armor-clad guards approached carrying pointed sticks and whips.

Timus unlocked the cell, and before the beast could move, the guards' metal-gloved hands caught his chains and dragged him toward a low, wooden table in the far corner of the room.

Honey Wine folded her arms across her chest and watched as the prisoner struggled, nearly pulling the guards off balance. Her heart fluttered. For a moment, she thought he might break loose, but they twisted his chains, prodded him with the sticks and threw him face down on the table. Their metal armor and mail gloves dug into his flesh as they stretched his arms and legs into metal cuffs on corners of the table.

Now we'll see how haughty he is, Honey Wine thought as a tall, thickly-muscled metal smith stepped up to one of the smoldering fires built near the table. He chose a branding iron made in the shape of a tiny, curved sword, the traditional symbol of Sophianna. He heated the iron over the fire.

The prisoner's face was turned away, so he didn't know what was planned, but he did comprehend it involved pain. His expression tensed, flesh pulled tightly over his prominent cheekbones. He seemed to struggle to regulate his breathing. *Fear.* She smiled. *It's about time.* Honey Wine shook her head. The rituals of the prison had always disgusted her. Was she becoming as violent as her sister? *No, it's just him.* What was it about him that made her dislike him so much?

The smith stood with the iron, and Honey Wine's fingers bit into her arms as she crossed them tighter over her chest.

At the first touch of the iron to his muscled shoulder, the beast's eyes widened, frantic with shock and pain. He struggled futilely in the bonds. For a moment, his eyes fixed on Honey Wine's with a pleading expression. An agonized, guttural sound rose in his throat.

The brand was removed, but the odor of burnt flesh permeated the room. The iron sizzled as the smith dropped it in a bucket of water by the fire.

The beast was taken from the table and dragged back to his cell. He stumbled a bit, still unsteady from the branding, and dropped onto the bench.

"He's all yours, Honey Wine," Bron sneered before walking away.

"This beast's tough," Timus whispered to Honey Wine as she passed.

"That should make my sister happy. He'll last a long time...up there." She approached the prisoner. "Let's hope the smith did his job cleanly. It will save him from having to do it again."

The beast's gaze snapped at her, as if he understood. Perhaps he did. She smiled wickedly, and for the first time his expression changed. It grew hard, hateful, but only for a moment.

Honey Wine examined the mark on his back. It appeared red and painful, so she cleaned it with more gentleness than she'd treated him the previous day. Afterward, she applied salve. As she worked, he leaned his forehead against the jagged rock wall and closed his eyes, but when she bent to shut her supply case, his hand touched hers.

With a gasp, she jerked away and reached for a pair of shears, but the only motion he made was to pass her a wad of clean cloth she'd placed aside and forgotten.

Glaring at him, she took the cloth and tucked it into the box. She stepped out of the cell, vaguely hearing some comment Timus made, but unable to shrug off the sensation of the beast's hand on hers. His touch had been faint for such a large hand. He'd touched her more tenderly than she'd cared for any of his injuries. He had to, or else he knew he'd be punished, she told herself. A glance over her shoulder revealed the beast lying face down on the bench, one of his long fingers trailing along the dirt floor.

* * * * *

The following afternoon, Honey Wine paused by the training pit on her way to the herbarium. Timus guarded the gate, and they exchanged greetings. The pit was a vast cave about the size of the great hall in the palace above, empty, save the herd of leather-clad men who paced and wrestled on the packed dirt floor. Barbed wire gates, the height of a war ship standing on end, blocked the entrance.

Honey Wine stared in, wondering if she would ever grow hardened to the horror of the prison and the Entertainment it provided. Ten of the beasts fought with each other, sparring matches to sharpen their skills for the Entertainment. The beasts knew the importance of their training. Only the strongest and the best would survive when they were called above.

Two of the largest, most heavily muscled ones grappled in a corner, raising clouds of dust until one finally pinned the other to the ground. Their panting breaths echoed throughout the cave and into the corridor. Dirt clung to their perspiring bodies.

As the dust cleared, Honey Wine noticed *him* squatting alone by a mossy wall. The muscles of his legs strained against the leather pants, and though he watched the others, he seemed indifferent to their squabbles.

"He won't last long." Timus nodded toward the newest prisoner. "He won't practice. He'll die."

"Perhaps it's what he wants," she said. "Better than living here."

"Will you be silent," Timus hissed, genuine fear in his eyes. "Talk like that is what got you here in the first place. Sister or not, the next thing The Mistress will do is kill you."

Honey Wine curled her lip in irritation, about to reply when shrieking sounded down the corridor. Bron dragged a short, scrawny peasant toward the pit, pinning the man's wiry arms behind his back. Terror shone in the peasant's dirt-streaked face as he shouted, "No! Let me go! Have mercy on my family. I have a wife, children. I…"

Bron ignored his pleas and hurled him through the gate which Timus had opened. The clanging metal rang through the corridors as Timus locked the gate.

All the beasts inside turned to the cowering man, their eyes gleaming with blood-lust, growls erupting from their brawny chests. They advanced on him, all except one.

The silent newcomer stood, brow furrowed, watching the crowd.

The beasts raced toward the peasant who screamed in fear and ran to the gates, grasped the bars and shook them, so lost in terror he didn't notice the barbs digging into his flesh.

"Is this really necessary?" Honey Wine hissed through clenched teeth.

"It whets their appetites for the Entertainment." Bron shrugged. "Like dogs before a fight."

The beasts inside tore the peasant from the gate, kicking and shoving him as he fought their hulking forms with his meager strength.

"This is wrong," Honey Wine stated.

Bron laughed. "You always were too soft. It's amazing you ever made it into the guard."

"I got into the guard by passing the test and beating out the likes of you!" She glared at him, her hands balled into fists at her sides. She ached to fight him, tear him apart as the beasts inside devoured the poor wretch behind the bars.

"Hey! Look at this," Timus called.

Bron and Honey Wine turned back to the spectacle inside.

The newcomer stood in the midst of the others. He fought with a panther's speed, using fists, feet, elbows and knees. He dodged blows, took many, but never lost concentration. Prisoners flew into the dirt, several crawling away, cradling injured wrists and arms, others simply lying where they fell.

"I never would have guessed..." Timus murmured.

Even Bron's eyes narrowed in surprise as he watched the fight.

A foot caught the newcomer in the abdomen, and he staggered, blocking a meaty fist from one side but missing an elbow on the other. Blood splattered his face, but he returned the three blows, sending the last of the beasts crashing into the rock wall.

Except for several groans and the men's harsh breathing, there was silence.

He stood in the center of the cave, fists raised, his gaze sweeping the pit for anyone willing to continue the fight.

"Why do you think we chased him so long yesterday?" Bron whispered. "He's a Knight of the Ruby Order."

Timus and Honey Wine shot disbelieving looks at Bron.

"You stole one of them?" she said.

"Why not? He was on our land."

"What in the name of the Twin Goddesses was he doing?" She placed her hands on her hips. "Administering aid to a bunch of sick women and children?"

"Something like that." Bron shrugged. "It's their own fault if they get caught. Bunch of troublemakers. There are many who want their Order wiped out."

"And many who think they're important," Honey Wine argued, looking to Timus for support.

"Mostly peasants." He shrugged. "Women, children, the old..."

Her disgusted look switched between the two guards, then back to the prisoner who offered his hand to the terrified farmer. Suddenly a dagger embedded in the small man's chest. His mouth opened in a silent, bloody froth, and he reached for the Knight who grasped his arms and lowered him to the dirt as he died.

Bron shrugged. "I had to kill him. We can't be housing bait on top of everyone else."

The Knight stood, his blood-streaked face frozen in its usual calm expression. He walked to the gates. Honey Wine expected him to focus his enraged eyes on Bron, the one who'd struck the fatal blow. Instead he looked at her. He didn't speak, just stared until she felt like she was trapped inside those dark blue orbs, a prisoner for a crime she didn't commit.

She drew a deep breath and returned his glare before continuing down the corridor. *Damn him! Damn his arrogant carcass to hell*!

Honey Wine heard Bron shout, "Clear these beasts back into their cages and get rid of that stinking body! We'll need some healers to look the beasts over. Honey Wine!"

"I'll be there in a minute!" she bellowed. "I need fresh supplies!"

In the herbarium, Honey Wine gathered what she needed, but her thoughts whirled with the fight she'd just witnessed and the knowledge she'd acquired about the new prisoner. A Knight of the Ruby Order. They were healers and great warriors who trained not to fight for land or power, but to lend aid. They lived like monks in a fortress miles from her kingdom of Sophianna. Their Order, though fairly small, was revered by the peasant folk who benefited most from their hospitable ways. Not to say that they were holy men. They fought and killed when driven to it, but they were known to use violence only as a last resort. Several monarchs had attempted to hire them for their skills, but the Knights of the Ruby Order were not mercenaries. Money didn't tempt them, therefore they could not be controlled. Many monarchs grew to despise them, and few were willing to join an Order which was constantly under royal scrutiny.

Honey Wine walked to the holding cells and assisted another healer in seeing to the beasts' cuts, sprains and breaks.

When she reached *his* cell and stepped inside, she was surprised that he refused to look at her. He sat on the bench, staring at the wall in front of him.

She took his chin in her hand to clean the blood from his face. His lower lip was swollen from the previous day's beating and the fight in the pit. Even so, she noticed for the first time the endearing shape of his mouth. His upper lip was slim, almost delicate, the lower lip a full upside-down arch, the tips of his front teeth visible against it.

She looked up sharply and caught him watching her stare at his mouth.

"If you're a Knight of the Ruby Order, then I know you understand everything we're saying. Are you mute?"

She waited for his answer while examining a bruise above his right eye. He said nothing and made no motion to respond.

"Not that I care, but I'll give you this advice," Honey Wine continued. "Do what they want you to. You're never getting out of here. As you might have guessed, the Entertainment above is fights. You beasts are pitted against each other as well as prisoners from other kingdoms. My sister isn't the only one who enjoys these spectacles. Ah. You look surprised. Yes, The Mistress of Sophianna is my sister. So if she does this to me, imagine how little she thinks of you, her dog, her cock."

Honey Wine's words dripped venom, whether directed at him or her sister, even she wasn't sure. Though she'd finished treating his injuries, her fingertips smoothed the fine lines of concentration from his forehead.

"You're not getting out," she repeated.

He lifted his hand and touched her brow as she touched his. Startled, she glanced over her shoulder, hoping Timus or any of the other guards didn't notice. Timus was talking to the guard posted in the cell beside them.

"Don't ever do that," Honey Wine whispered. "Do you want to get us both killed or worse?"

He smiled, that familiar, arrogant smile. She packed her supplies quickly and left.

Chapter Two

"Why do you do it?" Honey Wine hissed.

It was close to midnight. Only a few low-burning torches lit the vast room of holding cells. One guard stood watch at the far corner and another at the door. They paid no attention to the healer as she crouched close to the bars of the Knight's cell.

She'd watched him for weeks, her hatred of him tainted by increasing interest and the carnal dreams that disturbed her sleep almost every night.

"Why do you fight for those pathetic ones when they're brought to the pit? You know they always end up dead no matter what you do. Don't you understand you're not a Knight anymore? In here, the Ruby Order is dead. Everything of the outside world is dead."

He sat on the ground in front of her, gazing through the bars.

"You're going up there tomorrow," she said. "And if you try your stupid heroics, if you refuse to kill your match, you will die."

He continued staring at her, and she lost her temper. Her hand shot through the bars and grasped his wrist, her short nails digging his flesh. "I know you understand everything that's said and everything that goes on here. Why won't you talk? Say something, anything! What's your name? I'm Honey Wine." She spoke slowly, as if to a fool. "H-O-N-E-Y-W-I-N-E. Who are you?" She released his wrist and poked a finger into his hard chest.

Even in the darkness, she noticed him trying to control his smile. He took her hand and held it firmly, his thumb caressing her palm.

"Let me go!" she snapped, forcing her voice to remain quiet so the guards wouldn't hear.

He continued with the slow massage, moving to her inner wrist. Did he feel her pulse racing?

"Let me go, or I'll call the guard right now."

Instead of releasing her, he tugged her closer, his hand moving from wrist to forearm to biceps. Their faces were so close their noses touched.

"Do what they want tomorrow," she said through clenched teeth. "That's all I came here to tell you."

He loosened his hold so she could slip away. Cursing herself for acting like a fool, she slid her hand down the sinewy length of his arm as she drew back. His skin felt warm, the muscles beneath hard.

She walked to her chamber and fell into uneasy sleep.

* * * * *

Honey Wine's eyes flickered open and she stared at the wall from where she lay on her side in bed. Shadows from a low burning candle danced across the room, and she sighed.

Suddenly she became aware of movement beside her. Heart pounding, she rolled over and found herself staring into *his* eyes.

He spoke with his eyes. Lust. Desire. Tenderness. One of his large, graceful hands lifted to stroke her cheek. It felt warm, rough and gentle at the same time. Honey Wine took it in her own and kissed his palm. She ran her tongue over the calluses and nipped the tips of his long fingers. She licked between each finger and kissed the back of his hand, feeling the few sparse dark hairs close to his wrist tickle her lips.

Unable to resist her own desires, Honey Wine sat up, hands pressed to his chest as he settled onto his back. His eyes studied her carefully as she straddled him, her fingers gripping the hard muscles of his chest. She splayed her palms over his pectorals and swept down his ribs before she bent to kiss his breastbone.

Honey Wine's lips trailed lower, to his belly. She dipped her tongue into his navel and felt his abdomen clench and quiver. One of her hands grasped his balls while the other curled around his stiff cock and guided it into her mouth. She tasted the head and ran her tongue along the underside.

His breathing quickened, matching her own. Heart pounding in her chest, she knelt over his hips and guided him inside her heated pussy. The prisoner's big hands clasped her waist, and his hips thrust upward as she bounced atop him, hands clutching his biceps as she raced toward a mind-shattering climax.

When Honey Wine opened her eyes, she found herself in a large chamber in the upper palace, lit only by a fire burning in the hearth across the room.

The prisoner stood in front of the fire. Flames cast dancing shadows on his tall, chiseled body. Honey Wine's heartbeat quickened. The man was absolutely magnificent. She stared, unable to move, as he turned sideways, his long, thick cock resting in his hand. His fist curved around the steely flesh and stroked. When she managed to tear her gaze from the carnal sight of his self-arousal, she found his dark blue eyes burning into hers.

Honey Wine rose as if summoned, allowing the sheet to fall from her naked body as she walked toward him. She felt the heat of the flames as well as the warmth of his body as he drew her into his arms, his cock pressed between them.

"Why won't you talk to me?" she asked him, running her hands over his chest, feeling the muscles ripple as he reached down to clasp her buttocks. He lifted her off the ground, his gaze intent on hers, communicating with her through his look alone.

Placing her on a stool by the wall next to the fireplace, he pressed her to the wall, thrusting his cock into her pussy. Honey Wine clung to him, his body hot against hers, his muscles so steely and his breath a warm rasp in her ear.

* * * * *

Again Honey Wine awoke quivering and drenched in sweat. As she stood, pulling on her robe, she realized the night had actually grown warm. Still, there was no excuse for the wetness of her pussy and the slow ebbing of the intense orgasm caused by yet another dream of *him*.

What was going to happen to him tomorrow? Would he take her advice and perform as was expected of a beast, or would he risk his life to uphold the vows of his Order?

Honey Wine knew she wouldn't fall back to sleep soon, so she slipped on her boots and stepped into the hallway. She heard laughter from the opposite end of the prison and moved toward it. A group of guards were gathered around the door of the breeding pens, where favored beasts were made to mate with servant women chosen by The Mistress. It had been her sister's plan to begin a new breed of beast, one that ensured constant wins at the Entertainment. She believed if she bred the strongest and most attractive beasts and women and raised them like animals from birth she could accomplish this. The entire situation sickened Honey Wine who, at great risk to herself, had been supplying most of the women with herbs that would ensure no child would be conceived by them. If her sister ever found out, Honey Wine knew she would most likely be executed, but to her it was worth the risk.

There were two mating pens. A private one for the shyer beasts, and an open one, used for the guards' entertainment as much as for the mating. The guards were gathered around the open one. Honey Wine could see a tall, chestnut-haired girl from the palace wrapped in the arms of a tall, blond beast with a thickly muscled form, scarred from past battles. Honey Wine recognized the girl as a volunteer—one who actually liked the idea of bedding the beasts. Some women were attracted to their hulking forms and animal lust. Until she'd set eyes on the Knight, Honey Wine hadn't understood their interest.

The young woman had dropped to her knees in front of the beast, her hands clutching his large, tight ass while she sucked and licked his straining cock. The beast clutched the bars of the pen, his eyes closed, and head thrown back as his chest heaved. He growled his passion until Honey Wine thought he'd come without even entering the woman. She almost wished he would and avoid the chance of conception.

Suddenly he grasped the woman by the shoulders and pushed her onto the straw scattered on the bottom of the pen. She raised herself onto her elbows, watching him with gleaming eyes, but fell back hard when he shoved her legs apart and buried his face between them.

The woman moaned, head arched backward, the veins and tendons standing out beneath her pale skin as he lapped and sucked her clit while he slid several fingers into her pussy.

The guards laughed and cheered when the beast mounted her and thrust like an enormous, pale-skinned bull.

Shaking her head, Honey Wine turned back down the hall, only to find herself staring at Bron.

The guard grinned. "The sight of those two got you wet? Want some satisfaction?" He clutched his groin and gave himself a few pumps.

Honey Wine's lips curled in disgust as she shoved her way past him and returned to her chamber.

* * * * *

In the morning, five selected prisoners walked, in chains, out of the corridor. The Knight was among them. Honey Wine stood by the well, her fingers biting into the rock rim as she exchanged glances with him. Her heart pounded as if she was the one going to the Entertainment instead of him.

When did I stop hating him?

"Get moving, you lazy beasts!" Bron ordered, cracking his whip at their heels as several guards guided the prisoners down the corridor.

Honey Wine strained to listen until the clattering of their chains faded and finally stopped.

That day, concentrating on her work proved difficult. She wondered which of the beasts would be brought back wounded, and which would not return at all. It depended on the mood of the onlookers whether or not the losers lived, providing the winning beast wasn't so excited by the blood lust that he killed his opponent without waiting for a signal.

When the time came, would the Knight heed her advice, or would he sacrifice his life for the beliefs the Ruby Order had instilled in him? She didn't doubt he could become her sister's finest champion if he relied on the warrior instinct that enabled him to put down the beasts in the pit each time bait was tossed in.

But it's the bait he's fighting for, not himself.

Ignoring the unfamiliar weight of sadness in her breast, she told herself he would not be returning, and it would be better for her if he died. She was becoming too fond of him, and she could no more rescue him from his fate than she could save a hog from slaughter.

At midday, Honey Wine sat in her chamber, twirling her spoon in a bowl of stew but lacking the enthusiasm to eat it. Her stomach felt strange, like a hummingbird was trapped inside, beating its wings furiously to get out.

Outside, Bron bellowed orders and chains clinked. The prisoners were returning, no doubt with wounds that needed tending.

Honey Wine opened her door a crack and peered out, her gaze riveting to the Knight chained between two of the beasts. So three of them had survived and two had been forfeited to The Mistress' bloody desires. The faces of men behind and in front of the Knight were bruised and bloody, and one of them staggered, clutching a dirty bandage swathing his hirsute chest. By the look of him, he'd need immediate attention. At first Honey Wine thought the Knight was untouched. Then she noticed one of his arms was bound with a blood-soaked cloth.

She stepped outside and hurried past them to the holding cells, calling for the other healer on duty to assist her.

Honey Wine moved toward the Knight's cell, but Bron called to her, "You're the most experienced on this shift. This beast needs your attention." He nodded toward the man with the bandaged chest.

Cursing the truth of Bron's words, she went to where she was most needed. She felt the Knight's gaze on her but refused to look at him. The idea that Bron or another guard might notice her growing fondness for him disturbed her.

She set to work on the beast, giving him an herbal drink to ease his pain. He tore the mug from her hand and gulped it, then lay back, groaning to himself as she cleaned and stitched the wound on his chest. A sword slash, she guessed. As part of the Entertainment, the beasts were allowed their choice of weapons.

"What happened up there today?" Honey Wine asked Timus softly as he watched from outside the cell.

"The one you're working on won a match. The other lost, but was salvaged. The Knight won three matches. He would have been The Mistress' champion, except he refused to kill. She's ordered him to be punished by The Lady."

Honey Wine drew a sharp breath, willing her hands to remain steady as she stitched the beast. He'd fallen asleep with the aid of the potion, making her chore easier. The coming evening concerned her greatly. Punishment by The Lady would cause the Knight excruciating pain but wouldn't do permanent or serious damage to his body. Honey Wine's sister couldn't afford tortures that might render a champion unable to fight. Some had died under The Lady's hand, ones who had expired from fear and pain intolerance, but The Mistress only shrugged at those losses. They wouldn't have been strong enough to last in the Entertainment.

The Knight was not a killer, but Honey Wine's sister was determined to make him one. None of the beasts failed to do exactly what was expected of them after one meeting with The Lady.

Honey Wine finished with the beast, washed his blood from her hands, and moved to the Knight's cell. Timus unlocked the door, and she stepped inside.

The Knight sat quietly while she unraveled the bloody bandage from his biceps. Some of the blood had dried into the bandage, and she tried to cause him as little discomfort as possible as she peeled the gory wrapping from his flesh.

"You should have done what she wanted," Honey Wine whispered, refusing to look at his face. She couldn't bear to meet those proud eyes, gaze at that adorable mouth, all the while knowing what he'd be facing that night. A horror worse than the Entertainment.

"You're a fool, you know," she continued. "Are you prepared to suffer tonight?"

She didn't expect him to answer. After she'd stitched his arm and applied a clean bandage, she withdrew several leaves from her supply box. Pressing them into his hand, she whispered, "Eat this. It'll dull the pain when you meet The Lady."

Instead of keeping the leaves, he dropped them back into the box.

"Take them, fool!" she hissed.

He motioned slightly toward Bron and Timus. So, he understood better than she thought. If he came before The Lady, drugged, The Mistress would realize it. She'd want to know who'd supplied him, and Honey Wine was the only healer who'd tended him. She'd known that risk when she'd given him the leaves, realized that her own punishment could be as mild as removing her privileges to visit above or as harsh as a visit to The Lady herself.

Now that she really considered the rashness of her action, Honey Wine trembled.

"Honey Wine! Are you done in there?" Bron called. "The Mistress wants you to administer to some of the guest's beasts in the visitors' cells."

"I'm coming," she shouted to him. She hesitated before closing the supply box, her gaze darting from the Knight to the leaves still within his reach. He stood and walked to the opposite end of the cell.

"If that's how you want it, see if I care," she muttered as she left him alone to ponder the coming evening.

* * * * *

That evening, Honey Wine cursed her own cowardice as she locked herself in her chamber so she wouldn't have to watch the Knight being taken to his punishment.

However, she wouldn't escape his suffering. Bron knocked on her door shortly after dusk.

A smile twisted his thick lips as he said, "The Mistress requests your presence above."

"Why?"

"I've no idea. Most of us know better than to question The Mistress."

Honey Wine would have replied, but how could she remark on his weakness when she'd hoped to spend the night cowering in her room while a truly brave man suffered above.

She reached for her wooden supply box, and Bron scoffed, "That's foolish. Nothing in that box can help him tonight."

"I'm a healer now, remember? I feel comfortable carrying my tools just as I once carried weapons."

"Once," Bron sneered.

Honey Wine followed him down the corridor and up ten long flights of stone steps to The Lady's work chamber.

Four torches lit the round chamber. The only window was a tiny circular hole close to the high ceiling. Far from the ground and secluded from the rest of the palace, the room's location ensured no one could hear the screams sounding from The Lady's victims as she worked.

Manacles dangled from chains hanging from the ceiling in the center of the room, and on the floor below them ankle cuffs waited to hold the victim completely immobile. When the prisoner was tied, The Lady would have full access to his entire body, back and front. Honey Wine knew how devilishly she used this advantage. She'd seen her work before.

A stone couch cushioned in brown velvet was positioned before the chains so that The Mistress could observe the punishment. She didn't order such tortures often, but saved them as a treat to herself and lessons for those rare champions or enemies of state foolish enough to cherish their desires above hers.

Bron left Honey Wine alone inside, and she paced the room, wishing to be anyplace but there. How could she watch this punishment without revealing what she felt for the Knight? What would happen to both of them if her sister found out, and worse, how could Honey Wine plan their escape if The Mistress knew she cared for him?

The door burst open and guards dragged the Knight inside. They fitted his hands in the manacles above his head and his ankles in the cuffs on the floor so his long, sinewy body stretched almost immobile. She tried not to look at him, but couldn't help herself. An inkling of fear gleamed beneath the endless patience in his dark blue eyes.

"Ah, Honey Wine!" The Mistress swept into the room, her straight, black hair hanging to her buttocks, her tall, curvaceous body covered in a robe of black silk, a red sash about her narrow waist. Her pale skin made her molasses-colored eyes look even darker.

Many considered her a beautiful woman and often remarked on how much Honey Wine looked like her, except Honey Wine's body was more thickly muscled and her skin tanned from spending days on the field. Or at least it had been tanned once. Now she bore the same pallor as everyone else who spent their lives in the prison below. Only Honey Wine's eyes were different from her sister's. They were light brown, almost tan, thus her name Honey Wine.

"It's been so long since this chamber has been in use, and I know how you love to watch The Lady work," The Mistress continued, voice dripping sarcasm. Everyone knew how Honey Wine despised such punishments, particularly since it was never criminals who suffered them.

"This is unworthy even of you, Alva," Honey Wine said.

"Why?" She smiled and walked to the Knight. "Because he's of the Ruby Order? Because some consider them untouchable and holy? He looks quite touchable to me. Quite handsome."

Alva splayed her hands across the Knight's lean chest, her fingers biting into muscle. She stood on tiptoe, and her tongue snaked across his mouth. He turned his head in disgust, and Honey Wine's fists clenched at her sides. Maybe if she lunged quickly, she could break The Mistress' neck...

Too late. Guards stepped inside, carrying a round stool and a narrow table covered in leather, The Lady behind them.

The Lady scarcely reached Honey Wine's shoulder in height. Her golden hair was pulled into a severe bun on the very top of her head, causing her narrow blue eyes to slant. Her face was thin, cheekbones prominent. Though at first glance her lips appeared lovely and full, if one looked closely enough, they were merely thin, shapeless lines embellished by red paint. A green tunic covered her frog-like body, and gold hose disappeared into soft, green, thigh-high boots.

"He's haughty," Alva said to The Lady, hands still clutching the Knight's chest. Suddenly she slapped him hard across the face, her palm leaving a red imprint on his skin. "But he'll learn to appreciate me."

"Don't you ever tire of this, Alva?" Honey Wine tried to sound bored.

"No." Her sister smiled and floated to the couch. She sat and patted the seat beside her.

"I'll stand," Honey Wine said.

"As you wish, but it will be a long two hours." She nodded for The Lady to begin.

The blonde woman's small, gloved hands tore the leather from the table, revealing the sharp silver needles gleaming on a cushion of black velvet. There were hundreds of needles, hundreds of moments of pain, and The Lady knew how to use each one to squeeze out delicious agony without killing her victim.

The Lady chose one of the needles and placed it strategically through the Knight's skin. Honey Wine's nails bit into her palms as he tensed.

The Lady stood before him, a half-smile on her lips, her head cocked to one side like a curious dog. She chose a second needle, then a third.

The Knight's fists clenched, his wrists twisting in the manacles until blood dripped down his forearms.

Alva laughed and stretched out on the couch, the front of her robe parting. Her long, pale hands stroked the cleft between her breasts, and she sighed with contentment. "Seems he'll take his punishment with the same strength he took his opponents during the Entertainment. What do you think, Honey Wine?"

Honey Wine refused to acknowledge Alva. If she so much as looked at The Mistress, she'd strangle her and bring the guards in fighting. At that moment, Honey Wine didn't care for herself, but without her help, the Knight would not escape, and she was determined to find a way to free him from this hellish place.

"How many needles do you think it will take before he screams?" Alva asked The Lady.

"Just one more," The Lady chimed in her high-pitched voice, positioning the stool before the Knight and standing on it so she could better reach his upper body.

At the touch of the next needle, he shrieked as The Lady predicted.

Honey Wine's heart pounded, her head throbbed with the desire to kill both Alva and The Lady, to make them suffer as he was suffering.

He'd no sooner regained his composure from the last excruciating attack when The Lady added another of the metal demons to his trembling flesh.

Honey Wine circled the room like a caged animal, trying to avert her gaze from the spectacle in the center of the floor, but compelled to watch.

"Why don't you sit down?" Alva called to her. "You'll be tired of all that walking by the end of the session."

"Your soul is damned, Alva," Honey Wine hissed.

"Who really knows what the afterlife will bring? I believe in entertaining myself now, while I can enjoy it." She turned her dark eyes back to the Knight, stroking her nipples through the silk to the rhythm of his tortured breathing.

Alva approached the Knight and raked her nails over his chest, scraping his flat nipples. "Goddess, what a magnificent body he has."

"Then why are you ruining it?" Honey Wine snarled.

Alva continued running her hands over his body. "You know the needles will leave no mark. But I might."

Alva sank her teeth into his chest, drawing blood and causing the Knight to gasp. Honey Wine's fists clenched so tightly her nails cut into her palms as she watched Alva slip a dagger from the folds of her robe and slice off the Knight's loin cloth. His cock dangled, thick but flaccid. Alva ran her tongue over his abdomen, clutched his hips, and took his cock into her mouth.

The Knight closed his eyes, but not before Honey Wine saw the disgust and shame burning there. In spite of himself, he grew hard beneath Alva's skilled tongue and lips.

I'm going to kill her, Honey Wine thought. *One way or the other, I'm going to kill her.* But she would bide her time. There were other, more important tasks to complete before she sought revenge on the savage monarch who, to her revulsion, shared her blood.

Chapter Three

ை

"Swear that you will kill when ordered to do so during the Entertainment." Alva, the sash about her waist discarded, her black robe parted to reveal her nude body, stood before the Knight. "Look at me."

His eyes were closed tightly, his sweat-slicked body pierced by dozens of The Lady's wicked needles. The end of the session neared, and Honey Wine's sister grew impatient. For the past hour, she'd repeated the same words to the Knight. She wanted acknowledgment from him that he would do her bidding during the Entertainment. Other than his raw screams that echoed through the chamber, he hadn't spoken.

The air reeked of the disgusting mixture of Alva's strong perfume and urine puddled at the Knight's feet. The dangling position combined with the agony of The Lady's needles made breathing nearly impossible for the Knight, and Honey Wine noted he seemed to be losing the struggle for breath as exhaustion overcame him.

"I told you a hundred times, he's mute!" Honey Wine seethed. "He hasn't spoken a word since he was captured."

"He doesn't need to speak." Alva turned to Honey Wine, the ridges of her white cheeks stained pink with frustration. "He can make a motion that he understands. You said yourself he's not ignorant." Alva turned back to The Lady. "Use another. One way or the other, he'll do what I want."

For the first time, The Lady looked hesitant.

"He could die from this, Alva," Honey Wine said quietly. "The Lady knows it, just as you and I do."

"This session has been longer and more extreme than expected, Mistress," The Lady said.

"You've both seen this before," Honey Wine said. "If he hasn't done what you want by now, he's not going to. Think about it, Alva. Killing him would be a waste."

"Because he's a Knight of the Ruby Order?" Alva scoffed.

"Yes. Because no one has their fighting skills. He might not kill, but I'll wager he's been the finest Entertainment you've ever seen. Do you really want to kill him and waste all that talent, or wouldn't you rather keep him alive to compete? Eventually, he'll be here so long he'll forget about the life he once had. They always do. Even the most human of them become beasts in the end."

Alva flashed a beautiful smile. "I still think you're too rebellious, Honey Wine, but you've learned much serving below." She turned to The Lady, took the small woman's chin gently in her hand, and brushed a tender kiss across her brow. "You did very well tonight. His stubborn nature is not a reflection on your abilities. Take back your sharp little toys and meet me in my chamber."

The Lady looked past Alva and smiled belligerently at Honey Wine before she began removing the needles from the Knight's tormented body.

"Alva," Honey Wine said. "I think you should let me examine him. His wrists need care."

Alva picked up her sash and fixed it about her waist. "Honey Wine, you are such a good little girl. However, that irritating part of your personality is what always gets you into trouble. You want to help the beast so much, then you can spend the night up here with him. It gets so dark and cold, and you did just stand here and watch him be tortured. Once he gets his strength back, I wouldn't want to be trapped up here with him. He might not kill, but I've heard the Ruby Order knows methods of torture similar to The Lady's, only they use their hands to inflict the pain. If I was him, I'd give you a taste of it. Sweet dreams, sister."

Alva swept out of the chamber, one of the guards following her, the remaining ones standing in a circle around the room.

The Lady removed the last of the needles, and the Knight sagged in his bonds, his head bent toward his chest.

The Lady snapped her fingers for one of the guards to remove her table and stool.

As she left, the guards released the Knight from his bonds so his arms and legs were bound only by his usual chains. He dropped to the floor and lay there, stunned and panting, as the guards left, locking the door behind them.

With the torches already burning out, Honey Wine worked quickly.

She knelt beside him and opened her supply box. His entire body trembled with the aftershocks of The Lady's needles, and when she touched his shoulder, he jerked away. Honey Wine dropped her hand, understanding at that moment, he didn't want to be touched. The Lady's needles had left no visible marks on his skin, only on his mind.

Honey Wine used water from a flask to cleanse his flesh beneath the bonds where the metal cuffs had chaffed them. She was treating one of his wrists when he murmured, "Torn."

She paused and drew a sharp breath. He'd spoken!

"I know they are," she told him. "They won't hurt so much after I bandage them."

"No. My name is Torn."

"Oh." She smiled slightly though her throat suddenly constricted with anger and sadness at what he'd been forced to endure, at what so many of them who slaved below were forced to tolerate every day.

"It's not your fault." He glanced at her through half-closed eyes. "At first I thought you could do something about it, but you can't."

"Maybe," she said, and applied the bandages.

Using a cloth dampened with rosewater from her supply case, she started washing away urine from his legs. He caught her wrists and took the cloth from her to clean himself. Honey Wine knew even slight movement must have been an effort, yet she sensed his embarrassment and resisted the urge to continue helping him.

He had no reason to feel shame. Honey Wine had never heard of anyone not wetting himself during a session with The Lady, and it wasn't unheard of for victims to loose bowel control as well, particularly in the moments before death. The latter hadn't happened to the Knight, though Honey Wine guessed if the session hadn't stopped, it certainly would have occurred.

Once he'd finished cleaning himself and lay back down on the floor, Honey Wine shrugged off her cloak and placed it over his bare chest. The chamber had grown cold, but at least her dress was long-sleeved and woolen.

In the fading light, she traced a finger across Torn's full lower lip. She stroked his cheek with the back of her hand.

"That feels nice," he murmured.

"I'm sorry you're here," she said. "But it might not be forever."

"No. Eventually we all get to die."

* * * * *

Honey Wine awoke in blackness to the unfamiliar but pleasant sensation of another's warm flesh beneath her cheek. She realized that sometime during the night, she and Torn had moved to the couch. Her body was half draped over his, and he'd spread her cloak over both of them. Honey Wine lifted her face from his chest and strained to see in the darkness.

"Are you all right?" he asked, his hand touching her hair. His voice sounded deep, penetrating, even though he spoke softly.

"I should be asking you that question."

"I'm fine now. The Lady," he sneered her name, "is very skilled at her craft."

There was a question that had to be asked. "Why have you never spoken before?"

"Would it have done me any good? We're just beasts. No one here cares, except you."

Honey Wine wasn't sure how to respond. Finally she said, "I didn't act like I cared. Fear does that to a person. I never used to be afraid, but I was young and stupid. I thought I was so strong because I was a guard."

"The ability to fight is one kind of strength."

"Not the kind that matters. I don't see any guards rebelling against the Entertainment."

"You did."

"And look where it got me!" she snapped. "I've learned to be smart, Torn."

"Not a fool like me?" He flung her own words back at her with such gentleness that anger eluded her.

"I still think you're a fool," she whispered, "but a strong one."

"Because I can fight?"

"Because I've never seen anyone defeat The Lady. How did you get caught, Torn? How did my sister's guard capture you?"

"I was passing through your land on my way back to the Order. Fire swept through a small village, and I stopped to help. A troop of your soldiers must have seen the smoke and rode up to investigate. I was in the middle of tending some of the burn victims when one of the guards noticed by my clothes that I was of the Ruby Order. That's how I was taken."

"You said earlier you thought I could do something about the Entertainment. Why would you think that?"

"It was the look in your eyes. You hated what was going on around you, and you're strong."

"Like I said before, I was once…"

He cupped her chin in his hand, though she didn't know how he managed to find it so quickly in the darkness. "At first I didn't think you were a prisoner too, but you are. When you offered me those herbs this afternoon, it was the most selfless act I'd ever seen. Thank you, Honey Wine."

The sound of his voice caressing her name made her tingle. *You're becoming a fool for this man, Honey Wine!*

"You were more courageous for not accepting them," she said. "If I could have killed both of those bitches and gotten away with it, I would have, but we never would have made it past the guards. We have to find another way."

"Another way?"

"To escape from here. You don't really want to spend the rest of your life here, do you?"

"No!" he answered so quickly she would have laughed if their situation hadn't been grave.

"Then we'll find a way out," she said.

"You've already risked enough for me. I don't want you to be hurt any more than you already have been."

She blinked in the darkness. She'd been hurt? He was the one who'd resembled an embroiderer's pincushion that night!

"You won't get away without my help," she said. She knew one way or the other, this place would kill him, and he didn't deserve to die here. "Besides, I've had about all I can take of licking my sister's boots. One of these days, I really will kill her, and she's always surrounded by guards, so where would that leave me? You can either help me get out of here or not."

"Where will you go once you get away?"

She shrugged. "I'll find a place."

"You'll be safe at the Order, at least until you decide what you want to do."

"You're asking me to stay with a bunch of Knights?"

"Why not? You once stayed with your sister's guard."

"Stayed with?" Honey Wine huffed. "I *commanded* my sister's guard."

"If we escape, will you come home with me, Honey Wine?"

"When we escape, I will."

"Honey Wine, please understand if I don't speak again. I can't in front of them. If I did, I might succumb—"

"I understand," she whispered. "It's our secret."

The cloak had fallen off her shoulders, and she shivered in the coolness of the chamber. She pulled the garment over them and lay back on his chest. His arms encircled her, and she moved a hand over his hard pectoral muscles. She allowed herself to fantasize about what it would be like to make love with him, to have his tall, lean body dominate hers. What would it feel like to kiss that funny, sensual mouth of his?

As if sensing her thoughts, his hand caressed her cheek, his fingertips traced her lips, and he tilted her face upward.

His soft lips brushed hers, and she closed her eyes. He kissed her upper lip, her lower lip and then full on the mouth. She entangled her fingers in his hair, opening her mouth to his gently probing tongue and meeting it with her own.

"Honey Wine," he said in a husky whisper, his hands caressing her back.

She trembled. How many nights in her dreams had she kissed and touched him? Now it was really happening, and in spite of the horrors of earlier that evening, she felt weak with desire.

"Oh Torn," she breathed, changing her position slightly so she could touch his chest. Where Alva had bitten him, the wound felt sticky. She'd completely forgotten about it but had been more concerned with his wrists and the aftereffects of the needles. Groping blindly for her healing supplies, she managed to wet a cloth with water from a flask and sat on her knees beside the couch, cleaning the savage teeth marks on his chest. When she'd finished, she touched her lips to the injury while her hand splayed across his hard pectorals. She felt his nipple against her palm and stroked lower, her fingers caressing the nub.

Placing a hand behind her neck, he drew her face to his for another kiss. This time his tongue slipped into her mouth, exploring every corner, every moist nook. Honey Wine closed her eyes tightly and uttered a soft moan as she climbed on top of him.

Her throbbing pussy felt so hot and wet, and more than anything she wanted to feel him inside her. She felt his cock pressing against her clit, even through her dress, and she began rocking upon him as his deep kisses continued plundering her mouth.

She heard his chest rumble in a groan of pure desire, and that sound combined with the feeling of his rock hard body beneath hers sent her over the edge. She throbbed and gasped into his mouth, feeling blissful waves of orgasm warming her against the coolness of the chamber.

This time when she fell asleep, she didn't need to dream. Her body was already entangled with the Knight's.

Chapter Four

೫

Honey Wine had hoped to plan her escape before Torn was sent to the Entertainment again, but their actions would have to be certain before they moved or else it would lead to their deaths. The belowground prison was well guarded, and escape seemed almost impossible.

That night in The Lady's chamber was the only private time the two of them shared. Other than while routinely healing the minor injuries he sustained in the Pit and during Entertainment, Honey Wine communicated with Torn through words whispered through the bars of his cell in the middle of the night.

"I can't think of a way out of here," she murmured in frustration one evening.

"There's got to be," he whispered. "We're just not seeing it."

His hopeful attitude amazed her. Even though he'd never lost a fight and, to The Mistress' dismay, he had yet to kill in doing so, Honey Wine knew one day he would meet someone who would match his skill and destroy him. It happened to all the beasts eventually. The life of a champion was short.

Either he'll be killed or end up a beast like the rest of them, she thought. No matter how firm his beliefs, in time such a life of violence would take its toll. To survive, he would surrender to that which he hated. Then Honey Wine's Knight would truly be dead, more so than if he was slaughtered in Entertainment.

Somehow, her sister guessed Honey Wine's interest in Torn, or else she was told by Bron who had remarked several times on her fondness for the beast.

"I do believe you're starting to think of him as a pet." Bron's breath was hot on Honey Wine's neck as he leaned close to her one afternoon by the well. "It's all right, Honey Wine. I once had a favorite guard dog. He was half wolf and had to be destroyed for killing sheep. Yes, I certainly liked that dog. . . "

Bron's voice drifted off as he walked back to his post.

Soon after that, Honey Wine was "invited" by Alva to observe the next Entertainment. She said that the Master of the kingdom just south of Sophianna had a match for the Knight, one that was sure to challenge him, unlike the other ill-bred beasts he'd been pitted against.

"So who is it, Alva?" Honey Wine demanded the evening before the Entertainment. She'd sought a meeting with her sister since receiving her message, but The Mistress been deliberately slow in granting her an audience.

Alva's sensual mouth smiled at The Lady who perched beside her on the velvet couch. "Isn't she beautiful when she's angry?"

The Lady shrugged, her narrow eyes raking Honey Wine from her demurely braided black hair to the tips of her worn leather boots. Even in slave's clothes, Honey Wine sensed The Lady's jealously of her strong, curvaceous body. Honey Wine might not be as exquisite as Alva, but she knew she was not a woman to be passed over, and all the lip paint and fine clothes couldn't give The Lady the physical beauty she craved.

"I suppose you want to know the sort of beast the Knight will be fighting? Sorry," Alva yawned, "but I can't disclose that information. It would ruin the surprise. Just know there will be no more of his obstinacy. With this new opponent, he will either kill or be killed."

"You're sick, Alva, beyond the help any mere healer can give."

Alva stood, her face almost touching Honey Wine's, her white teeth grinding. "Your problem, sister, is you never learned how to have fun. All that training for war. You're like a man. A boring man. Now get out of my sight, or I'll give you to The Lady to practice her craft."

At this, The Lady did smile.

Honey Wine's fists clenched, and her gaze darted from Alva to The Lady. She could kill them both in seconds, but two guards stood by the fireplace, and two more waited outside the heavy oak door.

She turned and left the women on the couch, their fingers entwined, ignoring her like she was one of the caged yellow birds in the corner of the chamber.

* * * * *

Honey Wine was in the midst of a terrifying dream of Torn being slaughtered by twenty beasts armed with hatchets when she was awakened by knocking on her door.

"Honey Wine!" Bron bellowed.

Slipping on her robe, Honey Wine flung open the door. "What? Eh! What are you doing?"

Bron had motioned for two guards to chain Honey Wine and drag her down the hall toward the mating chamber.

The guards flung her inside and slammed the door shut. Bron leered at her through a slit in the door. "You're to mate with the Knight, per your sister's order. If he dies tomorrow at the Entertainment, she at least wants to breed him once."

Honey Wine's heart pounded with combined anger and desire. Anger at the idea of being forced to make love with Torn and desire at the thought of doing so. She'd dreamed of him for so long, had even kissed and touched him, but the thought of feeling him deep inside her made her legs weak and her belly clench with desire. Yet there was no way they would put on a show for Bron who would most likely watch the mating through the slit in the door. Never would either of them engage in such a lewd performance! Yet what choice did they have? If they didn't make love, she was certain they'd be punished.

"We know he's your favorite, Honey Wine." Bron continued taunting her. "You'll love every minute of being the beast's slut, I'm sure."

Moments later, the door opened, and several guards dragged Torn inside. They shackled him to the wall, and he stood, sympathetic eyes fixed on Honey Wine.

The door slammed, and Bron's piggish eyes continued staring at them through the slit. He sneered, "I have to watch to make sure you mate."

"Damn you to hell!" Honey Wine roared, throwing herself at the door, her fingers jamming through the slit. If Bron hadn't leapt away, she would have blinded him.

"You bitch!" he growled. "If you don't do what you're supposed to, I'll put you in the open cell and you can put on a show for the every guard down here! Now either lift up that dress or take it off!"

"I'd rather be tortured by The Lady!"

"Well that's what's going to happen to you, per The Mistress' order, if you don't fuck that beast!"

Honey Wine froze, her heart throbbing in her chest before she gathered the courage to shout, "Fine, let her—"

Torn's hand clamped over her mouth and he dragged her to his chest. She turned, glancing up at him and saw the fear in his eyes as he shook his head.

"It's all right," she told him, her entire body trembling. "You went through it."

"But not you!" He embraced her so he could whisper in her ear without the guards noticing. "I would rather be dead than see you at her mercy."

"Torn," she whispered back, slipping her arms around him and holding him tightly. "What are we going to do?"

"Pretend."

"What?"

"Hey! What are you two doing in there? I want to see some fucking going on!" Bron growled.

Torn shoved Honey Wine against the wall, grasped her wrists, and pinned them above her head as his mouth covered hers. His tongue traced the shape of her lips and slipped into her mouth as her own caressed it.

He ran his hand over her ribs, just grazing her breasts.

"It's all right. You can touch them," she murmured. They had to make the show look good, but as Torn's large hand cupped one of her breasts and his thumb stroked her nipple through the fabric of her robe, she wondered if it was a show anymore. Her heart pounded as he dropped her hands and cupped her other breast. He rolled both nipples between his thumb and forefinger while he continued kissing her and nuzzling her neck.

One of his hands untied her robe, baring her body to him alone and shielding her from Bron's prying stare. She felt his cock brush her belly, then press between them as he deepened the kiss. His steely chest crushed her breasts, and she felt him panting against her ear.

"Don't worry." His whisper sounded strained. "I won't penetrate you."

Honey Wine almost wanted to scream, *No, penetrate me! Shove it in, for the Goddess' sake!* Yet she refrained. Instead she slid her arms around him and held him tightly as his erection remained firmly trapped between their bellies, part of it rubbing her clit and causing her to ache with impending climax. She knew she was going to come if he didn't stop his movements, and she didn't doubt he would as well by the sound of his breathing and the slamming of his heart she could feel through his chest.

Suddenly her legs lost all their strength as she throbbed and shook in frenzied orgasm. She would have fallen had Torn not held her upright.

As her breathing returned to normal, she realized his was taking a lot longer. His cock still felt rock hard.

"Stay here a minute," he whispered, pushing away so he no longer touched her. He remained, his hands braced against the wall, eyes closed, until his cock returned to its flaccid state as if by his force of will alone.

He turned away from her suddenly, and Honey Wine, hands trembling with desire and anger at the spectacle they'd been forced to act out, tied her robe and stared at the door.

Chuckling, Bron strode in, followed by several guards to drag Torn back to his cell.

"I think you really liked that." Bron grinned at her.

"Apparently so did you." Honey Wine sneered, nodding toward the wet patch on the crotch of his leather pants. She shoved past him, muttering, "Pathetic."

* * * * *

The following evening, Honey Wine's face was covered with a black hood as she sat beside Alva in her carriage. Her hands, bound with chains similar to the beasts', were concealed beneath the folds of an expensive, fur-trimmed cloak The Mistress had insisted she wear.

"Understand that all guests are of the purest blood," Alva said. "Though your father was common—the Goddesses only knows why our mother chose to slip down with such a peasant—you can at least look the part of a lady. You might even find you enjoy the Entertainment, particularly when you see the Knight at work."

"I have no interest in your perversions," Honey Wine said.

Alva giggled, still lost in her own dreaming. "I'm so glad you convinced me not to let The Lady kill him. Watching him fight is ever so much fun. It's like grasping a lightening bolt out of the sky and containing it in a sorceress' crystal ball. He's glistening energy just waiting for the chance to explode into a full-fledged storm! And he will, Honey Wine. Tonight, he will!"

Honey Wine gritted her teeth in disgust as Alva's excited fingers bit into her upper arm. Her mind churned with thoughts of the sort of beast who inspired such added pleasure to Alva's decadence. From what she'd overheard from the guards' conversations in the holding cells, Torn's victories had been almost effortless. Even guards from other kingdoms had begun to wager on him over their own beasts, and the royals were becoming frustrated by The Mistress' champion. They were losing interest in the Entertainment, until the announcement at the last match. Bron had gloated over Master Sparro's boast that he'd been training a beast for months, one he'd kept from Entertainment to specifically hone his skills to such a vicious state that guards slipped his food beneath a barbed wire cage and had drugged him with a dart so they could bring him to the Entertainment field.

Though Honey Wine feigned indifference, she feared for Torn. He was skilled, but he was not a beast. At times she wasn't even certain he'd have made a decent guard. He was strong, a great fighter and knew how to bury his own fear, but he felt for others. A severe fault in both guards and beasts. She knew that first hand. Her own empathy had cost her everything.

The carriage stopped, and Alva jerked the hood from Honey Wine's face. She squinted in the dusk. Set in an enormous clearing in a wood, a round rock building stretched toward the treetops. Torches rimmed a cobbled walk from Alva's carriage to the wooden double doors guarded by ten warriors, two from each of the participating kingdoms. She noticed none were from Warefield, the official city of High King Verick who presided over most of the Islands of Travelle. Only the Ruby Order's official kingdom of Rubyshire and the Opal Hill, owned by the Knights' female counterparts, the Dames of the Opal Order, were beyond Verick's control. His absence lent Honey Wine the slightest relief. At least the High King was not involved in the Entertainment, not that it helped anyone in The Mistress' land.

"Ready, Honey Wine?" The Mistress smiled. Honey wine noticed a shiver running down her spine, though she was draped in a mink robe dyed the color of blood. "Oh, and before you forget yourself and start preaching against Entertainment, remember that everyone here loves it as much—if not more—than I do. They would be all too pleased to vote to drop you into the ring, and I, being the hostess, would be unable to deny their pleasure."

Honey Wine glared at her before guards ushered them both out of the carriage, down the walk, and through the doors to Alva's private hell.

Inside, they walked up a narrow stone staircase opening to a balcony that surrounded the vast room. The black, white and red tiles on the dome-shaped ceiling depicted various methods of execution, the richness of the design a strange contrast to the dirt floor below. There was only one door in the single, enormous room below, and that door was encased by a small square cage of barbed wire. Honey Wine later realized the cage protected the guards from the fighting beasts once they were turned loose.

Guards lined the back wall of the balcony, and cushioned seats were placed close to the railing so the onlookers had a perfect view of the battles below. Nobles, many whom Honey Wine recognized, already filled most of the seats. High born respected lords, ladies, and monarchs. If she hadn't been so worried for Torn, Honey Wine would have laughed aloud at their hypocrisy.

She took her place beside Alva who perched on the edge of a chair and laughed with a tall, red-haired man whose hands were covered with sapphire rings.

"Sparro, this is my sister, Honey Wine," Alva explained at the man's curious glance. So, this was the man who claimed he had a beast who could destroy Torn. "She's rather simple and doesn't get out much, but I thought she deserved to share in the excitement at least once." Alva glared at Honey Wine before she could comment. "She doesn't talk much either. She's rather shy."

Honey Wine understood her sister's implication. Unless she acted the way Alva expected her to, she'd suffer.

"Too bad." Sparro placed a hand on Honey Wine's knee. "Maybe I can get her to relax."

"You wouldn't want to be bothered." Jealousy sparked Alva's eyes. "She has some common blood in her—though I wouldn't want you to spread that information around."

Sparro's gaze fixed on Alva and he edged past Honey Wine to placed his bejeweled hands on The Mistress' shoulders. "Perhaps you could convince me to keep my silence."

"Of course," Alva smiled, her expression full of lust as she looped her arms around Sparro's neck. She glanced at Honey Wine. "Do you see what I'll do to protect your reputation, my dear?"

Honey Wine didn't try keeping the disgust from her face as Alva and Sparro's mouths met. Their tongues visibly raked each other's lips, then met, caressing and stroking as Alva's hands parted Sparro's robe and dipped into the waistband of his satin trousers.

"Such a marvelous cock," Alva whispered. "How I love to make it crow."

"And you do it so well," Sparro purred. He tugged down the front of Alva's gown. Her breasts popped free and he bent, taking one of her nipples between his lips while he pinched the other with his thumb and forefinger.

Alva's eyes slipped shut and a flush darkened her skin as he parted the folds of her skirt, brushing aside lace and revealing a carefully hemmed slit in her dress that Honey Wine hadn't noticed, so well was it disguised.

Sparro's hand disappeared in the slit and by the quickening of Alva's breathing, he'd found her clit and pussy quite easily.

Alva's stroking of Sparro's cock slowed as his hand sped up in its ministrations.

At her moment of crisis, Alva threw back her head, her entire body tense, her breasts heaving, and her ribs threatened to break her tightly corseted gown.

"I think you really owe me, my dear," Sparro hissed close to her ear.

Alva grinned, her hand once again pumping faster beneath his trousers.

"Wait!" Sparro gasped, his orgasm imminent by the rasp of his breath and the glaze of his eyes. With trembling fingers, he withdrew a smooth platinum ring from the satin pouch at his hip.

"I see." Alva's lips slid into a wicked smile and she removed her hand from Sparro's trousers. He tugged them down, freeing one of the largest cocks Honey Wine had ever seen. It was thick and ruddy, the veins weaving along its shaft prominent. He adjusted the ring at the base and cupped his huge, hair-dusted balls before gesturing to Alva to continue.

Alva dropped to her chair, placed her hands on Sparro's hips, and tugged him close, her mouth engulfing his cock—or as much of it as she could take in. Sparro placed his hands on her shoulders as she sucked, one of her hands kneading his balls.

Sparro's breath came in hard pants as Alva's attack increased. His buttocks squeezed and released, as if seeking an orgasm he was doing his best to hold at bay.

Alva drew back slightly, revealing his dark red cock, glazed with her saliva. It looked ready to burst and Honey Wine watched in repulsed fascination. Never in her life had she imagined people so disgusting as her sister and these lords and ladies. Even when she averted her gaze to the other seats, most of the onlookers were engaged in sexual play of one kind or another.

A low groan seemed dragged from Sparro's throat as Alva ran her teeth along his cock. The tip of her tongue traced one particularly prominent vein before running over the head, paying close attention to the little eye. She rotated between sucking him deep and using her teeth on him. A glaze of sweat glistened on Sparro's brow, and his chest heaved.

A horn sounded, and Alva pulled away so fast that Sparro staggered backward from the shock. Teeth clenched, his expression annoyed, Sparro hitched up his trousers.

He and Alva stared at the door below that opened to the fighting ground. Guards dragged two chained beasts out of the cage. They were dark, burly, hirsute creatures who tugged so hard on their bonds that Honey Wine thought the guards' arms might tear from their sockets. Protecting themselves with whips and hot irons, the guards released the creatures, hurried to the safety of the cage, and tossed swords through the bars.

The beasts scrambled for the weapons and attacked each other with little skill, merely brute strength. The fight lasted through several bloody moments before one of the creatures, his body slashed almost in half, dropped to the dirt. The victor, also dripping blood and panting loudly enough for onlookers in the balcony to hear him remained standing for several seconds before collapsing beside his dead foe.

The crowd cheered, laughter echoing throughout the room. Honey Wine repressed the urge to vomit. Death during war was bad enough, but this carnage for the fun of a wealthy, wicked audience was beyond evil!

She sat through two more matches, all the while thinking she had been wrong. The men forced to fight were less bestial than those who insisted they do so.

"It's them!" Alva squealed, nearly jumping out of her chair.

Honey Wine's heart pounded so hard for a moment she couldn't see clearly, then she focused on Torn as he walked between his guards. Unlike the other beasts, he appeared calm. Honey Wine was probably the only person in the room who noticed the faint signs of discomfort by the stiffness of his posture. His steps were uncharacteristically slow, and his face bore a strange expression she'd never seen before.

Behind him stalked his match. Tall, muscled, his skin marked with scars, Torn's opponent was held by many guards. Though, like Torn, he didn't act as wild as the other competitors, Honey Wine saw, even from such a distance, an animalistic expression in his shifting eyes. His fists flexed in his manacles, and he growled at Torn. Both men, like all others in the match, wore daggers at their hips.

The two were released and weapons tossed to them, a sword to Torn's opponent, and a staff to Torn.

A Staff! Honey Wine nearly screamed with terror and leapt out of her chair. Was Torn mad? He could have had the weapon of his choice, yet he picked a staff to use against that maniac's sword?

Master Sparro turned to Alva and smiled. "Now we'll watch that champion of yours die. You're not the only one who possesses a Knight of the Ruby Order. We captured that one down there months ago, and unlike yours, he's completely forgotten his vows. I guess that's what proper training does."

Shocked, Honey Wine stared at Torn and the other Knight below. They circled one another, and she thought she heard them exchange words but was too far away to be certain.

Torn's opponent attacked first. Beneath her cloak, Honey Wine clasped her manacled hands so tightly they ached.

The Knights attacked each other with such strength and swiftness that many of their movements were imperceptible. They seemed matched in skill, so Honey Wine knew eventually Torn's staff would fail against the other man's sword.

The crowd had fallen silent, until Torn's arm was slashed by the tip of his opponent's sword. Several people cheered. Though Torn had slipped the brunt of the blow, blood still ran down his arm. He knew better than to pause to look at the wound.

For several more moments, the battle raged. Finally, Torn's staff landed a powerful blow across his match's face. As the man staggered, Torn struck him between the legs, then knocked the sword from his grasp.

The other Knight regained himself and kicked Torn in the mid-section, sending him sprawling onto his back. He lunged on top of Torn, the staff between them, the beast — for he truly was no longer a Knight—pressing the weapon down toward Torn's chest. Torn's wounded arm must have hindered him, still he managed to break the man's hold.

"Amazing," Alva murmured. "I've never seen anything like this. It's beautiful. Like a dance. They're two perfectly matched partners."

"Yes." Master Sparro's gaze remained fixed on the warriors. "But your Knight has never killed. Mine does so on a weekly basis."

Alva turned to Honey Wine briefly and gloated. "I think that will be his downfall."

Below, the Knights had drawn their daggers, since Torn's staff had also been knocked out of the battle. They circled each other, eyes shining with battle-lust, bodies streaked with blood and sweat.

Torn shook his head. The other man shrieked in fury before he attacked.

They stabbed and slashed, dodged and ducked. The dirt flew under their feet, raising clouds of dust.

It happened so quickly Honey Wine thought she'd imagined it. The beast lashed out, Torn didn't move quickly enough, and the dagger plunged into the upper left part of his chest. His bellow of pain sounded throughout the arena, and before his opponent landed the deathblow, Torn's own dagger drove deep into the man's heart.

The crowd rose, and so did Honey Wine, however she didn't cheer. She watched in horror as the Knight dropped to the dirt floor, Torn on his knees beside him. The fatally wounded man touched Torn's hair, the motion gentle, almost grateful, before he dropped his hand and died.

Alva switched her gloating look to Master Sparro who dropped back into his chair, staring in disbelief at the scene below.

Guards were already walking into the arena, and Honey Wine said to Alva, "Let me go down."

Alva glanced at Sparro. "Sweet child. She wants a closer look at the winner."

Together Honey Wine and Alva descended the steps. They walked to the holding cells below the arena. Torn lay on a cot, Bron and Timus standing over him while another healer, an ancient, wrinkled old woman, examined the wound. Honey Wine shoved her way past the guards and looked at Torn with concern. His face was ashen, and blood soaked his woolen vest. By the unfocused look in his eyes, she thought he might lose consciousness.

"Is he salvageable?" Alva asked.

The healer was about to speak, but Honey Wine was quicker. "Yes. Let me out of these damn things!" She shook open her robe and held up her hands.

Alva glanced from Torn to Honey Wine and shrugged. "Untie her and let her help. It would be a pity to lose him now that he's finally killed."

Timus unlocked Honey Wine's bonds and she didn't even bother rubbing her sore wrists.

She set to work with the healer as Alva walked away.

Before they began, the old woman forced Torn to drink a foul-smelling mixture for pain. Still, Timus and Bron were required to hold Torn immobile while Honey Wine and the old woman removed the blade. The ancient one murmured to herself as she worked, and at first Honey Wine thought her mind had been ravaged by age, but her gnarled hands were deft. Honey Wine soon realized the woman knew more about healing than she did. While she cleaned and cauterized the wound, Honey Wine assisted.

By then, the herbs and blood loss had rendered Torn unconscious. The guards left them alone and helped in moving the beasts who hadn't been severely injured back into the wagons that would return them to their kingdoms.

Unhindered by the guard's scrutiny, Honey Wine let her hand stray to Torn's face. She was becoming desperate, and she knew they had to escape soon.

She dropped her hand suddenly when she realized the old woman had stopped her muttering to watch her.

"Don't concern yourself," the old one whispered. "I won't tell anyone."

"Tell them what?" Honey Wine used her height advantage to glower down at the woman, disguising her fear of discovery behind a daunting facade.

"That you care for him."

"He's just a beast."

"Not that one. Not yet. The Mistress banished me to this place years ago. I live here, healing the beasts after Entertainment. I've watched this one. There's still a soul in him, and I might be old, but I haven't forgotten what it's like to care for a man."

"You're wrong," Honey Wine stated. Torn moaned in his sleep and she turned to him. When she looked back, the healer smiled, though not unkindly.

"I understand," she continued, talking more to herself than to Honey Wine. "I've kept secrets, and now that I'm nearing the end of my life, I look back and don't like what I see. So much blood spilt, but no wars since I was a child. Her mother started it, you know."

"Whose mother?"

"The Mistress'."

My mother, thought Honey Wine.

"When I was a girl, younger than you, I was betrothed to a beautiful man. He was so handsome. His eyes were so dark...so dark..."

She closed her eyes, and for a moment Honey Wine thought she'd fallen to dreaming.

"He was a brilliant architect. Designed palaces and walls, towers, entire villages. The Old Mistress, this one's mother, asked him to build her palace. There were passageways and dungeons with vast chambers and torture devices...I shudder to think of them. Of course, my betrothed had nothing to do with the tortures, or so he thought, but his design has enabled these games to be hidden so well."

For the first time, Honey Wine felt genuine interest in the old woman's story. "In The Mistress' palace, were there hidden passages leading to and from the dungeon?"

She smiled again. "Yes. There was a single passage."

Honey Wine glanced around to make certain no one was paying attention to them. She leaned closer to the woman. "Where is it?"

"The well. Swim deep then high, and it opens into a pool in the courtyard."

Honey Wine's heart pounded. Could she trust this old woman, or was she a spy commanded by the guards or Alva?

"You say your betrothed created the palace. Did you never marry him?"

"I would have, but The Old Mistress had him executed. If she knew he'd told me his secrets, I would be dead as well. By the life I've led in this horrid arena, I believe I would have been better off."

"I'm sorry," Honey Wine told her. She couldn't help feeling a bit guilty since her own mother had caused this woman so much grief. Honey Wine often wondered why she'd never been able to love her mother. She believed it was because her mother had never loved her. For the first years of her life, Honey Wine had lived with her father on his farm, then her mother had sent for her and had her trained in the guard. She was to protect Alva. Protect Alva! It was the world which needed protection from her! Alva had questioned their mother's decision to carry the child of a peasant. She'd told Honey Wine so when she was ten years old and sprained her arm in training. Their mother wanted someone of strong stock but of royal blood to defend Alva. That might have been partially true, but Honey Wine also saw the way her mother lusted after her peasant father's rugged looks and rough ways.

Their mother was just like Alva, spoiled, vicious, and evil.

"Your secret is safe with me," Honey Wine told the old woman.

She sighed. "Part of me almost wishes you'd tell the guards."

"I'd never do that."

"Then at least let me leave this life knowing you'll use my secret well."

Honey Wine knew better than to trust anyone with her plans for escape, but the old woman did look genuinely disturbed about all she'd known and seen. Honey Wine said, "If there's ever a chance some good will come of it, you have my word."

That seemed to satisfy her.

Timus and Bron approached and lugged Torn's unconscious body to the wagon. None of the beasts were ever left in the arena. Many died on the journey back to the dungeon, but Torn wouldn't. He couldn't. Not when he and Honey Wine finally had a means of escape.

Chapter Five

Back in the dungeon, guards dropped Torn on the bench in his cell.

Honey Wine retrieved a bucket of water, staring into the blackness of the well as she did so, unable to see the water, let alone the bottom. She brought the bucket and her supply box to Torn's cell.

"Let me in," she ordered Timus.

The guard raised an eyebrow. "What for?"

"He can't be left alone tonight. His injury is too serious."

"I can't let you spend the night in a cell."

"The Mistress wants him alive for Entertainment. If he dies, I'll tell her that you were at fault for not allowing me to perform my duty."

Bron, who had been listening to the entire conversation, nodded at Timus. "Let her in."

Timus shrugged and unlocked the cell.

Bron glanced at Honey Wine as she passed. "All dogs die eventually, Honey Wine."

"Hold that thought, Bron. Your day will come."

The cell door clanged shut behind her, and Timus turned the key.

She knelt beside the bench and examined Torn's wound. She and the old healer had worked hard to get it clean, and Honey Wine hoped there would be no infection. To her relief, his skin was cool to the touch. She covered him with the tattered blanket at the foot of the bench.

His hand brushed hers, and she cast an anxious glance outside. Timus had his back to them, and no one else was paying attention.

She turned back to Torn and found herself staring into his dark blue eyes.

"I killed him," he murmured.

"Just rest, Torn."

"His name was Redly. I knew him for five years."

"I'm sure he was no longer the man you knew."

"I'm no longer the man I used to be. This place changes everything."

"You've never killed before?"

"Never like that. In the heat of battle, as defense. Never for someone's pleasure. Never one of my own."

"You were fighting, Torn. It was an impulse. Self-preservation. Anyone would have done the same. I don't know how you've repressed your own survival instincts for so long...in here."

"I never thought it would be like this..." His voice trailed off, his eyelids drooping. He swallowed audibly. "He didn't deserve to die like that."

"Nor do you, but that didn't stop him from trying to kill you."

"He wanted to die."

"Then you did him a favor."

"I almost wish he'd killed me."

"Almost." She touched his forearm, wishing she could kiss him as they'd kissed that night in The Lady's chamber, but she couldn't risk being seen. Maybe later, when the cells were dark with only a guard or two posted. "Almost, but not quite. You have the will to survive, Torn. I still plan on getting us out of here."

"Once I'm recovered, we can try." He used his fingertips to slide a blade from his bloodstained pants. "There's a hollow space under the bench. Put it there for me."

"Where did you get it?" She hid the blade against her palm and forearm as she slipped it discreetly under the bench.

"It's the one you removed from my chest. I took it off the tray after the guards left, when your back was turned."

Honey Wine marveled at his deftness, even in such a vulnerable state. "I thought you were unconscious."

"I was for a while, then again in the wagon. Even now it's a little hard to concentrate."

"You lost a lot of blood."

He nodded, closing his eyes. After a moment, she thought he'd fallen asleep, but he said, "You don't have to stay here."

But she did. She hadn't exaggerated when she'd told Timus about the severity of Torn's condition. Until she was satisfied that he was out of danger of infection, she planned on watching him closely.

He pushed himself onto his elbows and looked around the cell, dazed.

"Will you stay down!" She pushed him back onto the bench. "Or else the guards are likely to think you're attacking me and come in here and do worse damage."

"I just want some water."

She filled a mug from the bucket, added several drops of an herbal mixture she knew would put him to sleep and held it for him. He placed his hand over hers as he drank, then lay back down, murmuring, "I don't want the guards to think you favor me. It could be bad for you."

"Let me worry about that," she said too loudly.

Timus glanced over his shoulder. "How's that? Are you talking to yourself, Honey Wine? Or has that beast decided he's not mute after all."

"Of course I'm talking to myself," she snapped. "Why shouldn't I? No one else in this damn place listens to me."

Timus shook his head and walked closer to the next cell.

When Honey Wine looked back, Torn was deeply asleep, lips slightly parted. She impulsively traced his mouth with her fingertip. Tomorrow, she would slip into the courtyard and see if the old woman's story about a passage beneath the well was the truth or a fable created by an aging mind.

She wrapped her cloak around her shoulders as she sat on the floor of the cell, her back braced against the stone wall, and closed her eyes.

When she awoke, the torches outside the cells had burned low. Other than a guard posted at the door and Timus who stood watch several cells down, there was no security. The cages were of solid steel bars and locked. Only Timus and Bron held keys. If a passage truly existed through the well, escape from the dungeon itself would be easier than she'd hoped.

Torn was still asleep. She placed her palm to his cool forehead and sighed with relief. So few survived fevers under the dirty prison conditions, but Torn was strong and healthy, and if he survived the night, she had few doubts he would completely recover. She knew he wouldn't be expected to return to the arena until he was healed, and by then, their escape plans would be set.

Glancing over her shoulder, Honey Wine made certain Timus wasn't watching before she bent and placed a brief kiss on Torn's mouth. His eyes flickered open, and he smiled slightly. His knuckles brushed across the back of her hand, and their fingers entwined, squeezing gently. They didn't speak, but their eyes communicated everything they felt.

She sat on the floor close to his bench, facing outward so she would know if Timus approached.

"Tell me about your home," she whispered.

He took so long to answer that she didn't think he'd heard her. Finally he said, "It's a fortress in Rubyshire. Tall. Gray. But inside, it resembles the cathedrals in the countries south of here."

"It's said your Order is rooted in religion but you don't worship the Goddesses. Is that true?"

"Most of us believe in a Spirit who has no gender."

"What does your family think of this?"

"The Order is my family. My parents died when I was an infant. I was raised by Knights. Mahir, he's our leader, is like a father to me."

Honey Wine smiled slightly, sadly when she thought of how much Torn must be missed. In cells all around them were men who were missed. Men who had been forced to become beasts. For the first time, she wished she could free them all, but she knew that was impossible.

"It doesn't matter what deity you worship," she told him. "Your Order does good. That's all that matters. They don't take women, though, or else I might have joined once we get out of here."

"The Opal Order is exclusively female. Some of the Knights have wives, sisters and daughters who serve that Order. They could introduce you."

Honey Wine smiled and shook her head. "No. I don't think I could be like you. My temper is too bad. I hate too much."

"Funny you can say that after what I did tonight. How am I going to explain about Redly?"

"He tried to kill you!"

"That wasn't him."

"Then you didn't kill him. He was already dead."

"Honey Wine," he drew a deep breath, and she saw him struggle not to wince against the pain in his chest, "there's so much you don't understand about the Order, things I don't agree with…"

"Not nearly as much as I don't agree with about the rules here. Nothing is perfect, Torn."

"But—"

"Shh! Timus is making his rounds." She slipped away from Torn as Timus walked past the cells and stopped in front of theirs.

"Is he still breathing?" Timus asked.

"He's doing as well as can be expected."

"Fever?"

"No fever."

"Good. Bron told me to ask how long you think it will be before he can participate in Entertainment again."

"Not for a couple of months at least."

"A couple of months?" Timus shook his head. "The Mistress won't like that."

"The Mistress should be glad that he's salvageable."

"That's true," Timus said. "He's the strongest one we've had down here in a long time. Truth be told, he's not all that bad as beasts go. I wish they were all as simple to handle."

"It would make our jobs so much easier, wouldn't it?" Honey Wine wondered if Timus caught the underlying disgust in her voice.

"Sure would. You really want to stay there until morning?"

She nodded. "At dawn, you can let me out so I can wash, then I'll come back and get my morning rounds done. I'll catch some sleep after that."

Timus smiled at her and nodded before continuing down the room.

"You should have told him to let you out," Torn said as Honey Wine sat beside him. "Maybe you should forget about what we planned. I don't want to cause you any harm. I know I agreed to plan our escape. I wasn't thinking about what's best for you."

His words made her tingle with anger. "I'm not a child, Torn. I don't need you to look out for me."

"Then why are you looking out for me?"

Her anger dissipated. "The truth is, if I hadn't met you, I never would have found the courage to even try escaping. This is just as much a chance at freedom for me as it is for you."

"I don't want you to be hurt—"

"Then think about how I must feel watching you suffer. Not only you, but also everyone down here. For years, I've shielded myself against how I really feel because I thought there was nothing I could do. I might not be able to rescue everyone, but we can escape together. You can go back to your old life, and I can find a new one."

"Even if we escape the palace, we're sure to be chased. We'll need weapons of some sort."

"I don't have any access to weapons. Alva had Bron make sure of that."

"Can you get a blowpipe?"

"I suppose I could find something like that. Why?"

His blue eyes darted to the stone ledge above the bars of his cell. "I've been saving the bones from meals and making darts. The guards never actually come into the cells, so I've been storing them on that ledge. I've seen the herbs in your supply box. Some of them are poisonous. We can treat the darts with poison, and if you can get us pipes to shoot the darts, we'll have weapons."

She glanced at him as if seeing him for the first time. Her gentle Knight could be crafty when the situation required it. She nodded. "You've been doing quite a bit of planning for this escape, and I want you to know I've been doing my part. Today, if everything goes as I hope, I'll have useful information for you."

"What sort of information?"

"I'll tell you later." She leaned close and kissed him again quickly.

"Just be careful," he told her. "And if at any time you want to abort this plan, I'll never hold it against you."

"I've never wanted anything this badly in my life," she said. *Except, perhaps, you...*

Chapter Six

After leaving the prison that morning, Honey Wine went directly to the courtyard under the pretense of bathing in the pond. As she'd assumed, it was empty. Only Alva or her guests ever ventured into the courtyard, and knowing her sister, Honey Wine guessed it would be hours before she rose from the comfort of her bed and the arms of whichever lover she'd taken the night before.

Honey Wine slipped from her dress and into the chilly water. Drawing a deep breath, she swam out to the pool's center and dove. She swam deeper than she'd ever tried before, past green vines and goldfish until she neared a cave at the rocky bottom. A glance behind her revealed the sunlight melting through the water's surface.

She could certainly swim, but was not a diver by any means and knew that soon she would need air. Still, the cave was the only possible tunnel, if the old healer had been speaking the truth. She swam through the stony opening, and the water grew murky. A faint, eerie glow shone above. Rocks were hard and slippery beneath her feet as she pushed off from the bottom toward the strange light. As she broke the surface, she tried not to gasp loudly as her every breath echoed in the slimy stone tunnel where she found herself. Just above her, she heard voices. She recognized Timus, Bron and several other guards. So it was true! She was at the bottom of the well.

The bucket dropped into the water beside Honey Wine, nearly striking her face. Honey Wine bit her lip to keep from crying out in surprise. She'd better swim away before she was knocked unconscious and drowned. The thought made laugher stick in her throat, as she felt giddy with the hope of escape and the challenge it provided. For too long she'd lived in the drudgery of the prison. Slowly, her own warrior's soul woke from its slumber. For the first time in years, she felt willing to fight for her freedom.

She drew a deep breath and swam back down the well. As she emerged, her heart pounded, and she became momentarily disoriented. If she didn't remember which way to swim, she could drown since the pool was the only surface point she remembered passing.

Finally, she broke the surface and climbed out of the pool, wiping water from her eyes. Her hands trembled with excitement. She could scarcely wait to tell Torn what she'd learned, but it would have to wait. Both must be careful not to give away their plan.

After dressing hastily, she returned to the prison. Though tired from spending the night on the floor of Torn's cell, excitement coursed through her. She knew that even when she retired to her chamber, sleep would elude her.

In the dungeon, she checked several sick and injured beasts. When she reached Torn's cell, he lay so quietly on his bench she thought he was asleep. She no sooner stooped beside him than his gaze met hers.

She leaned close as she changed his bandage and whispered, "I've found a way out of here. Down the well, there's a passage—" She stopped speaking as Bron approached and watched her work.

"So we finally made a killer out of him," Bron said.

"And you sound so happy about it," she said.

He shrugged. "Truth be told, I'm glad he's alive. Wagering on him is an easy way to earn some coins."

She wound the bandage across Torn's chest, then touched a hand to his shoulder, guiding him back onto the bench. The urge to brush a wavy lock of hair from his eyes was overpowering, yet she resisted.

"You understand you have no soul left, Bron," Honey Wine stated. "None of us down here have any souls. We're complacent, and that's as much a sin as Alva supporting the Entertainment. This...beast...was the only creature down here who had a soul."

"Had, that's the important word, Honey Wine." Bron winked. "Now he's one of us, eh? When he recovers, I can hardly wait to watch him tear apart bait in the training cell."

"Just because he killed to protect himself doesn't mean he'll kill defenseless people."

"Don't fool yourself, Honey Wine." Bron nodded in Torn's direction. "He has the taste for blood. Besides, if you're supposed to have such sympathy for these creatures, you should be happy he's finally learned to play the game. Or did you get some sort of perverse pleasure from seeing him suffer? Maybe you want to watch another session of him with The Lady."

Honey Wine stood, fists clenched at her sides, and took a furious step toward Bron. Behind her, out of Bron's sight, she felt Torn's hand on her dress. He tugged gently, and Honey Wine stopped, willing herself to remain calm.

Torn was right, of course. If she kept control of herself, once he was recovered, both would be free. Or die fighting for their freedom...

* * * * *

During the next two weeks, while Torn recovered, Honey Wine stashed supplies for their escape. She prepared small amounts of the poison he'd requested for the darts and hoarded healing supplies beneath her mattress. She had a second cloak made, and saved what little coin her sister allowed as her wages.

"When's the next full moon?" Torn whispered one evening as Honey Wine changed his bandage before retiring to bed.

"Tomorrow night," she replied. Their escape would have to be on a clear night of a full moon, or else they'd never find their way through the murky water. "But we'll wait for the next. The wound is healing quickly, but you're not recovered enough to travel."

"I can," he said. "If I wait until the next moon, I'll be sent to Entertainment. I won't go there. Not again."

Honey Wine finished applying the bandage and let her fingers stray to his neck. She traced the strong shape of it and touched the hollow of his throat. He was right. If they waited too long, he'd be forced to fight again, and she knew he would sooner destroy himself than kill unjustly. However if they attempted escape before he was strong enough to make the journey, they could both be destroyed.

He took her hand and met her gaze. "I'd never endanger you. Believe me when I say I'm ready."

Honey Wine nodded. He had healed with remarkable swiftness, and she well knew his strength. It was time for them to move on.

"Then we'll do it tomorrow at midnight, just as we planned."

She stooped to retrieve her supply box, and he grasped her arm. When she turned, he was so close that their lips almost touched, and her heartbeat quickened.

"You're the most courageous person I've ever known," he said. "I wanted you to know that and thank you for what you've done for me."

She nodded, her fingertips brushing his before she left his cell.

The following morning, Honey Wine could scarcely concentrate on any of her duties. She both dreaded and desired the coming night. It might be a wonderful beginning for her and Torn or it could be an agonizing end.

"Honey Wine!" Bron grasped her arm as she stepped into the prison. "You and the Knight are to start breeding again."

"No!" She snarled, suddenly fearful that if Torn left his cell it might be searched and the tools for their escape discovered.

Bron grinned, running his tongue over his thick lips. "You haven't got a choice. I'll tell you, it does my soul good to see the former Captain of the Guard being pawed by a beast. No better than a common whore, you are, Honey Wine."

"You probably enjoy watching so much because no woman will take you to her bed. I remember seeing that pathetic little cock of yours in the bathhouse. I've seen mice with more to brag about."

Bron's face reddened and his fingers bit into her arm. "Fucking whore!"

He dragged her toward the breeding pen, but she jerked away from him. "I'm not going in the disgusting pen again! If I must breed with him, then I'll do it in his cell."

"In his cell?" Bron's anger was replaced by a leer. He bellowed with laughter.

"At least I know I clean it every day after I tend him!"

"Oh, this I've got to see!" He grinned, shoving her back into the prison.

Torn appeared surprised by the expression that must have been showing on Honey Wine's face as Bron unlocked the cell and shoved her inside.

"Go to it."

Torn stood and shrugged in question.

"We're supposed to mate again," she said, jaw taut.

Torn's eyes took on a chilling expression as he approached the bars, his teeth visibly clenched with fury.

Bron laughed, though he moved out of Torn's reach. "I don't think he likes the idea of fucking you again, Honey Wine."

She folded her arms across her chest. "If he doesn't then, there's not much point. You can't make a man perform."

"Oh no?" Bron suddenly lunged forward and Torn jumped back, but not before the guard had managed to stick a tiny needle in his neck. Torn jerked it out, staring at the pointed, reddish tip.

"The Lady said he won't be able to resist mating now." Bron snorted with laughter, dragged a stool in front of the cage, and sat. "If it works on him, I might ask The Lady for some myself."

Torn glanced at Honey Wine, and she saw panic in his dark blue eyes. Within moments, the aphrodisiac began its work. Torn paced the cell, expression tense, and Honey Wine couldn't keep her eyes from his cock that stood, stiff as a pike, before him.

Her heart pounding, she tried pretending they were alone, that Bron wasn't leering at them from several feet away and that other beasts and guards stood around the prison.

None of them, besides Bron and a few passing guards, could actually see what was going on in the cell, anyway.

Grasping Torn's wrists, she tugged him toward his cot. His eyes pleaded with her, telling her he was no longer in control of himself. She tried to tell him with her own eyes that it was all right. Soon, they would be out of this horrible prison and free to live a life of dignity where they could make love if they wanted, when they wanted and with the privacy such intimacy deserved.

Honey Wine lay on her back, and Torn's body covered hers. She was again surprised when he didn't penetrate her. Pressing his cock between their bellies was enough to send his drugged body into a frenzy. Closing her eyes, Honey Wine grasped his buttocks as he lunged against her. Within seconds she felt his seed against her belly and breasts, but almost magically, his cock was hard again. Two more times he came, the last dragging her with him. Her pussy ached for him, and she slid her hand between them, clasping his steely cock and guiding it toward her hot, wet slit, but he grasped her hand and pulled it away. He moved lower, drying his essence from her flesh with his blanket. He ran the rough blanket over her pebble-hard nipples before taking one of them in his mouth and running his tongue over it.

Honey Wine gasped, eyes tightly shut, and pressed his head closer. His tongue laved both nipples before he slid up her body and sat up. She stared at him, panting. His chest was heaving and his eyes were glazed with passion in spite of the flickers of anger in their blue depths. She didn't blame him for despising what was being done to them, but in spite of his rage, the aphrodisiac had him hard as a steel club. He stood, glaring at Bron who stared at them from his stool, one hand clutching his groin, his own breathing quick.

How Honey Wine hated him! One day, she vowed to repay him for every bit of humiliation he caused both her and Torn!

As Bron approached, with the key to the cell, Honey Wine noticed Torn's fists clench and saw by his temper he was on the verge of attacking the guard.

She placed a hand to his chest and said, "It's almost over."

"It is over," Bron stated, though he had no way of knowing she meant their time in captivity was almost over. Torn nodded almost imperceptibly and walked to the back of the cell, his entire body tense with combined rage and sexual desire. At least he was smart enough not to risk their escape by a foolish attack on Bron.

The guard continued speaking as he released Honey Wine. "He can spend the rest of the day playing with himself until that herb wears off. Yes, I'll be talking to The Lady about getting some of that for myself."

One day, you bastard, you'll regret everything you've ever done to us, Honey Wine thought. *I don't care how long it takes, but right now, I have more important plans. Tonight, Torn. Tonight we'll be free.*

* * * * *

Before she left the holding cells that evening, she slipped Torn one of the blowpipes he'd asked for as well as poison for the darts.

Their eyes met before she went to her chamber. There she filled her supply case and hid a satchel of food and clothes beneath her cloak. She took her usual walk to the courtyard and hid the case and the satchel behind several small, clipped bushes. She slipped off her cloak and hid that, too.

Back in her chamber, Honey Wine lay on the bed, heart hammering. Unable to relax, she alternated between sitting on the bed and pacing the chamber.

Shortly before midnight, she slipped from her chamber and to the holding cell. As usual, a single guard stood at the door.

"A little late for you to be here, isn't it, Honey Wine?" he asked.

"I realized I left behind a medicine bottle. I have to get it."

"Can't that wait until morning?"

"It's a very strong potion, and I'm afraid that if I left it in one of the beast's cages, the creature might poison himself. It'll only take me a moment to find it."

The guard nodded and unlocked the door. Almost as soon as she stepped inside, her eyes riveted to Timus who lay in an unconscious heap on the floor beside the branding table. The guard hurried to Timus, and as he stooped to examine him, Honey Wine took a branding iron from the wall and struck him in the head. He crumpled.

Several of the beasts stirred, but drifted back to sleep. Honey Wine rushed to the door and locked it from the inside, then took the keys from Timus and released Torn.

"We have to hurry," she whispered. "Everything's ready in the courtyard."

Torn nodded, and she noticed beneath his calm veneer, his eyes looked as tense as she felt.

They hurried to the well and she sat on the edge. Torn grasped her wrists and lowered her downward. Her toes touched the cold water, and he let her drop. She landed with a soft splash. Seconds later, waves dashed against her face as Torn sank in the water beside her.

In complete blackness, she groped for him.

"Hold my skirt so we won't get separated," she whispered, her palms braced against his shoulders. "Wait a moment."

"What?"

She felt for his face in the darkness and kissed his mouth. His lips were moist from the water. One of his strong arms snaked around her waist and pressed her to the hard length of his body.

"All right, let's go." She tugged free of his embrace, drew a deep breath, and dove beneath the surface. Below, the black water faded to deep blue. Once out of the well, the water was terrifying in its darkness, but far ahead, moonlight rippled, and she knew the pool in the courtyard waited above. Torn must have seen it as well, and as they neared the lighter water, he released her skirt and swam beside her, his inky hair blending with the waves.

They broke the surface simultaneously, blinking water from their eyes as they searched for guards. To their relief, the courtyard was empty.

"Come on," Honey Wine said, swimming toward shore. They stepped out of the water, and she handed him their cloaks. She'd attached a rope to her supply box so she could sling it over her shoulder and across her chest. Torn took the satchel, and they walked to the fence. The walls were high and completely smooth. There were no footholds.

Honey Wine said, "I'm tall enough to reach the top if you give me a boost. There's a rope in the satchel so I can lower it to you and help pull you up."

He narrowed his eyes at the wall before he stooped so she could stand on his shoulders. When he rose to his full height, she had little trouble grasping the top of the wall and pulling herself up. He tossed her the satchel, and while she searched for the rope, he landed in a squat on ledge beside her.

She nearly fell off the wall in surprise as she looked from the ground below into Torn's amused eyes.

Her brow furrowed. "How did you do that?"

"Years of practice." He grasped her hands and lowered her over the edge of the wall. From where she dangled, the drop to the ground was merely a few feet. He released her and she landed, bending her knees against the impact. The satchel landed near her, and Torn followed.

Forest loomed in the distance, and Honey Wine sensed freedom.

Torn gazed up at the moon and said, "We have a few hours until dawn. We'll have to make good time."

"We can head for the forest and travel upriver to hide our tracks," she told him.

"Good. Rubyshire is on the other side of the forest. We can reach it by midday if we keep a steady pace."

"If we—"

"Hey! What the hell are you two doing?" shouted two guards who had been circling the palace.

"Get him! It's one of the beasts. He's got Honey Wine!"

The guards drew their swords and raced at them. Honey Wine reached for her blowpipe and darts and took aim as Torn met the warriors head on. Her heart pounded as he dodged the slashing blades, certain he'd be killed. He swept one of the guard's feet out from under him, sending the man crashing to his back. The second guard nearly tripped over the first, and Torn took his moment of distraction to kick the sword from his hand. While Torn dealt with the second guard, Honey Wine shot a dart into the man on the ground. With two serpentine hand strikes, Torn rendered both soldiers unconscious.

Honey Wine shot a dart into the second man, to ensure that he, like his companion, would remain asleep for several hours.

Torn, his breathing even as if he'd just awakened, took up the satchel.

As they ran toward the woods, she said, "I still find it hard to believe it took only eight of my sister's guards to capture you."

He glanced at her, but didn't reply. Neither of them spoke again, but concentrated solely on reaching the woods. Several guards they could lose, but an entire troop would follow as soon as the others discovered the prison break. Then they'd ride them down and kill them, no matter how well she and Torn fought.

Torn knew in which direction to travel and therefore set the pace. Considering the severity of his injury such a short time ago, his stamina surprised Honey Wine. As they trudged upland through the water at a brisk, steady pace, she was reminded of the forced marches on which she'd accompanied her troops before her banishment to the dungeon. By dawn, they were miles from the palace and deep in the woods.

As the sun rose higher, they stopped for a brief rest. They drank from the river, ate some of the bread and cheese she'd packed in the satchel, and sat together on a wide, flat stone overlooking the water. She opened his cloak and unraveled the bandage from his chest. The injury was healing well, and she was glad their escape hadn't caused any further damage.

"Are you doing all right?" he asked.

"Of course. The faster we move, the better. Thank the Goddesses no one's followed us. Yet."

"As long as we keep to the water, they won't be able to track us. We'll be home in a few hours." He suddenly looked sympathetic and covered her hand with his. "I guess I've taken you from your home, haven't I?"

She snorted with laughter. "Some home. The only real home I knew was when I grew up with my father and grandmother. Then my mother took me to the palace when I was ten years old. I didn't even know my father was killed until days after his death. I should have left Sophianna years ago, but life as a guard was all I knew."

"You'll be welcome at the Order for as long as you want to stay."

She glanced down at her rough hands, for the first time feeling apprehension about meeting the rest of Torn's Order. She knew how courageous, strong and just Torn was. He'd chosen a life of service, but she'd lived a life of violence. There was a vast difference between a guard and a Knight of the Ruby Order. Yes, she'd become a healer in the dungeon, but again, she'd been forced. She'd lived a life among rugged men, fighting with them, becoming one of them.

"What will they think of me?" she asked softly.

He smiled slightly and touched his fingertip to her chin, tilting her face up toward his. "I'm sure they'll be charmed. As I was."

She shook her head, feeling an uncharacteristic blush creep into her cheeks. "That's only because you were imprisoned. If you'd been able to think clearly, you'd never have felt that way."

"No matter where we met, I'd have felt the same."

She drew a deep breath and gazed at the rippling water. "Will I like the Order?"

He tilted his head and looked both amused and perplexed. "I hope so. You'll appreciate Mahir, I think."

"Your foster father? The leader of your Order?"

Torn nodded. "He's outspoken, and he knows many things."

They stood and continued walking.

"How many of you are there?" she asked.

"As of now, five thousand Knights. Some are married and their wives and children live in the fortress or in houses throughout Rubyshire. A few are married to Dames from the Opal Order and live with them. Of course, not all of us are there at one time. We travel wherever we're needed. Your healing skills will be useful to us while you're there, and there will be more for you to learn, if you're interested."

"I am," she said, allowing herself to fantasize about what it would be like to marry Torn, to live and work at the Order. "I guess they'll be glad to get you back."

His blue eyes flickered sadly toward her. "I don't know. After they hear about Redly —"

"Torn, that wasn't your fault."

"It was my hand that killed him. No one forced me."

Honey Wine sighed and shook her head. If all the Knights were like him, she wasn't sure she'd be able to understand them.

A couple of hours later, Torn stopped suddenly and grasped her arm. He stood still, his gaze shifting through the trees.

"Do you hear that?" he whispered.

"Hear what…" she paused, then met his gaze, panic tightening her chest. "Dogs, damn it!"

"Up!" he stated.

They grasped the overhanging branches of a nearby tree and climbed. She watched him from where she clung to the branches above his head. Glancing up at her, he placed a finger to his lips.

Below, two muscular dogs with short tawny coats bounded into the water's shallow edge, barking so loudly she was sure she felt the vibrations through the tree branches.

"Wait a second." Torn swung down to a lower branch. "I know those dogs. Melinda! Roland!"

The dogs stopped, their squashed black and tan faces searching around, then upward. Upon seeing Torn, they barked with new enthusiasm, their stubby tails wagging.

"What's going on you two?" a man's voice shouted to the dogs. "What have you chased up a tree? Squirrels most likely."

Honey Wine strained to see through the leafy branches. A large man with curling black hair and a full beard rode a shaggy, big-boned chestnut stallion into the clearing. The man wore black leather trousers and a black thigh-length tunic with a red circle of thorns embroidered over his heart, a single ruby glistening in the center. The uniform of the Ruby Order. A quiver of arrows hung over his shoulder, and he carried a bow.

"Rain!" Torn called, dropping to the ground.

The horse pawed the ground, its movements expressing the surprise on its master's face.

"Torn?" The Knight dismounted, smiling, his dogs clamoring for attention around his ankles. "Where the hell have you been? We thought you weren't ever coming back." Rain's black-gloved hands jerked Torn's robe open to inspect his bandaged chest. "You've been wounded?"

"Two weeks ago. It's healing."

Honey Wine climbed down from the tree and into Torn's waiting arms.

"Who's this?" Rain demanded, though not unkindly. Honey Wine noticed he was even taller than Torn and several years his senior. Deep laugh lines marked his mouth and eyes, somehow adding to his charming appearance.

"This is Honey Wine. I've been imprisoned in her land of Sophianna. She helped me escape. It's a long story. I want to get back to the Order because we're most likely being tracked."

Rain's expression became serious as his eyes swept the area. "Let's go. You two take my horse. You look like you've traveled hard."

Honey Wine and Torn mounted the tall stallion as Rain fell into step beside them, Melinda and Roland trotting ahead, their noses lowered to the ground.

She slipped her arms around Torn as they rode, her breasts pressed to his hard, straight spine.

"Mahir will be glad to see you," Rain said as they moved onward. "They all will. You've been missed. Blaze has been very concerned. He didn't speak of it, but I think he thought you were dead. It's not always clear for him."

Honey Wine felt Torn sigh, and she tightened her arms around him as they continued their journey in relative silence.

Chapter Seven

The trees thinned as the forest opened into a hilly green field. In the distance, a vast gray fortress reached toward the midday sun. A section of the field in front of the fortress served as a mock battlefield for Knights on horseback, practicing archery, and training in hand-to-hand combat. Even to Honey Wine's trained eye, the Knights of the Ruby Order were formidable warriors. Their methods of hand fighting were unusual, as they executed strikes, holds and kicks, used by none of the soldiers in surrounding kingdoms.

"I think I'm privileged," Honey Wine remarked, her gaze intent on the warriors. "I don't imagine too many people get to see Knights of the Ruby Order training up close."

"It is a sight." Rain smiled, his eyes glistening with humor and pride. "Tomorrow you can come with me for archery practice."

"I'd love it." She looked at the Knight, unable to disguise her excitement. It had been too long since she'd held a weapon. Too long since she'd known freedom.

"I'm watching you, Rain." Torn cast the handsome older man a sidelong glance that caused Rain to laugh harder.

"So you're not immune after all," Rain commented.

"Immune? From what?" Honey Wine spoke close to Torn's ear.

"Torn is very serious about his vows." A smile played around Rain's full lips partially concealed by his wavy beard. "I trust they're all still intact?"

"I see you haven't been awarded extra guard duty since I've been away," Torn said. "We'll have to fix that, Rain."

Rain laughed. "Pulling rank on me, Torn? Perhaps I was closer to the truth than I thought…"

The exchange between the Knights was not only amusing, but it also revealed parts of Torn that had been concealed in the prison. Honey Wine said, "This is the most interesting conversation I've heard in years."

"Thank you." Torn glanced over his shoulder, an eyebrow lifted, his voice laced with sarcasm.

She smiled and squeezed his waist. One of his hands covered both of hers, and a feeling of warmth spread throughout her body. Now that they were away from the prison, maybe they could explore more deeply the feelings rising between them.

"I'm curious about these vows," Honey Wine said to Rain. "Tell me more?"

Rain shook his head, his smile fading though his eyes still glistened with good humor. "I'd best hold my tongue or else he really will give me an extra shift."

As they approached the fortress, several Knights rode up to them, calling to Torn and staring curiously at Honey Wine.

"Back off!" Rain said gruffly. "He'll be with you soon enough."

They rode through the open gates of the fortress directly to the stables where Honey Wine and Torn dismounted. Rain placed his horse in the care of a young boy. As Honey Wine walked with Torn and Rain across the courtyard, she admired the beauty of the flowering trees and clipped bushes. A square pool stood in the center of the courtyard, the castle walls and vegetation reflecting in its crystalline surface. Children played a game of tag under the supervision of a group of women mending clothes. Upon seeing Honey Wine and her escorts, the women looked up from their work, and several of the children stopped their game and pointed.

"Look," they said. "Sir Torn is back."

"Who's that with him?"

The women's whispers were much softer, but it was obvious they were talking about Honey Wine as well.

They walked into a spacious hall furnished with rows of long, wooden tables, benches on either side. A fireplace took up one wall, and embers burned, the smoky scent filling the room. Though the weather outside was warm, the enormous stone rooms had the chill common to all castles, and the fire was necessary. They stepped through the hall, into a long, narrow corridor lined with closed doors, and up a flight of winding steps. They stopped in front of a wooden door, and Torn knocked.

"Enter," spoke a deep, masculine voice from inside.

Torn opened the door, and they stepped into a mid-sized room completely filled with books and scrolls. Shelves lined all four walls from top to bottom, save the space where the fireplace stood. An older man of average height with blue eyes and gray hair hanging past his shoulders sat at a round table also covered with books and maps. He stood, gaze fixed on Torn.

"You're back." The slightest smile touched the man's stern lips as he strode across the room and embraced Torn.

"Mahir." Torn returned his foster father's hug.

Mahir pulled back, having felt Torn's bandage, and inspected the wound.

"It's almost healed," Torn shrugged, "thanks to Honey Wine." He turned to her and said, "Honey Wine, this is Mahir, leader of The Ruby Order."

"Pleased to meet you, Sir." She curtsied, unsure if that was the proper greeting for a man of his station.

"Honey Wine?" Mahir glanced at Torn.

"I owe her my life," Torn said. "Without her, I wouldn't have made it home."

Mahir nodded, his gaze fixed on Honey Wine. Though she wanted to look away from his soul-stripping gaze, she met his eyes with determination and a bit of her own discrimination.

"You're welcome here, Lady." Mahir bowed to her. "A friend of Torn's is a friend of mine."

"Thank you. I must accept your hospitality for a time since I can't return to my home right now." She glanced at Torn, hoping he'd continue with the explanation of where they'd been and what had happened to them.

"Seems these two have had quite a time of it," Rain said. "I'll see about getting a room for Honey Wine. They haven't slept in nearly two days, and I'm sure she's tired."

Honey Wine nodded at Rain who tossed her one of his boyish smiles, rather charming on a man of his rugged appearance. It seemed that not all of the Knights were as serious as Torn, but she had also known him in prison where there was little call for silliness. Though she liked Rain's easy manner, there was something gentle yet powerful, alluring, and sensual about Torn that drew Honey Wine to him.

Mahir placed a large, callused hand on Torn's shoulder. "After you've rested, I'll need a report from you."

Honey Wine wondered if anyone noticed the surprise in her expression at Mahir's words. His foster son had been missing for months, and he hadn't even asked where he'd been! He was willing to wait for a report?

Torn nodded, and Honey Wine followed him and Rain to the door. Torn glanced over his shoulder to Mahir who had returned to his reading. "I'm glad to be back."

"I'm glad you've come back, son." Mahir nodded, the expression in his blue eyes revealing the emotions his calm face did not.

They walked back down the stairs to the hallway lined with doors.

"This one's empty." Rain stopped in front of one of the doors and opened it for Honey Wine. The small room contained a quilt-covered bed with a trunk at the foot of it. The stone floor was covered with a rope carpet, and a fireplace took half of one wall.

Rain stepped inside and kindled a fire. "Would you like me to find you something to eat?"

Honey Wine shook her head and thanked him as he left her and Torn alone. She walked to the bed and sat on the edge of it. Torn stood in the doorway, so tall his head almost brushed the top of the door, his hands folded in front of him.

"My room is next to yours, to the right, if you need anything," he said.

Honey Wine nodded slowly, her heart throbbing as she gathered the courage to speak the next words. "You're not married, are you, Torn?"

He chuckled. "No."

"Thank the Goddess, right?" She grinned. "After all we've shared together."

"Honey Wine," he walked to the bed and sat on the edge, "I know we were forced into some things, and I regret how it was done, but I don't regret you."

"No?" Her smile softened.

"Never. You're a magnificent woman."

"If I ask you something, will you answer me honestly?"

"Yes."

"I don't want you to do this because you feel you owe me. I wanted to escape just as much as you did, so all we did was help each other."

"What do you want, Honey Wine?" His dark blue eyes stared into hers. They were so calm, so powerful, those eyes she'd become accustomed to. What she had once seen as arrogance, she now knew to be strength. She could no longer recall what it felt like to hate him.

"Will you stay here with me today?"

He paused so long that her stomach twisted. He was going to refuse.

Torn locked the door. Shrugging off his clothes, he turned down the bedcovers, and stretched out on the mattress. She lay beside him, suddenly hesitant to touch him.

He pulled the blankets over them and tugged her into his arms. Her cheek rested against his smooth, hard shoulder, one of her legs entwined with his.

"Do you know how many nights I dreamed of this?" she asked, tilting her face up to his.

He kissed her. His tongue caressed hers with long, soft strokes while his hands warmed her ribs and belly.

"I want to touch you," he whispered against her lips.

She took his hand and placed it on her breast, closing her eyes as he kneaded the soft mound. His hands slid around her so his fingertips could caress her nipples.

Honey Wine moaned, reached for his trousers, and tugged his cock free.

"Honey Wine," he groaned as she tightened her fist on his cock and stroked him. She ran her thumb over the head and her fingertip along the underside, then pumped the entire shaft until he pulled her hand away and pushed her onto her back.

Pinning her hands above her head, he lifted her shirt and took one of her breasts in his mouth, rolling his tongue over the nipple and sucking the hard little nub until she moaned. His hand stroked her inner thighs, slipping higher until his fingers dipped into her wet pussy, gathering her juices before he circled her clit.

Honey Wine's hips thrust against his hand until she throbbed with pleasure. He continued caressing her sensitive nub and moist folds of flesh until her passion ebbed and she relaxed completely. He took her hand and placed it over his chest, holding it there so she felt the steady rhythm of his heartbeat against her palm.

For the first time since she was a child, she slept without worry.

* * * * *

Honey Wine awoke warm, content and encompassed by Torn's scent. She smiled, remembering the hours she'd spent in his arms, but when she reached for him, the bed beside her was empty. Disappointment overwhelmed her.

She sat up, wiping sleep from her eyes, and glanced at the fire burning in the hearth. A tub full of water stood in front of it, clothes folded neatly on a plain wooden stool nearby.

Stretching, she slipped out of the bed and into the tub. The warm water soothed her body, still sore from the previous day's journey. She smiled wryly. There had been a time when such a hike would have been routine for her. Now that she was out of the dungeon, she'd have to sharpen the skills, which had lain dormant. She washed her hair and skin with the scented soap and braided her damp tresses down her back. She slipped into a green wool tunic and pulled on a brown skirt. There was no mirror in the chamber, and she wondered how she looked. Funny, before meeting Torn, she'd never thought of such things, but she wanted him to find her attractive.

She walked down the corridor and into the great hall. Several black-garbed Knights as well as women and children lined the wooden tables. Rain waved to her from where he sat with two other Knights, one blond, and the other flame-haired. She approached, feeling slightly out of place, but the men stood and greeted her with friendly smiles, and soon she was seated beside Rain enjoying a breakfast of bread and fresh fruit.

"Did you sleep well, Lady?" Rain's eyes glistened with good humor as he popped a fat, red berry into his mouth.

Honey Wine nodded, realizing that the blond and the redhead were staring at her in a manner that might have been offensive had their expressions not been so amiable.

"So you're from Sophianna?" the redhead asked in the clipped accent of the western lands where Honey Wine had once traveled with Alva.

"I am."

"Torn speaks highly of you," the blond said.

"Tell these rogues to mind their own business." Rain chuckled. "They don't even have the decency to introduce themselves before questioning a lady."

"Excuse us." The redhead reached for an apple and took a juicy bite. He tapped his chest with the fruit and said, "I'm Mage, and this here is Warrant."

"Charmed." Warrant took her hand and bowed his curly blond head over it. He winked one of his turquoise eyes at her. "And I must say you're even more beautiful than Rain described."

"A lovely compliment," she cast him a teasing smile, "from one so handsome."

Warrant released her hand and grinned. "I see Torn has found himself a formidable woman. I'm not at all surprised."

"Me either." Mage finished the last of his apple, tossed the core on his plate, and reached for a thick slice of bread. "He's waited long enough to find one."

Honey Wine lifted an eyebrow. "Find one?"

"Yes." Mage paused in his chewing. "Torn is careful with everything. He thinks things through. All his words and actions are means to a well-planned end. He doesn't waste time with—"

Rain interrupted him with a long, chastising whistle. "Risky, Mage. You know how Torn dislikes gossip."

Mage gave a snort of laughter. "You worry about him. I'm out of his faction and in charge of the home guard now."

"What faction is Torn in charge of?" Honey Wine asked. The more she heard clips of the Knights' conversation, the more curious she was becoming about Torn's position in the Order. He was obviously high up and well respected.

Mage's green eyes met Honey Wine's and he shook his head, his smile fading. "I'm sorry, Honey Wine, but we're not at liberty to discuss Torn's faction."

"Go on, make her more curious, why don't you?" Warrant leaned back in his chair, the black silk of his tunic pulling across his broad chest, masses of wild, curly hair tumbling over his shoulders and down his back.

Mage shrugged. "I am sorry."

"No he's not." Warrant glanced at the redhead. "Mage's area of expertise isn't training guards, it's aggravation."

"Clam up, the both of you." Rain tore a piece of bread with his teeth. "You're boring the woman…and me."

As she ate, Honey Wine couldn't help smiling at the playful banter of the Knights. Though none of them were blood-related, she noticed they were much like brothers. She wondered how many of them, like Torn, had been raised in the Order.

"Where's Torn?" she asked.

"Speaking with Mahir," Rain said. "They've been in his study all morning, so I guess they'll be finishing up soon. In the meantime, we can go to the field and then riding, if you'd like."

"In that case, I'll go back to my room and change into trousers." Honey Wine stood, and the Knights also rose. She felt a little uncomfortable, not accustomed to the Knights' formal manners, which surfaced sporadically. One moment they were bowing over her hand, and the next they were gulping food like starving dogs. Most of them weren't at all like Torn. He was so reserved and reflective, as if his mind was always churning. She wondered if some of that churning revolved around her?

Her room was close to the stairway, and as she paused to open her door, she heard angry conversation from the corridor above. She tried not to listen, but when she heard Torn's voice, she ventured partway up the steps. She'd never heard him raise his voice in anger, even through the worst tortures of Alva's prison.

"I will not continue with this lie any longer, Mahir!"

"This attitude is unreasonable and unacceptable." Mahir's deep voice was tinted with his own repressed fury.

"What you propose is unacceptable."

"What good would it do to tell her, Torn? Don't you see it doesn't really matter now? It was one deception, and keeping it quiet will both serve our Order and protect her feelings."

"I can't believe I'm hearing this. It goes against everything we stand for!"

"We stand to protect the weak!" Mahir snapped. "And we must do anything to ensure their safety."

"Don't stand there and tell me what I have to do! I've done it! Do you have any idea what it was like in that prison?"

"I don't deny you've suffered," Mahir's voice softened, his anger fading, "but I still say telling will not help her or us."

"I killed Redly," Torn continued, paying no attention to his foster father's words. "One of my own men. One of us. I trained him, and I killed him."

"You acted on instinct. You can't blame yourself for that."

"If it hadn't been for Honey Wine, I'd be dead or worse. I'd have ended up like Redly."

"You know that I'm forever in her debt for what she did for you, but don't you understand that if you tell her, she might be hurt and angry. Like it or not, Torn, we still need her help."

"She'll give it."

"You can't be sure—"

"I'm sure! You don't know her like I do. In spite of all she's endured, all she's seen, her heart is true. She was imprisoned for speaking against the Entertainment. Do you honestly think she'll deny us the information required to end it forever?"

End the Entertainment? Honey Wine's thoughts raced. How? What was the lie Torn spoke of? What was he keeping from her?

"I'm telling her, Mahir. I owe her that."

"Torn, you've always been a reasonable man. Think this through."

"I've had months to think this through! The only thing that stopped me from telling her weeks ago was my loyalty to this Order."

"You're endangering our duty if you tell her."

Drawing a deep breath, Honey Wine decided it was time to find out for herself the topic of their discussion. She knocked on the door.

"Enter," Mahir called.

She stepped inside and said, "Tell me what?"

"Honey Wine," Torn said.

For a moment she stared at him. It was the first time she'd seen him out of prison clothes, and she was stunned by his beauty. His tall, sleek body was draped in the traditional black silk uniform of his Order, a circle of red thorns embroidered around a ruby over his heart. Black leather trousers tucked into calf-high boots encased his long, muscled legs. A sheathed sword dangled at his hip, and black gloves covered his hands. His black hair was combed back from his face and tied at his nape with a strip of leather. For a moment, her heartbeat skipped, then she forced herself back to reality.

"I'm sorry for listening, but I heard shouting. What have you lied about, Torn?" Honey Wine looked directly into his dark blue eyes.

He drew a long breath, and she noticed Mahir watching them intently.

"Make sure you're saying this for her sake and not to cleanse your own soul," Mahir warned.

"Torn?" she pressed.

He turned from her and looked at Mahir. "I'm sorry, but she has to know."

Mahir nodded, smiling slightly. "Then I will give you privacy." He walked to the door, pausing for a moment in front of Honey Wine. "You can believe whatever he tells you. Torn is honest to a fault."

Honey Wine lifted her chin and met Mahir's eyes. "I would consider such integrity a virtue, not a fault."

"Don't misunderstand me, Honey Wine. Torn is a magnificent Knight. The Spirit knows, he's upheld all his vows, something few of us, including myself, can say. But it's always a pure heart which shatters, is it not? His integrity is what worried me from the first."

Mahir closed the door behind him, leaving Torn and Honey Wine facing one another. His eyes gleamed with too many emotions to discern, and she noticed a pulse beating in his throat. She longed to touch him, but resisted the urge and folded her hands behind her back as she said, "Tell me."

He walked to the table, his long fingers playing with a book's leather spine. The last time she'd sensed such tension in him was when he'd been tortured by The Lady. Suddenly she was terrified of what he was about to say.

"I wasn't captured by your sister's guard," he began. "I *let* myself be captured."

Honey Wine stared at him, aghast, momentarily unable to comprehend the absurdity of his words. Finally she said, "What do you mean, you *let* yourself be captured?"

"We've heard rumors about the Entertainment, but the participating kingdoms have kept it so well hidden that no one had any proof. Mahir is a friend of the High King, and he's been pressuring him for years to investigate the possibility of the Entertainment. Such an investigation would cause trouble in the kingdoms, and the Entertainment sounded so incredible that the King was not willing to risk disturbance. However if we found proof that it existed, he promised to put an end to it, no matter what the consequences. All of us have different functions here, in addition to our required duties of healing and protecting the weak. I lead a faction of spies. Redly was one of them. Last year, he was sent to find proof that the Entertainment existed. He never returned."

"So you went after him?" she murmured.

"Yes. I expected severe conditions, but nothing like what I experienced in there. Your sister's security is very good. Once I got in, I couldn't get out. You saved my life, Honey Wine."

She walked to a bookshelf, staring at the leather-bound volumes without really seeing them. The intimate moments they'd shared suddenly made her cringe. "I understand. You needed me to escape. I would have done the same in your place."

"I wanted to tell you." He placed a hand on her shoulder. She stiffened and jerked away. "Honey Wine, please."

"You don't have to say anymore." She shrugged. "It doesn't matter. In my own way, I needed you just as much as you needed me. Without you, I never would have dreamed of escaping. Now, I heard Mahir say you need me for something else?"

She turned to him and noticed a strange expression on his face. She knew what he'd just told her was difficult for him, but she didn't care. She had been falling in love with him, and he'd been using her to escape.

"Now that we know the Entertainment is real, we can stop it. Would you be willing to help us do that?"

"How?"

"We plan on attacking the fortress in the woods where the fighting takes place. To do that, we'll need to get to your sister. You know the palace. We want you to give us a map."

"You want to go back there? Are you mad? If she gets you again—"

"She won't. This time, I'll be going in fully armed and prepared. I'll have others with me. Will you do it, Honey Wine? Will you help us?"

She folded her arms across her chest and sighed. "On one condition."

He lifted an eyebrow.

"I want to go with you."

Chapter Eight

ಬ

"You cannot go with us," Torn stated.

Mahir, Honey Wine and Torn sat at the table in the library, negotiating the price of her help in mapping out her sister's palace.

It was an hour after she'd learned the truth about the Ruby Order's plan to put an end to the Entertainment. Though she understood Torn's secrecy about his purpose while in the dungeon, she couldn't help feeling hurt that he hadn't trusted her enough to confide in her before their escape. Though she hoped he'd finally told her because he'd grown to love her as much as she loved him, she was not foolish enough to believe such a fantasy. More likely he'd told her because he could no longer endure her kisses and her intimate touches. He'd probably only tolerated them to ensure her help in his escape.

"Because you think I'll try to warn my sister?" Honey Wine snapped at him.

His blue eyes bore into hers. "No. Of course not."

"Then why? Because I'm a woman? I assure you, when I was in the guard I was far more skilled than most of the men under me."

Torn shook his head, an exasperated smile tugging at his lips. "You're absurd! I thought you were skilled enough to plan an escape, but suddenly I'm judging you by your sex?"

"If I don't go, then I'll draw no plans for you."

"Fine!" Torn's eyes flashed with seldom-seen anger. "Then we'll do it without your help. I'm not about to put you or the rest of us at risk for stupidity."

"This has nothing to do with your skill as a guard, Honey Wine." Mahir's voice sounded soft but stern. "Torn and his spies are elite. There are few of them within our Order. We wouldn't even use members of our own infantry for this mission."

She nodded, lowering her gaze to the empty piece of parchment on the table in front of her. What Mahir said made sense. Every military organization had factions specially trained for certain duties.

"Help us now, and when the time comes to bring down the Entertainment, we'll need as many able warriors as we can find," Mahir continued. "I promise you'll have the opportunity to fight with us then if that's your desire."

Torn narrowed his eyes at his foster father. "Mahir, I don't want her endangered."

"Since when?" She shot Torn a furious look. "We both were in danger while escaping, but the risk seemed to be fine with you then!"

"And you think I won't carry that guilt to my grave?"

She forced herself not to reveal her elation at his words. Instead, she turned to Mahir and said, "Has he always spoken like the hero in a poorly-written drama?"

Mahir's blue eyes glistened with humor, but Honey Wine guessed he refrained from smiling out of respect for Torn. "It's a wonder the two of you ever planned an escape together. The way you fight, one would think you hated each another."

Torn's eyes met Honey Wine's across the table and she immersed herself in those beautiful, familiar blue depths. She thought she'd hated him once, but that was only because from the moment she'd seen him, she must have known how deeply she could fall in love with him if she let herself. Such strong feelings for a man had terrified her, but how did he feel about her? How did he *really* feel?

"Honey Wine, I'm told you once wanted to stop the Entertainment, that you were imprisoned for your belief in freedom. Do you still believe in it? Will you help us?" Mahir asked.

She picked up a quill, dipped it in ink, and placed the pointed tip to the parchment. It sounded scratchy as she drew. "I know most of the entrances and exits. There's an old woman in the arena who knows more, but I have no idea where the arena is located. I was hooded during the ride there."

Mahir nodded. "Draw everything you remember. Torn, send for the men you've chosen to accompany you. We'll start making plans today."

Less than an hour later, Rain and Warrant had joined them at the table. Honey Wine had drawn, in as much detail as she could recall, the entire palace at Sophianna.

"We'll be in and out quickly." Rain folded his arms across his chest and stared over her shoulder at the map.

"All we need is one guard from the dungeon," Warrant said. "No one will know where he disappeared to, and he'll give us directions to the arena."

Honey Wine shook her head. "Don't think it will be easy. The guards in the dungeon have all been hand-picked by my sister. They're devoted to her, and they fear her wrath."

"Honey Wine is right," Torn nodded, "but we have our own methods of discovering what we need to know. We'll take the young guard Timus. From what I observed, he'll be the easiest to work with."

Honey Wine felt a pang of concern. She'd known Timus all her life and liked him. She said, "Do you plan on harming him?"

"We don't want to harm him, Honey Wine," Mahir assured her. "We just need information."

Their mission was necessary, and as she remembered how many times Timus had stood by and watched Torn suffer, she felt less concerned about the Knights' means to and end.

"We'll wait another couple of weeks so we can plan it to the last detail," Rain said, "and give Torn's chest a bit more time to heal. We'll all need to be at our peak."

"Thank you for your help, Lady." Warrant bowed his curly blond head in Honey Wine's direction. "You've done humankind a service."

"I just hope you succeed in doing what I was imprisoned for," Honey Wine said.

When they emerged from the library, it was late afternoon.

Torn caught her hand as they walked down the corridor toward the great hall. "Ride with me?"

She looked up at him, raising her emotional shield against the onslaught of tenderness in his eyes.

His palm slid up her arm. "Please?"

"Please?" Her voice was almost mocking. "Ah, I think I like the sound of that."

He dropped his hand. "This is my own fault. You'll never believe another word I say."

"What's left to say?" She shrugged. "You and your Order have gotten everything you wanted from me. As soon as the Entertainment is ended, I'll be going."

"Going where?"

"To start a life, Torn." She didn't try to keep the hard edge from her voice. "Like you belong to this Order, I need to find someplace where I belong. I liked being a guard, and after working in the dungeon, I have healing skills as well. There's a world out there for me, and now I have the chance to discover it."

He looked about to speak, but instead touched her face then let his hand drop as he brushed past her down the hall.

She watched him go, her throat tight with unshed tears, and scolded herself for being stupid.

"Honey Wine!" Rain approached her. "Would you still like a tour of the training field?"

She smiled at the handsome Knight and accepted his arm. "I'd love it."

Together, they walked to the stable where Rain saddled his chestnut war stallion and offered Honey Wine a sleek white mare. She mounted, pleased with the graceful, spirited horse as they rode out of the fortress. Rain was a talkative, humorous companion, and after they observed some of the Knights training, they rode through the empty meadows behind the fortress. In the distance, she noticed another black-garbed Knight on a blue-black horse galloping at break-neck speed, jumping fallen trees and the remains of old fences.

Rain laughed and shook his head, murmuring, "Someday one of them is going to die. Warrant exercised that black demon while Torn was away. Threw him twice. Nearly broke his ass. . . Forgive me, Lady." Rain nodded almost sheepishly.

Honey Wine shook her head in dismissal and continued watching the rider, "That's Torn?"

"Young and wild," Rain nodded. "Worthy, though. He'll be named leader after Mahir."

Torn had caught sight of them and turned his horse in their direction. Honey Wine's heart pounded as he approached. He looked so handsome, all grace and power on a lithe black stallion.

He edged his lathered horse alongside Honey Wine's mare and stared at her through locks of damp, windblown hair. "I didn't think you were in the mood for riding."

She shrugged and smiled in Rain's direction. "I changed my mind."

Torn glanced at them. "I see."

"Actually, I have training to attend to." Rain bowed from the neck toward Honey Wine. "If I might leave you in Torn's company?"

"I think I can live with it." She smiled at Rain. "Thank you for a lovely afternoon."

"It's been my pleasure." His eyes danced as he turned his mount back to the fortress.

"We can go back," Torn said. "I know you'd rather be with anyone but me."

"Not true," she said. "I prefer you to my sister any day."

He didn't reply, but cast her a glance that conveyed exactly what he thought of her humor.

"You like him?" Torn nodded in the direction of Rain's retreating form.

"He's very nice."

Torn lifted a thick black eyebrow as his horse plodded alongside hers.

Halfway back to the fortress, he stopped.

"Something wrong?" she asked coolly.

"No."

Her gaze bore into his.

"Yes." He shook his head. "I can't say. I've been selfish enough when it comes to you."

Honey Wine sighed. "Torn, I'm not thrilled that I didn't know the truth about your mission before we escaped, but I do understand."

"You do?"

"Yes. I probably would have done the same if I'd been you. I respected you before, but I admire you even more now. Not many people would have willingly risked themselves as you did. Not many people could have endured the dungeon, the arena, and The Lady and not given in."

"Not many people would have had someone like you supporting them," he said.

As she looked into his eyes, she felt her control slipping. She longed to feel his arms around her and his mouth against hers.

"We should go back," she whispered, kicking her horse to a walk.

"I love you."

Honey Wine stopped breathing at his words. Her hands trembled on the reins as she tugged the mare to a stop. She swallowed audibly and collected herself before turning to him.

His dark blue eyes fixed on her, his expression uncharacteristically tense, as if he feared her response.

"There's really nothing left for me to tell you," she said. "No more information. Nothing I'm keeping. Nothing I've lied about. You don't have to continue playing this game with me, Torn."

His eyes narrowed. "I'm not playing any game, Honey Wine. I know you want to find a new life. I know you deserve one, but I can't help wishing that you want me to be part of your life. You said I belong to the Order, and I do. I'm loyal to it, but I'm in love with you."

She closed her eyes for a moment. "You're not in love with me, Torn. I was kind to you during your imprisonment. It's common for victims to develop feelings for jailers who display kindness."

"I'm not a fool!" he snapped. "I know the difference between being grateful and being in love. I want to know if you can still feel anything for me at all after learning what I did."

She hesitated. Should she tell him the truth? Should she trust him?

He nodded, his eyes lowering slowly until they fixed on the windblown forelock between his horse's ears. "You don't have to say anything. I just had to tell you how I felt."

"I do care for you," she murmured.

His gaze darted to hers. He dismounted and took her hand. "As a friend or as something more?"

"As a friend?" She gave a snort of laugher. She'd never dreamed of doing with a friend half of the things she'd done with him. She stared at their entwined fingers then slipped from the horse and into his arms, whispering into his ear, "As both."

His grip tightened on her so her cheek pressed against the damp silk of his tunic. Hot from riding, his body smelled of clean sweat, summer breeze, leather and horse. She felt his heart thrumming steadily against her ear and enjoyed the caress of his gloved hands on her back.

After a moment, he tilted her chin upward and kissed her mouth. She closed her eyes, losing herself in the warmth of his lips, in the moist, tender strokes of his tongue. She reached up, and loosened his hair from the strip of leather binding it at his nape and threaded her fingers through the silky black waves.

As the kiss broke, he sank to one knee on the grass in front of her, one of her hands swallowed by his large, gloved ones.

His eyes bore into hers as he said, "Marry me, Honey Wine?"

Her heart throbbed, and she knew he felt her hand trembling. Marry him? Should she? Could she?

She cleared her throat and asked calmly, "When?"

"Tonight."

She lifted an eyebrow.

"Not soon enough?" The slightest smile played around his adorable mouth.

"No." She shrugged. "Tonight's good."

He laughed, and before she knew what was happening, he'd stood, caught her by the waist, and tossed her up into his arms.

She giggled, clutching his neck. As he lowered her to her feet and kissed her, she knew for the first time in her life where she truly belonged.

Chapter Nine

೫

Mahir was authorized to perform weddings within the fortress, and he immediately gave his consent to marry Honey Wine and Torn that evening. Though he didn't speak of it openly, she sensed genuine gladness as he embraced them both.

"You should find Blaze," Mahir told Torn before they left his library for the second time that day. "He returned this morning from a settlement outside the Zaltanian border. The war in the south is causing heavy casualties and more healers are needed."

Torn and Honey Wine walked hand-in-hand down the corridor toward the great hall, and she asked, "Who's Blaze? Rain mentioned him earlier as well."

"Blaze is a good friend. I've known him all my life. He's lived with the Order since he was five. Good man. Once you get used to him, you'll like him."

"Get used to him?" Honey Wine lifted an eyebrow.

"Yes, he's a bit—"

"I sense it's you and not an apparition." A tall man with shoulder-length, unkempt auburn hair and beard called to them from the end of the corridor. Honey Wine noted he wore the traditional black uniform of the Order, except a wide, olive-green sash swathed his narrow waist and dangled to the end of his tunic.

"Blaze." Torn smiled as the man crossed the hall in several long strides and jerked Torn into a rough embrace. He was close enough for Honey Wine to note the details of his appearance. Unlike Torn's straight, slightly upturned nose, Blaze's was large and might have been his most prominent feature had it not been for wide eyes of such a pale blue that they shone like opals against his tanned skin. His mouth beneath the beard was finely drawn, the upper lip forming a perfect, delicate V.

Blaze drew back, one hand still clasping Torn's shoulder while he wagged a finger at Honey Wine's husband-to-be. "One month I searched for you. 'He's in the land of the raven-haired queen,' they said. There I went and was told you'd never been seen. How chastised I was when I returned home. Did I think the spy needed a keeper? He's a leader of men!"

Torn's broad smile reflected some of the confusion she felt at Blaze's strange speech, though when he replied to his friend, she sensed he was well accustomed to Blaze's nature. "Thank you for looking, Blaze."

Blaze shook his head, his smile fading, his eyes taking on a haunted expression. "I saw such things. Your suffering. Unlike our noble leader of swords and sewing needles, I cannot bury what I feel. Mahir waited in silent agony, that I knew. But I had to do something. Alas, that's why he is our leader and I wear the sash of the weaponless warrior." Blaze looked almost apologetic. "My life."

Torn placed a hand on one of Blaze's broad shoulders. "You truly serve, Blaze. Not many in this Order have the courage to wear that sash."

"What courage?" Blaze shrugged. "I must live with the souls I take. I must hear them, see them." Blaze stared past Torn for such a long time that Honey Wine glanced over her own shoulder, wondering what had captured his attention, but the corridor was empty. Blaze shook his head and turned to Honey Wine with a charming smile. "A Mistress who'll rule with a just hand and compassionate heart. You and Torn are well matched." He took her hand and bowed over it. "Sweet Liquid. Your father is proud."

"Thank you...I think." Honey Wine returned the strange Knight's smile.

"Honey Wine and I will be married tonight, Blaze. Will you witness?"

"Only barred doors would keep me away." Blaze laughed. "When the time is right, dissipation of innocence is beautiful."

He released Honey Wine's hand carefully and continued down the hall. He paused and turned back to Torn. "Don't punish yourself over Redly's death. He bears you no ill will."

Blaze disappeared up the steps, and Honey Wine looked at Torn. "What in the name of the Twin Goddesses was he talking about?"

"Most of the time I still haven't the faintest idea. He sees things not of this world. Spirits of the dead talk to him. They're constantly with him, and he can't always tell what is flesh and what is vision. As a child, he was considered mad by his parents and sent to live with us, but I assure you he's as rational as you or I. He just sees more. It makes him difficult to understand, but his heart is pure."

"Why does he wear that green sash?"

"He's a true healer. Those of our Order who wear that sash carry no weapons, even in battle. Their only function is to heal. Oh, they're very skilled in empty-handed fighting, but they prefer never to fight at all. You won't see many of those sashes."

"I can understand why." Honey Wine shook her head at the idea of entering battlefields weaponless. Then she turned her thoughts to the coming night. "So what are weddings like here?"

* * * * *

The marriage ceremony took place late that night in the courtyard. Mage's sister, Iris, who was visiting from their home village and was about Honey Wine's height, loaned her a floor-length tunic of pale blue. After slipping into the garment, Honey Wine sat on a stool in her chamber while Iris braided her hair.

"This is so exciting," Iris said. "Weddings are rare here. Some of the Knights marry, but most of them spend their lives traveling and doing other…Knightly things… My mother keeps hoping Mage will marry."

Honey Wine glanced in the mirror at Iris's reflection behind her. Like Mage, she was tall and slim with a waist-length mass of wavy red hair. Freckles sprinkled her pert nose, and her lips were dark, cherry red. She wasn't beautiful, but exuded charm that made her more attractive than pretty-faced women.

"Are you married?" Honey Wine asked.

Iris laughed. "No. I've always been a bit boyish. I've never mastered the art of flirtation. Unfortunately."

"Neither have I, but Torn doesn't seem to care."

"Torn's very sweet. He looks past the surface of everything and everyone." She laughed again. "I think my mother arranged for me to visit Mage hoping I'd find a husband among all these fine Knights. They're a decent enough bunch, but not all of them are as true to their vows as Torn. Mage's friend Warrant, for instance. The man is a master of flirtation, and my own brother is no better."

"So you haven't found a potential mate here?" Honey Wine smiled.

The slightest blush crept into the sharp ridges of Iris's cheekbones. "There is one, but he wouldn't be interested in me."

"Who is it?"

"I couldn't. I'd feel silly."

"I won't tell anyone."

Iris took her full lower lip between her teeth and thought for a moment before saying, "Sir Rain."

Honey Wine smiled at her. "Rain is very nice. Have you approached him at all?"

"Oh, I wouldn't. I'd end up making a fool of myself. I'm fine around men if I'm riding or hunting, you know, like one of them. But to approach one as a woman..." Iris shook her head.

"Rain is hardly intimidating. He seems to like riding. Go riding with him."

Iris didn't speak of Rain again as she finished with Honey Wine's hair.

A tap sounded on the door, and as the women stepped outside, Blaze awaited them. He'd attempted to bind his wild auburn locks at his nape, but random pieces escaped the leather strip and sprang in several directions.

"I'm to be your escort, Sweet Liquid." He offered Honey Wine his arm, which she accepted hesitantly. She found his strange ways unsettling, but she trusted his large, blue eyes.

"My name is Honey Wine," she told him.

"Of course, Sweet Liquid, Mead. A fitting name for gentle amber eyes. This marriage will be good. Very good. Spirits whispered of your courage and strength. You've reached the unreachable, breached the chaste defenses of the pure-hearted."

Honey Wine glanced over her shoulder at Iris who followed behind them. The young woman dipped her head in Blaze's direction and shrugged, confused by the Knight. Honey Wine repressed laughter and continued walking to the courtyard.

As they stepped outside, Honey Wine stared in wonder at the beauty of the place. Black garbed Knights and their families assembled along the round walls of the courtyard. Hundreds of candles lined the cobblestone walkway leading from the great hall to the gate. Two rows of Knights stood behind the candles. At her approach, they drew their slender, straight swords and raised them, creating a tunnel of glistening silver. In the center of the walk, Mahir and Torn awaited her, the older man shadowed by Torn's height. Firelight reflected in Torn's eyes, and Honey Wine saw him draw a deep breath and smile as she walked toward him, still holding Blaze's arm.

When she reached the center of the courtyard, Blaze took her hand and Torn's, placing them together before stepping aside.

Honey Wine smiled up at Torn as Mahir spoke the words that bound them forever.

"We're here to witness the union of Torn and Honey Wine. They've been joined by the Spirit and have accepted that joining.

With the strength of the Spirit, I bless them as husband and wife." Mahir glanced at the couple. "Torn, do you promise to be Honey Wine's husband until the Spirit reclaims your soul?"

"Yes, I promise." Torn's eyes bore so deeply into Honey Wine's that she nearly missed her part of the vows.

"Honey Wine, do you promise to be Torn's wife until the Spirit reclaims your soul?"

"Yes, I promise." Her hand tightened on Torn's.

"I, Mahir of the Ruby Order, stand as witness and mediator between your souls and the Spirit. You are, from this day forward, husband and wife."

Cheers sounded from the onlookers on the wall, and Mahir and Blaze embraced the couple. The clink of steel sounded through the courtyard as the Knights along the walkway raised their swords. Torn and Honey Wine walked to the great hall followed by Mahir, Blaze and the other guests.

Food was spread on the tables inside, and everyone laughed, ate and drank. Torn and Honey Wine sat with Mahir, Blaze and Rain. Within moments, Mage, Warrant and Iris joined them. Honey Wine discreetly motioned for Iris to sit beside Rain.

"Watch out, Rain." Mage chuckled from across the table. "Iris might chop off your hand to get at the food. Ever since she was a child she's had a mean appetite for a skinny girl."

"I think your sister is a lovely woman, Sir Mage," Honey Wine said.

"Course she is." Mage lifted his wineglass. "Runs in the family."

"Not only that, what do you mean by calling her skinny?" Torn's eyes glistened with humor. "My wife's wearing one of her dresses."

Mage threw back his head and laughed. "I'd best keep quiet and eat."

"A wise idea." Rain smiled in Iris's direction. "Has he always been a fool, missy, or has he acquired the skill since joining the Order?"

Iris blinked several times at Rain, and Honey Wine nudged her.

"Yes," she smiled wickedly in Mage's direction, "he's always been a fool."

Rain laughed and offered Iris a glass of wine.

Happy at her first attempt ever at matchmaking, Honey Wine looked at Torn. Beneath the table, he reached for her hand. Neither ate much that night and excused themselves early.

"Honey Wine," Rain called as she followed Torn out of the great hall. She glanced back at the Knight, and he winked. "Be gentle with him."

Torn shot him a look of death, and Honey Wine laughed. Knights were certainly strange creatures.

Torn took her hand as they walked down the corridor to his chamber. His palm felt warm and rough against hers, and her heart leapt at the thought that within moments, she'd be pressed to the heat of his body. Marrying him was like a fantasy, one she knew might end all too soon should he be discovered when he and the others breached the palace guard at Sophianna. *Don't think about that now*, she told herself. *Tonight is for us to be happy.*

"You know I've never seen your room before," she said as he unlocked the door.

"It's not much." He smiled. "We don't keep many things."

They stepped inside, and while he crossed the room to rekindle the fire, Honey Wine glanced around. It wasn't much larger than the chamber she'd been given. There was a bed in one corner with a trunk at the foot of it. On top of the trunk sat a basin and pitcher of water. A chair and a small, round table stood by the fire. Two books rested on the table, and a sword and several daggers were mounted above the mantle. No rug covered the floor, and as she slipped off her boots, the smooth stones felt cold beneath her feet. She shivered.

Torn glanced over his shoulder from where he squatted in front of the hearth. "It'll warm up now that the fire is going."

"I'm sure we'll make our own heat." She smiled and slid her arms around his neck from behind, her palms smoothing over his hard, strong chest beneath the black silk.

He took her hands in his and guided her to the front of him as he stood. His mouth descended on hers in a kiss so passionate she was almost taken by surprise. She closed her eyes and clung to him as his soft lips opened against hers. His tongue traced the shape of her lips, then slipped inside to taste hers. He explored every inch of her mouth, his every stroke a heady mixture of tenderness and lust.

She felt his fingers loosen her braid and sift through her hair, spreading it over her shoulders. His palms splayed against her back and held her closer. Honey Wine's breasts pressed to the hardness of his chest, and her entire body felt as if it had turned to liquid. She wondered how much longer her legs would continue to support her, but she needn't have worried. Torn swept her into his arms, his mouth never breaking contact with hers, and carried her to the bed.

He placed Honey Wine on her back, and she stared up at him.

"You're so beautiful," he murmured. "I can't believe you're mine."

She smiled. "Until the Spirit reclaims our souls."

He traced the shape of her face with his fingertip, touched her eyebrows and lips.

"I want to make you happy," he said.

"You do."

He stood, walked to the fire, and gazed at the flames. Honey Wine sat up, watching him.

"Honey Wine, I have a confession of sorts."

"Oh no." She tensed. "What now?"

He shook his head. "Nothing terrible, at least I don't think it is, unless it proves to be a problem tonight, but if it does, it won't last long. I learn fast."

A smile played around her mouth. "Torn, you're starting to sound like Blaze. You've lost me completely."

His gaze remained on the fire. The snapping sound of burning wood filled the otherwise silent room.

Finally he said, "I've never... I haven't actually had intercourse with a woman."

His words took her slightly aback. After this morning, she'd expected some horrible confession, like he didn't really love her. It had never entered her mind that Torn was a virgin—especially after all the times they'd kissed and fondled each other and all the times he'd given her such marvelous orgasms. Still, looking back, the only time he'd ever climaxed with her had been when he was under the control of the aphrodisiac, and even then, his desire to penetrate her had been almost tangible, yet he'd refrained.

"Well," she couldn't help smiling, "I wish I could claim to be as pure, but there were a couple of men when I was in the guard..."

He shook his head. "You don't have to tell me. I don't want to know."

Honey Wine stood, and he drew her into his embrace. She rested her head against his chest and listened to his heartbeat.

"Are you disappointed?" he asked.

"No. Not at all. A bit surprised. You're a handsome man, Torn. Surely there was some woman?"

"We take a vow of abstention here. Sexual intercourse is allowed only after marriage. It's an old custom and isn't enforced so strictly anymore, provided discretion is used."

"But you've upheld that vow—or tried to?" She shook her head. "I know you have. How awful it must have been for you in the prison, between my sister pawing you, the two of us forced into those disgusting mating rituals. All that time you tried to hold onto that custom of yours."

"I think it's a good custom. And I'm glad the only woman I've ever felt complete physical pleasure with is you."

"Then are you disappointed because I've been with men before?"

"No. You're with me now. That's all I care about." He took her face in his hands and kissed her.

She tugged up his tunic and pulled it over his head, baring his warm flesh to her touch. His body was lean and hard. Dark hair dusted his chest, tapered to his flat, muscled stomach and disappeared beneath his leather trousers. She touched her lips to the healing pink wound on his chest. Her fingers splayed against it, clutching solid muscle dusted with soft hair.

He sank to his knees in front of her and lifted her dress. He kissed her from knee to thigh to abdomen as he pushed the dress over her head and dropped it on the chair so she stood completely naked before him. His hands warmed her shoulders, and his eyes ravished her body, lingering on the generous curves of her firm breasts. Honey Wine took his hands and placed them on her breasts, covering them with her own and squeezing gently. As his thumbs brushed her nipples, she dropped her hands and closed her eyes. He kissed her cheek, her neck. Every inch of her breasts and ribs were covered with kisses while she stood helpless before his carnal exploration. With frustrating gentleness, his hands trailed over her calves, knees and thighs while he pressed his cheek to her stomach.

"So soft," he murmured, touching his lips to her abdomen. His tongue traced her navel, and she shivered, fingers tightening in his hair, pressing him closer to her body. "I've wanted to love you like this for so long, without being forced. I've dreamed of you almost every night since I saw you, Honey Wine."

"I want to feel you," she said, tugging him to his feet and yanking the waist of his trousers. "All of you. Take these bloody things off."

He willingly obliged, and by the time he stepped out of the trousers, Honey Wine awaited him on the bed.

"Turn over," he said.

"Why?"

He rolled her onto her stomach, sweeping aside her hair and kissing her nape. His lips brushed her shoulders and back while his hands encircled her waist, cupped her buttocks and caressed her hips. Her entire body felt both relaxed and aroused beneath his touch. When he turned her over, she looked up at him through half-lidded eyes. The tip of his tongue moistened his lips before he lowered his head to her breasts. His tongue flicked over one nipple, then the other. Honey Wine moaned, aching for him, yearning to be devoured. He sucked on one of her nipples, and she arched her back, pressing his head closer.

She reached for his cock, her fingertips tracing the veins and flesh she already knew well, but wanted to know more, without being gawked at by the guards or without concern for their safety. Her fist tightened gently as she stroked him, feeling him swell even more beneath the velvety skin.

His body tensed at her touch. She leaned forward and kissed his neck, his shoulder. He relaxed a bit, though when she placed her hand to his chest, his heart slammed against her palm.

Smiling mischievously, she pushed him onto his back, knelt between the muscular, hair-roughened length of his legs and took his cock between her lips. She licked the underside and laved the head before sucking him deep into her mouth. His cock head brushed the back of her throat and she heard him panting with desire. She pulled back slightly and buried her face in the root of his cock. She licked upward, paying close attention to the veins and the ridge on the underside of his cock. She lapped the head, the tip of her tongue caressing the little eye and tasting the first of his essence. One of her hands squeezed and kneaded his sack while she continued tasting and teasing his cock.

His hands trembled on her hair then slipped from her head to grip the sheets. Unsure of how much longer he could endure her exploration of his finely-shaped weapon, she drew back only to slide up the length of his body so they lay, breast to chest, lips inches apart.

He caught her hips, and gently tossed her onto her back. He parted her thighs, his callused fingertip touching her slick passage, caressing her heated softness. Torn's face lowered to her swollen clit. His exploration was tentative at first, but as she tightened her fingers in his hair and quivered beneath his lips and tongue, his ministrations became more sure and thorough. He tasted every soft fold of flesh and stroked her pussy with his tongue. Following the positioning of Honey Wine's hands, he noted the ragged sound of her breath until she teetered on the verge of ultimate fulfillment.

"Do it now," she panted, tugging him onto her, guiding him to her heated pussy. His fingers entwined with hers as he pressed her hands into the pillows. She opened her eyes and stared directly into his burning blue eyes. His first movements were deliberately slow. Too slow. She was starving for him, and by the sound of his ragged breathing, he was just as hungry for her. Eyes closed, she clenched the hard muscles of his shoulders and back, urging him to move faster. Her hips matched the frantic thrusting of his while her legs clutched his lean, strong body. Suddenly she throbbed in a warm, blinding, orgasmic swirl. She held him tightly as he joined her in ecstasy, his long, hard body pumping into hers. His weight pinned her to the bed and his heart beat in wild time with hers.

After a moment, he rolled onto his back and pulled her into his arms. Her cheek rested against his chest, and she stroked his ribs with her fingertips.

Then she laughed.

"What? What's funny?" His voice possessed a defensive edge.

She raised herself onto her elbow and met his gaze. "If your 'first' time was this good, then I'll have many happy years ahead of me."

He smiled and guided her hand to his cock, which, to her surprise, swelled beneath her touch. "They say practice makes perfect."

Grinning, she slid back down his body, her legs entwining with his. It was going to be a wonderfully long night!

Chapter Ten

ಸ

Early the next morning, as Torn and Honey Wine entered the great hall to break their fast, she wondered if she looked as glowing as she felt inside. Their wedding night had been more pleasurable than her deepest fantasies, and already she looked forward to the coming evening.

As they joined Rain, Iris and Mage at one of the tables, Mage smirked, "I'd ask how the wedding night was, but I'd probably get my teeth knocked out."

"Only if you're lucky," Torn replied, tearing a slice of warm bread and offering Honey Wine half. He glanced at Rain. "Are you and Warrant ready to get to work this morning?"

"Warrant is on the field waiting for us."

"I won't be late again tomorrow," Torn, said.

"I was a little surprised to see you so soon." Rain took a long drink of water. "When we get back, you ought to take some time off. Show Honey Wine the valley. Women love that place in the summertime."

"Why is that?" Iris glanced at Rain.

The bearded Knight shrugged. "All the wild flowers, I guess."

"Iris wouldn't care about such things," Mage said of his sister. "She'd rather race horses on the shoreline."

"Didn't know you were such an able rider." Rain glanced at Iris.

Mage laughed. "Don't start with that, Rain. She'll probably challenge you to a race."

"Surely she knows her limits." Rain chuckled with good humor.

"Apparently better than you know yours." Iris's cheeks flushed with anger, and Honey Wine nearly laughed. Obviously her attraction to Rain didn't tame her high spirits.

Rain's eyes widened with surprise as Iris continued, "The weather today is perfect to race, unless you're afraid of losing to a woman, Sir?"

Mage smirked at Rain. "Told you."

"I'm afraid this race will have to wait until later." Torn stood. "Rain, we'd better find Warrant and start training."

Torn dropped a quick kiss on Honey Wine's cheek before he and Rain walked from the hall. Mage also excused himself, leaving Iris and Honey Wine seated alone.

Iris dropped her head onto her folded arms and moaned, "Oh, Honey Wine. See what I mean? How flirtatious is that, challenging him to a horse race?"

Honey Wine shrugged. "By the look in his eyes, I think he found it exciting."

Iris looked up, her expression hopeful. "Do you really think so?"

"Yes. Not all men like women who spend their days stitching tapestries and feigning fragility. I know Torn surely doesn't."

"I heard you were Captain of the guard in Sophianna. How about teaching me how to handle a sword? Mage wouldn't show me."

"I'd be glad to."

Honey Wine was thrilled to find a female companion who shared her interests. Mahir was kind enough to loan them some weapons, and they rode off to an empty field behind the fortress where they spent the day training, swimming and hiking in the nearby woods.

By the time Honey Wine returned to the Order, her body ached pleasantly, and she felt freer than she had in years. It was wonderful to pick up her active lifestyle and begin to sharpen skills that had lain dormant during her captivity.

Shortly before dusk. Torn, Rain and Warrant joined the women in the great hall. Rain and Iris excused themselves to see to their wager, Iris's expression competitive, Rain's indulgent. Honey Wine smiled inwardly. She'd seen Iris's skill on horseback that day and wondered if Rain would look so smug when they returned. Even if she didn't beat him, she'd give him fiercer competition than he planned.

Torn sat quietly beside Honey Wine at the table, and she immediately sensed his preoccupation.

"Are you all right?" she whispered, touching her hand to his knee.

He nodded and smiled at her. "Just thinking about the plans we've been making."

"A river of apprehension, like lava beneath the fragile ground," Blaze said as he took the seat beside Honey Wine. He shook his head at Torn. "Spat up from the pit only to be thrust back into it."

Honey Wine nodded slowly, finally starting to understand the peculiar Knight's manner of speaking. He too sensed Torn's fear of returning to Sophianna.

Blaze gestured toward Torn, holding his palms up. "Admiration, Sir Knight, not only mine but all those with branded flesh who paid forced homage to the raven-haired queen."

Torn gave a wry laugh and muttered, "One wrong move and they can thank me in person."

"Torn..." Honey Wine reached for his hand.

He shook his head and offered her a comforting smile. "But that's not going to happen. Let's forget about it for tonight."

"I'm told you heal, Sweet Liquid," Blaze said. "It's my life's dedication. We could share our knowledge."

"I'm sure I could learn far more from you than you could from me," Honey Wine said.

Blaze looked to the empty space beside her and pointed. "She is. She is progression. Observational and bold." His pale blue eyes focused on Honey Wine. "Save some time for me, with your husband's permission."

Honey Wine glanced at Torn who shrugged. "Blaze heads the Green Faction. If you're interested in expanding your healing skills, he's the man to see."

"I'd appreciate your help," Honey Wine told Blaze, hoping she could understand him enough to retain what he taught her.

He bowed from the neck. "The honor is mine, Sweet Liquid."

"Her name is Honey Wine, Blaze." Torn sighed, a half-smile on his lips.

"Forgive me," Blaze said. "For so long before we met, the spirits whispered your name. Sweet Liquid, Mead, the drink of...I speak too much, the shadows say."

The auburn-haired Knight fell silent and didn't speak again throughout the entire meal.

They'd almost finished eating when Rain and Iris, both looking hot and dusty, entered the hall. Rain's mouth was pressed into a serious line, his brow furrowed. Iris skipped ahead of him, smiling, and dropped into an empty chair beside Blaze. Dirt smudged her cheek, and her red hair was disheveled, but she didn't seem to care as she took a meat pie from one of the trays.

"Don't tell me." Mage shook his head disgustedly at Rain. "She won?"

"Only by a nose," Rain said.

Iris smiled. "It could have gone either way."

"You cheated," Rain said. "If you hadn't pretended to lose control of that horse, I never would have tried to help you and lost."

Iris shook her head. "By the time you began judging me as an opponent instead of a woman, the race was already won."

Rain smiled humorlessly at Mage. "Charming girl, your sister."

"Told you." Mage shook his head.

"A toast to the winner." Honey Wine lifted her glass, and the others, even a grudging Rain, drank with her.

When they finished eating, Torn and Honey Wine retired to their room where they made love and fell asleep wrapped in each other's arms.

Honey Wine awoke around midnight and reached for Torn but found the bed empty beside her. Shrugging on a robe, she walked barefoot down the corridor, thinking he might have gone to the great hall, or perhaps taken a walk in the courtyard. He had been so restless with thoughts of the mission back to Sophianna, not that she blamed him.

The night had grown cool, and Honey Wine shivered as she stood in the doorway of the great hall and glanced around the moonlit courtyard. A noise in the corner caught her attention, and she noticed two figures beneath one of the taller trees. Blaze knelt on the grass, his face buried in his arms resting on a gray stone bench. Torn squatted beside him, one hand on Blaze's shoulder. It took Honey Wine a moment to realize the auburn-haired Knight was sobbing.

Torn waited several moments before he stood and approached the great hall. His gaze met Honey Wine's, and he sighed.

"What's wrong with him?" Honey Wine whispered as Torn drew her into his arms. Together they walked back to their room.

"He doesn't tell us half of what he sees," Torn said. "The rest of us experience our own problems, but he experiences those of the dead. I don't begin to understand it. Who knows what he's seeing right now, what he's feeling? Sometimes I wonder how he keeps any semblance of sanity."

Honey Wine squeezed Torn's hand and said, "He's lucky to have you for a friend."

"And I'm lucky to have you." He paused outside their door and kissed her. Her arms slipped around his neck as he tugged her into his embrace, kicked the door shut behind them and carried her to the bed.

"Blaze did give us a belated wedding present," he said between kisses.

"What?"

Torn pushed himself off the bed only to retrieve a small vial of blue glass from his trunk. He uncorked the bottle and sniffed it, then extended it to Honey Wine who held her nose over the vial.

"Umm," she said. "Nice."

"Get on your back," he said.

She purred, "Ohh, I like the sound of that."

Honey Wine tugged off her clothes, then sprawled naked on her back. Torn removed his trousers and tunic then knelt at the foot of the bed. He poured some of the oil from the vial into his palms and began massaging it into first one foot and ankle, then the other. Honey Wine's eyes slipped shut as he rubbed oil into each of her legs, then paused at her groin. She felt his breath blowing soft and warm against her clit before his tongue laved the nub to alertness.

Honey Wine's eyes opened halfway and she felt her heartbeat quicken, both from the feeling of his tongue and lips on her clit and from the sight of her tall, sinewy husband kneeling between her legs, licking and sucking her where she most loved to be touched.

"Oh Torn," she breathed as his tongue dipped into her pussy and swirled before returning to her clit. He tasted the moist folds of her flesh while his hands reached up to cup her breasts. His thumbs circled her nipples to the same rhythm as his tongue circled her clit, and within seconds she came, shaking and jerking beneath him.

Before the last ripples coursed through her body, he covered her, his cock filling her as he claimed her with long, slow thrusts that drove her toward another orgasm.

His hips thrust while his lips and tongue mated with hers and then moved to her neck. Her body heated with pleasure as she neared another climax. Increasing the speed of his thrusts, he drove into her fast and hard, extending her orgasm and only slowing his motions when the last ripples rolled through her.

Again he reverted to the slow, steady rhythm, and she clung to him, her nipples rubbing against his chest.

"Oh Torn," she panted as another climax neared. Her fingers sank into his shoulders and her tongue fenced with his as his movements increased. At the final moment, she tore her mouth from his, gasping and clinging to him as his hips lunged into hers.

Through a haze of passion, she began to realize he was a damn good lover—more than enough to literally take her breath away.

As another intense orgasm threatened to hurl her into blackness, she felt him cry out close to her ear. She slid her hands upward and rested them loosely around his neck, feeling the strong column tense and throb as he lunged into her. His fast thrusts didn't slow this time as he exploded within her, filling her hot, throbbing pussy with his essence.

* * * * *

Two weeks passed with unprecedented speed, probably because Honey Wine knew such a dangerous mission awaited Torn.

Too soon, she stood outside the fortress with Torn beside his saddled black stallion. Rain and Warrant were already mounted and waiting a polite distance from the couple. All three men wore black trousers and shorter black tunics, which allowed more freedom of movement than their traditional knee-length uniforms. She'd seen the dark masks that accompanied their outfits, allowing them to blend with shadows and move undetected throughout the palace. She hadn't been told all the details of the mission, only that if everything went as planned, they would return early the following morning.

"I'll be waiting for you," Honey Wine said.

"I'll be back."

His expression was calm, his eyes focused and confident, but when he drew her into his arms and held her tightly, she felt his heart pounding against her cheek. She knew how terrified she would be returning to the palace, risking capture, and death in the arena, or worse, by The Lady. Inside, she wept for him, and she prayed to the Goddesses, or the Spirit—whoever listened—to keep him and the others safe.

He kissed her once, then mounted his horse, and led the others toward the wood without looking back.

Honey Wine watched until he disappeared in the trees. When she turned away, she noticed Iris standing behind her looking as concerned as she felt. Honey Wine knew the young woman's heart was with Rain.

"They'll be back," Iris said.

Honey Wine nodded. They had to be.

"I'm going to study with Blaze for a while. Do you want to come?" Honey Wine asked her.

Together the women walked through the gates and to a room behind the stables, which served as Blaze's herbarium. Even before they reached the open door, the scent of herbs wafted on the air, blending with the scent of horses and leather. Inside, surrounded by shelves of potted plants, the auburn-haired Knight sat at a long, rectangular table mixing medicines. He stood upon seeing the women, so tall his head nearly brushed the herbs dangling from the ceiling.

"Sweet Liquid and the Brilliant Flower." He smiled. "Welcome to my workshop and sanctuary. Explore and ask. Tell me of your ways and I'll translate the work of healers from the beginning. They whisper, though not all are wise. Much like us?"

Iris stared at him, blinking, and Honey Wine repressed laughter.

"Stubborn, are they?" Honey Wine asked him. "I guess even spirits don't want to give up the old ways."

"I can't say much." He shrugged. "They did clear the path for us, after all. Yet they chatter amongst themselves, one clamors for this method, another for that."

"What's this?" Iris asked, picking up a glass bottle and inhaling deeply.

He laughed. "No real value there. A pretty scent. The wives asked for it. Rose, sandalwood, vanilla, all in glistening little vials. Woman things."

"Perfume." Iris smiled, passing Honey Wine the bottle.

She sniffed the lovely floral scent. "This would drive Torn mad," She smiled. "May I use some?"

Blaze waved his hand. "Take what you please, both of you. I've no use for it."

For the remainder of the morning, Honey Wine and Iris helped Blaze prepare medicines, then he excused himself to train with the other members of his faction. From what Honey Wine understood of his explanation, there were ten Knights who wore the green sash. They spent most of their time healing, but trained daily in the method of empty-handed fighting in which all of the Knights were proficient. Those of Blaze's faction trained only for defense, as they loathed violence.

Blaze saw the dead as clearly as he did the living, and he had no desire for the ghosts of those he killed to join the beings who constantly surrounded him.

Blaze's visions intrigued Honey Wine, and she couldn't resist asking if he knew what was happening to Torn and his party.

"They work in darkness," he said. "The spies are formidable. Their work tonight is important. They're determined to succeed."

"Will they?"

He smiled sadly. "Forgive me, Sweet Liquid. I can't always see clearly or so far ahead."

"Thanks for trying," Honey Wine said. She was beginning to understand Torn's friendship with Blaze. Though the auburn-haired Knight was difficult to follow, he was kind. Honey Wine wondered if somewhere a woman existed who could truly understand him. Though Blaze appeared to be content with his spirit companions, Honey Wine knew he must have human needs as well. Perhaps there was a woman who could wade through his rambling and provide him with the physical and spiritual bond she and Torn shared. She hoped so.

Chapter Eleven

೫

When Honey Wine retired to Torn's—to *their*—chamber that night, she lay in bed and stared at the ceiling until long after the fire burned down. Had Torn, Rain, and Warrant made it into the palace? Had they captured Timus, or were they dead or imprisoned? More than anything, she wished Torn was lying beside her. She longed to feel his arms around her, hear the sound of his voice against her ear.

If he didn't come back, she'd return to Sophianna and kill Alva herself. Surely it would mean her own death, but she didn't care. Life would never be the same without her strong, gentle, courageous Knight.

Honey Wine wasn't sure when she finally fell asleep, but her dreams were distorted visions of the dungeon, the arena and The Lady…

It was still dark when she heard voices in the corridor. She leapt from the bed, tugged on her clothes and boots, and hurried to the great hall. Torn and Warrant stood in the doorway talking with Mage, Blaze and Mahir. Honey Wine's heart leapt at the sight of his lean, black-garbed body and smooth, innocent face accented with eyes of innate sensuality and keen intelligence. She whispered thanks to whichever Goddess or Spirit had protected him.

Torn's gaze riveted to Honey Wine as soon as she stepped into the hall. She noted his expression looked strained in the torchlight. It had been a tense mission.

"Honey Wine." He held her tightly as she locked her arms around his waist.

"Rain?" she asked.

"He's preparing Timus for questioning," Torn replied, and Honey Wine nodded, relieved that all three had safely and successfully completed their duty.

"Would you accompany us, Honey Wine?" Mahir asked. "Your presence could prove helpful."

"Of course," she said.

"Let's get on with it." Mahir glanced at Torn and Warrant. "Then you both should get some rest. We have much planning ahead of us."

As the others filed out of the hall, Torn and Honey Wine shared another brief embrace.

"I missed you so much." She kissed his earlobe, then his mouth.

"I missed you too."

"Was it difficult?"

He shook his head. "Just tedious. Your maps were perfect. We were in and out in half an hour. If the rest of our plans go as well, the Entertainment will end. Forever."

They walked across the courtyard and up the steps to the fortress's highest tower. Timus sat in a chair in the center of the round, torch-lit room, Rain's hulking form shadowing his face. Honey Wine noted Timus wasn't tied, but stared warily at Rain. His gaze locked with Honey Wine's as soon as she entered the room with Mahir and Rain, Warrant and Blaze following behind them.

"You bastards abducted her too!" Timus snapped.

"I wasn't abducted," Honey Wine said. "I'm here of my own free will."

Timus laughed humorlessly. "I always knew you were too self-righteous for your own good, Honey Wine, but I never suspected you were a traitor. And a fool. You think he cares about you?" Timus nodded in Torn's direction. "He's just using you to get what he wants. Once these...*Knights*...get information, he'll toss you aside."

"That might prove difficult seeing that we're married," Honey Wine said.

Timus' eyes widened in surprise, then narrowed. "It doesn't matter. Whatever you want from The Mistress, you won't get it. She'll raise armies against you. She has allies. When this Order is destroyed, you'll die with them."

Honey Wine shook her head. "You're delusional, Timus. Have you served in that dungeon so long that you think Alva is the most powerful ruler in the world?"

"I know how powerful she is." Timus held Honey Wine's gaze. "So do you. Whatever you want from me, I'll never give. No matter what kind of torture you inflict upon me, nothing would be worse than The Mistress' punishments should I betray her."

"We don't use torture," Mahir stated, "but you will tell us what we want to know."

Chairs lined the walls, and the Knights sat in them, facing Timus from every direction.

"We want the location of the arena and the date of the next Entertainment," Torn said.

Timus' eyes focused on the wall in front of him, his jaw set.

"You weren't cruel, Timus," Torn continued. "You never abused your authority as a guard like most of the others did. I don't think you agreed with the Entertainment any more than Honey Wine."

Still, Timus refused to speak.

"His fear deadens his tongue," Blaze said quietly. "Fear of the thorns of agony."

Honey Wine's gaze met Torn's, and she murmured, "The Lady's needles?"

Torn didn't speak, didn't move, except for his eyes which switched from her to Timus, glowing like strange jewels in the torchlight.

"Tell us what we need to know, and you'll be protected," Mahir said.

Timus snorted with sarcastic laughter. "You couldn't even protect two of your own from us."

"This is going to be a long day," Warrant muttered so only Honey Wine heard. He folded his arms across his chest and sank deeper into his chair. "We have methods of extracting information and could learn all that he knows in moments, but Mahir prefers to have cooperation."

As the day wore on, Timus refused to speak. Honey Wine sat, forcing her eyes to remain open as dusk approached. She'd scarcely slept the night before, and Torn, Rain and Warrant were nearing three days without sleep.

Finally, Mahir turned to Blaze and sighed. "He's yours."

"Sensible," Blaze muttered, withdrawing a vial from his cloak. "Potion of truth. Elixir of honesty will clear his mind and assist us. The liquid of—"

"Just give it to him already!" Rain snapped at Blaze who turned his wide blue eyes to Honey Wine and shrugged.

"Keep that poison away from me!" Timus leapt from the chair as Blaze approached. He flew at the auburn-haired Knight, fists flying. Blaze's stances shifted almost imperceptibly, and each of Timus' blows pummeled air. Rain and Torn grasped Timus and held him in the chair while Warrant and Blaze forced the potion down his throat.

"It's harmless," Blaze told the terrified guard.

Honey Wine had expected to feel sympathy for Timus, but his fear goaded her instead. As she'd watched the Knights' peaceful interrogation, memories of Torn's suffering in the dungeon had plagued her.

"How do you like being on the other side of the bars, Timus?" Honey Wine asked.

She restrained the urge to taunt her former comrade, knowing that indulging her own temper would do little to aid the situation.

Within moments, all tension and awareness faded from Timus, and he responded, trance-like, to every question the Knights asked.

They learned the exact location of the arena and discovered the next Entertainment was planned for two weeks' time. All the monarchs from the participating countries would attend with their most favored beasts.

When the questioning ended, Mahir motioned for Blaze to take Timus to the chamber that would serve as his prison until the Entertainment ended and the High King had the proof he needed to replace the guilty monarchs.

Torn took Honey Wine's hand and said, "Let's go to bed."

Yawning, she walked with him across the courtyard and up to their room.

"Do you really think we'll be able to stop the Entertainment?" she asked as they undressed and slid, naked, into bed.

"We'll have nearly every Knight not involved in the Zaltanian war surrounding the arena."

"There are guards in the arena from all the participating countries," she mused. "Still, none of the armies are as well trained as your Order, I admit that much. And you'll have me, for what little it's worth."

"On the contrary, we're lucky to have your skill with a sword, even though I'd prefer that you stay here."

"Not this time, Torn." Honey Wine snuggled close to him and rested her head on his chest, enjoying the warmth of his skin and listening to his heartbeat. "Both you and Mahir promised I could go this time, and I'll hold you to it."

"Mahir has sent word to the High King about our plan. I can't wait until all this is over." His voice sounded tired and his hold on her slackened.

She knew in moments she'd succumb to sleep as well, but during that time she savored the feeling of his body against hers and the comfort of knowing he was safe.

"I love you, Honey Wine," he murmured.

"I love you too, Torn."

She pressed a kiss to his chest and slept.

* * * * *

Hours later, Honey Wine awoke snuggled close to Torn's chest. She glanced up and in the dimness, saw his eyes fixed on her.

"Hello," she murmured, wiping sleep from her eyes.

He smiled softly and brushed her forehead with a kiss.

She embraced him, more thrilled than she could express that he was back in her arms. She'd told him how much she loved him, but she wanted to *show* him.

She sat up, and he tried to hold her, but she tugged away and whispered, "No. Just stay where you are. Close your eyes."

He did as she asked, his lips parted, the tips of his front teeth adorably visible between them. Pressing her lips to his neck, she traveled downward, licking and kissing every inch of his chest and stomach. She loved the sensation of his hair-roughened skin beneath her lips. Using her tongue, she circled his nipples as he'd so often done to hers, then traced the hard muscles of his abdomen. She licked the joining of his hips and groin and buried her mouth in his dark, curly pubic hair.

Honey Wine licked his cock from root to head and back again. The sound of his increased breathing, and the feeling of his heart pounding against his ribs when she rested her palms against them made her insides quiver with passion.

She sucked him deep into her mouth then laved the head with her tongue and ran her teeth gently along the shaft.

"Honey Wine!" he gasped when she continued the sensual ministrations until his hips bucked involuntarily. She released him just before he came, her fist tightly clamping the base of his shaft.

Grinning wickedly, she leaned forward and trapped his stiff cock between her breasts, pressing and rolling the soft, warm globes of flesh until he came, jerking and gasping as he sprayed them both with his creamy essence.

* * * * *

Over the following weeks, Honey Wine spent most of her time training for the coming battle, studying with Blaze and helping plan the attack on the arena.

During their free time, she and Torn often went riding or engaged in extra training with Iris, Rain and Blaze. She noticed how much time Iris and Rain spent together. To them, almost everything was a challenge, but beneath the competition—perhaps *because* of the competition—Honey Wine sensed attraction between them.

Blaze and Torn fought with similar styles. Honey Wine was amazed by Blaze's fighting ability and almost thought it a pity that he refused to touch a weapon. With his talent, he would have made a marvelous warrior. Torn once told her that Blaze had spent several years in a country across the sea, studying with the greatest masters of empty handed combat. The defensive techniques appealed to the auburn-haired Knight, and he'd carried his knowledge back to the Order. She understood the depth of Torn's friendship with Blaze and was glad of it. Torn could be so quiet, so serious, and Blaze was so odd that many wouldn't take the time to really know him. Honey Wine knew each of them might have been alone without the other.

"I'm glad you've taken so well to Blaze," Torn said one day as they shared a horse on a ride back from swimming in the river.

Honey Wine glanced over her shoulder at Torn. "He's really very sweet underneath all that…that…"

"I know." Torn smiled. "People laugh at him, look at him like he's crazy, but I wonder how they'd adapt to his life?"

Honey Wine placed her hands over Torn's as they rode across the sunny meadow toward the fortress. She tried to imprint upon her mind the sensation of his body against hers, the warmth she'd felt since coming to live with the Order. Not since she was ten years old had she felt as if she was part of a family. Now Torn's family was hers. She enjoyed the friendships she'd developed with Blaze, Rain, Iris and Mahir. Even Warrant and Mage were pleasant and amusing. She was comfortable in Rubyshire, and she belonged.

Gazing up at the cloudless sky, she wished her mind was as clear. She couldn't help worrying. In two days, their plan would unfold.

* * * * *

The gray stone arena loomed in the clearing, and Honey Wine shivered. The last time she'd seen the dreaded place had been on the night Torn had killed Redly, the night he had almost lost his own life.

Torn and his spies had been the first to approach the arena, and she guessed they'd already infiltrated the walls. Mage led the second wave, the majority of the Knights—the infantry— who surrounded the arena, disguised in the shadows and leaves of trees.

Honey Wine held her position alongside Blaze and his faction who followed up the back, ready to aid the casualties. It wasn't that she feared combat, but her decision to remain at the back seemed to pacify Torn, and she knew his concentration couldn't be hindered. He and his spies were in the most dangerous location, directly inside the arena.

She clutched her sword and glanced at Blaze who squatted with his back against a nearby tree, his pale eyes looking eerie in the darkness. She wondered how he could appear so calm, sitting there weaponless. Though they were at the back, they would be thrust into the battle once it began.

"Now flows the sanguine stream," Blaze whispered. Honey Wine lifted an eyebrow. He searched for the words and said, "It's beginning."

She strained to see in the darkness. Everything was still, but minutes later, the fighting broke out.

Shouting and clashing steel sounded from within the fortress walls.

Honey Wine's heartbeat quickened as Knights dropped from the trees and rushed the fortress. Several troops formed a tight circle around the building while others forced their way through the open doors. Torn and his men had done their work well.

"Onward, Sweet Liquid," Blaze bellowed above the noise. Honey Wine followed him toward the fighting, two members of his faction at their heels.

Within moments, she lost sight of the auburn-haired Knight as they mingled with the rush of guards from the fortress as well as beasts who had been freed or turned loose during the scuffle. A guard swung his heavy sword at Honey Wine, and she blocked and attacked, every thrust of his weapon jarring her. She felt a rush of excitement she hadn't experienced in years. Her warrior's heart still thrived after all.

She dispatched several guards before catching sight of Blaze amidst a small group of armed men. She was amazed at how he held his own, weaponless, against the sword-wielding guards. If he was so quick and powerful with simply his hands and feet, her spine prickled to think of how formidable he'd be if he abandoned his code of ethics.

Honey Wine forced her way inside, desperate to find Torn. Several of the Knights lay injured with the bodies of guards and beasts, and she prayed she wouldn't find him among the dying.

She raced into the arena and glanced up at the balcony. Rain, Warrant and several other Knights held the monarchs at sword-point.

The arena itself resembled a small battlefield. Bodies of guards and beasts sprawled on the bloody dirt floor. A group of guards battled in a frenzied cluster around two Knights. Mage and Torn! Back to back, the two created an unbreakable defense. Torn's eyes glistened with concentration as he blocked blows with his short, straight sword and struck several attackers with snapping kicks, sending them flying to the arena floor.

"I should have known!" bellowed a familiar voice from behind Honey Wine.

She whirled in time to block a deathblow from Bron's sword. The guard's strength nearly ripped her arms from her shoulders, but she spun and slashed his leather chest plate.

"Bitch!" he snarled. "If it's the last thing I do, I'm going to kill you, Honey Wine. I always said a woman shouldn't be a guard, and I was right. Tell me, does that mute beast's tongue feel so good on your cunt that you would betray your own people!"

"Your fun is over, Bron," Honey Wine snapped. "No more beasts to torture. The Entertainment ends tonight along with Alva's reign."

Bron and Honey Wine met one another blow-for-blow until she slashed his sword arm. His weapon dropped and his eyes met hers with fury.

"That's why a woman led the guard," she hissed. He pulled out a dagger and lunged at her. Reflexively, she shifted her stance and ran him through.

His eyes widened with horror as he dropped at her feet, blood running from his chest and streaming from his mouth.

She pulled her sword free of Bron's body and turned to the center of the arena. Mage cried out as an arrow embedded in his chest, and he fell, leaving Torn alone amidst the guards.

Honey Wine's gaze swept the arena, and she noticed a single guard loading a second arrow into his bow. She raced toward him as he took aim at Torn who still fought the small troop surrounding him. Even as she ran, she knew she wouldn't reach the guard before he fired.

Blaze leapt through the door onto the archer, knocking him to the ground and rendering him unconscious with a strike to the head.

Releasing her pent-up breath, Honey Wine swung around to aid Torn, but he'd already subdued his attackers and stepped through the group of bleeding, groaning soldiers to assist Mage who lay incapacitated.

Honey Wine and Blaze also hurried toward them.

"A safe position," Blaze said, gently examining Mage's wound. "The Spirit was with you."

"Easy for you to say," Mage muttered through clenched teeth.

"Are you all right?" Torn reached for Honey Wine, his black-gloved fingertips brushing blood from her face.

"I'm not hurt." She took his hand and squeezed it.

His sapphire eyes met hers for an intense moment before he stood and said, "I have to make sure the fortress is secure then send a message to Mahir. He's on the outskirts with a troop from the High King's army. They're waiting to make the arrests."

"You think they would have helped us fight." Honey Wine shook her head in disgust.

"Monarchs, no matter how just they try to be, are all stitched of the same thread," Blaze said, then smiled. "Forgive me, Sweet Liquid. You are the exception."

"But I'm not a monarch," she said.

Blaze didn't speak again as he continued tending Mage's wound.

"By the Twin Goddesses, Torn!" Honey Wine clutched her husband's sleeve. "The old woman! The one who told us how to escape from the dungeon!"

Together, they raced to the holding cells from which the beasts had been freed. The chamber was empty, the cell doors flung open, the furniture and healing tools broken and scattered on the floor.

A closet creaked open, and they spun, hands reaching for their weapons.

"Is it safe?" The old healer emerged from the closet, her eyes wide in her wrinkled face. Upon seeing Honey Wine and Torn, she smiled. "I guess I told my tale to the right woman."

"Thank you," Honey Wine said to her, "for everything."

"May I ask a favor?"

"Of course. Anything," Honey Wine said.

"Do you think you could help an old woman find a place to live now that the arena is gone?"

Torn grinned. "I think we can manage something."

He cast Honey Wine one last glance before leaving her to see to his troops. Honey Wine offered the old healer her arm as she led her out of the fortress to freedom.

Within the hour, the High King's army arrested all the participating monarchs and their surviving guards. The beasts were taken to determine which were capable of entering into society again and which, unfortunately, would be forced to live out the remainder of their lives in confinement.

Several Knights had been injured, but remarkably only two lost their lives. Honey Wine didn't know the ones who died, but she sensed the sadness of the entire Order.

A funeral service was held for them that night. Their bodies were burned and the ashes scattered over the river running through Rubyshire.

Chapter Twelve

ಜಾ

The following evening, Mahir sent for Honey Wine and Torn. As they entered his study, they were surprised to find High King Verick sitting at the table. He nodded his gray head at them, and Torn and Honey Wine bowed.

"As you know, new monarchs have been chosen for the countries which participated in Entertainment." The High King's voice was a deep rumble throughout the room. "Due to your lineage and your outstanding service and skills, I name you, Honey Wine, the new Mistress of Sophianna."

Honey Wine glanced at Torn, and she was shocked that his dark eyes reflected none of the surprise she felt. He smiled at her.

"Do you accept?" the King asked.

"I don't know."

"Honey Wine, as Mistress, you can repair all the damage Alva did to your kingdom. You can rule fairly," Mahir said.

"But what about you?" She turned to Torn and reached for his hand. "I'm your wife. Your place is here and my place is with you."

"You can be my wife and be The Mistress," he said. "You deserve this, Honey Wine, both you and your people."

"He can go live with you, Honey Wine," Mahir answered Honey Wine's unasked question. "Some of the Knights live with their families outside of Rubyshire."

"I'm still required to report here and carry out my duties," Torn explained. "But some of those duties would have required me to travel at times, anyway. The choice is yours, Honey Wine."

She paced the room, her mind reeling. Her, The Mistress! There was so much good she could do. The first would be to empty the dungeon…

"All right." She bowed once again to the High King. "I accept."

* * * * *

One day later, Torn and Honey Wine traveled to Sophianna. Upon arriving, they learned that as soon as the High King's troops marched on the palace, The Lady had thrown herself from her chamber window. Several relatives of the men who had died at her hand tore her body apart and burned the pieces in the village square.

Rain, Iris, Blaze, and Mahir traveled to Sophianna later that day to witness Honey Wine's coronation.

"My faith, Sweet Liquid." Blaze bowed his head as she mingled with guests in the great hall after the ceremony.

"And you have my faith as well, Sir." She smiled at him. "I hope you'll still find the time to teach me."

"Always." He looked to Torn. "The orphan becomes the consort of a Mistress. How strange the tapestry of the Spirit."

It was nearly dawn when Torn and Honey Wine retired to one of the palace's upper chambers. Eventually, they would move into Alva's rooms, but Honey Wine wanted them to be emptied of her sister's belongings first. Alva was imprisoned for life in the High King's tower, a fate too good for her, in Honey Wine's mind.

Anxious to be rid of the royal finery she'd worn for the coronation, Honey Wine tugged the thick gown of black and gray velvet over her head and let it fall to the floor. She kicked it aside as she approached Torn who stood by the fire.

"Honey Wine," he murmured, drawing her into his embrace.

She locked her arms around his neck. Her sweet Knight. Bravery, wisdom and innocence all existing in one man. "I love you, Torn. As much as I hated serving in the dungeon, one good thing came of it. I found you."

"You've shown me a kind of love I never thought existed." He took her face in his hands. His palms felt warm and rough against her skin, and his soft lips brushed her forehead and mouth. "I feel I'm the luckiest man in the world because I have you."

Torn swept her into his arms and carried her to the bed. He dragged off her clothes while nipping and licking her ear, causing her to giggle and squirm. When she lay naked beneath him, he stretched out beside her, fondling her breasts. He gently squeezed and kneaded each warm globe, then rolled the nipples between his thumb and forefinger. He took one in his mouth, his wet tongue lapping the tip of it and circling the sensitive little peak before moving to the other.

Honey Wine made a soft sound deep in her throat as she guided his hand between her legs. His fingers sifted through the dark curls covering her pubis. He caressed her slick folds of flesh then rubbed her clit, carefully stroking the side. Honey Wine tried to restrain a moan.

"Let me hear you," he said in a husky voice. "I love hearing you."

"Oh Torn," she murmured, crying out sharply as his fingers sped up, driving her to orgasm. While one hand rubbed her clit, two fingers of his other thrust inside her, exploring her wet, throbbing pussy as she came.

Before the last marvelous bursts of orgasm ceased, he slid down her body and covered her clit with his mouth, caressing the hard little mound with his tongue. He laved and lapped. He traced the shape of it with the tip of his tongue until she came again.

"Torn, oh Goddess. Torn!" she cried, fingers gripping his hair as he continued licking and tugging at her soft clit with his lips. Her belly clenched as another orgasm neared. This time as she came, he thrust into her. Her pussy clutched his stiff cock, and their hips ground together. Torn grasped her buttocks, two fingers gently pressing the sensitive flesh deep between the soft globes.

His mouth covered hers, absorbing her moans of pleasure as she came again, this time dragging him with her. As they merged, body and spirit, she knew their souls had joined and she had found her true mate.

The End

Knights of the Ruby Order:
Crag

ഗ

Chapter One

☙

Lily's daughter sickened in winter.

Her husband had been dead for nearly a month, killed in the war with the kingdom of Zaltana.

Battles continued to destroy village after village, forcing many to surrender to the powerful, vicious Zaltanian army. Lily's home had been long destroyed, and she and her daughter had been living in the mountains with a small group of villagers who'd taken to hiding. They scratched out an existence under overhangs and in makeshift shelters. Even by the first snow, most of them were cold and hungry. Lily believed their poor living conditions caused her daughter's illness, but hiding had been her only course of action. The Zaltanians killed their enemies' children, all except the ones old enough to work in the mines. Women and men were raped and taken into slavery. Better for Lily and her daughter to die in the mountains than at the hands of some Zaltanian pig.

Still, part of her had believed she and Vina would survive. The belief was strangled at the onset of Vina's fever, at her sudden lack of appetite and at her incessant crying for which there was no comfort.

"Twenty miles north is a village called Tanek which has managed to fend off the Zaltanian army," said Cormac, one of the only other survivors of Lily's village. "It's a long walk, but if the snow holds off, you should make it."

"What good can they do me?" she asked, tired from spending the past several nights tending Vina, and hungry since there hadn't been enough food for more than a meal a day for each adult in the settlement. At that moment, she wished the Zaltanians *had* killed her.

"They fought off Zaltana because they're backed by Knights of the Ruby Order."

Lily drew a deep breath, feeling the first glint of hope in months. Knights of the Ruby Order were known throughout the land as the finest warriors and healers, but they only fought for just causes, never for profit. If anyone could help Vina, it would be them.

Immediately, she packed her few belongings and set off on foot with Vina in her arms. She didn't relish such a long hike with a sickly infant, but it was her only choice.

The day remained sunny and warm as she waded through calf-high snow. Ice melted from the trees and rocks, and the sound of running water might have been musical had she been in the frame of mind to listen. She simply felt too tired and worried to care about the beauty of the countryside. Trees, some green, others skeletons decorated with glistening icicles, covered the mountains. She passed streams of rushing white water where she stopped for a drink and sat on a rock, attempting to feed Vina. The infant took some milk, but was promptly sick.

Lily rocked her, whispering to her, wondering if the baby sensed her mother's desolation.

It was dusk when Lily saw the welcoming fires of Tanek, and she could have cried from relief. Her feet ached, her arms felt sore and her stomach hurt from hunger.

As she neared the settlement, some of her hope waned. Though its people had chased off the Zaltanians, Tanek had suffered. Most of the houses lay in ruins, and people and animals huddled under lean-tos scarcely stronger than the ones in her own mountain hideaway.

She noticed some rebuilding had taken place, but it was not an easy task in the middle of winter. Several men dressed in black tunics, a red circle of thorns embroidered around a ruby over their hearts, trudged through the wreckage. She closed her eyes and whispered a prayer of thanks as she recognized the uniforms of the Ruby Order. The Knights carried themselves with pride and determination, even the ones whose arms and legs were bandaged. They had obviously fought hard for Tanek, and she knew more of their troops still battled throughout the continent, attempting to force the hated Zaltanians into submission.

As she neared the settlement, a tall, bearded Knight with two muscular, tawny dogs at his side, approached.

"Please help me," Lily said. "My village was destroyed months ago. I've walked twenty miles to find you. My daughter is sick, and we have nowhere to go."

The Knight glanced down at Vina. He offered to carry Lily's pack of belongings and bid her to follow him to one of the long, wooden buildings still standing amidst the rubble.

"We have survivors from most of the villages in the north," he told her. "Tanek has other settlements similar to this one. I'm afraid our resources are spread rather thin. Most of the settlements have one or two healers to look after everyone, but you're welcome to stay."

He opened the door of the longhouse, and Lily nearly gagged. Stuffy from smoke, the place reeked of herbs, blood, sickness and death. Water from melting ice dripped through holes in the ceiling, and men, women and children covered the dirt floor, some leaning against walls, others sprawled in the center of the single large room. She saw movement in the dim loft and knew there were even more people pressed, back-to-back, above them.

She gazed down at Vina's flushed face and felt a lump form in her throat. This place was scarcely better than where they'd come from. Still, the Knights were here. The Ruby Order possessed the finest healers in the world.

"Right this way, missy," said the Knight who'd escorted her in. They edged around people, stepping over some and nudging others aside, to the more open space in the center of the room.

Lily glanced at the hearth and saw two women turning a deer over a spit. At least they had food. The sounds of coughing and sneezing mingled with moans, soft conversation and the snapping of flames from the fires and torches throughout the building.

The bearded Knight paused behind a man draped in a gray tunic stained with dirt and blood. Dark brown hair was tied with a piece of rope at the man's nape. Lily noticed his neck was rather thick and his shoulders broad in spite of his slimness. He applied a bandage to the stump where his patient's hand had once been. The patient was an older man with grayish hair and a battle-scarred face. Eyes closed, he gritted his teeth against the pain.

The healer finished with the bandage, and the bearded Knight said, "Crag will take good care of you, missy."

The healer's head jerked over his shoulder, and Lily stared at him. His cheekbones were high and wide, a rich brown beard covered his face beneath. A full lower lip peeked out from beneath the wiry hair. The tip of his straight nose was gently rounded, a streak of dried blood running down its tip. Blue eyes glanced from beneath thick, dark brows. Lily noted those eyes didn't look at all welcoming.

"Crag, this woman has walked twenty miles with a sick baby to get here. Where would you like her?"

Crag looked at Lily hard, his expression saying he'd like her to go anywhere but here. He stood, his shadow falling across Vina's face. He was very tall, very lean, and Lily noted his face looked nearly as gray as his robe. He appeared more like a nightmare than a healer. Surely he wasn't a Knight? Yet a circle of red thorns was embroidered over his heart, the symbol of his Order.

"Space is limited, Sir Rain," Crag said, his voice a low timbre. The sound of it might have been comforting had his expression not been colder than the snow outside. "But we'll find a place."

"Of course you will." Sir Rain placed a hand on Lily's shoulder, then turned to leave.

"Sir," Crag followed Rain, "have the reinforcements arrived yet? We have close to two hundred people in our settlement now, and with just me and Sir Wood—"

"Crag, I'm sure the Order is sending more men as quickly as they can. We'll just have to make do in the meantime. You're doing well." Rain nodded and left.

"Doing well," Crag muttered under his breath, his jaw working.

Vina wailed, and Lily did her best to quiet her. Hesitantly, she said, "Sir Crag, where can I get some water?"

"Just Crag," he said. "I'm not yet a Knight. I'm serving here as part of my training."

Lily didn't really care about his training. She only wanted some water, food and a place to rest. He seemed to sense her thoughts as he pointed to the women by the spit. "Go ask them. They'll tell you where to find supplies. Come with me first. I'll get you a place to stay and examine your baby."

"Help! A healer! I need a healer!" shrieked a woman from across the room. "My husband is not breathing!"

"Just find an empty space somewhere," Crag called over his shoulder as he stepped over people and wooden supply trunks toward the woman crying for help. "I'll be with you as soon as I can."

Hoisting Vina over her shoulder and rubbing her small back, Lily muttered, "Some Knight he's going to make. The epitome of manhood and compassion."

She found a place beside an old woman who reeked of must and rotted teeth. Lily noted that her odor had to be especially foul if it was discernable above the general stench of the place. At least the hearth was nearby, and if she turned her back, the scent of smoke and burning wood overpowered the old woman's pungency. She dropped her pack and rested Vina against it before turning to one of the women by the spit.

"Is there anyplace I can get some water?"

"Surely." The woman smiled, and Lily wondered how she was able to remain cheerful in such horrific surroundings. "The well is outside. Here's a bucket." She edged the large wooden pail toward Lily with her foot. "We need more water in here anyway. I'll keep an eye on your baby while you fetch it."

Lily hesitated, glancing at Vina. She didn't know the woman. She didn't know anyone there, but she desperately required water since Vina not only needed to be changed, but was covered in drying vomit.

Sighing, she took the bucket and walked outside. The well was located in the center of the settlement, and she took several moments to inhale the cleansing winter air while she filled the bucket. When she entered the building again, the smell wasn't so intolerable, and eventually, she'd learn to ignore it.

As she approached her space, she noticed Crag kneeling beside her pack, examining Vina.

He glanced at Lily, an eyebrow raised. "I hope you plan on using some of that water to wash her."

She dropped the bucket beside him, some of the water splashing on his filthy tunic.

"You look like you could use some washing yourself," she snapped, tired and angry from the long, tedious walk, the worry she felt for Vina, the nagging hunger in her belly and the memories of the life she'd once had.

"You try staying clean in this place." His blue eyes flashed anger. "We have two healers right now. Me and Sir Wood who's been ministering to the ones in the lean-tos all morning."

"Well you try keeping a vomiting baby clean over a twenty mile walk in the middle of winter!" She shook her head. He was, after all, the healer. She'd traveled all this way for him to help Vina, and if she didn't hold her temper, he might not bother with her at all. Lily murmured, "I'm sorry."

"Bathe her in cool water. I'm going to prepare a medicine which should help settle her stomach. The truth is, I've seen a lot of this illness since I've arrived here. The outlook isn't good. I'm sorry."

Her stomach clenched and her head throbbed. *The outlook isn't good. I'm sorry...* His blue eyes held hers, and she noted he actually did look sorry.

Lily cleared her throat and said, "The man whose wife just called you. Is he all right?"

Crag stood, wiping his hands on his rough gray robe. "No. He's dead."

He disappeared across the room, and she sat beside Vina and bathed her. Tears slipped from Lily's eyes, dripping off the tip of her nose as she thought, *I should have just stayed in the mountains...*

Chapter Two

"Here, love. You look like you could use this."

Lily glanced at the woman squatting in front of her, the same woman who'd given her the bucket earlier. She held out a chunk of bread and a wooden bowl full of stew. Bits of meat and vegetables floated in the brownish broth, and Lily's stomach rumbled.

She accepted the food and began eating. The bread was hard, but the meat tasted tender and flavorful. In truth, it was the best food she'd eaten since the Zaltanians attacked her village.

"Sir Rain and some of the villagers hunt often. You won't starve here, that's for certain. By the way, I'm Coral." The woman sat on the floor, her feet tucked under her. Wisps of hair had loosened from the bun on her head, and she blew them from a face streaked with ashes from the hearth. Still numb from stifled hopes since arriving in Tanek, Lily didn't answer. Coral asked, "What are you called?"

"Lily," she murmured. Vina awoke and let out a piercing shriek. Lily placed her food aside and reached for her, but Coral picked her up and said, "You finish eating. I'm good with babies."

Taking another bite of the bread, she watched as Coral rocked Vina and whispered endearments. Lily asked, "Do you have children?"

Coral shook her head. "My betrothed was called to fight against Zaltana before we were married. That was a year ago. But growing up I was the oldest of five, so I often cared for my brothers and sisters."

"Is he alive?"

"My betrothed?" Coral sighed. "I hope so. It's been months since I've gotten a message from him. At times I think this war will never end. Since the Ruby Order became involved, the Zaltanian army has known more defeats than ever before. I don't think there are enough Knights to silence them completely, but at least Zaltana won't conquer the continent as they'd planned to."

"I hope every last one of them dies where they stand," Lily snarled and glanced up sharply as a shadow fell across her bowl.

Crag squatted beside her, his eyes as cold as frozen pools, his mouth a grim line. He held a vial in one hand, and reached for Vina with his other. Coral placed her in his arm, and the baby vomited on the front of his tunic. He glanced at the yellow stain, not that it was particularly noticeable since his tunic was plastered with dirt, blood, and other indiscernible body fluids. Still, Lily felt the need to apologize.

"Doesn't matter," he muttered, wiping Vina's face with a piece of cloth and forcing a bit of the vial's contents into her mouth. It took him several moments to administer the medicine since the baby screamed and spat. Lily placed her food aside, her hands twisting in her lap until the tedious chore was completed. Still, she noted he was far more gentle and patient than his miserable expression had led her to believe.

When he'd finished, he passed Vina to Lily and watched her for several minutes.

"Call if you need me." He stood. "I'll be nearby."

"Thank you."

He walked away, and Lily turned back to her daughter.

"He's been here for a year and a half," Coral said, her gaze following Crag as he made his rounds. "All the Knights are trained as healers, but most of the ones here are used as guards. Sir Wood is an experienced healer, and there have been others who've come and gone. There have been weeks at a time when Crag is the only one. Too bad he's taken his service during the Zaltanian attacks."

"I imagine they all take service in desperate places," Lily said. "From what I understand, the Ruby Order's training is rigorous."

Coral nodded. "Which is why they're elite. It's still not right, how they've left him here. But I guess it's not right that any of us are here. Look at your daughter, for instance, and the other children. Is your husband fighting?"

"He was killed during the attack on our village."

Coral's brow furrowed. "I'm so sorry."

"He was a good man. Not a fighter, though."

"But you are." Coral offered an encouraging smile. "I can tell. You're a survivor, Lily."

"Sometimes I think that's more of a curse than a blessing."

"I have to get back to work. There's food to prepare and the washing up to do. Consider me a friend."

Lily smiled at her. "Thank you. Think of me as the same."

Over the next couple of hours, Vina slept peacefully. Whatever Crag had given her had stopped—or at least postponed—her queasiness. Lily noted that he passed them often, stopping to look at Vina. It wasn't until later that night that she, quite by chance, discovered why he hovered so close.

She'd slept for several hours and awoken thirsty. Buckets of water with ladles were stored at the far end of the longhouse, and she hoped they were still partway full, since she didn't relish the idea of leaving the warmth of the house for a cold walk to the well. She picked her way over snoring men and women to the buckets standing outside a patched leather curtain. She'd seen Crag disappear behind that curtain often and emerge with herbs, supplies and bandages. Tilting one of the buckets, she heard water slosh, and dipped in a wooden ladle. As she drank, one of the black-garbed Knights passed her. He was of medium height and build with sandy hair falling straight to his shoulders. A short scabbard hung from his hip, and as he passed, she noticed his uniform was bloodstained and almost as dirty as Crag's gray tunic. His green gaze caught hers, and he nodded before stepping behind the curtain. Her stomach tightened. Whenever one of those Knights crossed her path, she felt as if she should salute or curtsy. Many other people felt the same. She saw it in their eyes when in the presence of a member of the Ruby Order.

"I rode to the nearest settlement this afternoon," came a hushed voice from behind the curtain. Lily guessed it was the Knight who'd just stepped inside. "Their supplies are as limited as ours, but I know reinforcements will be coming soon. You seem to have everything under control here."

"Yes, Sir Wood." Lily recognized Crag's voice. "We do need back-up. People are still coming in from other villages."

"How is that baby you asked me about earlier? The one whose mother brought her in today?"

Lily dropped the ladle and listened intently.

"She's stopped vomiting, so the mixture worked."

"Good."

"I dislike working with babies," Crag stated.

Lily's face burned, and her stomach clenched as tightly as her fists. *Dislikes working with babies?* She knew by looking at him he was a wretched man. Some healer he was. He didn't seem to like anybody at all, not only babies. Still, to say such a thing!

"The medicine worked," Crag continued, "but the wrong amount of herbs could have killed her. I don't like working with something so small."

The wrong amount? Lily nearly tore through the curtain and cursed both of them, Ruby Order or not. Didn't he know how much to use? Shouldn't he know? To think that Vina—not to mention the rest of the settlement—was at the mercy of some charlatan! And she had been stupid enough to think the Ruby Order possessed the finest healers in the world! What bothered her most about his revelation was not knowing if he had been concerned with killing Vina because he cared for her life, or because he didn't want to appear stupid in front of Sir Wood and the rest of the settlement.

"All part of our duty, Crag. All part of our duty. With more experience, you'll be fine."

"I've been here for quite a while. The battles show no sign of ceasing. Wouldn't I be of more use fighting in the front lines?"

"You came to us with martial skills," Sir Wood told him. "You knew when you entered the Order all Knights must be trained in the healing as well as the fighting arts. We're not mercenaries, Crag. We undertake missions of mercy. Your fighting skills are important and will be an asset to our Order, but you've already fulfilled your military service. Now you must do your time as a healer. We need you here. You can see that. Unless you feel you can't rise to the occasion?"

"No, Sir."

"Good. Now, I'm going to get a few hours sleep, then you can wake me and rest yourself. As always, if you require my assistance—"

"Thank you, Sir."

Crag stepped from behind the curtain, and nearly stumbled over Lily. Their gazes met, and for the briefest moment, she thought he looked as bewildered as she felt.

"Is your baby all right?" he asked.

"Vina. Her name is Vina. Yes. She's as well as can be expected."

He nodded and reached for a ladle of water. No sooner had he raised it to his lips than someone across the building bellowed, "Crag! My stitches tore!"

Crag flung down the ladle and kicked the bucket so that water splashed onto the leather curtain. Cursing under his breath, he trudged in the direction of the voice.

"Why doesn't he just leave," Lily muttered, "if he hates it so much?"

Suddenly, Vina's familiar cry echoed through the relatively quiet room. Sighing, she hurried back to her.

Lily picked up Vina and tried feeding her. The infant settled against her breast, and for a few moments, there was almost total silence—until Sir Rain and another Knight burst in, dragging an enormous, armor-clad man whose hair and face were streaked with fresh blood.

"Let me go! I have to find the Captain!" bellowed the man. In spite of his injuries, he possessed enough strength to drag the two Knights off balance.

Several people who had been sleeping by the door grabbed their children and scurried away. Though Lily stood across the room, she impulsively held Vina tighter.

"Crag!" Rain bellowed, but Crag was already on his way to assist them. Rain continued, "This man is the only survivor of an attack on a village just east of here. He's gone mad."

Crag shot Rain a look that said, *Really, I failed to notice!*

"He's bleeding badly," Rain said. "You need to stitch him up."

As Crag approached, the man's thick leg kicked at him. The healer dodged the blow just as the warrior broke free from the Knights' arms. Crag lunged at him, and the two struggled while Rain and the second Knight pulled out ropes to tie the madman.

"I must inform the Captain!" he ranted. "They're all dead! Zaltanian bastards!"

Lily's heart pounded as she watched the scene, amazed that Crag still had a grip on the man who had to be at least twice his weight. Crag was tall and big-boned, but this warrior was a giant. No wonder he'd been the only survivor of a Zaltanian attack.

"By the Twin Goddesses," Coral said as she stood beside Lily, her freckled nose wrinkling. "I've seen other people go temporarily mad from the horrors of battle, but why did it have to be a man the size of a draft horse?"

Suddenly one of the warrior's flailing elbows struck Crag in the face. Blood gushed from the healer's mouth, and Lily winced. Instead of dropping his charge, Crag wrestled the man's arms behind his back and knocked his legs out from under him. Panting, fury glistening in his blue eyes, he held the man fast while Rain and the second Knight bound his wrists and ankles.

"Good," Rain said, wiping his brow on his sleeve. He glanced at Crag. "Are you all right?"

Crag nodded.

"We can handle him from here," Rain said. "I'll tend the wound. Go clean yourself up."

Crag stalked directly past Lily, and Coral muttered, "Didn't think he had it in him."

"He was a warrior," Lily told her.

"How do you know? Crag never speaks about his life before joining the Order—or his life since, for that matter."

"I overheard." Tucking Vina in the crook of her arm, Lily approached Crag.

He sloshed water around in his mouth and spit in a wooden bowl. Blood and a tooth landed with a splash.

"Damn it!" he muttered.

"Is it a front or a back tooth?" Lily asked.

"Sort of the middle." He placed a hand to his jaw.

"Hold on. I'll be right back."

She asked Coral to watch Vina for a moment and left the house. Outside, she knocked an icicle off the roof, crushed it against a stone, and wrapped it in one of her kerchiefs.

She brought it to Crag and held it to his jaw. "This should help. When I was little, my sister and I got into a fight and she knocked out my two front teeth. Ice helped."

"I know." He half smiled. "Healers pick up on little tricks like that."

She wondered if she looked as sheepish as she felt.

"You look good for a woman with no front teeth," he said.

"They were baby teeth, so they grew back."

"Speaking of babies, how's... "

"Vina," she supplied.

"Sorry. I feel a little muddled right now."

"You have a lot of people to remember."

"Yes." He looked far off for a moment.

"Crag!" Rain called. "I need salve for this man!"

Still holding the ice to his jaw, Crag continued with his work.

"Lily, she got sick." Coral thrust Vina into her mother's arms.

"Oh no." Lily sighed, those few moments of somewhat pleasant conversation with Crag forgotten. If Vina continued to expel all nourishment, she'd die. Lily didn't need a healer to tell her that.

Chapter Three

The next few days fell into a dismal pattern. In between caring for Vina, Lily made herself useful by fetching water and helping prepare meals. Her body moved, yet her thoughts remained fixed on her daughter, who, in spite of Crag's careful ministering of herbs, showed no signs of improvement.

One afternoon, Lily stood by the well, a bucket full of water beside her, and stared up at the cloudy winter sky. What had happened to her life? It seemed like so long ago that she'd lived in a prospering village with a husband she cared for and a healthy child. Hers had been an arranged marriage. She and her husband had grown up together and had gotten along well. He was a decent man who paid attention to her and Vina. Lily missed his laughter and his kindness. She missed sharing meals with him and walking in the field behind the home he'd built. Though she had never experienced that weak-kneed attraction so many women described feeling for their lovers, Lily had liked her husband. And he'd liked her.

Her thoughts were interrupted as Crag stopped by the well to fill one of his buckets. Outside of the dim longhouse, he looked even paler. His eyes were shadowed beneath, and part of his lower lip was still swollen from the whack he'd taken several days before. For the first time, Lily realized how tired he looked. She scarcely saw him sleep, and knew he had little time to eat. It seemed as soon as he picked up a bit of food, someone called for him, either a villager or one of the Knights. Not that everyone didn't work hard. The healthiest people were still rebuilding the destroyed houses and barns, and the Knights hunted and trained diligently to prepare for any future attacks. Sir Wood made his rounds along with Crag, but he also traveled between the settlements of Tanek and was able to leave the longhouse for several hours a day. Crag seemed tied to it.

"Why have you chosen to become a Knight?" Lily asked.

His blue eyes turned to her, surprised. For a moment, she thought what a lovely shape and color his eyes were. If he cleaned up and got some sun, he'd be rather attractive. His lips twisted in a sarcastic smile. "Glamorous life, isn't it?"

"It seemed that way."

He looked down at his bucket. "It's the uniforms."

She raised an eyebrow. "Is that all?"

"No. Just my attempt at a bad joke."

They stepped aside as others approached the well.

"You don't have to answer," she said. "It's really none of my business."

"Two and a half years ago, I was fighting in a village that was rescued from Zaltanian rule by the Ruby Order. I was a warrior, but when I looked at those Knights, I saw men who didn't fight for any particular land or for profit. They fought for the oppressed. They healed everyone who needed help, Zaltanians included. To me, that kind of aid was unheard of. I was sick of killing. I wanted to save lives instead of take them. I wanted people to look at me like they looked at those Knights. Sounds selfish, doesn't it?"

Lily shrugged. "In a way, but not the part about saving lives. The instinct to lend aid isn't at all selfish."

"I was wrong about everything. Since I've begun my training, I haven't escaped killing. I see just as much—more. Except now it's worse. Now I'm not fighting back. I'm cleaning up. There's no glory to Knighthood."

"But you're saving lives."

"Am I?" His cool eyes stared into hers. "You see what it's like here. We need more supplies. We need more help. Rebuilding is too slow and people are piling in too fast."

"If everything is so hopeless, then why don't you leave?"

"I don't know," he murmured. "I guess because eventually, once I'm Knighted, I'll request to be placed where I can do the most good."

"And where is that?"

"In battle."

"I thought that's what you were trying to get away from? Haven't there been enough battles?"

"I'm a good fighter, or at least I was. I haven't picked up a sword in months. There's been no time."

"You're not a good healer?" She was almost afraid to ask that question, after the conversation she'd overheard between him and Sir Wood several nights ago.

He glanced at her but didn't reply.

"How bad can you be, if you're in charge of this place by yourself?"

"Sir Wood—"

"Is not here as much as you are."

He paused outside the longhouse and asked, "Where is your husband? Fighting?"

"He's dead."

Crag nodded. "So you're alone with... " He thought for a moment, and this time she let him search for her daughter's name. "Vina?"

"Yes."

He pushed open the door, and let Lily pass through first. Before she took back Vina from Coral, she glanced over her shoulder at Crag. His back was to her, and firelight danced off his gray tunic as he stooped beside a crippled old man. She wondered if he had a family somewhere, a wife and children. What did they think of his leaving them to pursue Knighthood?

Living in Tanek, she could understand his frustration and disillusionment. Even so she would have thought a man who aspired to Knighthood would somehow possess more nobility than an average person. Yet Crag was just a man. Still, part of her rebelled against the notion that he had fears and desires like everyone else. Once his service was complete, he was to be a Knight of the Ruby Order. He'd don the black uniform, and people would look up to him. They'd expect him to defend the weak and lend aid where it was required. He would be expected to do all that, a man who "disliked working with babies" and who kicked buckets of water when someone called him to fix their stitches. He'd be summoned to fight, this man who hadn't picked up a sword in months.

Crag might have been disillusioned, but not nearly as much as Lily was.

After seeing to Vina, Lily asked Coral if she needed help baking bread for that evening.

"It would help if you could get more flour from the storage house." Coral grinned, holding up her hands and forearms coated with bread dough. "I'm a little stuck."

"Be glad to. Just keep an eye on Vina for me."

As Lily walked way, she realized she had no idea where the storage house was. Since arriving in Tanek, she'd rarely left the longhouse except to haul water. She was about to turn back and ask Coral when she noticed Crag standing in the doorway, inhaling fresh air. Suddenly it struck her how much alike they were, both trapped in misery from which death was the only escape.

She approached him, and his gaze instantly fell upon her.

"Where's the storage house?" she asked. "We need more flour."

"I'll help you. Those sacks are heavy."

"I know you're busy—"

"I have a moment of peace, and I'll take any chance I can get for clean air."

Together they left the longhouse and walked across the frigid ground toward a shed at the end of the settlement.

Crag opened the door, and they stepped inside. Lily glanced at the collection of sacks and barrels, grains and salted meat.

"At least we won't starve," she said.

"That's one good thing," he muttered. "Flour is this way."

While he reached for one of the sacks, she stood on tiptoe to slide a box on a top shelf to a less dangerous position and stumbled into Crag.

He caught her, steadying her against his chest. "Are you all right?"

She nodded and tilted her face up to his. Her breath caught in her throat. It might have been a trick of the light in the dim shed, or perhaps it was spending so many months without the touch of another human being, aside from her infant daughter, but her body tingled when Crag's gaze held hers.

"I'm fine," she murmured.

"Are you?"

"What...what do you mean?"

"Are any of us fine in this place?" His dull eyes suddenly looked wild—or desperate. Even that spark of light in their depths rendered them as beautiful as polished sapphires.

She swallowed, knowing she should leave. His fingers gripped her upper arms, not enough to hurt, but enough that she'd have to make a conscious effort to pull away. Would he let her go? Of course he would. Did she want him to? She'd disliked him from the first, but there was no denying the kinship they shared.

"I miss life before the war," she whispered, tears clogging her throat. She swallowed them. Crying was of no use.

"I don't know what it's like not to be at war." His brow furrowed. "There was always some battle, some skirmish, some...bloodshed. I've been fighting since I could hold a sword."

"I remember what it's like to live in peace, to walk without fear. I remember what it's like to wake up and do something because I enjoy it, whether it be a walk in the field or picking flowers. By the Spirit, sometimes I just wish I could escape. I wish I could—"

"Do something for myself." He released her and paced, his fists clenched. "Have a moment unclouded by other people's pain and my own anger."

Without thinking, she grasped his arm. His head snapped toward her. They stood so close she noticed the pulse beating in his throat, saw the fine lines about his eyes and the weary shadows beneath. Still, his eyes shone with a burst of yearning she understood all too well.

He cupped her cheek, and before Lily could stop herself, she stood on tiptoe as he bent and covered her mouth with his. The kiss was tentative at first, but when she didn't pull away, his tongue slipped between her lips. Hers reached out to meet it, stroking and tasting. Crag took her face in his hands as he explored every moist corner of her mouth. His callused hands stroked her cheeks and forehead with such gentleness Lily felt near tears again. It had been so long since she'd been held and caressed. The only man she'd ever known had been her husband, and while she enjoyed his touches, something in the way Crag stroked and kissed her made her heart catch fire. Her entire body felt weak, yet she slipped her arms around him and clung to him like a sailor clings to a mast during a storm. She needed contact that much.

For a moment, she wondered why he kissed her. Was he just a man desperate for sex, or was he a human being in need of comfort, just like her? Maybe that in itself was a lie. She wanted sex, not just as a form of release, but as a way to rebel against whatever power had sent her life tumbling down the path to hell. *Go on. Take away my happiness,* her mind shrieked. *You can't crush my desires completely!*

Lily closed her eyes, enjoying the softness of his lips and tongue and the roughness of his beard against her skin. She ran her fingertips down his blade-sharp cheekbones. She gripped his shoulders, relishing the hardness of his lean muscles beneath his tunic. Beneath her palms, his chest felt so solid and strong. In spite of his slimness, he was such a tall, big-boned man.

His hands opened against her back and swept down to her buttocks. He cupped the fleshy globes and squeezed gently. Lily moaned when his lips moved to the tender flesh behind her ear. He nipped her lobe and kissed her neck, his beard tickling until she shivered. One of his hands caressed her breasts through her rough woolen gown before he slid it down her shoulders, baring her nipples. The cool air as well as her arousal stirred them to hard peaks. Crag sat on a barrel and tugged her between his knees so his mouth was level with her breasts. Capturing one nipple in his lips, he laved it with his tongue.

"Oh!" Lily mewled, clutching his head close. His fingertips caressed the flesh beneath her breasts while he sucked one nipple, then the other.

Lily's pulse raced and her breathing grew ragged. Wetness seeped between her legs. Crag tugged up her dress, his large hands roaming over her outer thighs and hips. While one hand grasped her buttocks, his other dipped between her legs, gathering moisture. His wet fingers circled her clit, and that alone sent her over the edge. She gasped and clung to him, her hips thrusting against his rapidly stroking hand.

As she leaned against him, catching her breath, she slid her hands downward, grasped his tunic and yanked it up. She found the waist of his trousers and unknotted his rope belt.

"Lily..." he began then his voice trailed off when she wrapped her hand around his cock. It felt hard and warm. Her finger traced veins and the smooth head. Moisture leaked from the eye, and she smeared it along the underside with one fingertip while her opposite hand grasped his sac and squeezed. He groaned, his arms tightening around her.

Lily touched her lips to his neck, feeling his pulse throb. As she pumped his cock and kneaded his sac, his breathing quickened. She doubled her motions, stretching her thumb to caress his slick cock head as she continued rubbing the shaft. He grew harder and bigger in her palm and he panted.

As she guided his cock to her aching pussy, his hands covered hers. For a moment she thought he might stop, but he grasped her bottom and tugged her onto his lap, burying himself to the hilt inside her.

Lily gasped and clutched his shoulders, raising herself so his cock nearly left her, then dropping back down so he filled her again. She rode him fast and hard, clinging to him, her face buried in his neck.

Another orgasm built inside her, tingling, tightening, until she burst. As she throbbed around his cock, he stood, his hands still clutching her buttocks and holding her close. He walked several steps without ever slipping from her pussy and pressed her to the wall. Keeping his knees bent, he drove into her so rapidly she thought he'd come in an instant. His movements continued, extending her orgasm and pushing her toward another. It was slower in coming, but it wound so tightly she knew when it happened, it would be shattering. She only hoped he could sustain the wicked pace until she reached her climax. He seemed to have no intention of stopping. His mouth covered hers in a probing kiss, his tongue thrusting in time with his hips. Lily gasped, running her fingers through the sweaty hair at his temples. His body felt so hot, but so did her own.

"Oh don't stop! Don't stop, please!" she gasped. The most fantastic orgasm was so damn close! She exploded, her legs gripping his waist, her arms probably choking him, though at that moment she didn't care.

"Ah Lily! Gods!" he cried out, plunging in to the hilt, his body pinning hers to the wall as he surged in ecstasy.

For several moments they stood, panting in each other's arms. She opened her eyes and found him staring at her, all her doubts, shame and guilt reflected in the blue eyes holding hers.

"By the Spirit, what have I done?" he murmured.

Simultaneously they broke apart, Crag adjusting his trousers and tunic and Lily fixing her dress.

Her heart still pumped wildly and her hands shook. By the Gods, what kind of a person was she? Her husband was dead, her daughter might be dying, and she'd just fucked a Knight-in-training who should have been tending to his duties in the longhouse!

"I'm so sorry." He reached for her, but she stepped away.

"It was as much my fault as it was yours," she said. "Please, can we pretend this didn't happen?"

Anger sparked his eyes and he looked about to protest. Finally he nodded. "Of course. That would be best."

He walked across the shed and picked up a sack of flour, swinging it over one of his broad shoulders. "Lily, please don't think my behavior is a reflection on the Ruby Order or their beliefs. I—"

"Don't worry. This slut won't think any less of your Order."

"You're no slut."

"What kind of a woman would do what I just did?"

"What kind of a man would have taken advantage of you?"

"I'm not a child! I wanted it as much as you!"

"Don't be so sure about that. I wanted it badly."

"So did I," she admitted, "but we can't do it again. It was—"

"Wrong. That's why I'm sorry."

"And it never happened."

"Lily—"

"Never!"

For a moment, they held each other's gaze before Lily said, "Coral needs the flour back at the house."

Crag nodded, the fire in his eyes fading to dullness again as they stepped out of the shed and back to the real, dreary world they'd been delivered from for such a painfully short time.

Chapter Four
ೊ

Vina died exactly one week after arriving in Tanek. Though Lily lived through that final day like a blurry nightmare, she later remembered it clearly.

When she awoke in the morning, Vina's fever had soared higher than the night before. What worried Lily most was that she didn't cry. She made no sound for most of the morning.

When Crag stopped to examine her, he didn't say much, but Lily knew when he didn't bother administering the herbs that her trip to Tanek had been a waste. Lily didn't cry. She didn't speak. Between her chores, Coral joined Lily's vigil. She sat with her and tried talking a bit at first, then took her friend's hand in silence.

In fairness to Crag, he spent more time with Vina than usual. There were times when Lily knew he could have slipped away for a meal or some rest, but sat with them instead. He held Vina when she died. Lily panicked when her breathing became difficult and thrust her into his arms. He used a mixture of Eucalyptus to aid her breathing, but both mother and healer knew it wasn't congestion.

Lily stared as Vina grew silent and still in his arms. After a moment, he passed her to Lily and murmured, "I'm sorry."

She nodded, but couldn't speak. Tears stole her voice as she buried her face in Vina's blankets and cried. She felt Coral's arm around her, felt Crag's touch on her hair, but she couldn't look at either of them.

She wasn't sure how much time passed, but she finally allowed Coral to take Vina's body to prepare for burial. Once they were gone, Lily sat, numb, for several moments before she stood and ran out of the longhouse, leaping over people, buckets and trunks.

Crag had just reached the doorway, two full buckets in his hands. She shoved him out of her way, causing the water to drench his tunic and boots. He muttered a curse then called to her, but she didn't want to speak to him or anyone. She wanted to be alone because that's exactly what she was. Completely alone with no living connections to the family she'd once had.

* * * * *

Vina was buried the following day along with several other villagers who'd died of disease or battle wounds. Coral stood with Lily, and she felt grateful for her friend's support.

Crag didn't attend the funeral. A new group of villagers had arrived that morning, keeping him busy inside.

Sir Rain approached her after the funeral. "My condolences, Lily."

She nodded, her eyes hot and dry. She hadn't cried since those first moments after Vina's death. What was the point? Tears did no good.

"Will you be staying with us?" Rain asked.

"I have nowhere else to go, but if you want me to leave, I understand."

"You're more than welcome here." The Knight bowed from the neck. "Coral and the other women said you've been helpful in the longhouse. We need as many healthy workers as we can get, and if you decide not to settle here permanently, I'll put in a word for you with the leader of our Order. We'll find a place for you in our fortress."

"Thank you, Sir Rain. You've been kind to me from the first."

"I can always sense a good woman." He placed a hand on her shoulder. "Again, I'm very sorry."

"Thank you."

Inside the longhouse, Lily joined Coral and the other women in baking bread. She wrapped a kerchief around her head, rolled up her sleeves, and kneaded a soft heap of dough. Others conversed around her, but all she thought of was Vina. Several times she looked over her shoulder, thinking she had to check on her. Then she'd remember and blink back tears.

"Looks like we might have seen the last of the winter storms," Coral observed.

"I hope so," remarked a gray-haired woman beside her. "My bones ache so terribly in the cold. Crag gave me a salve which helps, though."

"He's a good enough healer," said the last woman in their circle, a middle-aged redhead with a plump face even more freckled than Coral's. "Even if he is Zaltanian."

Lily's gaze shot up. "Zaltanian?"

"I heard that rumor," Coral stated. "Lily said he was a warrior."

"Oh yes," said the redhead, "A captain in the Zaltanian army."

Lily flung the dough hard on the wooden table and punched it with all her strength. Zaltanian! "That bastard! What the hell is he doing here if he's Zaltanian?"

"He's no longer Zaltanian." Coral's eyes opened wide. "He's of the Ruby Order. They're a kingdom in themselves."

"Once a Zaltanian, always a Zaltanian!" Lily turned from the table and searched the room for Crag.

He stood examining a woman's arm and didn't see Lily approach.

Crag was far too tall for her to reach his head, so she punched him in the back even harder than she'd punched the bread. He grunted and spun around, pressing a hand to his lower back.

"What the hell are you, mad?" he snapped.

"Zaltanian pig!" Lily sensed everyone's eyes upon her, but she didn't care. Her pulse pounded and she trembled with utter rage. Zaltana had ruined her life, and she'd been sharing quarters with one, had even placed her daughter in his care! Lily didn't think about how sick Vina had been, or that Crag had never set foot in her village during the attack, since he'd already begun his training for the Order. He was still a Zaltanian bastard, and she'd even given him her body! Oh, they both pretended it had never happened, but she'd still been soiled by the filthy, murdering savage! She ranted, "No wonder why you're a lousy healer! Your kind is only good for killing! So eager to go to the front lines, are you? Want to get back to your own people and away from sick babies. You probably let Vina die! You probably poisoned her! And what you did with me! You perverted bastard!"

The woman Crag had been examining leapt fearfully from her chair and stood a safe distance away, cradling her injured arm. Lily picked up the chair and flung it at Crag. He lifted his arms to block the blow, and the chair dropped to the floor, raising a cloud of dirt and dust.

"Will you calm down!" Crag's voice was just shy of a bellow.

"Murderer!" she screamed, flying at him with clawed fingers. He grasped her wrists and cursed as her knee jabbed him between the legs. He held her so tightly she couldn't move no matter how hard she struggled, yet his grasp wasn't painful. His arms were warm, strong and comforting—just as they'd been when they'd made love in the storage house. Against her will, Lily relaxed enough to completely give in to her grief. It really wasn't Crag Lily was furious at, but everyone involved in the bloody war. She was angry at life and at fate. She choked on tears and sobbed, "Zaltanian bastard. Why can't I hate you? Why can't I?"

His grip loosened, but didn't release her. His fingers threaded her hair as he held her close to his chest. She wasn't sure how long they sat there, but eventually her crying ceased, and she heard the rhythm of his heartbeat against her cheek and felt the comforting rise and fall of his chest as he breathed. His fingers were warm and gentle on her hair. She sat up, her face hot and her eyes stinging. She pushed away from him, too ashamed to meet his gaze, and left the house.

At the well, she hauled up water to wash her face, then stood outside until she shivered from the cold. At least she felt more in control of herself. Completely foolish, but in control.

When she walked back inside, several people looked her way, but no one except Coral mentioned the incident. She approached and asked if Lily was all right.

"I will be. I should never have attacked him like that."

Coral smiled slightly and shook her head. "You're not the first. Few knew he was a warrior before joining the Order, but almost everyone knows he's from Zaltana, and there are others who've confronted him for the same reason."

Lily felt a bit guilty. Though Crag had committed his share of violence for his homeland, he'd done his best to help Vina, of that she was certain. And he worked as hard as anyone in Tanek. Every kingdom had soldiers, who fought, and no one here had the right to blame him for performing his duty, particularly after all he'd done for the settlement.

As she returned to baking, she looked for Crag. He was involved with his patients, and if he glanced at her at all, she didn't see. But she remembered. She remembered the feeling of his arms around her. For the first time in months, she'd felt as if someone cared for her suffering, though he probably didn't. He'd just wanted to shut her up before she caused trouble for the entire house. By watching him subdue the man who'd attacked him days ago, and according to Coral, he was accustomed to quieting madmen—and madwomen.

Nearly an hour later, Lily was gathering dirty bandages to be boiled when Sir Wood strode into the longhouse.

"Good news, Crag," said the Knight, stooping beside the apprentice healer and watching as he applied salve to a man's burned back.

"Sir?" Crag spoke softly, his eyes focused on his work.

"Two apprentices from the small settlement just north of here will be joining us on the morrow."

Crag's gaze shot up, and he sighed. "It's about time...Sir."

"That was the good news." Wood offered a sad smile. "The bad news is, all the ill from the settlement will be moved here. Word has come from the Order that it will be safer to merge the smaller settlements with the larger ones. That way the guards will be more centrally located."

"But if the same healers are coming with their same charges, what real difference will it make to us?" Crag asked. "The work will be the same for us all."

Sir Wood shrugged. "Work something out. Cover one another's shifts."

"Sir, now we have over two hundred people in this settlement alone, many who need constant care. It's impossible to—"

"Nothing is impossible, Crag," Sir Wood stated. "Not to the Ruby Order. You'll do well not to forget that."

Crag nodded. "Sir, now that you're here, I was wondering if you could take over for me for a couple of hours? I could use some fresh air and washing."

Sir Wood shook his head. "Not right now, Crag. I have to get a couple of hours sleep. Rain needs me to help with guard duty tonight."

"Guard duty? But there are many guards around the settlement."

"Rain has sent most of them north to move the villagers here. Give me a few hours, then I'll relieve you before I start guard duty."

Sir Wood crossed the room and disappeared behind the leather curtain. Lily glanced at Crag who stared straight ahead for several moments, looking like a stunned deer who'd just been shot by a hunter's arrow.

Good. The Zaltanian bastard should do the worst kind of penance for the acts of his people, she thought, though deep in her heart, she didn't believe her own words. Still, she walked away from him and continued her own miserable day.

Chapter Five

The following morning, the first of the people from the north arrived, and by dusk all had been moved from the smaller settlement, including two apprentice healers. The new group moved into two small houses recently built.

Lily saw the apprentices by the well. Like Crag, they wore gray robes with red thorns embroidered over their hearts. They looked almost as miserable as he did, but they didn't realize the benefits they had. At least they were assigned to the new buildings that didn't reek like the old longhouse, and there were two of them to Crag's one. Of course, Lily heard them argue that though Sir Wood had divided his time between the settlements, he had lived at Crag's station and was therefore more readily available.

Lily stood nearby as the two new apprentices expressed this view to Crag. His reply had been a loud, humorless laugh before returning to the hovel most everyone called home.

Over the following days, Lily busied herself with cooking, sewing, sharpening weapons for the Knights and making arrows. She did anything that allowed her mind to remain numb to the inconsolable pain of Vina's loss. She often saw Crag in passing. While living in a one room shelter, contact with him was inescapable. They rarely spoke, and during those first days after her attack on him, did their best to avoid one another. Still, she often found herself watching him, dragging herself from the frigid prison she'd built around her heart and soul to observe the Knight-in-training. He scarcely smiled, not that he had any reason for happiness. For a man training for such a revered vocation, his life was no better than the rest of theirs — worse in some ways. She'd never noticed before how much healers were depended upon and how dedicated they were to their craft, at least Crag was. Though she'd only known him a short time, Lily realized how much he'd learned during his service with the Knights. For a man who'd only begun studying the healing arts no more than two years ago, he was more knowledgeable than he gave himself credit for—more than she'd given him credit for. There was so much to know, first deciding what was wrong with a person, then choosing and preparing the correct herbs to treat the problem.

She often watched Crag, Sir Wood and the other apprentices treat men, women and children who fought like animals, at times injuring the healers. Crag excelled at restraining people without hurting them, and Lily knew that particular skill came from his years of studying fighting. He must have been excellent at hand-to-hand combat. The Zaltanian army had lost a good warrior, of that she was certain. Their loss was the Ruby Order's gain.

When had she begun to respect him? A Zaltanian?

As the days became weeks, she wondered about the whereabouts of the reinforcements Crag and Sir Rain had spoken of on the first day she'd arrived in Tanek. Surely they would be coming soon, for there were more sick and injured than ever before. The battles still raged, and as many as could travel made their way to the infirmary Tanek had become.

Among the newest arrivals was a woman in the last weeks of pregnancy. Lily scarcely noticed her when she arrived, and had never even learned her name. It was quite by chance that they both stood outside the longhouse when her labor started. She was taking some air while Lily beat the dirty rope rugs that scattered the floors inside.

Her sudden gasp made Lily glance in her direction. She stared at Lily with startled eyes, one hand clutching her back.

"Goodness, I think I strained a muscle," she murmured.

Lily stood, dropping the rugs in the snow. "Why don't you go inside and rest? It's cold out here."

"I wanted to get out of that stuffy room for a while. It's horrible in there."

Lily nodded. The woman had only arrived a couple of days ago, and the smell was bound to be more noticeable to her. She remembered how it had been during her first days in Tanek. Now she scarcely noticed the stench, or rather accepted it as a part of life, just as she accepted the pain of losing Vina. She had no choice.

Looking at the woman, she felt a pang of jealousy. Soon she'd have a baby. Most likely Lily would never have another. Her husband was dead, and she had no intention of marrying again.

"It's not the most pleasant place in the world, but it's shelter," Lily said, gathering up the rugs. "Come on. I'll go with you."

"It's funny. My backs been hurting all morning."

"Has it? You might be in labor."

"But I still have a few weeks." Her eyes widened. "That's what the healer at my home village had told me."

"Have you mentioned the pain to Crag or Sir Wood?"

She shook her head. "Sir Wood left about an hour ago, and Crag seems so busy."

"Crag is always busy." Lily guided her inside and passed the rugs to Coral. She joined the pregnant woman in her space in a corner of the house and helped her to lie down.

The woman gasped sharply and closed her eyes. After a moment, she smiled at Lily and said, "Perhaps you're right."

"I remember the feeling well enough," Lily told her. "What's your name?"

"Gem."

"I'm Lily. I'll get you some water and find Crag. Let him know what's going on."

Gem's eyes widened. "There's no midwife here?"

"Crag is a very good healer."

"But he's a--" Gem stifled a shout as another pain gripped her. "I think he'll do just fine. Just fine."

Lily found Crag in one of the lean-tos outside, setting a young boy's broken leg. She told him what was happening to Gem, and he stared at her. "How long do you think before she delivers?"

"Me? How should I know? You're the healer."

"Yes, but you had a baby."

"I don't know, Crag. Her pains are still several moments apart."

"I have to finish up here, then I'll be in."

She nodded. "I'll sit with her in the meantime. I don't think she has anyone."

"What did you say her name was?"

"Gem," she told him. Then, remembering his trouble with names, scratched it onto the dirt at his feet.

His lips flickered in a slight smile. "Thank you for staying with her."

"Not a problem."

By the time Lily returned to the longhouse, Gem seemed more anxious. Lily explained Crag would arrive soon and tried conversation to keep her mind off the impending delivery.

She learned that, like Coral's, Gem's husband was fighting Zaltana. They'd been married for two years, and this was their first baby.

"You said you have children?" Gem swallowed nervously as another pain faded.

"I had a daughter. She passed on recently."

"I'm so sorry."

"How about after your baby is born you let me help you?"

"I'd love it... If I get through this."

Lily smiled. "Oh, you will. Trust me."

Crag arrived within the hour, just in time for Gem's labor to begin in earnest. Lily remained with her, holding her hand and offering words of encouragement. She noted Crag looked almost as grateful for her presence as Gem did. He prepared an herbal drink to lessen her pain, but as Lily well remembered, nothing short of a blow to the head could deaden it completely.

In less than two hours, Crag announced that he could see the head and ordered Gem to push.

"By the Goddesses, Lily, this hurts!" she snapped, sweat beading her brow and upper lip.

"You're doing fine," Lily told her. Indeed she was. Her labor had been very short and relatively simple.

Within moments, Crag announced the birth of a healthy boy. As he caught the slippery infant in his large hands, he smiled at Gem. It was the first genuine smile Lily had ever seen him wear, and she was nearly as bewitched by it as by the birth she'd just witnessed. Somehow, helping Gem had rekindled a part of her she thought was dead. She was still able to feel happiness in spite of everything she'd lost.

Gem uttered a giddy laugh as Crag placed the infant on her stomach. She gazed at her son and said, "My first baby."

"Mine too," Crag told her, and the three of them laughed.

Lily helped him clean Gem and her son, making them comfortable. Coral offered to assist her while Crag and Lily washed themselves.

"Thank you so much," Gem told Crag before he left the house.

"You're very welcome," he said.

Lily waited for him at the door, and together they walked to the well.

"That was an experience," she said.

"Hmm."

"You know that's the first time I've ever seen you smile like that."

"It's the first time I've had a reason. If only all situations could turn out like that one. Usually I'm stitching someone up, cauterizing a wound, causing them pain. People need me, but they hate me at the same time, and not just because I'm Zaltanian."

Lily glanced at him. It had been so long ago that she'd bombarded him with verbal and physical abuse that she thought he'd forgotten. Apparently, her accusations had affected him.

"I'm sorry about what I said before. I was angry and miserable about losing Vina." She swallowed hard. It was the first time she'd spoken her daughter's name since she'd died.

"You don't have to explain." He gestured around the settlement. "Heaven knows there's been enough misery around here. A person can only take so much."

"You're sorry to be here, aren't you?"

"Sometimes," he admitted.

"You can't ever go back to Zaltana, can you?"

"Sure, if I want to be executed. Sometimes that doesn't sound so bad."

"Don't say that."

"Why? It's true."

"If you weren't here, who would have helped Gem just now?"

"Another healer." He shrugged. "We're all expendable. Besides, I wasn't the only one who helped her. You were very good yourself."

Lily smiled. "Thank you."

"Maybe you should be a midwife."

She tilted her head to one side. "I never thought about it, but I will now."

"Think hard," he warned. "A healer's life isn't easy. Believe me."

"But don't you think it's worthwhile?"

"Crag! We need help over here!" Sir Rain bellowed from behind the barn. "One of the horses has gone lame!"

Crag looked at Lily and shrugged before stalking off to the barn. She never did receive an answer to the question she'd asked him. At least not then.

Chapter Six

Coral, Gem and Lily sat together sewing, the baby nearby, when the first direct attack struck the settlement.

"Everyone, stay inside!" One of the Knights apprentice rushed into the longhouse, his face as pale as his dirt-stained gray robe, his sword drawn. "Zaltanian raiders are bombarding the village!"

Sir Rain stepped inside, his sword drawn, a silver helmet on his head. He pointed the tip of his blade at the apprentice. "You stay here and bolt the door behind me. I need volunteers to guide those in the lean-tos to the houses."

Lily stood along with a handful of men and women. Crag dropped the bucket of bloody water he held and approached Rain. "I can fight, Sir."

"No," Rain stated. "Healers with your skill are too valuable to waste on the defense line. You either stay here or help with moving the others."

"But, Sir—"

"Another word from you, and I'll slap you with a formal reprimand," Rain told him before he strode out the door.

Lily glanced at Crag as they joined the others hurrying to help the villagers in the lean-tos.

"Be careful, Lily!" Gem shouted to her friend.

Coral caught Lily's arm before she stepped outside. "Are you crazy? You could get killed out there!"

Lily jerked from her grasp and followed the others. She knew she could die. She didn't care.

Outside, the Knights and apprentices formed a circle around the settlement. Some, mounted on horseback, met the charges of galloping Zaltanian raiders.

The guards were outnumbered, and the Zaltanians were powerful fighters, but the Knights again proved they were the most skilled in the land as they defended the settlement against the raiders' onslaught.

Lily approached the nearest lean-to and helped a man with a leg injury to his feet. When he was safely deposited in the longhouse, she ran for others.

Around her scurried men, women and children. Knights clashed with the sword-wielding Zaltanians. Terror momentarily gripped Lily, and she nearly dropped the old woman she was escorting to race for the safety of one of the houses. She noticed Crag a short distance away, stooping beside a Knight who'd sustained a severe arm injury.

It was then she realized several Zaltanians had completely breached the settlement's defenses. They galloped their horses into several lean-tos, stabbing terrified villagers with their swords and trampling supplies. Flashes of her own village's destruction leapt across Lily's mind, and she screamed. That scream became a bellow of shock as she saw Crag snatch the wounded Knight's sword and race toward a raider about to stab a woman sprawled in the snow. The raider turned in time to block Crag's thrust and counter with his own swipe, but almost before Lily could discern his motions, Crag had slain the Zaltanian. Two others attacked him, and she watched in terror and awe as he spun and struck with his blade in the most dangerous and graceful motions she'd ever witnessed. Within moments, he'd cleared several Zaltanians from the lean-tos so Lily and the volunteers were able to drag the survivors to safety.

By then, the Knights had driven off the attackers. Lily stepped out of the longhouse to see who required help and noticed Crag had dropped the sword and knelt by the bodies of a dead Zaltanian and a slaughtered Tanekian woman. He stared at his bloody hands and shook his head.

"Crag." Lily touched his shoulder.

His head snapped up, and she couldn't clearly discern the emotions warring in his eyes.

"By the Spirit, what a mess!" Sir Wood approached. He stared hard at Crag for a moment before he ordered, "Come. We have plenty of work to do. Many wounded to care for."

Silently, Crag joined the healers who were attempting to be everywhere at once. Coral and several others from the houses joined Lily in searching for those clinging to life among the corpses.

Lily sighed as she gazed at the bloody snow and the ruins of several lean-tos.

It wasn't until very late that night, when most of the mess had been cleaned, that they were finally able to rest. Outside the longhouse, Lily sat behind a barrel and gazed at the moon, pulling a woolen robe tightly under her chin. The nights were growing even colder, and she sensed an impending storm in spite of how the earlier warm weather had tricked them into believing winter might end.

She heard footsteps, and glanced at the shadowed figures of Crag and Sir Rain. Hidden from them, she overheard another conversation not meant for her ears.

"In spite of the lives you saved fighting off the raiders, you deliberately disobeyed orders today, Crag," Rain stated.

"Yes, Sir."

"I, personally, agree with the decision you made. Your instincts weren't bad, and I might have done the same. However, the rules of our Order demand that you be punished for insubordination." Lily heard Rain sigh. "When the reinforcements come, we had intended to ship you out to join the cavalry for the remainder of your service. To pay for your actions today, you will stay here instead."

Lily squinted in the dimness and saw Crag swallow hard. He drew a deep breath and nodded. "Yes, Sir. Such an assignment is probably better for me. After today, I have no intention of ever picking up a weapon again as long as I live."

Rain lifted an eyebrow. "I'm surprised to hear you say that, Crag. Is there a problem you'd like to discuss?"

"A few days ago, I helped bring a life into the world, Sir. Today I killed six men, perhaps more, if the ones I wounded also die. Over the time I've spent here, I've seen many die. I wasn't able to save them, but I also didn't kill them."

"You were a soldier before you took up your training. I know you've killed before."

"Yes, Sir, but I've changed. I've had enough blood on my hands without putting more there myself," Crag stated. "May I go, Sir?"

"Yes." Rain touched Crag's arm. "You may change your mind about fighting with weapons, however, if you don't, there is a faction of our Order—a small faction, grant you—which have dedicated their lives completely to healing. They carry no weapons. Ever. They are, however, highly trained in hand-to-hand combat. It's difficult for a Knight to enter this faction. The training is rigorous and the ultimate decision about who is accepted falls on the faction leader, Sir Blaze. Still, it's something for you to consider."

"Thank you, Sir," Crag said, but Lily saw no interest in his eyes, only desolation.

She nearly followed Crag inside, but instead remained seated, hugging her knees. After all, the Zaltanian's problems—and his decisions—were none of her business. She had her own troubles to wallow in.

* * * * *

Aiding in the delivery of Gem's baby had made Lily think about her own existence. Her family was dead and her village destroyed. But she was still alive. Unless she chose to take her own life—a thought which had crossed her mind—she would go on. Slowly, she opened her heart to life again.

One afternoon, between chores, she approached Crag who knelt, cleaning and stitching a leg wound on Tanek's blacksmith who had been injured while shoeing a horse. One of the Knights apprentice, a man training in the guard, held the man as still as possible while Crag worked. In spite of the blacksmith's desire to remain still, it was difficult when Crag's quick, gentle ministrations caused such pain to the raw injury. The apprentice struggled against his charge's strength.

They were positioned in one of the only empty spaces left in the house, directly by the hearth. Even in the dead of winter, the constantly burning fires made the longhouse hot and stuffy, but the temperature by the hearth was most unbearable. Unfortunately, it was also the brightest place in the house, therefore easiest for Crag to see the injuries he worked on.

Lily paused for a moment, watching his bloody hands as they carefully removed dirt and bits of rock from the wound then stitched it. It amazed her that such large hands could be so graceful and gentle, yet she well knew just how tender their touch could be. Her heartbeat quickened when she recalled how his hands felt on her body. No! How could she think of such a thing at a time like this? He turned his head, attempting to wipe a tendril of sweaty hair from eyes that were bloodshot from smoky air and lack of sleep.

"Here." Lily brushed back his dark brown hair and retied the strip of rope that had loosened at his nape.

"Thanks," he said. "I should just cut it all off."

"I know women who'd kill for that hair," she told him.

"It's hot as hell's belly in here," he muttered. "And outside your fingers could fall off from the cold."

"We need a perfect spring day."

The blacksmith snapped through clenched teeth, "There are no perfect days left. All because of those Zaltanian bastards!"

Lily's gaze flew to Crag's face, but his expression only betrayed concentration on his work. She asked, "Can I help at all?"

"I could use some fresh water."

Immediately, she filled a bowl and brought it to him. She continued watching him, and once the wound was stitched, he showed her how to bandage it.

"I can teach you how to change dressings," he said. "If you want."

"Would it help?"

He gave a wry laugh. "Do owls hoot? With so many people, it seems like I spend half my life changing bandages."

For the remainder of the day, she followed Crag as he worked, watching him and assisting in any way she could. This mostly meant fetching water and bandages and talking to people to keep their minds off his ministrations. For the first time in weeks she focused on something other than Vina and her old life.

It was long after dusk and most people were asleep when Lily and Crag finally stopped for a meal. She took half a loaf of bread, and he picked up two leftover bowls of stew. He walked toward that mysterious leather curtain, and Lily stopped outside, knowing it was off-limits to all but the healers.

He glanced over his shoulder. "Don't you want any stew?"

Hesitantly, she followed him behind the curtain. It was a small space, but large enough for them to sit comfortably on a rug. Shelves of powders, liquids, dried herbs, bandages, needles and knives lined the walls from ceiling to floor. Blankets were piled in the corner, and two leather bags, one she guessed belonging to Crag, the other to Sir Wood, sat side by side against a barrel.

As they ate, she glanced at Crag. He stared into space, chewing silently.

"I can help you again tomorrow, if you want," she offered. "I know I'm not much help, but—"

"No, you are." His blue eyes focused on her. "Thank you for all you did today."

"I'm glad to be useful for something more than cooking and mending." She placed her bowl on the floor, bowed her head and closed her eyes, rubbing the back of her neck, sore from weeks of hauling water and supplies.

Crag's hand nudged hers aside. His strong fingers massaged the tight muscles in her neck and shoulders, and she allowed herself to relax.

"I'm sorry Zaltana ruined your life," he said.

She looked up at him. "You don't have to apologize. You didn't kill my husband or destroy my village."

"The warriors of Zaltana follow orders, just like anywhere else."

"Your orders are to kill and enslave. Men, women, children, no one's safe from you—I mean them. Surely you must see the wrong of what they do. Why else would you have left?"

"Change will take time. For a kingdom like Zaltana, change may never occur."

"It can as long as there are Zaltanians like you."

"Like me." His eyes frosted. "I was a killer, Lily. In my own way, I'm still a killer. When the injured are brought to me, I often have to decide who lives and who dies. Who should get my attention first? When should I summon Sir Wood? What herbs should I give and how much? Much of what I do is guesswork. How does that sound? Guesswork from a healer, from a person people bring their sick children to and say 'help them.' Our supplies are dwindling, yet more sick are brought in every month—no, every week. I haven't left this place in over a year and a half. I'm tired of the dirt and of watching people suffer. I'm tired. I can't remember the last time I slept a full night. Sometimes I wish these people would disappear or… "

"Die?" she asked.

"Does that make me a terrible person?"

"No," she replied honestly. When she'd first arrived in Tanek, she would have been horrified by such a revelation from a man training for Knighthood. That was before she lived here.

"I don't think they're ever going to let me leave here," he whispered. "Not until this bloody war is over, and knowing Zaltana, that could take forever."

"Don't say that." She shook her head. The thought of the war never ending was too terrible.

"It's true, isn't it?" His hand moved to her shoulder, then her neck. His eyes, glistening with frustration and yearning, bore into hers, yet for the first time she noticed another emotion.

Once again drawn by mutual desolation, they leaned closer to one another. Her eyes focused on his full, soft-looking bottom lip peeking through his dark beard. She remembered how it felt and longed for his kiss.

"I know we're not supposed to mention it," he whispered against her lips, "but I want you again, Lily. I want you so badly."

"I know," she murmured, taking his face in her hands. Her gaze held his and her pulse throbbed.

"You're an ache, Lily, a sweet, powerful ache." He buried one of his hands in the hair at her nape and kissed her temple then her cheek. "I could take you right here and now."

"Do it." She clutched handfuls of his hair. "Do it!"

He needed no further encouragement. His mouth covered hers, his beard rough and his lips and tongue soft and moist.

Lily closed her eyes and untied Crag's hair from its leather strip. She threaded her fingers through the thick waves. His arms tightened around her so his chest crushed her breasts. His strong, hard body felt so good! Disentangling her fingers from his hair, she grasped his back. Through his tunic she felt the play of muscles as he moved. Her fingertips pressed along the length of his broad shoulders, feeling the thickness of his bones. When in his arms, she found it difficult to remember he was a healer. The ones in her village had been slim, studious and a bit condescending. While lean, Crag's muscles felt rock-hard and sculpted. Beneath her touch, his body radiated strength such as she'd never felt. Intelligence shone in his eyes, yet he was never condescending. Sullen, perhaps, and she understood why.

"I need you, Lily," he murmured. He kissed her upper lip then her lower.

Burying his face in her neck, he tickled her flesh with his tongue. Lily shuddered at the sensation, her heartbeat quickening when he slipped down the front of her dress. His thumbs circled her nipples. He traced her areolas and her nipples tightened to tingling peaks. Her pussy grew wet and Lily fought to keep from moaning. Only the curtain separated them from the others sleeping in the longhouse. What if another Knight—Sir Wood, perhaps—decided he needed healing supplies? Lily nearly mentioned this to Crag, but his lips fastened on one of her nipples as his tongue caressed the peak, and she no longer cared who might discover them.

Crag's hands slid beneath her dress and stroked the curly triangle between her legs. He gently explored her pussy and a shiver of desire ran down her spine. A wet finger stroked her clit, running up, down and along the underside.

"Oh Goddess!" Lily whispered, trying not to gasp too loudly.

Two fingers slid inside her. She clenched her inner muscles and thrust against Crag's hand. His fingers explored her hot, moist inner-flesh while his thumb circled her clit. All the while his lips and tongue continued their delightful torment on her nipple.

Lily's heart throbbed out of control as she approached her climax.

Suddenly Crag's hands and lips left her. Her eyes flew open as she started to protest.

She paused. Crag, his own chest rising and falling with agitated breathing, fumbled with his tunic and trousers. His lips parted slightly as he tried panting in silence. Within seconds, his cock was free. Though dark, Lily caught the outline of it and her pulse leapt. It was long and thick, arising from a cushion of dark spirals. Suddenly she longed to see the rest of his body. She knew how powerful he felt, and she'd seen the breadth of his shoulders and chest, but what did his flesh and muscle look like beneath the drab gray tunic?

Crag's gaze met hers, burning with desire and the same desperate need she felt. Again it struck her how much they were alike, she and the Zaltanian.

"Lily," he whispered, his body covering hers. She felt him slip inside her, filling her with his hard, warm flesh.

For a moment, neither moved. His breath was warm and quick against her neck. Every muscle in his body felt tense.

"I never want this to end," he whispered, pressing his body even closer to hers.

Neither did she, but their bodies wouldn't listen to their emotional desires. He thrust into her with long, slow strokes. Lily grasped his shoulders and hooked her legs over his, pressing him deep inside her. His thrusts became short and fast and she knew it was as difficult for him to keep silent as it was for her. Gripping his sides, she felt his heart knock against her palms, its pace so frantic she doubted he could last much longer. The idea of being caught was nearly as arousing as the sexual act itself and had pushed both of them to the edge of control. Lily's pulse raced and she tightened her grip on him.

Suddenly his thrusts slowed, teasing her with long sweeps that left her aching on the edge of orgasm with each stroke. He certainly wasn't making it any easier to remain quiet and not draw attention to themselves. His hips thrust fast again. This time he didn't stop. Lily's mouth opened in a silent shriek as her pussy clenched and pulsed around his cock. His motions slowed again, extending her orgasm to the last marvelous ripple.

Lily had expected him to come fast. Instead he continued his steady thrusts. The sensations felt almost too wonderful to her stimulated flesh. Another orgasm built slowly inside, forming a tight ball of heat in her pelvis. His thick, hard cock, slick with her juices, drove in deep then pulled out almost to the tip before rushing back in. Crag's mouth covered hers, his tongue thrusting in time with his hips. He absorbed her cry when she came, squeezing him tightly as she quivered and pulsed. Rather than slowing his movements, he increased them, grinding into her, stroking and licking her shoulder and neck. The rough fabric of his tunic stimulated her excited nipples. Crag grasped her buttocks with one hand, hauling her even closer as he thrust. Lily exploded in a third orgasm, short but intense.

As the sensations waned, her body felt aflame. The excitement of their precarious position behind the curtain was so incredibly exciting and the sensations of their bodies so intense that she wondered how he managed to keep control of his passion.

Lily opened her eyes halfway and felt a new wave of desire. Crag's eyes were closed, his expression tense. The tip of his tongue flicked once over his kiss bruised lips. Perspiration misted his forehead, a droplet running down one of his temples and streaking his cheek. As his thrusting quickened, his head arched slightly, tendons and veins standing out beneath the moistening flesh of his neck. She sensed he was holding his pleasure at bay as he sought to give her another climax.

"Crag," she murmured, raising her hips and locking her legs tighter around his waist. Though incredibly aroused, her orgasm was slower in arriving. She felt his excitement and wondered if he'd last long enough for her to reach a fourth, greedy peak, knowing that when it happened, it would surpass all others.

"Almost," she whispered, "Oh, Goddess don't stop! Just a little more!"

Before her eyes fluttered closed, she noticed an expression of pleasure/pain cross his face. His nostrils flared slightly and a shiver ripped down his spine as he slowed his movements. He pulled out to the tip of his cock, then swept down. Lily's mouth opened in a silent shriek as an orgasm tore through her, so intense it was almost agony.

Crag stiffened, surging and trembling as he came so hard he collapsed on top of her. His hot body pinned hers to the blanket. Lily's hands rested on his back, feeling his fast breathing and his heart pounding.

As she recovered, Lily's stomach lurched. Again! She'd made love with him again, and worse, she'd been *desperate* for it. What kind of a woman was she?

She pushed him gently, and he lifted his head, his eyes almost drowsy following such a powerful release of desire. He stroked wisps of hair from her face. "Should we pretend this didn't happen, too?"

"I am a horrible person," she muttered, more to herself than to him.

His brow furrowed. "What?"

"My daughter is dead and you and I—"

"Lily, you're not horrible. You're a human being. I'm the disgrace."

"Why you?" It was her turn to look surprised. From what she could see, he'd done nothing except act upon his normal male urges. He hadn't forced her. Quite the contrary. She'd wanted him, though she hated herself for it.

"I took a vow of abstinence when I joined the Order. Until marriage, Knights aren't supposed to bed women. I've broken so many of my vows, Lily. First by disobeying Sir Rain, and now with you. I didn't mean to take advantage of you, but I—"

"You didn't take advantage."

He drew a deep breath and caressed her face. "I felt if I didn't get some kind of release I'd go insane."

Lily took his hand and squeezed it. "I know. That's just how I felt. I won't tell anyone what we've done, Crag."

"I'm not worried about that."

"I am. Vina's dead," she said, as if that explained everything.

A strange emotion flickered in his eyes. For a moment, she thought her implication had hurt his feelings, then his face returned to its usual stony expression.

"Healer! I need a healer!" a man bellowed from somewhere in the longhouse.

Crag muttered a curse but straightened immediately and adjusted his clothes.

"Do you want me to help you?" she asked.

He shook his head. "Get some sleep."

As his warm body left hers, Lily felt empty. She'd loved being in his arms again. Through her own guilt, it had never occurred to her that Crag might have felt just as wretched by their impulsive lovemaking. She had no idea Knights took a vow of celibacy—at least until after marriage. Still, she didn't blame Crag one bit for breaking some of his vows. He'd been stuck in this hellhole for so long, just as Lily had endured her own pain and sorrow. They were just two people in need of escape, clinging to each other out of instinct for emotional survival.

Lily sighed as she snuggled deeper into the blankets. If that was the truth, then why did she still feel so damn guilty?

Chapter Seven

Two days later, light snow began falling, driving most of the villagers and the Knights not on guard duty indoors. Lily was helping Crag clean and rearrange the herbs and mixtures in the healers' space when one of the Knights apprentice joined them.

"Crag, Sir Wood and Sir Rain want to see you. Something about the reinforcements—"

Before the apprentice had finished speaking, Crag hurried out of the house, forcing Lily and the apprentice to run to keep up with his long strides. By the well, Wood and Rain spoke with another Knight draped in a long wool robe covered with frost from traveling. The pushed-down hood revealed wavy auburn hair cut just below his ears. Even from the respectful distance Lily kept from the Knights, she noticed the man's large eyes were of the palest blue she'd ever seen. Just beneath a hawkish nose, a reddish brown growth of beard dusted his face.

"Crag, this is Sir Blaze," Rain said.

Crag bowed his head in deference. Earlier, he'd told Lily what little he knew about Sir Blaze. Apparently, the redhead was the leader of a small faction of the Ruby Order that placed healing above all else. They never carried weapons, though they used their healing skills in the thick of battle. Blaze himself was the leader of the healing arts for all the Order, and he held a high rank, just below the second-in-command of all the Knights. Crag had also said it was rumored Sir Blaze spoke with the dead and had visions. Crag himself didn't seem to believe the story, and Lily found it difficult to accept as well.

"Jagged Peak." Blaze offered Crag a slight smile.

Crag looked confused. "Sir?"

"Jagged Peak... Rough Mountain... Crag."

Crag stared at the Knight who paid no attention to the apprentice's uneasy expression and continued, "I'm told you've tossed your blade to the furnace. You've decided to walk weaponless among armies of steel."

"If you mean I no longer want to carry a weapon, that's true," Crag said.

"Was this decision rash or pondered?"

Crag looked thoughtful. "Rash at first, but I've thought about it since and my feelings haven't changed."

"You wish to wear the green sash?"

"Green sash?"

Blaze opened the folds of his cloak, revealing his black uniform beneath, a silky green sash about his narrow waist. "The symbol of madmen, according to many of our Order."

Rain laughed. "We can't argue there, Blaze. There's no way I'd march into the front lines without my sword."

Several Knights apprentices approached.

"Sir, may I ask if you've brought reinforcements?" asked one of the healers.

"Only myself." Blaze opened his arms wide, his expression almost apologetic. Lily smiled. He certainly didn't seem like a man who wielded the power she knew he possessed. In spite of his odd manner of speaking, Blaze seemed pleasant, approachable. "I traveled from the south, and I fear battles thrive there. Five of the green sash and ten of our finest armed healers rode with me, but were detained. However there are fresh supplies on my beast."

"Fifteen healers?" Sir Wood shook his head. "And only you could come to us, Sir? The war must be worse than we thought."

"Even the spirits are restless." Blaze sighed, his smile fading. "Six miles from here is a settlement of men near death. Without care, they cannot be moved here. I need two volunteers, preferably a healer or an apprentice who's completed his healing service, to join me. We must lend aid and speed the wounded here or guide them comfortably to the world beyond."

All the apprentices, including Crag lifted their hands. Lily knew to him anything would be better than staying another night in the longhouse.

Blaze glanced over the group, and his gaze fell on Crag and a young Knight apprentice beside him. "You'll both do well. Ready yourselves. We leave within the hour."

The Knights dispersed, and Blaze turned to Lily. Her hands fidgeted, as his eyes seemed to read her very soul. He approached. "Water Flower they say is your name."

"Lily," she murmured. "My name is Lily."

He nodded. "Water Flower. Those you love are with you still. They won't wander without leaving a message. A husband and daughter."

Her heart pounded and tears stung her eyes. "What are you talking about? Why are you doing this to me?"

"Forgive me." He placed his gloved hand to her cheek. "My words aren't meant to wound. I speak with all of them… " He drew a deep breath, as if searching for the words. "With those beyond. Your daughter sleeps in your husband's arms. Their suffering is no more, nor do they want you to suffer but to find happiness with whomever you choose."

"You can really talk to them?" Lily's entire body tingled with a combination of shame and hope. If the spirits of the dead could indeed see the actions of the living, her husband must know about her and Crag. Was Blaze's message her husband's way of relieving her guilt?

"In truth, they talk to me. I merely interpret." He smiled and shook his head. "Stubborn. They say what they want, but rarely listen. At least not to me."

"But they're happy?"

He nodded. "They're at peace. I must go. Work to be done. Nice to have finally met you, Water Flower. They've been speaking of you for miles, your child and your husband. Nearly ran my horse into a frozen lake. Spirits don't realize how loud they can be," Blaze murmured to himself as he walked toward the longhouse.

He's either mad or some sort of prophet, Lily told herself. Regardless of what he was, his words did offer comfort.

Inside, she helped Crag pack supplies for his journey.

"He said he spoke with Vina and my husband," she said.

"Sir Blaze? Perhaps." Crag lowered his voice. "He's very strange."

"But he seems sweet."

Crag tossed her a look which said any man who'd sustained such a high position in the Order couldn't possibly be sweet.

"He said—"

"What?"

"Nothing," Lily murmured. Just because she might be free to act on her attraction to Crag didn't mean he had the same privileges. By making love with her, he'd broken his vows, and unless she became his wife—something for which she had no inclination—their intimacy must be kept secret or better yet, never occur again.

He slipped into a worn wool robe and slung his leather bag over his shoulder. He said, "One of the Knights apprentice will act as healer here until I return, and Sir Wood will also be around the settlement."

"Good luck, Crag," she said.

He nodded, offering a half smile, his eyes burning into hers. Before he swept out of the longhouse, he bent and quickly kissed her cheek. The softness of his lips and roughness of his beard felt so pleasantly familiar that she wished for a longer kiss, preferably on the mouth. She sighed, watching from the doorway as Crag, Blaze and the Knight apprentice disappeared over the snowy hillside.

* * * * *

Snow fell heavily that day, and by the next morning, the world seemed made of ice. The cold wind hurt to breathe as Lily stepped outside the longhouse, so unless water was required, she remained inside. With Crag gone, she realized how much she missed him. Though he didn't have the most pleasant disposition—she well understood why—he was familiar, and the times they'd made love seemed imprinted on her mind. He was dependable and a good teacher. She missed the sound of his voice and knowing any of them could go to him, night or day. In spite of the conditions he'd been forced to live under, in spite of what his own overworked brain thought at times, he cared about people. He, a Zaltanian.

Lily spent the days helping Coral with her chores and Gem with her baby. Often the three women sat together, mending or cooking, and talked about the life they might have after the war ended. They all knew they were simply fantasizing.

Lily used the slight knowledge she'd gained from Crag and continued assisting what people she could. If Sir Wood noticed, he didn't mention anything. At least he didn't tell her not to interfere, however he didn't offer any new learning either. She understood he was busy, but Crag had been busy too. Perhaps Crag had seen the sense in sharing his knowledge with a commoner.

It was two nights later that Crag and Sir Blaze returned to the settlement. Almost everyone was asleep, but Lily sat, propped against a barrel, staring at the hearth and allowing her thoughts to drift. She stood as the doors opened and freezing wind wafted through the entire house.

Crag and Sir Blaze, both covered with frost, stepped inside. Wood joined them, and Lily edged closer.

"Rain and his guards are helping the casualties we brought into the other houses where there's more space," Sir Blaze said.

"Good. We're cramped enough as it is in here." Wood glanced at the two men. "One of the women will bring you some warm water and blankets."

The two looked frozen and exhausted. Crag kept his hands buried in his robe, and he hadn't so much as glanced around the longhouse. He probably feared if he caught anyone's eye they'd shout for a healer.

"I'll get the water and blankets," Lily said softly.

Blaze offered her a tired smile. "My thanks."

As she walked away, she heard Blaze say to Wood, "Please avoid disturbing us until after first light."

"Of course, Sir," Wood said. "I imagine it's been a difficult time for you."

"Three sleepless days and nights," he stated. "But all is well. Many were saved."

Both Blaze and Crag sat close to the hearth and removed their frozen cloaks. After Lily set a pan of water to heating, she brought them blankets.

Blaze accepted a blanket from her and nodded toward Crag, "He needs water. His gloves are little more than ornament."

She glanced at Crag's hands and noted that his gloves, worn before the journey, were completely threadbare. He began removing them clumsily, as if his fingers were too cold to get a proper grip.

"You should have had new ones made," Lily said as she began removing the gloves for him, her stomach tense when she thought of the discomfort he must feel. His blue-tinged hands felt like ice, the fingers stiff. He was lucky frostbite hadn't set in.

"I didn't have much call for them around here," he said, a slight waver in his voice as he trembled violently. "I've never done so much stitching with hands that cold. I don't think I'll ever move them again."

He sat on the ground, leaning against a wooden trunk, the blanket draped over his shoulders. Lily filled a wooden bowl with warm water and placed it on his lap. He immersed his hands in it, and after a few moments, wiggled his fingers.

"Were there many people?" she asked.

"Enough. There was no real shelter. No food. Hardly any water. It's amazing so many survived, considering the seriousness of their injuries."

"Would you like something to eat?"

He shook his head, his eyes slipping shut. "Not now."

She nodded, watching him for a moment, resisting the urge to touch him and offer comfort for fear someone in the longhouse might notice the familiarity between them and guess their intimacy.

After a moment, she joined Blaze. "Would you like something to eat?"

"Don't trouble yourself."

"It's no trouble."

She stood and found bread and leftover broth to bring him. He ate with a heartier appetite than his slim frame had led her to believe.

"Do you... Do you really speak with the dead?" she asked.

He stopped chewing, and his pale eyes met hers. For a man of his age and position, his eyes appeared almost innocent, and she was charmed by such a rare, open expression.

"Yes. Dead to us, but still alive. To me, they're as real as you, Water Flower."

"You mean they're not like ghosts?"

"Not to me. They appear as flesh, though I cannot touch them. They speak as loud as anyone, yet in code, as they feel and as they see."

She narrowed her eyes. "It must be difficult for you, living with the dead."

"It can be distracting, yet I've grown accustomed to their ways."

"Are there many like you? Not who see the dead, but who wear that green sash?"

"Ah, the weaponless warriors. No. We are few. Ten in our faction, including myself." Blaze glanced at Crag. "Soon perhaps eleven."

"He's a very good fighter," she said.

"And a good healer," Blaze observed. "Wood told me, yet over these days, I've seen for myself. His instincts are good, and he's gained much experience in a short time. This is a difficult place in which to fulfill service."

"This place is hell."

"A palace can be hell, Water Flower."

Lily nodded. "I see what you mean, but don't tell me you like it here."

He laughed. "A point well taken."

"I'll let you sleep, Sir." She took his empty bowl and stood.

"Thank you." He touched her arm and again nodded in Crag's direction. "The life of a Knight is not easy. He's lucky to have found you."

Lily blinked. "I'm afraid I don't understand." The idea that someone had discovered her and Crag's secret both startled and relieved her.

Blaze offered a gentle smile, but said no more.

Lily discarded the bowl and sat for a time, watching Gem's baby sleep as she'd often watched Vina.

For some reason, she was unable to sleep herself. She approached the hearth and saw Blaze curled by the fire, his eyes closed. She glanced at Crag. He'd fallen asleep with his hands still in the water.

Shaking her head, Lily took a towel and knelt beside him, slipping the bowl from his lap. The water had already started to cool, and in a few moments would have defeated its earlier purpose. As she dried his hands with the towel, he jerked awake.

"What are you doing?" he asked.

"You fell asleep with your hands in the water. You'll get cold again."

He bent and straightened his fingers almost painfully. "At least I can move them now."

"Here." She took one of his hands in hers, using her thumbs to massage his palms. She rubbed his fingers and gently turned his wrists. "How does that feel?"

"Good." He sighed. "Very good."

"My husband's hands used to hurt. He said this helped." She stared down at the hand she massaged. Her husband's hands hadn't been as large as Crag's, yet in some ways, they were similar. Both had strong, graceful fingers. It disturbed her that simply touching Crag or looking at him made her entire body tingle and her belly tighten. Her husband had never evoked such feelings. He'd been a good man. She'd cared for him and mourned his death, but something about Crag made her ache with desire. Lily cleared her throat as she continued, "My husband was a stone carver."

"An artist?"

She nodded. "His statues were all over our village. They were destroyed during the attack."

"I'm sorry," he whispered.

"I'm learning to move on."

"Are you? That's good. I wish I could."

"Blaze said you're a very good healer."

"He said that?"

"Yes."

Crag leaned his head back and closed his eyes as Lily picked up his other hand and repeated her ministrations. She massaged his fingers until she was certain he slept, then covered him with another blanket. Instead of moving back to her own space, she sat beside him and drifted to sleep.

What seemed like moments later, she jumped awake when someone called for a healer.

Crag had thrown off his blankets and, out of habit, stumbled to his feet. Lily grasped his arm. "Sir Wood is going to them."

He squinted in the dimness and saw that she was right.

"You have until tomorrow to rest, remember?"

He settled back beside her. "I had the worst dream."

"What about?" Lily studied his profile, the flutter of his lashes against his cheeks and the straightness of his nose.

"The entire world was black and red," he murmured, his voice sleepy, though he reached for her hand and clung to it. "A herd of beasts, tall as houses with big, gray tusks chased me. Monkeys, demons and birds of prey swooped from trees stripped of leaves. The trunks were all black. There was blood on my hands."

"It was just a dream." She touched his shoulder with her free hand, her fingers gently gripping.

With a sigh he sat up, walked to a basin of water and splashed some on his face. Shrugging on his cloak, he glanced at her, "I need some air."

She stood, reaching for her own cloak. "I would have thought you'd had enough of the cold over the past few days."

Without a word, he headed for the door, slowing so Lily could fall into step beside him. They paused in the doorway, and he held her gaze. "I missed you, Lily."

"You did?"

He nodded.

Why did his words make her feel so warm? He stared at her, as if waiting for a response. Did he want her to say she missed him as well? She had. Quite desperately at times, but some part of her, a part that still hated Zaltanians, refused to let her tell him.

Crag stepped into the cold, and after a moment's hesitation, Lily followed. Moonlight brightened the snowy settlement, so she had no problem following Crag's dark silhouette to the supply house. Her heartbeat quickened at the thought of the last time they'd been there together. Did he really need supplies, or had he hoped she'd follow him?

When she stepped inside, he stood staring at the door, one of his shoulders leaning against the wall.

"You did come." He stepped close to her, placing his hands on her shoulders.

"We shouldn't be doing this, Crag."

"I know, but I can't seem to stop myself, Lily." His eyes burned into hers. A pulse beat madly in the base of his throat. He took her hands and held them to his chest. "It used to be when I had even the briefest moment to myself, I wouldn't think at all, just sit, numb. Now, during those moments all I think about is holding you."

"Why are we doing this?" she sighed, closing her eyes, her fingers gripping the hard muscles of his chest. "Are we like animals taking what pleasure we can while we can? Once this is over, if it's ever over, will we regret what we've done?"

"It's too late to take it back."

"I know." Lily looked up at him, at the familiarity of his beautiful eyes, the hollows beneath his sharp cheekbones, the color of his beard, and the shape of his lips. She stood on tiptoe and kissed him. His tongue met hers while his hands caressed her face. Suddenly she wanted to give him something that he'd always remember, even after they separated.

She parted his cloak and caressed his chest and abdomen as she sank to her knees before him, lifted his tunic and slipped beneath it.

"Lily, what are you doing?" he murmured, but already she sensed his excitement and desire.

She unfastened his belt and tugged his trousers down to his knees. She sighed with pleasure upon feeling the steely muscles of his hair-roughened thighs. By the Spirit, he was built like a lean, granite statue!

Lily pushed down his soft leather boot, lowered her face to one of his ankles and kissed it. She ran her lips over his shin while her hands kneaded his calf, loving the sensation of hard muscle beneath a mat of hair. When she reached his knee, she traced the shape of it with her tongue, then licked her way up his inner thigh to the joining of his hip and pelvis. She buried her face in the dark thatch between his legs and nuzzled him, cupping his heavy balls in one hand and squeezing.

Crag drew a sharp breath when her tongue moved to his other leg. She lapped from thigh to ankle, then kissed her way up again. Lily cupped his smooth buttocks as her breath fanned his cock. The hard muscles of his bottom were clenched with desire. Her fingers gently parted the globes and teased his sphincter with feather-light touches. She rubbed her cheek against his cock, enjoying the smooth hardness. Burying her lips at the base, she kissed its length and took the head between her lips.

"Lily, oh Gods!" he panted, his bottom tightening even more in her hands. She lapped his cock head and ran her tongue along the underside. Kissing her way back down the straining rod, she moved one hand to cup his balls. Squeezing the hair-dusted globes, she continued lapping and sucking his erection. Her other hand wandered up to caress his torso. Her palm rested against his ribs, and she felt his heart slamming against bone and muscle. As she sucked deeper and harder, the rhythm beating against her palm quickened even more. His cock felt so steely that she wondered if it could get much harder. Her teeth raked the length of him and the tip of her tongue played around the little eye, tasting the first droplets of his essence. She'd never done such things with a man before, and she wondered how long she could continue before he reached the end of his tolerance? Lily slowed her pace, then sped it up. She sucked fast and deep, then licked slow and long. All the while she listened to his breath as it changed from soft panting to ragged sobs. She gauged the beating of his heart beneath her hand, noting that in spite of the coldness of the storage shed, his flesh had heated. So had hers. Arousing him had her nipples hard and her pussy drenched.

"Lily, that's enough!" he finally gasped, his hips thrusting against her face. She thought he might try pulling away, so she clutched his buttocks as she continued exploring every inch of his cock with her tongue. She found a long vein along the underside and traced it with the tip of her tongue before laving the smooth head. Taking the tip in her mouth, she sucked in a quick, steady rhythm that soon had him writhing, his hands clutching her head.

"I can't, Lily!" His voice sounded ragged and she felt him tremble as he tried holding his orgasm at bay. Lily wouldn't allow it. She sucked harder, her rhythm faster. His grip loosened on her hair and he said in a raw voice, "Stop now or I won't be able to control myself."

She didn't relent, but kneaded his buttocks and thighs as she continued licking and sucking his cock head.

"Oh Gods, Lily! Don't stop!" She nearly smiled. He'd changed his mind quickly enough. Not that she blamed him, considering the force of her attack. She'd leave him no opportunity to surrender.

Suddenly he lunged against her and stifled his cry of pure pleasure. His entire body surged and shook as he gasped her name.

Giving his soft cock a final lick, she slipped from beneath his tunic and watched as he hitched up his trousers with trembling hands.

She couldn't conceal her smile as she stood, particularly upon noting the color darkening the ridges of his cheekbones. Had she possibly resurrected sheepish feelings in a former Captain of the Zaltanian guard?

He moved so swiftly she hadn't a chance to react before he grasped her waist and pressed her to the wall.

"Crag, we should get back to the longhouse—"

"Before you get your due?"

"What if they need a healer?"

"I have until morning, as you so recently reminded me."

"Yes, but—" she gasped, her eyes closing in ecstasy as he dropped to his knees, lifted her skirts, and fastened his mouth on her clit. The sensitive nub was already swollen and aching, just from arousing him, and within moments his moist caress would hurl her into orgasm. Or so she thought.

Crag seemed to know just when she was about to explode. He stopped caressing and simply rested his tongue against her stimulated flesh. Lily trembled in an effort not to move. She knew even a tiny thrust against his tongue would be enough to push her over the edge. He reached up, tugging down her dress and freeing her breasts to his hands. He cupped the warm mounds and kneaded them. His callused palms felt so good against her nipples, but not nearly as good as his fingertips when they circled the hard little peaks.

"Oh Crag!" she panted, her pulse throbbing in her ears. She leaned against the wall as his tongue resumed its ministrations. This time, he swirled it inside her pussy, then returned to her clit. He paused, allowing his breath to caress her.

Crag's hands left her breasts and cupped her buttocks. Lily was grateful for the change of position because seconds later, he began lapping her clit with fast, gentle strokes of his tongue that sent her into an orgasm that nearly knocked her off her feet.

"Crag!" she gasped. "Oh, don't stop! Please don't stop!"

He continued licking and tugging at her with his lips as she clutched handfuls of his hair, her pelvis squirming against his face. Finally she sagged against him as her breathing returned to normal.

He waited until she stirred before suggesting they return to the longhouse.

"You can still have a few hours of sleep before morning," she said.

"I think I'll sleep very well." A smile played around his lips.

She grinned. "I'll wager."

She adjusted her clothes and headed for the door, but he caught her arm. "Lily, I want you to know that, if a child comes from anything we've done, I'll do what's right—"

"There won't be a child."

"How do you know?"

"Because of this." She tugged a pouch from the folds of her skirt. "I'd been having problems with my monthly showing and the healer from my home village gave me a supply of this herb. It helped with my regularity, but another result is that I won't conceive children while using it. So you don't have to worry, Crag. I won't shame you."

"I wasn't thinking of myself." His voice sounded rather cold, but before he turned away, she noted an unfamiliar look in his eyes. If she hadn't known better, she would have thought it was disappointment.

"Until we find the next spare moment," he said, brushing her mouth with a kiss far more passionate than his cool words before sweeping out of the storage house.

Cold air blew in, and snowflakes dusted Lily's face as she blinked against the wind. Shaking her head, she followed Crag back to the longhouse, puzzled by the strange quirks of men.

Chapter Eight
℘

Lily awoke covered in blankets, her head resting on a folded cloak, a bowl of water for washing beside her. She blinked her eyes clear, running a hand through her hair and searching for Crag. Kneeling by the fire, his back to her, he prepared an herbal mixture. Across the room, Blaze ministered to an elderly woman.

Lily sighed. Crag had returned, and nothing had changed. They'd made love last night, but again it was to be their secret and life in the longhouse would continue as usual. She stretched and stood to begin the day.

Days fell into the same familiar pattern. Though she and Crag spent hours together during which she watched him and learned. Neither initiated lovemaking. Not that there was time. The injured still poured in from the battles raging across the continent. Sometimes, during a moment of rest, Lily caught Crag staring at her and her pulse would quicken. His eyes expressed his desire for her, the same yearning she felt for his body. Perhaps it was more than just his body. If circumstances had been different, if she hadn't been recently widowed and he hadn't been Zaltanian, would they have seriously pursued each other? Rather than drive herself mad thinking about what might have been, Lily immersed herself in learning all she could about the healing arts.

Sir Blaze offered knowledge as freely as Crag, allowing Lily to listen as he instructed the apprentices in the use of herbs and the preparation of medicines.

One afternoon Lily stood with Crag behind the curtain, helping to dust and replenish supplies.

"Blaze knows things about healing I've never imagined," Crag said. "Watching him, I feel like I know nothing."

"I wouldn't worry about it," she told him. "I've seen Sir Wood look just as bewildered as you say you feel around Blaze."

"It is funny that a man with Blaze's skill and power in the Order isn't the least bit intimidating."

"Not like many of the others," Lily admitted, passing him a bottle of ointment. He reached for it absently, and his hand covered hers.

Crag turned, and their gaze met. He took the bottle with his other hand and placed it aside, not loosening his hold on her. Lily's heartbeat quickened as she stared at him. He was so tall and strong, and it seemed like forever since they'd made love.

Crag shook his head, looking almost annoyed.

"What?" she asked softly.

"We've been living in the midst of a stinking hell hole and all I've been able to think about is being with you again and not just in private. I want to tell the whole damn settlement."

She swallowed, wondering if he felt the tremor running down her spine. She wanted to make love with him, but he had just taken their relationship a step further. He had been thinking about making their feelings for one another public. He'd said a Knight could only make love with a woman he married. If he announced their courtship, then marriage was sure to follow. No! She could never even consider it. Zaltana had destroyed all she loved, and no matter what she felt for Crag, giving the rest of her life to him would make her feel like a traitor, something that would eventually destroy them both.

"I'm sorry," he said. "I know we weren't supposed to talk about it."

"I just… "She lowered her eyes. "I'm just not ready for that, Crag. Not now."

He cupped her chin in his hand and tilted her face toward his. "I know. Forget I ever said it." In spite of his reassuring words, she didn't miss the disappointment in his eyes.

He turned back to the shelves, and Lily continued passing him supplies.

They'd just finished their task when Blaze stepped behind the curtain.

"The snow has stopped," he announced. "Come outside with me, Jagged Peak."

Silently, Crag followed Blaze who called over his shoulder, "You shriek curiosity, Water Flower. Satisfy it."

Even after such a short time, Lily had grown accustomed to Blaze's odd manner of speaking. Sensing her interest, he was bidding her to follow.

Outside, Blaze led Crag to a clearing behind the barn. No sooner had they stopped and faced each other, than Blaze struck out at Crag with his fist. Crag just missed dodging the blow.

"Sir!" he snapped, eyes flashing surprise. His hands rose to a defensive position as he and Blaze circled one another.

"You've passed the test for healing skills," Blaze told him. "Rain sings praises of your fighting talents. I must see for myself."

Lily's fingers tightened on her skirt as Blaze attacked Crag with a barrage of fast, powerful kicks and punches. Blaze had so perfected the art of fighting that he appeared graceful as a dancer, yet she knew each of his strikes was potentially fatal. To Crag's credit, he blocked and dodged most of the blows, yet he seemed unable to breach the auburn-haired Knight's defenses, in spite of how he struck back.

Lily well knew Crag was a skilled fighter, yet Blaze was almost inhuman in his precision. He spun, and the back of his fist struck Crag in the cheek, almost staggering him. Crag attacked with greater force, his foot finding a momentarily unguarded place in Blaze's mid-section, his kick knocking the auburn-haired Knight onto his back. Blaze sprang up, caught one of Crag's arms as his fist flew, and jerked him into an arm lock that sent him crashing to the icy ground.

Crag's blue eyes gleamed with fury as he struggled in Blaze's unbreakable hold.

Blaze released him and stood, brushing snow from his uniform and smiling with approval. Crag pushed himself to his feet, his expression wary, as if awaiting another attack. Both men's breaths came in visible puffs in the frigid air.

"Just as good as most of my own men," Blaze said. "Rain was accurate in his recommendation."

"What recommendation?" Crag demanded.

"Of you to join my faction. At times the guards choose men they think are ready, yet few truly are up to wearing the green sash. Once your service is complete, I extend you an invitation to our faction. Do you wish to join the madmen?" Blaze's pale eyes glistened.

"I don't know what I want. And as for being a madman, I already qualify."

"You have time to decide. It's often long after he's Knighted that a man decides to join our faction. My conscience only allows me to choose the best healers and the best fighters. I cannot send a defenseless man weaponless into the thick of battle. The green sash adorns few."

"Where I come from, I was considered elite," Crag said. "I've never met anyone with your talent for hand-to-hand combat. Where did you learn?"

"First, from the leader of our Order, then in my travels. Join my faction, and all I know will be yours." Blaze turned back toward the house. "We're needed."

Lily joined Crag and fell into step beside him. "Are you all right?"

He shrugged. "Fine."

"Are you going to join his faction?"

"Right now, I only want to think about surviving the war. Knighthood, the green sash, those decisions can come later."

She glanced down at her feet as they plodded through the snow, thinking that it felt as if the war would never end. But, as she already should have learned, all things end.

One month after Blaze and Crag's sparring match, the snow and ice had melted and gave way to the warmth and freshness of spring. The longhouse was still stuffy, yet outside warm breezes carried the scent of wild flowers. Lily, along with many in the settlement, took daily walks to the brook in the nearby woods to bathe.

In spite of the pleasant weather, springtime saddened her somewhat. She'd been married in the spring.

Though most of the winter casualties had either healed or died, others continued pouring into Tanek. Lily helped Crag and Blaze deliver two more babies and began to train seriously as a midwife under Blaze's instruction. It was strange learning such skills from a man, but when it came to the healing arts, Blaze overflowed with knowledge.

"You should come to Travelle," Blaze had often told her. "Our sister group, the Dames of the Opal Order, have fine midwives. You should learn from them."

"Perhaps I will."

Delivering babies reminded her that there was still hope in the world, a difficult thing to remember when she watched Crag or Blaze lend aid to the fatally wounded.

One morning in early spring, while she assisted Crag who was removing an arrowhead from a soldier's chest, the longhouse doors burst open.

Rain, his black hair tousled, a broad smile on his lips, bellowed, "The war is over! Zaltana has retreated!"

For a full minute there was silence, then loud cheers erupted throughout the room. Coral stood beside Lily, her hands full of freshly washed clothes. She dropped the clothes, and the two women embraced tightly, neither caring about the blood on Lily's hands.

Laughing in spite of her tears, Lily turned to Crag. His expression hadn't changed as he concentrated on stitching up the man's chest. When he finished, he washed and dried his hands.

She approached him and slipped her arms around his waist. He hugged her so tightly she felt his heart beating wildly against her cheek. His fingers threaded through her hair. Neither spoke, and when the embrace ended, they continued with their work as if nothing had changed.

Chapter Nine

That night, a celebration was held outside. The healthy attended, as well as the off-duty Knights and apprentices. Coral, Gem and Lily spent the day cooking the meat Sir Rain and several villagers hunted that morning. A few men and women who had managed to salvage flutes and stringed instruments from their homes spent the day huddled in a group practicing so they could entertain that night.

"We're going to sing," Coral told Lily, motioning with her head toward Gem. Gem didn't seem to notice as she kneaded bread, the smile on her lips never fading. The Knight who had brought the message that the war had ended had also brought news of Gem's husband. He was doing well and his regiment would be arriving in Tanek within days. Lily said a silent prayer that Coral's betrothed would also be so lucky.

"I used to sing all the time," Lily said.

"Were you good at it?" Coral asked. "Because Gem and I can just about carry a tune."

She shrugged. "I was told I didn't cause any severe headaches." In truth, her voice had been praised in her village, but it was just a small part of the world.

"Why don't you sing tonight?" Gem suggested, glancing up from the dough.

"Oh, I don't know. I haven't felt like singing since my village was attacked."

"Yes, but now is a time for celebration," Coral told her.

She was right. One song couldn't hurt, and for the first time in what seemed like forever, Lily wanted to sing.

That evening, fires burned outside the houses. People talked, danced, and ate. Lily stood beside Crag who, like the other healers, lurked in the doorways so as not to be far from their charges.

"I can't believe it's really over." Lily looked up at him.

He nodded, unsmiling, his arms folded across his chest.

"Are you all right?" She stood so close to him their arms brushed. "I know you must feel torn about this, since Zaltana is your homeland."

He shook his head. "I'm glad they retreated. Not a bit of good came of this stupid war."

"Lily!" Coral, tugged her arm. "Time for you to sing."

"Sing?" Crag raised one of his dark eyebrows.

She smiled at him, feeling a sudden wave of shyness. "Just pray my voice doesn't crack. It's been a long time."

She felt his gaze on her as she approached the group of musicians by the fire. They played a familiar folk song she knew about the birth of the Twin Goddesses.

At first she felt a bit nervous, but after the first smooth notes, she relaxed and enjoyed the song. Somehow, singing provided comfort and release she hadn't felt in over a year.

When she finished, the crowd shouted, clapping. Lily smiled and curtsied. Apparently she hadn't lost her talent over the months her voice had rested.

"Lily, that was wonderful!" Gem shook her shoulder.

"Why didn't you tell us you had such talent?" Coral scolded. "You could have been singing all winter and gave us escape from the gloom."

Lily smiled softly. "I just didn't feel much like singing."

Turning back to the steps, she noticed Crag and Blaze standing in the doorway together.

"Your words are sweeter than any songbird, Water Flower," Blaze told her. He opened his mouth to speak again, but inside came the call for a healer.

Crag turned to answer, but Blaze shoved him gently aside. "I'll go."

The Knight left Crag and Lily alone, staring at each other.

"That was beautiful," he said.

She glanced down at her shoes. "My husband used to think so."

"You never told me his name."

"Daran."

"He was lucky. So lucky." Crag's knuckles brushed her cheek before he disappeared into the longhouse.

Her face tingling from his touch, she watched him go and sighed. Now that the war was over, what was to become of them? He'd surely return to Travelle, to the fortress of the Ruby Order, and she...she still had no idea where she wanted to go or what she wanted to do. Suddenly she realized she might never see him again, and the thought was almost too much to bear. It was almost like losing someone she loved again. She thought about the desire he'd expressed to make their feeling for each other known. Perhaps he'd been right. Lily shook her head. She didn't want to rush into a relationship she might later regret, just because she feared parting from him now that the war was over. They'd clung to each other out of desperation, but they each had a life to lead. Crag was almost a Knight and Lily—well, for the first time she was completely free to choose her own path.

As Lily sat a shadow fell across the steps, and Lily glanced up at Crag. He extended his hand to her, and she took it, rising.

"Sir Blaze told me to take a couple of hours off." His lips twitched upward in the slightest smile. "I've almost forgotten what those words sound like."

"Are you going to rest?"

"I was hoping you'd walk with me."

Lily's hand tightened on his as they crossed the settlement. With everyone still celebrating, they slipped, unnoticed, into the storage shed.

"I'm getting a little tired of this," he said.

"Don't talk, Crag." She looped her arms around his neck. "Just make love to me."

"Lily," he whispered against her lips. Sweeping her into his arms, he took several steps and placed her atop a stool, so she was almost at eye level with him. His hands slipped inside the front of her dress and he caressed her breasts, his thumbs stroking her nipples. When her eyes slipped shut, he said, "No, look at me."

"But—"

"Look at me, Lily."

She stared into his eyes, nearly drowning in the emotions gleaming there. Crag kept much to himself, so much that at times he seemed more like the rock he was named after instead of a living, breathing man. Looking into his eyes reminded Lily of how human he was—how full of masculine desires.

His hand slipped beneath her skirt, and he gently explored the soft folds of her flesh. His fingertips caressed her pussy while his other hand continued stroking her breast. All the while, his eyes remained fixed on hers.

As his touch aroused her, his fingers grew slick from her wet pussy, and his caresses became quicker and more demanding. Lily's eyes fluttered as pleasure overtook her.

"Don't close them," he said in a husky voice. "I want to see pleasure in your eyes."

Oh, she was feeling pleasure! His long, strong fingers knew just where to touch her and exactly how much pressure to use. Lily's breathing quickened and her pulse throbbed.

"Crag," she said, her voice strangled with passion.

"I'm here, Lily."

"Please don't stop!"

"Never."

"Oh Crag!" she cried out, unable to keep her eyes from closing as an orgasm tore through her.

Before the last ripple left her, she felt Crag's cock slip into her. He grasped her wrists and pinned them to the wall, his mouth claiming hers as his hips drove against her. His tongue circled her lips, then thrust into her mouth in time with his ramming cock. Pleasure built again, so deep that Lily would have shrieked as she climaxed had his mouth not captured the scream.

Crag held her, stroking her hair, his cock still hard inside her. His chest rose and fell against her cheek, and she closed her eyes, leaning her full weight against him for several long moments.

"Come, Lily." Crag took her hand and tugged her to the floor.

She glanced at him in question, especially when he asked her to kneel. She did as he requested, craning her neck to see over her shoulder. He raised her dress over her back, blocking part of her vision, so she faced the floor and waited. Though she felt a bit awkward, almost animal-like, on her hands and knees with her privates exposed, the position was strangely provocative.

His palms caressed her buttocks and lower back, kneading and stroking. Sighing with pleasure, she wiggled a bit when he covered her entire bottom with kisses. His tongue laved her hips and lower back, then traced shapes on her buttocks while his fingertips stroked and teased her thighs. His touch was gentle but exciting, and her clit tingled for him.

One of his arms snaked around her waist and he used one finger to circle her clit. Suddenly she felt the tip of his cock pressing against her damp slit. Closing her eyes, she moaned as he entered her.

While he thrust slowly, tenderly, his hands warmed her back and buttocks. Lily wiggled with pleasure, her hands gripping the wooden floor and her heart pounding.

Grasping her hips, Crag increased the speed of his thrusts.

"Oh Lily," he murmured, slightly breathless as passion grew.

"Oh yes," she panted. "I love hearing your voice, Crag. Tell me how it feels."

"Good. It feels so good." His deep voice sounded husky with passion. "You're so hot and wet. So soft. I wish I could stay inside you forever."

Lily wished the same, but it was impossible. Already their desire had reached ecstatic heights. Neither could prolong it any further. Their cries of fulfillment mingled as he pumped into her. Lily shattered, throbbing and bucking. He kept a firm hold on her hips though she felt his hands tremble as he came, lunging hard into her straining body.

Crag's softening cock slipped from her before she sank deeper onto the floor. Crag gathered her close, leaning against a barrel with her cuddled on his lap.

Lily squeezed him tightly and whispered, "What we've shared has meant much to me, Crag."

"And to me, Lily. You've been the only relief I've had in longer than I can remember."

Relief. He was right. That's all they were to each other.

"Now the war is over," she drew a deep breath, "and so this has to end."

His gaze held hers and he swallowed as he gently pushed her from his lap and stood. "If that's what you want."

"It has to be. You're going to be a Knight and I—I'm not ready for another relationship. Not now."

"I understand." He ran a hand through his hair and glanced at her, his brow furrowed. "Such decisions can't be rushed. Even if we take years to make some choices, we still can't know we've made the right ones."

Lily nodded.

"I'm going back to the longhouse," he said.

"Why? I thought you wanted to get away."

"I did."

Before she could say anymore, he was gone. Lily sighed. Her mind told her she'd made the right decision, but somewhere in her heart—a heart that still mourned Vina and despised Zaltana—she couldn't believe what she and Crag shared was truly at an end.

* * * * *

One week after the war ended, the casualties finally stopped arriving, and a week after that, those who were strong enough to travel left to find new homes or return to their old villages to help rebuild. Some wished to remain in Tanek and make it their home. Lily decided to stay for a time. Crag was still there as well. As she'd asked, he made no attempt to bed her again. He seemed as distant as when she'd first met him, and such an attitude made it much easier for her to realize she'd made the right decision. Perhaps he was actually relieved she'd made their parting so simple and hadn't been the sort of clinging woman who'd try to interfere with his life in the Ruby Order.

Relief finally came for the healers and the Knights on duty. Fresh Knights and brand new apprentices rode in, all draped in black or gray on fresh mounts. It was time for a rotation of service, and Crag, along with the other Knights apprentices who'd done their duty in Tanek, would be given the first step toward Knighthood in a ceremony preceding their dubbing in Travelle.

Though there was still much work to be done, rebuilding had proceeded smoothly, and with so many new, healthy Knights, apprentices and villagers, Tanek scarcely resembled the pit of suffering and death it had been for so long.

Now that Crag had some free time, Lily noticed he spent much of it practicing empty handed fighting with Sir Blaze. Sometimes, when he was off duty, she'd see him riding across the fields toward the woods. She learned that when he'd been placed in service in Tanek, he'd given up his horse to the guards for their use. Now that service was over, his animal was returned. It was a beautiful horse, tall, sleek and completely black except for four white socks.

One morning, Lily followed Crag to the stable for a closer look at the animal.

While Crag brushed him, the stallion lowered his lovely head for her to stroke his nose. His eyes were large, dark and calm, so unlike Crag's. In spite of his quiet demeanor, his eyes gleamed with inner sparks, like a burned-down fire desperate to rekindle into devouring flames. A few, blissful times she'd seen those sparks turn into an inferno. Lily wondered what he'd been like before entering his service, before his spirit had been twisted and restrained.

"You're a lovely, aren't you?" She rubbed beneath the stallion's forelock and glanced at Crag. "What's his name?"

"Pale Feet."

She smiled. Leave it to Crag to pick such a sensible name.

"I'm going for a ride. Do you want to come?" he asked, surprising her. It seemed like forever since they'd talked about anything except healing and impersonal daily happenings.

"Very much, but I've never been on a horse before."

"Nothing to it." He saddled up and gave her a boost.

She clasped the saddle, feeling a bit dizzy. Pale Feet was very, very tall, much like Crag. He mounted in front of her, and she clasped his waist tightly.

Glancing over his shoulder at her, he smiled. "Don't worry. I won't let anything happen to you."

Pale Feet loped out of the settlement and over the grassy hills. After a while, Lily relaxed and loosened her grip on Crag. It was then she became fully aware of his body, the hardness of his back and lean waist beneath her palms. His robe, freshly washed and no longer covered with blood, carried the pleasant scent of herbs. His unbound hair hung down his back in tight, dark brown spirals that tickled her cheek.

They dismounted by a lake and sat on the rocky edge, their feet immersed in the cool water. He turned to her, his eyes gleaming with a look she'd become accustomed to. She sensed he was about to speak of the forbidden, so she decided to keep them on the straight path and said, "Are you going to join Sir Blaze's faction?"

"I don't know," he murmured, glancing into the water. "I don't really want to talk about it."

She nodded.

"What are you going to do?" he asked.

"I don't know," she replied honestly. "I really don't want to talk about it, either."

"Lily, I—"

"Please don't say it," she whispered.

His jaw clenched. He picked up a stone and flung it so it skimmed across the water. She leaned back on her elbows and glanced at the cloudless sky. A flock of birds flew overhead, their black wings beating against a backdrop of blue. After several moments, they left the water, replaced their shoes, and plopped in the middle of the field where Pale Feet grazed. Neither felt much like talking anymore, and Lily had made it plain they weren't going to make love. Lying side by side in the sun warmed grass, they closed their eyes and took a short nap. It had been so long since they'd enjoyed peace without cold, fear, exhaustion and the threat of death. It felt good just to relax with someone else who understood. Lily hadn't known Crag for long, but they'd shared so much. Soon they would part, and after all her good intentions, she wondered if she'd truly have the strength to let him go.

* * * * *

Two days later, Lily stood in the field outside the settlement along with a large group of villagers, Knights and the new Knights apprentices. Two rows of Knights, swords at their hips, stood at attention, forming a long pathway at the head of which stood Sir Rain and Sir Blaze. A wooden table laden with a dozen swords stood between them. Crag had explained the ritual to Lily. The apprentices whose service had been fulfilled would walk up the pathway and accept the sword with which they would be dubbed when they reached Travelle. Only the leader of the Knights, a man called Mahir, could dub the newest members of the Order. This ritual was just a formality in which the apprentices accepted their new position.

Lily was lucky to have gotten a spot close to Rain and Blaze. Sir Wood stood beside her along with two new apprentice healers.

The ceremony began suddenly. The Knights, in single file, rode their horses across a shallow brook and dismounted at the foot of the path. They led their horses up to Rain and Blaze, the two Knights of the highest rank available, and extended their hands for the sword. Rain stood watch, but Blaze, being his superior, awarded each apprentice with his sword.

Each accepted his blade, some smiling, others serious, but all respectful. They bowed to Blaze and assembled in a row behind the table.

When Lily noticed Crag riding through the brook, her heartbeat quickened and her hands trembled. The way she felt, one would have thought it was the prelude to her own dubbing. She was so happy for him, knowing how hard he'd worked to achieve his goal and how dedicated he was.

Pale Feet's hooves thudded in the water. Crag sat astride him wearing a plain black tunic and trousers, no ruby yet over his heart, symbolizing a Knight. That would come after the dubbing ceremony in the fortress of the Ruby Order.

Crag dismounted, Pale Feet's reins in his hands as he walked up the pathway, his eyes focused on the horizon. He didn't look happy, didn't look miserable. He didn't look as if he felt anything at all.

He stopped before the table, and Lily noticed a glimmer of approval in Rain's eyes. Blaze took up a sword, holding it across both palms, and offered it to Crag who drew a deep breath. He took the blade, both hands gripping it tightly. For a long moment, he held Sir Blaze's gaze, then he flung the sword at the Knight's feet.

Expressions of shock shone in the eyes of the Knights, and a murmur of surprise swept through the crowd.

"What's he doing?" Lily whispered.

Beside her, Sir Wood's brow furrowed as he explained, "He's relinquishing his sword. He's decided not to join our Order."

"What?" She stared, dumbstruck. He couldn't do that! Not after all he'd gone through to become a Knight!

Blaze alone didn't appear surprised. He held Crag's gaze and nodded slowly before Crag led his horse away, joining the rest of the onlookers at the back of the crowd.

After the ritual, the crowd dispersed and everyone made their way back to the village.

Lily caught up with Crag in the stable.

"Why did you do that?" she demanded.

He glanced at her. "I don't want it. I thought I did, but I don't."

"But you've been through all that service, all that sacrifice!"

He began brushing Pale Feet.

"Don't you have anything to say?"

He glared. "I don't owe you or anyone else an explanation. My decision is none of your concern. We were nothing more than a few moments of pleasure to each other, isn't that right?"

Lily felt her face flush. His life was none of her concern, and no, she wasn't ready to build a relationship on a few moments of intimacy, but hadn't they shared enough to at least make them friends? Didn't he care at all about anything?

"Fine," she snapped. "Have a good life, Crag, if a miserable bastard like you can."

She turned on her heel and left just as Blaze stepped inside.

"Don't bother, Sir," she told the auburn-haired Knight. "He'll only chew your head off if you shown him any concern."

Blaze's large blue eyes widened in question, but Lily didn't wait around to explain. She plopped on the ground outside the stable. After a moment, she realized she could hear Crag and Blaze's conversation.

"I'm sorry for my decision, Sir," Crag said, though he didn't sound very sorry.

"It happens at times, that an apprentice feels unable to accept Knighthood, particularly when his service is performed under severe conditions such as yours. Yes, all apprentices are bombarded with duties, but yours were relentless and in the midst of war. Your work was admirable and your skills are desirable to our Order."

"I can't." Crag sighed. "I just can't."

"I understand. Your thoughts might change. All is not lost. We will not leave for the dubbing ceremony for two weeks' time. You have until then."

"Thank you, Sir, but I don't expect to change my mind."

Moments later, Blaze stepped out of the barn. His gaze riveted to Lily. He offered her the slightest smile before continuing on his way.

Lily wrapped her arms around her knees and sighed. Why had she thought there might have been something between her and Crag? Why had she even bothered wanting it? She should have known happiness with a man was not to be hers.

Chapter Ten

ಸಂ

"Lily, what's wrong?" Coral asked as the two women sat by the brook, scrubbing clothes against the rocks.

She sighed, squeezing the wet fabric of the skirt she washed. "It's just that I really don't know what I want to do with my life. I have no one. I can go anywhere. It's the strangest feeling."

Coral looked at her with sympathy. Both her and Gem's betrothed had come to Tanek, and both couples had decided to settle there. Though she was glad their families were reunited, she couldn't help feeling envious. The war had hurt everyone, yet some had been left with nothing, just as Lily had been. Still, some of it was from her own doing. She and Crag might have continued their relationship. He'd once wanted to court her publicly, but she wouldn't have him, and after their conversation at the stable, she realized she'd been right.

"There's a place about two miles west of here," Coral said. "It's called the crossroads. Years ago, people of the Ancient Religion would go there to pray for guidance. Not that I'm saying there's any truth to the old beliefs, but maybe it'll be a quiet place for you to think your life through."

As Lily continued scrubbing, she mulled over Coral's suggestion. That night, she packed her belongings. Before she left the following morning, she searched for Crag, hoping to make peace with him after their words from the day before, but he was nowhere to be found.

She sighed, saddened by the thought that the previous day might have been the last time she'd ever see him. After all they'd been through, she hated the idea of leaving with bad feelings between them.

The morning was sunny, but a breeze fanned her skin as she walked to the crossroads. The vastness of the place surprised her. Set in a field, woods in the distance, the crossroads was a large cobbled circle with four pathways jutting from it, like reversed wheel spokes. A fountain stood in the grassy center of the circle, four benches surrounding it.

Her brown leather boots were silent as she walked up the nearest pathway, crossed the circle, and sat on the grass near the fountain. She removed an apple from her bag and ate it.

Glancing around the empty field, she listened to birds chirping in distant trees and asked herself exactly what she was doing there. She felt too alone with her thoughts. Without chores to do around the settlement, all she could think about was her loss. Tears welled in her eyes, and she allowed a few to slip down her face before wiping them away. She sat, her knees drawn up to her chest, and stared at a group of ants crawling around the base of the fountain.

The sound of hoof beats echoed across the field. Glancing up, she saw Crag astride Pale Feet. He looked as forlorn as she felt as he rode up one of the pathways.

He slowed Pale Feet, his gaze meeting Lily's. They held each other's gaze for a long moment until she swallowed hard and looked away. Pale Feet's shadow fell upon her as he and Crag moved across the circle. She heard Crag's deep voice urge Pale Feet on as he kicked the stallion to a gallop and disappeared over the field and into the woods.

The relationship between her and Crag made her head spin. For two people who'd shared so much, why couldn't they talk to each other? Why would they rather remain alone with their pain? Why wouldn't he tell her his reasons for denying the Order? Why hadn't she agreed to be his woman?

She remembered the time he'd held her after Vina died, and the times they'd made love. If she closed her eyes she could almost feel his chest beneath her cheek, just as she could feel Vina's sweet weight in her arms. She shook her head, knowing she had to move on.

For close to an hour she rested by the fountain, then slung her bag over her shoulder and made her way to the edge of the forest. In the shelter of the trees, she set up camp, gathered wood for a fire, and removed blankets and a small metal pan from her bag to heat food.

It was close to dusk and she was about to build a fire when Crag approached. She jumped, her heart pounding, having been so lost in her thoughts she hadn't seen or heard him.

He dropped a rabbit he'd killed by her feet.

"I'll skin it if you cook it," he said.

Lily wiped dusty hands on her skirt. "That sounds fair."

"You looked upset earlier. I should have stopped. I'm sorry."

She shook her head. "I'm sure you're sick of handling other people's problems."

He touched her arm. "But you're different, Lily. You're not just anyone. You're the woman I—"

"Please don't." She shrugged off his hand, not exactly sure what she meant. Did she not want him to touch her? To talk to her? Just a few hours ago, hadn't she wondered why they couldn't express affection for each other?

"Lily, please don't push me away," he said.

"If you want to make love, find someone else. I told you it's over between us, at least for now."

"I do want to make love, but not with someone else, and not with you at this moment. Do you think the only reason I ever came to you was to bed you?"

"You're a man."

His teeth clenched visibly and he shook his head. He silently took the rabbit and began skinning it as she prepared a spit on which to cook it.

"What are you doing out here, anyway?" she asked.

"One of the villagers told me about the crossroads. It seemed a good place to think."

"About becoming a Knight?" she ventured.

He shook his head. "I don't think so."

"Isn't it a terrible waste?" she continued softly. "You went through all that work. You learned so much, and now... "

"Now what? I can step into a pretty black uniform and do it all over again for the rest of my life? Knights are just men, yet people look at us like we can perform miracles of healing and fighting."

"Is that what you thought?"

"Isn't it what you thought?"

She smiled sadly and nodded. "Yes. At first I guess I was expecting miracles from you. Instead I got understanding, protection. I got hope."

"Hope." He dropped the rabbit into the pan and gathered the scraps. Lily followed him to the woods as he buried the useless pieces and stooped by the brook, scrubbing his hands.

"You did give me hope. Especially you."

"Stop it," he said.

"Why?"

"Vina's dead."

"People die every day. I miss her, but you did all you could."

"You don't understand, do you?" he said. "No matter what I do, so often it's not enough."

"You're a healer, not a God." She narrowed her eyes, wondering exactly what he was trying to express, what he felt. She wondered what she could tell him to make him change his mind about the hasty decision he'd made.

"People want us to be, but we're not! I thought I was used to the expression in a person's eyes when I'd say his wife or child is dead. I honestly thought I didn't care anymore. This war is over, but I'll only be sent someplace else where this hell will repeat itself. I've been frozen for two years, Lily. Before that, I wasn't even alive. I was a creature of death. Kill and conquer.

There were absolutely no feelings attached to that life. Suddenly I can feel again, and I hate it."

"I know," she told him. "When Vina first died, I felt numb. As days passed, I thought about her more, but since feeling her loss, I somehow believe I can go on and have a life. You showed me that. When we made love, Crag, you proved to me I can still enjoy life."

"Vina's loss was the worst," he whispered. Lily knew he hadn't heard what she'd said. He stared straight ahead, as if in a trance, reliving the horrors he'd seen all over again. "I feel like I failed her, failed you. She had no life. No life at all."

He dropped onto the rock-and-root strewn dirt and covered his face with his hands.

Sitting beside him, she drew him into her arms. He clung to her, his face buried in her shoulder, his tears soaking her dress. She rubbed his back and threaded her fingers through his hair. She wasn't sure how long they sat there, but she didn't feel the need to cry herself. Somehow comforting him gave her strength. It made her feel like she was still worthwhile to someone, especially this man who had seemed so completely in control of himself, who had been the symbol of strength to everyone in the settlement.

Finally his sobbing stopped, but they remained locked in each other's arms.

"I'm sorry," he whispered.

"Don't be." She sat back and brushed dampness from his hot cheeks. The whites of his eyes were tinged red, somehow making his irises seem bluer. "You're just a person, Crag, but you've done so much good for so many. Don't forget that."

He hugged her before stooping by the lake and splashing his face with cold water.

"I'll go cook dinner," she said, leaving him to wash up.

Since it was nearly dark, Lily hurried to build the fire then placed the rabbit on the spit to cook.

As she sat watching the flames, Crag joined her. He'd gained control of himself again, and to her surprise, he smiled.

"Thank you," he said. "No one's ever... Thank you."

"It's been a rough time for everyone."

"What are you going to do, Lily?"

"I'm not sure. I might continue training as a midwife. Blaze said I should go to Travelle." She glanced at him, her heart pounding. She'd already rejected his courtship, but would he ask again? If he didn't, could she ask him to reconsider?

"I hope you do." He reached for her hand. "That way we'll get to see a lot of each other."

She smiled, meeting his eyes. "You're going to be a Knight?"

He nodded. "I...guess I had to get out what I felt. I didn't know how to express it. Now that it's said, I know I can continue. Thank you."

"You're welcome."

He took her face in his hands, and this time he didn't speak of a kiss—he acted. His mouth covered hers, his lips soft and his beard rough. She closed her eyes as his hands moved from her face to her neck, then down her back. Her arms slipped around his neck, her heartbeat quickening as her breasts pressed to his hard chest.

Her mouth opened to his gently probing tongue, her own tongue meeting it with soft, affectionate strokes. Her fingers sifted through his silky curls, and she felt like liquid in his arms. Never in her life had she felt such heat from a kiss, such tenderness. She'd loved her husband, but she'd never lusted after him. Crag was altogether different. Lily wanted to feel every inch of his tall, strong body against hers. She wanted to taste every bit of his flesh. She wanted his lips on her body. She wanted to feel him deep inside her, their bodies so close that they became one being.

His lips moved to her cheek and neck. He kissed her forehead and traced the shape of her lips with his thumb as he whispered, "Lily, listen to what I have to say this time. I love you. I think I have for a very long time."

"I love you, too." Admitting it felt strange, but it was love she felt for Crag. She wasn't exactly sure when she'd begun loving him. Maybe she had from the first, but had been too preoccupied with things more important than her own happiness.

"The moment you walked into Tanek, I thought you were the most beautiful woman I'd ever seen," he murmured against her lips.

She laughed. "I was a mess. I'd just walked twenty miles in the middle of winter."

"I don't care. I thought you were beautiful. I was almost glad to be so busy because whenever I had a second to think about you, all I could imagine was making love with you, and when we did, I thought the pleasure of it would kill me."

"Crag!" She giggled.

"It's true." He cupped her cheek in his hand and stared into her eyes. "Do you want to marry me? When we return to Travelle, after I'm dubbed?"

"You really want me to marry you?"

"More than I want anything…even Knighthood."

Her heart raced, giddiness nearly overwhelming her. She never imagined she could feel such happiness again. All her foolish doubts about spending the rest of her life with a Zaltanian vanished. Crag was no longer a Zaltanian to her, but the man she loved. "Yes," she smiled, "I want to marry you."

"Ah Lily." He crushed her to his chest, his lips caressing her hair. "I love you so much."

"I love you too, Crag."

They slipped apart only long enough to eat. Lily felt giddy as a young girl as she playfully fed Crag pieces of meat with her fingertips. He nipped and licked her fingers and palms, paying more attention to her than he did his meal.

The night was very warm and the full moon brightened the path to the brook where they decided to enjoy a swim. Lily's heart pounded with anticipation as she watched him undress. Even when they'd made love, they'd never had time to fully undress. She'd dreamed of seeing Crag's body, and when his baggy tunic and trousers fell away, leaving him in only a loincloth, she couldn't tear her gaze from him. His tall frame was very lean and lanky, his muscles hard and defined in spite of his slimness. His shoulders and chest were broad, the bones of his forearms and wrists thick. Sparse, dark hair dusted his chest and sleekly-muscled legs. He had the body of a warrior. His cock bulged against the loincloth, and when she reached out to stroke it, he caught her wrist.

"Your turn." He nodded to her dress. "I've been dying to see you naked."

His words made Lily's stomach clench, and her hands trembled a bit as she undressed. What would he think of her? Would her nude body please him as much as his pleased her? Her dress pooled at her feet, and she stepped out of it, leaving only a transparent shift.

Though she wasn't a tall woman, Lily's breasts were full and firm, her waist narrow and her legs strong. Glancing down, she noticed her pink nipples pressing through the thin shift. She turned to the water, but Crag caught her upper arm and dragged her to him for a kiss.

"You're so lovely," he said, his hands stroking her bare shoulders. "I could never have dreamed of a more beautiful woman."

"Or I a more handsome man." She looped her arms around his neck. He smiled, apparently pleased by her words.

They slipped into the brook and engaged in a playful water fight which ended with him pulling her into his arms and kissing her until she nearly lost her breath.

"Stop!" She gasped, laughing. "Oh please!"

"I'll make you beg me for something else." He caught her in his arms, stood, and walked to the shore. He carried her to the camp and stretched out on the blankets close to the fire. Looming above her, Crag stroked damp hair from her face and kissed her temple and cheek before covering her mouth with his.

It felt good to have her naked breasts pressed against his bare chest. The hard muscles were scattered with soft, curling hair that teased her nipples. As his lips and tongue moved to her neck, she clutched his back, enjoying the warmth of his flesh and the smooth, hard muscles beneath her grip.

Crag slipped down her body, his mouth caressing her breasts over and again, as if he couldn't taste enough of the warm globes and pebble-hard nipples. Lily writhed, entwining her legs with his. She rubbed her pelvis against his side and tugged at his hair.

"Demanding little wench, aren't you?" Crag's deep voice rumbled in his chest as he tugged her hands from his hair and positioned himself between her parted thighs. His tongue slid into her pussy and swirled. Fastening his mouth on her clit, he grasped her buttocks and squeezed gently. Lily moaned, threading her fingers back into his hair. One of his fingers probed the soft, sensitive skin between her bottom cheeks as he continued licking her swollen little nub.

Lily thrust her pelvis upward, and he held her fast, tugging with his lips, licking, and teasing until she exploded in a mind-shattering climax. He continued licking her damp folds of flesh, forcing her toward another orgasm almost before she recovered from the first.

"Crag, oh Crag!" she gasped, her body shaking and writhing in another ecstatic peak.

She felt him slide up her body and slip inside her hot, throbbing pussy. She clung to him with all her strength as he thrust long and slow until she climaxed again.

"Oh Lily, I love you," he panted against her lips before kissing her, his thrusts short and fast. Lily clutched his shoulders, her legs tightening around his waist, holding him as close as she could while her body met his thrust for thrust.

Crag tore his mouth from hers and cried out in ecstasy before collapsing on top of her. For several moments they lay, catching their breath and enjoying the feeling of lying in each others arms.

Crag rolled onto his back and Lily rested her cheek against his chest, listening to his heartbeat. She traced a long, thick scar across his ribs. "Did you get this during the war?"

He nodded. "Remember how I told you I was fighting in a village and the Ruby Order drove out the Zaltanian troop? I was seriously wounded. I would have died had it not been for one of the Knights. He saved my life."

"I'm so glad he did."

Crag's arm tightened around her and he kissed her hair. "What bothers me is I never knew his name. I don't even know if he's still alive. He might have been killed during one of the battles."

"Maybe when you go to Travelle, you'll find him."

"Maybe." Crag sighed as she lowered her face and kissed the scar. Her lips traveled over his chest and taut abdomen. His fingers threaded through her hair, and she slid on top of him, their mouths devouring one another's. Her knee brushed his cock, and to her surprise, it was already hard again.

Lily smiled and gripped his erection, pumping it and feeling it swell even more in her grasp. "How did a man with your appetite ever endure vows of celibacy?"

"It was fairly easy, until I met you."

"Really?"

He sighed, his eyes slipping shut as her hand moved faster along his shaft while her other squeezed his balls. "Most of the time I was too tired to think about it, but you're beautiful enough to defy exhaustion."

"And what happens when beauty fades?"

His eyes opened and his hands reached down to restrain hers. He rolled onto his side and tilted her face to his. "Your face and body are gorgeous, Lily, but I meant your whole person aroused me. You are beautiful through to your soul. That's why I needed you so badly."

Lily's heart fluttered. How could she ever have disliked him?

Chapter Eleven

∽

"Close your eyes," Crag ordered.

Lily did as he asked and felt the gentle sweeping of the horsehair brush over her eyelids. He'd mixed dye from the petals of crushed flowers, and they sat by the fountain at the crossroads while he painted her face. Using the brush he'd made from several strands of hair from Pale Feet's tail, he drew across Lily's cheekbones, around her eyes, and down the length of her nose.

"And this is some kind of warrior symbolism?" she asked.

"Yes. Not Zaltanian. My village was on the southern most shore of the continent. It was taken over by Zaltana when I was a boy, but the warriors there still kept the face painting tradition even after they fought for the Zaltanian army. When I decided to join the Ruby Order, I stopped wearing the paint."

"Do you miss it?" She opened her eyes to look at him.

He laughed. "Hell, no. It was an annoyance smearing on this mask all the time."

"It doesn't feel like you're just smearing this on. When can I look?"

"In a moment." He took her chin in his hand and placed a dot above each of her eyebrows.

"So do you really consider yourself Zaltanian?"

"Not anymore."

"I mean before you joined the Order."

"Yes. As I said, I was very young. Zaltana was all I knew." He sat back on his heels. "Finished."

She jumped up and leaned over the fountain, staring into the still water. What he'd done was by no means a simple smearing of paint. Her face was a beautiful mask of lines, circles, triangles, and spirals.

He stood behind her, his body warm against her back. "The more intricate the design, the more respected the warrior."

She smiled and turned, tilting her face up to him. "Then why did you put on so much? I wouldn't be so respected—if I was a warrior."

"After all you've been through, I've no doubt you're a warrior, Lily."

She gazed back into the water. His fingertips swept her hair across her back and draped it over her shoulder, baring her neck. She felt his lips on her skin and shivered with desire, her eyes slipping shut as his mouth trailed down her neck. He slipped her tunic partway down her arm and kissed her shoulder. She turned, locking her arms around his neck as their mouths met.

"Maybe I should wash this paint off before it smudges all over us," she said.

"You can't." He smiled against her lips. "It'll wear off in a couple of days."

"A couple of days!" The string of complaints that would have followed were silenced by a kiss so deep she forgot about everything but the sensation of his lips and tongue and the love she felt for him.

Lily buried her fingers in his hair as his tongue stroked hers. She licked the soft flesh inside his mouth and ran her tongue over the smoothness of his teeth. To her, everything about Crag was something to be explored and rediscovered.

"You're so beautiful, Lily," he said, taking her face in his hands. Her eyes opened, gazing into his. "Sometimes I wonder why we had to go through hell to find each other. I might have deserved everything I've gotten, but not you."

"Nobody deserved this war, Crag, but finding you has changed my life in a way I never thought possible. I never imagined finding love again. I didn't think I wanted to."

"I promise to love you always." His lips brushed her forehead before he kissed the tip of her nose then whispered against her lips. "Always."

Lily kissed him before slipping from his grasp and running toward the woods.

"What are you doing?" he called.

"Want me? You have to catch me!"

Lily grinned as she enjoyed her head start. Hoof beats sounded and she laughed. The cheat!

Suddenly she felt Crag's arm around her and she was hauled onto Pale Feet. Crag held her close, and she felt the sensual pressure of his thighs and chest against her.

He nuzzled her neck. "I like this kind of hunting. The prey is prettier than usual."

He kicked Pale Feet to a canter until they passed the crest of the next hill, then slowed the horse to a walk. Crag released the reins and placed his hands on Lily's hips and slid them up her ribs. He cupped her breasts, his thumbs stroking her nipples through her dress. Lily sighed, leaning against him and tilting her neck so he could kiss it.

He slipped her dress down her shoulders and over her arms so it draped her waist, baring her torso. His callused palms roamed over the soft skin and he tenderly rolled her nipples before using his forefinger to circle them. He teased and rubbed the tight little peaks, filling her with desire through to her core.

Lily's breathing deepened and she squirmed, yet he didn't stop caressing. He kneaded her soft breasts, gently rubbing his callused palms over her nipples.

"Lily, my beautiful Lily," he said close to her ear, moving one of his hands from her breasts and tracing each of her ribs with his fingertips. He tickled her navel before sliding his hand down the front of her dress. His skilled fingers gathered moisture from her pussy and circled her clit while his other hand continued rolling her nipple to the same rhythm.

Lily leaned against him, panting, her bottom squirming. Beneath them, Pale Feet lurched. Crag held Lily steady and nibbled her ear. He licked the back of her neck and covered her shoulder with kisses. She surrendered to him completely, lost in her need for this man whom she once thought she hated.

"Oh Crag!" She panted, writhing beneath his ministrations, her heart racing with a combination of excitement and embarrassment. They were on the back of a horse and he was teasing her to climax, yet she was past the point of wanting to stop!

"Yes, Lily," he purred close to her ear. "It's all right. Come for me, my love. Come for me."

Lily mewled, her head arching against his shoulder, her breasts thrust forward as his fingers quickened between her legs. Lily panted, momentarily fearful of tumbling off Pale Feet in her moment of crisis. She needn't have worried. Though the hand between her legs continued drawing out her pleasure until the last ripple, Crag's other arm left her breast and held her steady as he whispered endearments.

Lily sighed, resting quietly against him.

Suddenly Pale Feet snorted and Lily jumped, startled. She'd been so lost in pleasure that for a moment she'd forgotten—and hadn't cared—where she was.

"This is disgraceful, you know." She glanced around at him, warmed by the masculine smile on his lips and the glow of passion in his eyes.

Crag tugged up her dress and helped her back into it. "A little late to worry about it."

"You're right about that." Lily kissed him. "And I'm really not worried."

He grinned. "Somehow I didn't think so."

* * * * *

The next morning Crag and Lily mounted Pale Feet and galloped across the fields. Crag sat behind her, and she relished the strength of his arms around her, the warmth of his chest and the pressure of his steely legs.

He slowed the stallion as they crossed a brook, the water spraying their boots and drenching his trousers and the hem of her tunic. They stopped at a cliff overlooking the sea. Waves splashed against the rocks below, and wind blew hair across their faces. She drew a deep breath and smiled at him. He kissed her, then turned Pale Feet back toward the crossroads where he released the horse to graze.

Crag sat beneath a willow tree, tugging Lily between his knees. She rested against his chest.

Slipping his arms around her waist, he said, "Sing for me?"

She sang the folk songs of her village and lullabies she'd sung for Vina. It was the first time she could indulge those memories and not cry. Lily still ached from the loss of her daughter, but she realized she always would. She would never forget her, nor did she want to.

"I could listen to you forever," he murmured when she'd finished.

"Why don't you join me?"

He laughed. "I can't sing."

She tilted her head to face him. "Of course you can." She knew by the lovely, rich tone of his speaking voice he could sing. "What can it hurt to try?"

He shrugged. "If you want me to. But don't say I didn't warn you."

She sang a few lines, and he mimicked her, softly, almost hesitantly. As she guessed, he sang as beautifully as he spoke. With some practice, he'd be better than most of the musicians in her village.

They sang for most of the afternoon then fished for dinner in the brook. As they sat side-by-side, fishing poles dangling over the water, he said, "How can I thank you for all you've done for me? I feel like my entire life was nighttime with a moon hidden by clouds, and you've just pushed the clouds away and made everything light again."

His words warmed her entire body, and her stomach tightened with joy. "No one's ever said anything like that to me before."

He leaned closer and whispered against her lips, "Where did you come from, Lily?"

"Part of me feels like I've waited for you all my life. I never imagined loving a man as I love you."

"I'll have a crazy life serving in the Order, Lily, but I swear I'll always love you. I'll always try to make you happy."

They reached for each other simultaneously, starving for one another, each seeking nourishment from the other's soul.

"Oh Crag… "

"Lily… "

"Crag, I think I've got a bite."

"Um-hmm." He said absently, kissing her lips and throat.

"No, I mean it!" She pushed away as her line jerked hard. She yanked on her makeshift rod and flipped the fish directly into Crag's face.

Spitting, he grasped the slippery fish while Lily sat back on her heels and laughed.

Crag shot her an annoyed look, but it was impossible for him to look intimidating with a fish flopping wildly in his hands. He snickered as well, and the fish squirmed back into the water.

"There goes dinner," Lily groaned.

"Forget dinner." He tugged her into his arms. "Let's just have the sweets."

"I'm going to love being your wife."

"I hope so, Lily."

She didn't have to hope. She knew.

"Isn't this lovely!" a gruff voice taunted.

Lily's eyes flew open. She and Crag stared over their shoulders at a group of Zaltanian soldiers in tattered uniforms. Several of them ogled her and laughed at her painted face. Fear twisted Lily's gut, and she clutched Crag's arm.

"You." One of the soldiers, apparently the leader by the yellow marks embroidered on his collar, pointed at Crag.

"Jarib," Crag said. "You look like you and your men can use help. I know where you can get food and—"

Jarib threw back his head and laughed, exposing chipped teeth. His black hair was cut short, and his face smeared with dirt. His bulky hand closed over his sword, and the others reached for their weapons as well.

"Lily, go to the horse and get out of here," Crag said calmly.

She shook her head, groping for the nearest rock, preparing to fight alongside him if the need arose, though she knew they wouldn't have a chance. They were outnumbered by armed soldiers, and neither she nor Crag carried a weapon.

"Go back to the settlement," he repeated.

Yes, the settlement! She'd go to Sir Rain and return with Knights. But by then Crag could be dead.

"Luscious little thing." Jarib pointed his blade at her and licked his cracked lips.

"The war is over," Crag stated, rising to his full height. He was taller than the soldiers, and she knew he was a strong, able fighter, but it wouldn't be enough. Not against those odds.

"Yes, the war is over. Out here. But the Zaltanian army is all over the world. You know it, and I know it, Crag. You are a former captain turned traitor. As the only Zaltanian authority out here, it's my duty to punish you. Execution." He glanced at the soldiers. "Take the woman"

Two of the men moved forward. Crag shoved Lily behind him and bellowed for her to run for Pale Feet as he dodged the blades. As she fled, one of the men followed her, but she leapt on the horse's back and kicked the soldier in the face before galloping off. She noticed Crag had disarmed the two men who'd attacked him, but he didn't pick up a weapon to defend himself.

She cursed his integrity and the green sash faction he sought to join.

The hot wind stung Lily's face as Pale Feet galloped across the field toward the settlement. Blaze was the first Knight she found. He stood by the well, drawing water.

"Zaltanian soldiers," she gasped, not bothering to dismount. "By the river. They have Crag and want to execute him as a traitor."

One of the other Knights had approached, heard Lily's story, and shouted for Sir Rain while Blaze mounted Pale Feet behind her. They galloped toward the woods, Knights on horseback following them.

By the river, several Zaltanians soldiers lay unconscious, and Lily knew Crag had fought them.

"Blood." Blaze pointed to a red path in the grass leading to the woods. He kicked the horse onward, slowing only when the woods thickened.

Another soldier lay in a clearing. Sir Blaze slipped from the horse and stooped to examine the body. "Not wounded by a blade."

"Is he dead?"

Blaze shook his head.

Lily gasped as Crag dropped from a nearby tree. He pressed a hand to his side, blood dripping through his fingers and staining his tunic. Her heart dropped to her stomach, and she jumped off the horse. Blaze reached him before Lily did, examining the injury as Crag sank to the ground and leaned against a tree. His face was colorless and misted with sweat.

"Poison," he murmured. "Zaltanian soldiers usually carry poison arrows."

She noted the arrow had passed almost directly through Crag's flesh, the bloody head partially exposed.

While she helped Crag to sit under a tree, Blaze built a hasty fire. He took an iron from his bag of healing supplies and set it to heat over the flames before approaching Crag.

"Your assistance, Water Flower," Blaze ordered as he sat on his knees next to Crag.

She held him as Blaze began extracting the weapon. Crag gasped, his fingers tightening on her arm. Sweat streaked his face, and she knew he struggled not to cry out in pain. It seemed to take Blaze forever to remove the arrow, and as she glanced at the gory scene, she understood why. Behind the arrowhead, sticking out of the shaft, metal barbs hooked on muscle and flesh. It was a nasty weapon, made to inflict the worst kind of agony.

Lily drew a sharp breath as Crag's grip became painful. Finally the weapon was removed and his hold on her relaxed so completely she thought he'd fainted.

"Sorry," he whispered, his eyes half closed from pain and the poison.

"Shh." She brushed wet hair from his forehead and glanced at Blaze who'd removed the iron from the fire. He sealed the wound from the back, causing Crag to gasp and clutch Lily spasmodically. The cauterization from the front, where the arrowhead had come out, the vicious rows of teeth leaving a gaping hole, dragged a half sob from his throat. For a moment, his head dropped to her shoulder, his hot neck throbbing against hers as he composed himself.

Lily met Blaze's eyes and asked, "How can I help?"

"We need antidote."

"They carry it," Crag said.

Lily and Blaze both looked to the body in the clearing, but Crag murmured, "He doesn't have any. I already checked."

"By the river—" Blaze began, but before he could finish, Lily mounted Pale Feet and galloped to the other soldiers, not caring that she still felt unfamiliar with horseback riding. Rain and several Knights had already begun tying up the Zaltanians, and with Lily, they searched the prisoners thoroughly but found no antidote. Blaze joined them and shook his head upon hearing their report.

"Nothing." The auburn-haired Knight looked as frustrated as Lily felt.

They returned to Crag who lay as still as death, his face the color of wax. Sweat bled through his tunic, mingling with the blood, darkening the pale gray material. Lily and Blaze stooped beside him.

The Knight shook Crag's shoulder. "Stay awake."

Crag's lashes fluttered. Blaze lifted his lids and spoke firmly, "Crag."

Panic nearly overcame Lily, but she buried screams and tears deep inside. She'd just found Crag, and losing him so soon would be far too cruel.

"He could have taken their weapons to defend himself but didn't," Blaze said. "He's of my faction."

"He hasn't even been dubbed." Lily felt tears welling in spite of her attempt to remain calm.

"He is a Knight."

"Jarib," Crag murmured.

"One of the soldiers was called Jarib," she explained to Blaze.

"He shot me. He has it."

Lily needed no further incentive. Ignoring Blaze's shouts to wait for assistance, she leapt onto Pale Feet, kicking him deeper into the forest. If it was the last thing she did, she'd catch that Zaltanian bastard! She'd lost too much to Zaltana's greed and violence. Her husband. Her daughter. Her village. She would not lose Crag too.

As the forest became more twisted, Pale Feet was forced to walk, and Lily's stomach churned with fear, anticipation, and anger. She felt anger most. Rage at the war itself and the stupidity of people. Fury that men like the Knights risked their lives only to be rewarded with injury and death.

She heard water rippling and saw a Zaltanian soldier kneeling by the lake, examining his injured leg. One of his boots rested in the mud beside him, his bow and sword a short distance away, but not close enough for him to reach without scrambling. Obviously the pain of his injury had thwarted his common sense.

Quietly as she could, she dismounted and picked up a thick tree branch lying beside Pale Feet's hoof.

She'd nearly reached Jarib when he turned, glaring at her. His face was white with pain, and she noted the awkward twist and tremendous swelling of his ankle.

He looked at the branch clutched in her fists and laughed. Simultaneously he lunged for his sword and Lily dove at him with the branch, swinging hard.

He raised a hand to deflect the blow and grunted as the branch cracked against his arm. Apparently he hadn't expected her strength. She swung again, and he kicked her. Lily's legs flew out from under her, and she landed so hard on her back she nearly lost consciousness. Her stomach ached, as the wind was knocked out of her. Before she fully recovered, Jarib's body covered hers. His knee shoved her legs apart and his rancid breath struck her face.

Then she remembered his injury. She struggled, managing to use her heel to stomp hard against his ankle. He growled in agony, one of his hands loosening on her as he reflexively reached for his foot. She squirmed a hand free and punched him hard in the throat, a technique she'd learned from watching the Knights train. Jarib's eyes bulged as he rolled off her and clutched his throat, unable to breathe. Lily crawled toward the branch, and this time her blow hit its mark. Jarib lay unconscious in the rocks and mud.

Lily wasted no time searching Jarib's belongings, piling anything that looked like it might contain antidote into a leather bag. She mounted Pale Feet and hurried back to the clearing.

"Water Flower?" Blaze glanced at Lily with concern, his eyes raking her bruised, dirty face and torn clothes.

"Here." She slid off the horse and passed Blaze the bag.

While the Knight searched through the contents, she focused her attention on Crag. His eyes closed, his face paler than before, he appeared dead, except for the almost imperceptible rise and fall of his chest.

Blaze opened a small leather pouch, sniffed the contents, and inserted his fingertip. It came away covered with a fine black powder that he touched to his tongue. Lily noted his look of relief as he measured some of the powder and emptied it into a wooden mug then mixed it with water.

He shook Crag, forcing his sleepy eyes to open.

Blaze glanced at Lily. "Help him."

She slipped behind Crag, assisting him to a sitting position while Blaze forced him to drink the entire contents of the mug.

"It's not safe here," Blaze said. "We have to get him back to the settlement."

The auburn-haired Knight stood, and with surprising strength for a man so slender, lifted Crag onto his shoulder and carried him to Pale Feet. He mounted, positioning Crag in front of him so he could support him, and turned back toward the settlement while Lily followed.

At the settlement, Blaze carried Crag into the longhouse, Lily close behind. As soon as they entered the dim interior, Coral and Gem approached.

"What happened?" Coral demanded.

"We were attacked by Zaltanian soldiers. He was shot with a poison arrow," Lily explained quickly, wondering if she sounded as terrified as she felt.

"By the Goddess!" Coral said. "I'll get some water."

Blaze positioned Crag, who had yet to awaken, on a blanket by the fire. Lily watched as the Knight examined the wound. Finally he sat back on his heels and glanced at her. "He's resting easily. I believe he'll survive."

Lily released her pent up breath and covered her face with her hands. Suddenly her entire body felt weak. Blaze's arm slipped around her, and she rested her head against his sharp-boned shoulder.

"Your bravery rivaled a great cat in battle, Water Flower."

She shook her head. "Everything I did was out of fear."

"For him." Blaze motioned in Crag's direction, and she nodded. "Then he has all the wealth the world can offer. Watch over him. There are others who need my attention."

Gem brought another blanket, and Coral a mug of water. They checked on Crag often, as did so many others he had helped during his time in Tanek. Lily wondered if he realized just how much he was appreciated. It might have made life easier for him during the difficult times of his service.

As dusk neared, she lay down beside him and watched the rise and fall of his chest. Lulled by the warmth of the fire and tired by the events of the day, she felt on the verge of sleep when he moaned softly. Raising herself on her elbow, she touched his face. "Crag?"

His eyes opened halfway and took a moment to focus as he turned to her. "Lily?"

"How do you feel?"

"My side hurts, but I'm all right—I think. The poison…"

"We got the antidote. Blaze says you have to rest, though."

He winced as he moved to a sitting position and lifted a hand to her bruised face. "What happened?"

"It doesn't matter. Are you hungry?"

He shook his head. "A little thirsty."

"I'll get you some fresh water." Lily took the mug from beside him and left the house, taking deep breaths of the cool night air as she made her way to the well.

When she returned to Crag, Blaze sat beside him, applying salve and a new bandage to his injury. Lily noted that while Crag didn't appear completely well, most of his color had returned.

As she knelt beside him, his gaze held hers with such intensity she nearly dropped the mug. He reached for her hand and tugged her onto the blanket beside him. "You saved my life."

"As you've done for so many others."

"That's different. I've been trained for battle and for healing. You rescued me by your strength of heart alone. I'm very lucky."

"To have survived that arrow wound. I know."

"I mean I'm lucky to have you." He touched her cheek. "And you thought you didn't deserve the battle paint."

She held his gaze for a long moment before Blaze interrupted them.

"No infection, but you must rest."

"There's too much work around here to—"

"I don't take well to insubordination," Blaze said. "Though it is a fact healers make the worst patients."

"I'll try not to be difficult." Crag sounded a bit teasing.

"I'll make sure he rests," Lily told Blaze as he left them alone.

"Oh will you?" Crag lifted an eyebrow.

She nodded and kissed his forehead then his cheek. "Let someone take care of you for a change. You deserve it."

"I still feel like I should be doing something."

"Yes, resting. Close your eyes."

"I don't—"

"Do it!"

He obeyed, his protest silenced by her kiss. When she drew back, she noticed a slight smile on his lips, and her belly warmed. Crag's expressions and mannerisms seemed to become more adorable and endearing every moment they spent together. It was hard to imagine those times when she'd disliked him. He was a good man, and in spite of the horror of the conditions in which they had met, she was glad and grateful they'd found each other.

She touched her fingertips to his temples and massaged with a soothing, circular motion.

"That feels good," he murmured in a sleepy voice. The herbs Blaze had given him to dull the pain had obviously begun working. Within moments, his breathing became deep and even as he slept.

Lily settled beside him, her head resting against his shoulder, and fell asleep as well.

* * * * *

It took Crag close to a week to recover enough to do more than rest and perform the gentle exercises required by Sir Blaze to keep him mobile and ensure his injury healed properly. Once he began feeling better, it was all Lily could do to keep him from returning to his healing duties.

"Let him go," Sir Wood told her as she attempted to follow Crag during one of the usual midnight calls for help. Lily was about to argue with the Knight, whom she'd never particularly liked, but she noted an almost proud expression in his eyes as he watched Crag. "If he seems unable to perform, Blaze or I will relieve him. Resuming his duties is the best thing for him right now."

Lily nodded and snuggled back into her blanket, though her gaze kept returning to Crag as he worked. To think a man so dedicated had considered leaving the Ruby Order.

Several hours later, Lily stirred from a light sleep to Crag lying beside her.

"Are you all right?" she asked.

"I'm fine. Sir Wood sent me away." Crag glanced across the longhouse to the other Knight. "That's certainly not like him."

"A week ago you nearly died. You need rest yourself."

"I feel so ready, Lily." He turned to her, stroking her cheek, his eyes gleaming. It seemed like ages since they appeared dull and lifeless as when they'd first met. "I never imagined feeling like this. I think most of it's because of you."

"No." She rested her hand over his wrist. "It's because all the work you did has finally paid off." She smiled. "My husband will be a Knight of the Ruby Order."

"I want you, Lily," he whispered, then chuckled, "Don't think I'd be of much good to you at this point, but it doesn't stop me from desiring."

Lily's fingers entwined with his. "Do you feel up to a trip to the storage shed?"

His lips jerked upward in a grin and his eyes glistened with passion. "You have to ask?"

They stood, their fingers still entwined. As they took a step toward the door, she paused. "Wait. Are you sure this won't be too much for you?"

Crag bent and whispered in her ear, his beard brushing her cheek, "It's either you or my fist. Just ask which I prefer."

As they left the longhouse, Sir Blaze stopped them. "A strange time for a walk. Are you not well, Jagged Peak?"

"I …" Crag held the Knight's gaze, "I wanted to see if any dried fruit was left in the storage shed."

A quirky smile played around Blaze's lips. "I've been told some vows are less important to keep than others."

Crag's brow furrowed and his eyes widened a bit. "But…"

"Be careful. You've yet to fully heal and finding fruit can be a most strenuous exercise."

Lily stepped outside to hide her blush. As Crag joined her, he said, "Is there anything he doesn't notice?"

"There's more to Blaze than most people seem to realize, but he is right."

"About?"

"I wouldn't want you to hurt yourself."

"Liilllyyy…" His voice held a warning tone.

She smiled as they approached the storage shed and stepped inside.

"Come." She took his hand and guided him to a corner of the shed. "Sit."

He sat on a barrel while she opened his cloak and knelt between his legs.

"Lily…"

"Shhh." She pushed up his tunic and he lifted his hips as she slid down his trousers.

Grasping his balls in one hand and his half-aroused cock in the other, she stroked him in a steady rhythm as he grew beneath her touch. "Such a fine weapon. I'm glad this is one sword you can't throw down."

"Wench, you're not as shy or proper as I once thought." He grinned.

"You've corrupted me. Painted my face and made me a warrior." She bent, running her tongue from the base of his cock to the head. She laved the smooth, round bulb. She felt him tense as she licked back down and used her lips to play with his balls as she continued squeezing.

"Oh Lily," he groaned when she took the head in her mouth again, laving and sucking. His breathing quickened and his fingers tightened in her hair.

Lily closed her eyes, concentrating on the smoothness and the ridges of his cock and the shape of his balls. The tip of her tongue explored the veins along the shaft and the ridge along the underside. When she began sucking deeply, feeling him brush the back of her throat, his hips shifted and he panted.

"Don't stop, Lily! Oh, by the Spirit, don't stop!"

She would have laughed at the panic in his aroused voice had she not been so fully concentrating on her pleasurable task. When he came, he uttered a hoarse cry, his hips thrusting, though she knew he tried to control the motion as she continued sucking until he collapsed against the wall.

She gazed at him and smiled. His eyes were closed, his expression peaceful and completely fulfilled. She watched the rise and fall of his chest as his breathing returned to normal. Slowly, his eyes opened and his lips tugged upward in a pleased grin.

"Your turn?" he offered.

"No. You're still injured." She stood, tossing him a coquettish glance over her shoulder as she headed out of the shed. "But you owe me later."

"I can't think of a more pleasurable debt to pay."

He adjusted his clothes and they returned to the longhouse. Sir Blaze sat on the steps, mixing an herbal remedy. He glanced up, his large eyes sweeping them. "No fruit?"

Lily and Crag exchanged looks, and she felt herself blushing again.

"None that we found," Crag replied.

Blaze turned back to his mixing bowl.

"He didn't say a word, so why do I feel guilty?" Lily muttered.

"Why should you? You're not the one who broke a vow."

"Don't you feel guilty?"

"Lily." He kissed her cheek as they settled back into the blankets. "I sometimes think I was born guilty. Sleep well, love."

"You too." Lily rested her head against his shoulder. She could scarcely wait to become his wife so they could avoid storage sheds and little white lies.

Chapter Twelve
Two Weeks Later

ಞ

Lily stood beside Sir Blaze at the bow of one of the Ruby Order's ships as they approached Travelle.

"Ah, the source at last!" Blaze smiled, gazing at the foggy shoreline. "Our leader of swords and sewing needles will be pleased with these new Knights, and I, for the first time in seven years, can drape a green sash around another madman's waist."

Smiling, Lily glanced over her shoulder at Crag who stood with a group of Knights and apprentices preparing to unload horses and cargo. Blaze told her the dubbing ceremony would take place two days after their arrival, and he promised to speak with Sir Mahir, the leader of the Order about her marrying Crag directly afterward. He also promised to speak with the Dames of the Opal Order about allowing her to train with them as a midwife. Their fortress was no more than a few hours' journey from that of the Ruby Order, so she and Crag could live between the Orders while she trained.

Most of his time would be spent with Sir Blaze and the green sash faction. Truthfully, Lily worried about his decision. She knew he would be acting as a healer in the middle of battle with no weapon to defend himself. Though she understood his proficiency in hand-to-hand combat, she still worried. Yet she vowed never to mention her concern. He'd thought hard about his choice and how important the green sash was to him, and she felt proud of his decision. Few were brave, selfless, and skilled enough to enter Sir Blaze's faction.

The ship docked, and other Knights waited on shore. Lily and Crag shared his horse on the journey to the fortress. She sat in the saddle, Crag behind her, his body warm against her back.

New black gloves covered his hands, matching the simple black uniform.

"Is the fortress far?" she asked.

"No more than half an hour away."

"Is it very big?"

"Yes. It can hold several thousand Knights and their families, not including the hospice. Then there's the training grounds and the woods. The Knights not living in the fortress have settled in houses all over Travelle, most in Rubyshire, the Order's official land. "

Lily could scarcely wait to see the fortress. They rode over the beach and across several hills. She noticed villages, scattered cottages and farms, many of them owned by Knights, Dames and their families.

Finally a high stone wall loomed in the distance, an even taller building behind it. Outside the wall, groups of Knights practiced archery, swordplay and jousting.

"At last!" Blaze, who had been riding alongside them, kicked his horse to a gallop, passing the line of horses and gliding through the gates long before the rest of them reached the fortress.

They dismounted after passing through the open gates, and Lily stared at the massive gray walls, the beautiful courtyard filled with trees and flowers, and the black garbed Knights walking throughout the yard and great hall. Women and children—families of the Knights—also went about their daily life, staring at the newcomers with interest.

While Crag took Pale Feet to the stable and joined the other apprentices in training, Lily was shown to a room. She followed a cheerful maid—one of the Knights' daughters—up a stone staircase and down a long corridor lined with closed wooden doors on both sides. Lily's room was at the end of the hall. Though small and sparse with only a bed, table and trunk, it was spotlessly clean and had a window overlooking the training field. She thanked the maid as she closed the door behind her then squinted out the window, trying to discern Crag among the mass of Knights mingling below. She laughed at herself. They were all dressed exactly alike. About to turn away, she saw him. Taller than most, and so handsome, especially since the war had ended and he'd been able to get proper rest and food, he stood with a small group of Knights wearing green sashes. Lily smiled. Soon he'd be one of them.

After unpacking her belongings, she wandered down to the great hall where a tall, attractive woman dressed in a simple yet elegant brown dress approached her.

"You look a little lost." The woman smiled. "You must have just arrived. I'm Honey Wine."

"Lily." She accepted the woman's hand. The feeling of calluses on the woman's palm surprised her. In spite of her fine attire, she was obviously accustomed to work.

"Are you with one of the Knights?" Lily's new companion continued.

"My fiancé is to be dubbed in a couple of days."

"Oh, that's wonderful." Honey Wine smiled. "My husband will be presiding over the ceremony with Mahir and Blaze. Dubbing ceremonies are beautiful and there's a hell of a celebration afterward."

Lily laughed at the woman's brusque manner that conflicted with her almost regal beauty, yet somehow suited the callused palms.

"That's why Torn—my husband—and I came here," she continued as they walked to the courtyard. "He travels between here and my kingdom."

"Your kingdom?" Lily raised an eyebrow.

"Sophianna."

"You're a Queen?"

"We call it a Mistress," she said.

"Should I curtsy or something?"

She laughed. "No. I'm not fond of the royalty rubbish. Before I was monarch, I was a prison healer and before that a guard."

"How did you become a ruler?" Lily asked, fascinated. Honey Wine was by far one of the most interesting women she'd ever met. She wondered what her husband was like.

"It's a very long story," she said.

"Your husband must be high up to be presiding with Sir Mahir."

"He's second in command. He makes me a madwoman at times. He returned from the war several months ago. I'll tell you, there's nothing worse than waiting, not knowing if they're dead or alive." Honey Wine shook her head. "I don't want to think about it, but you must know exactly how I feel. You and your fiancé must have met during the war."

"We did. He's joining Sir Blaze's faction."

Honey Wine's eyes widened. "My goodness. So few get in. So few *want* to get in. He must be a special man."

"Yes. He is, but try telling him that."

"That's how the good ones are. The ones who strut around like arrogant bulls usually have far less to brag about."

Lily spent the rest of the day with Honey Wine, touring the fortress and grounds and meeting many of the Knights, families and servants. After eating dinner in the hall, during which Crag didn't appear, Lily retired to her room. She'd been in bed for hours when a soft knock roused her. Lily slipped on a robe and opened the door.

Crag stood outside.

"I'm sorry. I woke you," he said.

"I'm glad you did." She let him in, warmed by the sight of him.

"I'd hoped to spend more time with you today, but there was so much to do."

"I understand."

As soon as the door closed, he tugged her into his arms and kissed her.

"Blaze spoke to Sir Mahir," he said. "You have a choice. We can wait until the end of the week and have a big ceremony, or Sir Mahir will marry us in private directly after the dubbing."

"I don't need a big ceremony. I just want to marry you. Soon."

He smiled. "I feel the same way."

They lay on the bed, their bodies entwined, mouths fused, separated only by his clothes and her shift.

"Do you think you'll like it here?" he asked.

"Very much. I spent the day with Honey Wine. We had so much fun. She asked us to visit her in Sophianna after we're married."

"Honey Wine?" Crag narrowed his eyes. "Sir Torn's wife? The Mistress of Sophianna?"

Lily nodded.

He looked amused. "You pick lofty friends. He's second in command."

"Have you ever seen him?"

Crag shook his head. "Not yet."

"I'm curious to look at him. See what kind of a man married Honey Wine."

"What's wrong with her?"

"Nothing. She's very nice. Forceful, but nice. Did you know she was once a guard? You think our relationship was impossible, you should hear how she and Sir Torn met."

"You'll have to tell me all about it," he said, rolling her onto her back and kissing her throat.

She laughed, clutching his shoulders as his beard tickled her skin. "Keep this up and I won't be coherent."

In answer, his mouth covered hers. His tongue tickled the roof of her mouth and stroked the soft, moist flesh inside her cheeks. Lily explored his mouth and caressed his nape.

When the kiss broke, they held each other's gaze for a moment before shedding their clothes. Crag stretched out beside her and pulled her naked body close to his. Their limbs entangled and Lily sighed, loving the sensation of his hard, hair-roughened legs against her smooth ones.

She kissed the pit of his throat and ran her tongue over his collarbones while massaging his chest. He felt so hard and powerful, yet the quickening of his heartbeat and the soft moan of desire deep in his chest reminded her that he was flesh and blood. Passion weakened and invigorated him the same as her. She had power over his strong, virile body and could make him gasp and writhe. Pleasuring him thrilled her.

She slipped down his body, covering his chest and abdomen with kisses. Her tongue traced each of his ribs and teased his navel. Sliding her arms beneath his thighs, she buried her face between his legs. She licked his balls, her lips gently tugging at the soft, hair-dusted flesh.

"Lily," he sighed, threading his fingers through her hair. In spite of his easy stroking, she sensed the tension building in his body and nearly smiled.

She ran her tongue around the base of his cock then licked every inch of it. As she lapped and laved, his rod thickened and glistened with her saliva. His breath rasped when she took the head between her lips and sucked vigorously. The fingers stroking her hair tensed, though he never grasped her too hard. She knew it must have been difficult as his passion increased. His belly clenched and his buttocks tightened. She gripped the base of his cock, holding it steady in her mouth as his hips thrust.

"Oh yes, Lily! Ah!" He panted. "You're going to kill me!"

She grinned as well as she could around his cock. Her pussy felt hot and drenched. Her belly tightened with desire, all from arousing him.

Running her tongue along the ridge beneath his cock head, she cupped his balls and squeezed. He groaned, a sound of delightful agony. Suddenly he pushed her away. She gazed at him, noticing flames of desire in his eyes as he tugged a pillow to the center of the bed. Grasping her waist, he gently placed her on her back, her buttocks on the pillow. He knelt between her legs and entered her with a long, slow thrust.

Lily's eyes slipped shut and she arched her head back, her fingers stroking her nipples as he thrust. One of his hands held her hip while the other covered her clit and rubbed. His thumb circled her engorged little nub, and Lily gasped, her body surging against his.

"You're so beautiful, Lily," he panted. "I could never grow tired of touching you, looking at you…"

"I love you, Crag," she murmured, lost in sensation.

Both his hands grasped her hips as his thrusting increased. Lily's body tensed, striving for fulfillment. A few more fast, steady thrusts and she exploded, her pussy clenching and pulsing around his cock. Crag drew a sharp breath as he came, lunging into her heated body.

Though lost in the sleepy, contented haze following her climax, Lily felt him slip from her and tug the pillow from beneath her bottom. He dragged her close to his chest as he lay on his side and kissed her hair.

"I love you, Lily," he murmured before they both drifted to sleep.

* * * * *

The day of the dubbing ceremony finally came. Crag spent the morning training with the other Knights and apprentices. Honey Wine, also a trained healer, brought Lily to the herbarium where they helped Sir Blaze with his mixtures, powders and teas. As dusk neared, Blaze brought Lily a new black tunic with a circle of red thorns embroidered around a ruby on the chest.

"To cloak the Jagged Peak," he said.

She ran her hands over the black silk. Crag's uniform, the clothing of a Knight.

Blaze excused himself to prepare for the ceremony that would take place after dark in the training field behind the fortress.

She brought the uniform to Crag's room—the room they'd share after marriage—and sat on the bed, her stomach fluttering at the thought of the dubbing. If she was this nervous, she could scarcely imagine how Crag felt.

The door opened, and he stepped inside. Having just come from the field, he wore trousers and a black vest—a common training uniform. The black material clung to his body with sweat, and moisture beaded his muscled arms. His hair was tied at his nape, but several damp locks curled against his forehead. His blue eyes glistened as he looked at Lily and smiled. He had the most adorable smile, and she was still unaccustomed to seeing it so often. Since leaving Tanek, smiling had been easier for both of them.

"Blaze sent this for you." She held the uniform out to him.

He glanced at it, placed it on the bed, and grasped her shoulders, kissing her deeply. She stepped closer to him, locking her arms around his neck, pressing her body so tightly to his that she felt moisture from his flesh seep into her cotton tunic. Late that night, they would share this room—this bed—as husband and wife. Lily could scarcely wait.

"I'll be leaving soon for the ritual bath before the ceremony," he said. "I won't be able to see you again until after the dubbing."

"Then we'll be married?"

"Sir Mahir has arranged to marry us in his private study once the feast is underway."

"This is so exciting, a dubbing and a wedding all in one night. Are you nervous?"

He shrugged, but she sensed he was a bit unsettled.

"I love you," she told him.

"I love you, too." He brushed a kiss across her forehead just as several sharp knocks sounded on the door.

Two Knights, green sashes about their waists, stepped inside.

"Jade, Court." Crag nodded to the lanky red haired and the shorter, blond Knight in succession.

"We've come for him," Jade said seriously, though his green eyes glistened with humor.

"Oh yes," said Court, stroking his blond beard, "he's ours from now on."

Smiling, she clasped Crag's arm. "I hope you gentlemen don't mind sharing him."

"With such a beautiful lady?" Court bowed deeply. "We're honored."

"Congratulations are in order for you both." Jade winked at her. "Sir Blaze has allowed you the next two days off, Crag, due to your new marital state."

"Sounds fine to me." Crag glanced at Lily, and they smiled at one another.

"Let's go." Jade held the door for Crag who picked up his uniform and stepped into the corridor. "We have to get you washed, dressed and ready to be dubbed."

"And married," added Court.

"Lady," both Knights said in unison, bowing politely from the neck.

"I'll see you after the ceremony." Crag glanced over his shoulder at Lily. Her own longing reflected in his eyes. She could have kissed Blaze for awarding him the next few days off.

* * * * *

As a fiancée of one of the newly dubbed Knights, Lily was allowed to stand in the front row closest to where the ceremony would take place.

Again, rows of a hundred Knights on either side formed a pathway at the head of which stood Sir Mahir, a gray-haired man of mid-height with wizened, aqua eyes. To his left was Sir Blaze and to his right, a very tall, black-haired man, smooth-shaven and handsome, with a slight overbite that lent him a look of youthful innocence. Lily guessed he was Sir Torn, Honey Wine's husband.

Onlookers stood behind both rows of Knights. There were hundreds of men, women and children waiting to watch the dubbing. The apprentices, soon to be Knights, stood single file at the end of the pathway. Forty men were to be dubbed that day, yet only one would wear the green sash, Crag.

Lily watched with anticipation as the first thirty men passed. Finally it was Crag's turn to walk down the pathway. As she watched him approach Sir Mahir and kneel, offering the leader the sword sheathed about his waist, she felt an incredible wave of pride and admiration. Crag had put such effort into his training and would be a wonderful Knight. He had changed — battled his own demons and won.

Sir Mahir spoke in a calm, cultured voice. "Do you swear to uphold the sacred vows of our Order — to render help to those who need it, to protect the weak, to abstain from the pleasures of the flesh until entering the sanctity of marriage and to respect all life?"

"I swear," Crag stated without hesitation, his deep voice resonant in the quiet field.

"From this day forward, you are one with our Order. You and yours are entitled to our protection." Sir Mahir touched the sword to Crag's neck. Lily noted that unlike many who kept their gaze lowered, Crag's blue eyes remained fixed on Sir Torn. Mahir continued, "Arise, Sir Crag, and join your brothers."

"Sirs," Crag said, still kneeling, his gaze sweeping Mahir, Blaze and Torn. "I relinquish my sword and all weapons, save my own hands which will be used only for defense."

Crag offered up his sword which would be mounted on the wall of the great hall along with the swords of all those who wore the green sash. Lily realized that, as he did this, she held her breath. Slowly, she released it.

Sir Torn took the sword from Crag, and Sir Blaze stepped forward, a smile on his lips as he placed a green sash around Crag's waist and tied it twice.

The auburn-haired Knight embraced Crag before allowing him to take his place with the newly dubbed behind Mahir.

When the ceremony ended, the crowd broke and made their way back to the fortress where food waited in the great hall.

Lily approached Crag and hugged him. "I'm so proud of you."

He kissed the top of her head. "I have to find Sir Torn. He's the one."

She raised an eyebrow. "The one?"

"The one who saved my life."

"You won't have to wait long. Here he comes with Honey Wine. I asked them to witness our wedding."

"Congratulations, Sir Crag," Honey Wine said.

"Thank you, Mistress." He bowed, using her formal title, but again his eyes were fixed on her husband. "Sir Torn, I never got the chance to thank you for saving my life."

"Saving your... I'm afraid I don't understand." Torn's sapphire eyes narrowed in confusion.

"I didn't think you would." Crag smiled. "In a village called Trentendine, I'd been fighting for Zaltana and was wounded. You not only saved my life, but inspired me to become a Knight."

"Apparently I did well." Torn nodded. "You've made Blaze happy, and I have no reason to doubt you'll continue to bring exemplary service to our Order."

"I had to thank you, Sir."

Torn smiled. "You're welcome." He glanced at Honey Wine whose arm was linked with his. "Now, I believe we have a wedding to witness."

Crag smiled at Lily and took her hand as they made their way to the fortress.

In the great hall, the smell of pungent smoke from the hearth and torches lining the walls mixed with fragrant incense, cooking meat, fresh bread, sliced fruit and sweet pastries. Everyone stood solemnly until Sir Mahir motioned for the festivities to begin.

The sound of laughter and conversation echoed through the stone walls, reaching as far as the corridors leading to Mahir's private study. Books filled the walls of the round, windowless room. A wooden table, also covered with thick leather volumes, stood in the center of the floor, scattered with worn rope rugs.

Blaze already waited there, smiling. "A perfect day twice as magnificent for you."

"Yes." Crag held Lily's hand tightly.

Sir Mahir entered, followed by Torn and Honey Wine.

"Thank you for agreeing to this, Sir," Crag told Mahir.

"It means so much to us," Lily added.

Mahir's blue eyes, stern yet kind, held hers as he offered a smile. "The marriage of one of ours is considered as sacred a ceremony as a dubbing. You've agreed to share your lives — no simple decision."

"Particularly when one has decided to marry him." Honey Wine pointed a teasing thumb in Torn's direction.

"Still angry because I beat you at that little archery challenge this morning?" Torn grasped his wife's hand. "Perhaps I should have let you win."

"Let me win? I beat you quite often. You should win once in a while, considering you're on the field every day and I haven't as much time for practice while handling affairs of state." Honey Wine tried to jerk her hand from Torn's grip, but he held fast and kissed the back of it.

"Excuses, excuses," he quipped.

"I'm sure the two of you don't bicker." Mahir winked at Lily and Crag.

They exchanged glances, and she said, "I believe we argued within hours of meeting."

"Well, don't expect it to end," Honey Wine told them. "It only gets worse."

"But other things get better." Torn glanced at the Mistress from the corner of his eye. She didn't speak, but her smile revealed underlying passion.

"Let's begin," Sir Mahir stated, "before all the food is eaten."

Lily and Crag stood in front of him, Blaze, Honey Wine and Torn behind them.

Mahir began, "We're here to witness the union of Crag and Lily. They've been joined by the Spirit and have accepted that joining. With the strength of the Spirit, I bless them as husband and wife. Crag, do you promise to be Lily's husband until the Spirit reclaims your soul?"

"Yes, I promise." Crag's voice was as firm and reverent as when he'd accepted his Knighthood.

"Lily, do you promise to be Crag's wife until the Spirit reclaims your soul?"

"Yes, I promise." She looked up at Crag, and he cast her a loving smile.

"I, Mahir of the Ruby Order, stand as witness and mediator between your souls and the Spirit. You are, from this day forward, husband and wife."

Crag placed a gentle hand behind her neck and kissed her, a soft, chaste kiss, but heated with the underlying promise of what was to come later that night, when they were alone.

Honey Wine hugged Lily, and Blaze and Torn offered their congratulations.

"I hope you both realize the jewels you've uncovered," Blaze said to Crag and Torn. "True love is rare. I almost envy—"

"I've told you for years to look for a wife." Torn grasped Blaze's shoulder and gave him an amiable shake.

"With so many spirits sharing their thoughts, it wouldn't be right. I'm a madman, they say, for more than choosing the way of the green sash."

"They don't know everything," Crag told Blaze.

"I fear matrimony shall not enter my circle."

"You never know," Lily told him. Surely some woman would be taken with Blaze's gentle heart and large blue eyes which knew everything yet observed with innocence and honesty. He was a good man, and Lily knew the right woman would count herself lucky to win Blaze's heart.

* * * * *

Crag and Lily remained in the great hall for a short time, not even bothering to eat. Unnoticed, they slipped upstairs to his chamber and locked the door behind them. While he kindled the fire, Lily turned down the sheets and undressed. Sitting on the edge of the bed, she brushed her hair and watched as he shed his uniform and draped it over the chair by the fire. Her heartbeat quickened at the sight of his broad shoulders and lean, muscled body. His thick, curly hair hung loose down his back and firelight reflected off the muscles in his long legs as he approached the bed.

He took the brush from her hand and ran it through her hair. Lily closed her eyes, enjoying the feeling of the brush interspersed with his stroking fingertips. Finally he put it aside and lifted her hair over her shoulder. She tingled as he pressed his lips to her nape.

He kissed down her spine while his hands stroked her ribs and hips. When he reached her lower back, he guided her to her stomach and knelt beside her. Using his palms to caress her buttocks, he continued covering her back with kisses.

Lily sighed, lost in sensation. His hands and lips felt so warm and gentle, yet she felt consumed by passion.

Crag's kisses covered the backs of her thighs and traveled down one of her calves until he reached her foot. Taking her foot in his hand, he massaged, his thumb caressing the arch while his other hand warmed her buttocks.

"Turn over," he said in a husky voice.

She did as he asked, watching through half closed eyes as he stretched out by her hips and guided one of her legs over his shoulder. He cupped her buttocks as his head dipped between her legs. Lily gasped when his tongue lapped her slit, slipping inside her and exploring with warm, tender strokes. Threading her fingers in his hair, she moaned, urging him on with husky words of desire.

He laved her clit, using the tip of his tongue to tease the side of it. Tension built deep inside her until she exploded beneath the rhythmic probing of his tongue. Crag continued his carnal exploration, drawing out her passion until she lay still, except for the rise and fall of her chest as her breathing returned to normal.

Stretching out beside her, Crag drew her body close as his stiff, velvet-skinned cock slipped inside her. Lily opened her eyes and stared into his as their legs entwined. She noticed the spark of passion beneath their calm depths and her belly tightened.

"I love you so much, Lily," he whispered, stroking her hair with one hand while caressing her shoulder with the other.

She swept her palm over his hip and kissed him. "I love you, too, Crag."

Their bodies moved together in a slow yet perfect rhythm. Both kept their eyes open, holding each other's gaze even as desire grew. Through her own passion-glazed stare, Lily noted his eyes becoming soft and dark as his orgasm neared. Her own was seconds away, yet she forced her eyes open as long as possible, reluctant to look away from the perfect male beauty of her lover's face.

Just before she exploded, he rolled onto his back, his hands clutching her hips, his cock never slipping from her sopping pussy. She straddled his waist, her palms gliding over hard pectorals and his flat, tight belly. Slipping downward so they were pressed breast to chest, she extended her legs and her toes wiggled against his.

Suddenly his hands slipped under her arms, and he guided her back to straddle atop him. His hands caressed her breasts, then grasped her hips as his own lifted to match her rhythm.

In a fluid motion, he switched their position, pinning her beneath him. She gasped, her heart pounding, teetering at the edge of her control. She briefly wondered how she'd lasted this long. Crag grasped her wrists and held them above her head as his lean hips thrust against hers. His mouth absorbed her gasp as his steely cock drove her to orgasm.

Even after he released her hands, she clung to him tightly as his tantalizing rhythm continued, pushing her toward another peak. His hands slipped beneath her and cupped her buttocks, one finger stroking and pressing the tender flesh between her bottom cheeks. Lily's heart raced as she exploded in another magnificent climax. At her moment of crisis, his breath rasped in her ear and he gasped her name as his body surged into hers.

Across the room, the fire burned low, and there was a chill in the air, fended off only by the warmth of their entangled bodies. Cuddling close, they drifted to sleep.

Chapter Thirteen

৯

Several months later, Crag and Lily were stationed in a village called Marin Point that had been nearly destroyed by a storm. A message had been sent to the Order explaining that most of their people had been killed or wounded and their food supply dwindled. They begged for assistance, and Mahir placed Crag in charge of the rescue mission. He and Lily filled a wagon with food and healing supplies. With four Knights apprentices, they headed south.

After several days of hard travel, they saw what looked to be ruins along the coast. Several tents and lean-tos were assembled, as were two large funeral pyres. Handfuls of men, women and children wandered about, looking thin and gray from exposure and lack of food.

All eyes turned to the party as they approached, though only a few neared the wagon.

A bearded man of medium height, his clothes dirty and torn, strode toward Crag. The man's dark gaze swept the group, and his stern face grew even colder.

"We've come from the Ruby Order," Crag explained as he climbed from the wagon. Lily and the trainees stood with him as he turned to the villager. "I'm Crag. This is Lily, Sand, Wade, Lot and Starr."

"That's all? Four of you and a woman?" The man, apparently in charge of Marin Point, curled his lip. "And only one of you is a real Knight?"

"Are you the leader here?" Crag asked, completely ignoring the man's insults.

"I'm called Phillipos, and yes, this village is my responsibility."

"Where are you keeping the injured and what repairs are already underway?"

Phillipos scoffed, "Injured are everywhere. Our healer was killed during the storm. As for repairs, we're still trying to clear away the wreckage."

Crag glanced at Sand, Wade and Lot. "You three organize the repairs. Phillipos, introduce them to your able bodied workers so the rebuilding can begin right away. Starr and Lily, come with me so we can set up the infirmary."

Crag moved forward, but Phillipos placed a rough hand on his chest. "Wait a minute. Who do you think you are? These people are under my care. They're not going to take orders from you."

"I'm not giving orders. I'm stating facts. My direction is necessary to get this village on its feet. You sent a message to the Ruby Order, did you not?"

"Yes, but—"

"We're here to help, as you asked."

"Great!" Phillipos tossed his hands in the air. "They send a woman, four trainees who look like they're scarcely out of swaddling and a supposed Knight who doesn't even carry a sword."

"My faction of our Order has forsaken the use of weapons," Crag replied. Lily marveled at his calmness. His experience in Tanek had taught him the value of patience and self-control.

Beside him, she clenched her fists and willed herself not to give Phillipos a piece of her mind. They'd traveled to help his village, and now he was arguing with Crag? Instead they could be spending time with people who'd appreciate their help.

"Wonderful," Phillipos muttered. "Our village is in ruins. Most of our warriors are dead. We needed the protection of the Order as well as repairs! What happens if we're attacked?"

"Then we'll deal with the situation. Right now, we need to—"

"Phillipos! The Knights have arrived?" A young man, his leg bound with a bloody rag, limped over.

"One Knight, Randal." Phillipos looked disgusted. "One who doesn't believe in fighting."

The youth tossed a curious glance at Crag. "But Knights of the Ruby Order are known for their strength in battle."

"Right now it looks to me like you need healers and builders." Lily could no longer keep silent in the face of such ungratefulness.

"Why exactly are *you* here?" Phillipos raised an eyebrow at Lily. "I didn't realize the Ruby Order accepted women."

"They don't. I'm Crag's wife."

Phillipos slapped a hand to his forehead. "His wife! Wonderful. Just what we need. Another useless mouth to feed."

"Since we've brought the food, it shouldn't matter to you," Crag told him.

"Food?" Randal stared at the wagon that stood in the center of the village. Several people had already started unloading the food supply.

"Lily is a midwife," Crag continued. "Her skills will be useful."

"Midwife," Phillipos muttered under his breath.

"Where's your well?" Crag asked.

Phillipos glanced at Randal. "Show him, will you? I have work to do."

"This way." Randal limped across the rubble.

"I'll take a look at that leg for you," Crag said.

"Thanks. I was in one of the houses when it collapsed," the young man explained. "This is the worst storm we've seen since I was a boy. Don't mind Phillipos too much. He was expecting more Knights."

"Our troops have been spread thin since the war with Zaltana. Many villages need assistance."

"So you really don't carry a weapon? Must make it difficult in battle."

"Crag is one of the Order's finest in hand-to-hand combat," Lily stated.

Randal raised an eyebrow. "We could use some training like that here. We lost our best fighters."

"Martial training will be included in the rebuilding," Crag told him. "We have no intention of leaving until your village is self-sufficient and stronger than it was before the storm."

The youth laughed. "You're asking for a lot."

"Nothing is impossible."

Crag's gaze met Lily's, and she smiled, remembering Sir Wood had once said the same thing to a certain doubting trainee. Nothing *was* impossible. She knew that better than anyone. Not even a year ago, she never thought she'd marry and have children again. Now she had a husband whom she loved deeply, and in a few months would have another child. She hadn't told Crag yet, fearful that he'd have insisted she remain behind while he was stationed in Marin Point, but she planned on telling him soon.

The first day was incredibly long and difficult, since the village had little organization. Though Phillipos was looked upon as the leader, he'd been greatly disheartened by the destruction and lack of resources before the storm. Other than one or two elderly women who practiced herbal remedies mixed with superstitious rituals, there wasn't a trained healer in the village. Many were hurt and ill, keeping Crag, Starr and Lily working nonstop. The other trainees were just as busy organizing the repairs.

It was well after dusk on the first night when Lily retired to the lean-to she shared with Crag. Tired from the work as well as the changes in her body, she fell asleep almost immediately, awakening only when Crag finally joined her.

"How late is it?" she murmured.

"It'll be dawn in an hour or two," came his sleepy reply. He crawled beneath the blankets and pulled her into his arms, kissing the top of her head. "Are you sure you don't regret coming?"

"I want to be with you, and I'm glad I can help—even if it does benefit that fool Phillipos."

She felt him smile against her hair. "He'll get used to the changes. So will the others. It's not easy thinking positively when you've been subjected to constant hardship. I learned that the hard way."

"You're such a good man, Crag." She turned and stroked his face in the darkness. "You're going to be a wonderful father."

"I hope so, when the time comes."

"In about seven months."

He fell silent for a moment, and she waited, her heartbeat quickening with apprehension.

"Crag? Are you happy?"

"Happy isn't a strong enough word." His arm tightened around her. "I love you so much, Lily... I... Are you crazy coming out here when you're having a baby! This place is—"

"Where we need to be. You and I together. That's the agreement we made. As you said, I'm a midwife now. I'll go where I'm needed, and right now we're needed here."

"It's so strange, but some of the worst events of my life brought me the best thing I ever could have hoped for." He kissed her, and she clung to him. His soft lips and rough beard moved down her neck. He freed her breasts from her shift. When his warm, moist mouth closed over one of her nipples and his hand kneaded her other breast, Lily clutched his head, arching against him.

His tongue flicked then laved her nipple. He used the very tip to circle the sensitive peak before moving to the other. Crag's fingers explored her pussy, gently stroking, pushing deeper, gathering wetness. He used his moist finger to circle her clit then ever so gently rub the ultra-sensitive side of it.

Lily felt her body heat and her heartbeat quicken.

"Crag," she whispered, clutching him harder. "Oh Crag!"

His beard tickled her belly as he kissed the gently rounded flesh. His fingers caressed the soft skin along the joining of her thighs and hips while his mouth covered her clit. As he lapped and stroked, two of his fingers slipped inside her and his other hand caressed her buttocks. He squeezed the firm globes then slipped a finger between them, pressing and stroking the soft flesh in a manner she loved.

Lily's belly clenched as he continued his relentless ministrations until she dissolved in ripples of intense pleasure. She writhed and her hands spasmed in his hair. He didn't stop licking, sucking and stroking until she lay, spent, beneath him. The perfect moment was disturbed by rustling outside the lean-to.

"Crag!" Lot called. "I'm sorry to bother you, but I need help in the infirmary."

"I'll be right there." He offered Lily an apologetic shrug before giving her thigh a final kiss and left the warmth of a bed in which he'd rested for too short a time.

Lily sighed, trying not to feel disappointed. Then she thought of how Crag must also feel. She didn't envy her husband's job, but she was proud of him. There were far fewer pregnant women requiring her care at the settlement than there were sick and injured for him. Still, they would have other moments in what she hoped would be a long life together.

Wrapping herself in the blankets, Lily closed her eyes and thought *Goodnight, Crag. I love you.*

* * * * *

Like the time spent in Tanek, the days and nights were filled with hard work, particularly for Crag, since he was the Knight of the highest rank stationed with a handful of trainees. Lily noted how well he handled his responsibilities, never succumbing to the despondency that had plagued him throughout his training. Like her, he'd learned to appreciate periods of happiness and relaxation while realizing the importance of his duty during difficult times.

Though he'd forsaken the use of weapons, Lily considered Crag one of the strongest men she knew. His power exceeded the limitations of those who simply wielded a sword, and she wasn't the only one who sensed it. Over the months they spent in the village, the people had grown to like the quiet, gentle Knight who cared for them through sickness and injury and worked tirelessly to rebuild their village. The trainees also worked to the best of their ability, building homes, gathering food, and teaching the able bodied youths to defend during troubled times in the future. Crag tempered his firm guidance with understanding. Once, several months into their stay at Marin Point, Starr mentioned abandoning his training.

"It's impossible here," Lily heard the young trainee say to Crag as they stood outside the infirmary. "I can't even get a single night's sleep, and many of these villagers are so ungrateful. They look at me like I'm useless because I'm a trainee."

"Do you feel useless?"

Starr sighed, and even from where she listened by the door, Lily felt his despair. "Sometimes I do. There's so much I don't know."

"So much to learn," Crag said. "Training isn't easy, but you knew that when you joined the Order. I do understand how you feel, and I promise what you do isn't useless. The ability to heal isn't just curing disease or setting bones. It's offering comfort and letting people feel they can depend on you."

"Sometimes I feel I can't even depend on myself. When that happens, who should I depend on?"

"I know you will always be able to depend on yourself, but I'm here for you and the others. Always."

"I know." Starr sighed. "I don't mean to complain."

"Get some fresh air. I'll stay here until you get back."

"But you've been in the infirmary since last night."

"Just go and center yourself. Someday I might come to you and ask the same favor in return."

Starr walked away, paused and glanced over his shoulder. "I want to be a credit to the Order, Sir."

"You will be. I believe in you. Why else do you think I requested you for this assignment?"

Starr's eyes widened a bit. "I didn't know that. Thank you, Sir."

Lily smiled to herself. Crag had been allowed to handpick his trainees, and she knew he'd always felt a particular liking for Starr. The young man was serious, careful and a quick learner. In many ways, he reminded her of Crag. The youth may have moments of self-doubt, but Lily sensed he would make a fine Knight.

"You're good," she said as Crag stepped into the infirmary. He raised an eyebrow. "You know what I mean, Crag."

"Starr is right, though. Phillipos' complaining hasn't made our task here any easier. Many are skeptical of us. I'm used to it, but it's a little harder on the trainees."

"They'll make it, just like you did. And if anyone can turn this village around, it's you."

Though it took time, Lily's prediction came true. Even Phillipos eventually thawed toward Crag and the others, particularly when he saw the Knights making good on their promise of complete restoration. Lily made many friends in the village. Ironically, her closest female companion became Phillipos' wife, Zea.

The women spent much time in each other's company, and Zea helped Lily make clothes for her baby. Lily often wondered how such a pleasant woman had gotten saddled with an arrogant, ungrateful man like Phillipos. Though she had to admit, the man hadn't said much to Crag or the others since he'd seen their determination to rebuild the village was not in vain.

One evening while Crag and Lily sat by the fire outside the infirmary, Phillipos approached with a loaf of nut bread his wife had made.

"Looks good." Lily gazed at the loaf. At this stage in her pregnancy, she was ready to eat just about anything. "Tell Zea thank you."

"I've always been a skeptical man," Phillipos began. "It's my nature, but I try to be honest, as well. I was wrong about you and Crag."

Lily glanced at the man with surprise. They'd been stationed in the village so long, she'd thought Phillipos was too stubborn to ever show any gratitude. She looked to Crag who simply held Phillipos' gaze, unwavering.

"You've done much for this village—things I never expected for us even before the storm. I still don't understand your refusal to defend yourself with a blade, but you're a strong fighter and have trained our people well. At first I didn't think you were much of a Knight, but I was wrong. Thank you for all you've done."

"You're welcome."

Phillipos nodded and headed back to his family's home.

"Never thought I'd hear him talk like that," Lily said, breaking off a chunk of the nut bread and chewing. "This is delicious. Want some?"

Crag shook his head. "Enjoy it."

Lily did, and it wasn't until several hours later that she began regretting it.

She nudged Crag awake.

"What's wrong?" he asked, rubbing a hand across his sleepy eyes.

"I don't feel well. I think that bread made me sick."

He sat up immediately. In spite of all his experience as a healer, the fast approaching birth of their child had him a bit on edge. At times he seemed to watch her as if she was a volcano waiting to spout its top. "Are you sure it's the bread?"

"Sure I'm sure," she sounded annoyed as the cramps in her stomach spread to her back. "Don't you think I would know if it's…?"

"What?" He lit a lantern and she met his wide blue eyes, offering a weak smile.

"It's not the bread. My water broke."

Lily, though thrilled she'd finally meet the child she carried, didn't look forward to the hours to come as she remembered how painful Vina's birth had been. Over the past months, she'd helped several woman deliver babies and had tried not to think of her own approaching confinement.

This child's entrance to the world came as a pleasant surprise. The labor took only a few hours, without any hard pain until just before the birth. Crag remained with her throughout, leaving the trainees in charge of the village. Zea offered her assistance, and while Crag delivered the baby, she sat with Lily, talking to her and offering a hand to hold.

Almost before she realized, Lily heard the infant's screeching, and she pushed herself onto her elbows, blinking damp hair from her eyes. She stared at the squirming baby in its father's hands.

"What is it?" she panted.

"It's a boy." Crag smiled as he cleaned off the infant and brought him to Lily, placing him in her arms.

Lily stared at their son, unable to resist a happy laugh. She thought briefly of Vina and how much she'd missed having a child to care for. She prayed this baby's life would be longer and happier than Vina's had been.

"Congratulations. He's beautiful." Zea smiled. "What are you naming him?"

Lily and Crag exchanged glances, and he said, "It's your choice. You did all the work."

"I think we should name him after his father."

Crag's eyes shone, and Zea laughed. "I guess you'll have to call them Crag One and Crag Two."

Zea held young Crag while his father delivered the afterbirth and made Lily clean and comfortable. After returning the infant to his mother's arms, Zea left the hut, giving the family privacy.

"She's right. He is beautiful." Crag gazed at the boy before kissing Lily's mouth and stroking random hairs from her forehead. "Thank you so much."

"Thank you." Lily smiled. "You've given me back a life I thought I'd lost forever, Crag."

"You've given me one I never imagined possible. I love you, Lily."

"I love you, too."

He sat beside her, their son in his arms. She drifted to sleep watching them, knowing that to both of them, their child symbolized hope.

There would be difficult times ahead—like the months in Tanek—but also happiness. No matter what happened, they had known each other's love and would carry it with them forever. To them, their affection would always be the greatest hope of all.

Epilogue
Four Years Later
Somewhere in the Chaston Ocean

❧

"Hold on!" Torn's boots slipped on the wet deck of a Ruby Order warship tossed in the stormy waves. He clasped Rain's hands tightly, their grips sliding as an enormous wave crashed overhead, nearly capsizing the sinking ship.

Lightning had struck a mast, pinning one of Rain's legs beneath it. Crag, Blaze and two other Knights strained against the wood. Rain's bellow of pain was swallowed by thunder as they managed to lift the mast enough to free his mangled leg.

Torn, Rain and a handful of other Knights had been sent to a small island off the coast of the Western Continent to bring home Crag and Blaze who had been ministering to villages ravaged by battles with Zaltana. Though they had been pushed out of Tanek, Zaltana still occupied most of the Western Continent and had turned their greed toward kingdoms farther away from Rubyshire and the Knights.

"We're going down fast and the lifeboat has already sunk!" Crag shouted above the roar of the storm, glancing at the Knights struggling to keep afloat in the water. "We'll have to swim for the shore!"

"Crag and I will swim with Rain!" Torn ordered. "The rest of you, go!"

"Forget about me!" Rain snapped. "You'll be lucky to save yourselves in this strong water!"

"Our guardian has arrived!" Blaze pointed off the bow.

"What the hell are you blabbering about?" Rain hissed through teeth gritted with pain as Crag bound his leg tightly. "Guardian of—"

"He's right!" Torn narrowed his eyes against the wet, cutting wind. A flash of lightning momentarily illuminated the black water, revealing a small ship headed toward them. "Swim for the ship! Crag, help me with Rain!"

The ship lurched. Blaze and several Knights leapt overboard and treaded water while Crag and Torn, Rain supported between them, jumped.

As they neared the boat, its captain, a powerfully built dark-skinned man with a shock of kinky brown and white hair, gave one of the Knights a hand up. Then he leapt into the water himself. A powerful swimmer, the captain joined Torn and Crag, taking the burden of Rain from them and swimming toward the ship, appearing unhindered by the weight of another man.

On deck, Crag and Torn, waterlogged and relieved as the others, approached Rain. Blaze already knelt beside him, tending his leg.

Blaze glanced at their brawny savior who had pulled himself on deck. He whispered, "Mate of the Key. He will join our ranks."

"I think you swallowed too much seawater," Rain snapped. Blaze tightened the bandage on his leg. "That hurt!"

Crag approached the captain who sat on deck, catching his breath. The man's pale blue eyes fixed on Crag. He panted in a voice laced with a SothSea accent, "How many of you were lost?"

"We're it," Crag told him gratefully. "We're all here."

"All?" The captain narrowed his eyes at his passengers.

"Circumstances being what they are with the battles with Zaltana, there were few to send on this mission," Crag continued, stooping to assist one of the Knights nursing an injured arm.

Blaze approached the captain and touched the man's thickly muscled arm. "You listened when the Spirits spoke. Thank you."

The shoreline loomed in the distance, and the captain managed to dock without crashing.

"He has skill," Crag mentioned to Torn as they helped Rain off the ship.

"Plenty of it," Torn agreed.

"I wonder who he is?"

"I'm sure we'll find out very soon."

The End

About the Author

⋅∽⋅

A lifelong fan of action and romance, Kate Hill likes heroes with a touch of something wicked and wild. Her short fiction and poetry have appeared in publications both on and off the Internet. When she's not working on her books, Kate enjoys dancing, martial arts, and researching vampires and Viking history.

Kate Hill welcomes mail from readers. You can write to her c/o Ellora's Cave Publishing at 1056 Home Avenue, Akron, OH 44310-3502.

Read an excerpt from:

Knights of the Ruby Order: Lock
Book 3
© *Copyright Kate Hill, 2004.*
All Rights Reserved, Ellora's Cave, Inc.

"What's going on?" Sparrow looked up from the cart of apples in the marketplace toward the ensemble of guards leading two wagons full of prisoners into Blue Hollow square.

"The bounty hunters have come to peddle slaves," Shea-Ann, Sparrow's closest friend and former nanny, explained. "We missed the bunch they brought last year. Maybe we could take a look at this group before the punishments start."

Sparrow glanced at Shea-Ann. Twenty four years Sparrow's senior, Shea-Ann had known her since the day she was born. Sparrow had been the third daughter in the royal house of an eastern kingdom overthrown three years ago by commoners. Not that Sparrow blamed them for the uprising. Her brother had been on the throne, and unlike Sparrow, he thrived on cruelty. Taxes were indescribable and punishments brutal. The royal family had been thrust out of power and her brother beheaded. Sparrow, once a princess, now ran a small farm in Blue Hollow, and though at times she missed her creature comforts, she'd never been happier. She was proud to earn her keep through hard work and enjoyed living in a village run by women. Sparrow had never loved life as a princess. She'd always felt guarded, overly-protected, and she disliked watching the damage her brother inflicted while being powerless to stop his greedy rampage. When she left home, Shea-Ann had accompanied her, no longer as a servant, but as a companion. The older woman was a fine healer and midwife, and the people of Blue Hollow demanded her skills as much as they clamored for Sparrow's corn, potatoes, wheat, and milk.

"Why do we need to look at slaves?" Sparrow asked. "We have two farmhands who help us, and the farm isn't so big that I can't handle it on my own when I have to."

"It's a good way to have a look at half-naked men." Shea-Ann's dark slanted eyes gleamed with mischief. The woman was small, scarcely reaching Sparrow's shoulder in height, her body slender and supple, her skin fine and pale. Shea-Ann had always enjoyed escapades with men, even in the palace. "I just don't like to watch the punishments. Such cruelty is usually unnecessary."

Sparrow chose a sack of apples, paid the cart owner, and slung her goods over her shoulder. "All right. We can go look, but do you want to finish shopping first?"

Shea-Ann shook her head. "Always thinking with your stomach instead of your womanhood."

The companions bought fruit, smoked meat, fabric, and wool from several other carts in the marketplace, then brought the merchandise to their wagon.

Together, they wound through the crowd of vendors, women leading horses to the village blacksmith, and children playing in the streets.

As they approached the platform in the center of town, two tall, golden-skinned, black-haired men strutted across the planks, seemingly unhindered by the shackles and chains on their ankles. The hard muscles of their nude, oiled bodies flexed as they struck poses. Raising their arms, they squeezed their fists and their biceps bulged. They turned, revealing corded muscles beneath the smooth skin of their backs and shoulders. Long, sinewy legs stretched into wide stances, their erect cocks saluting their audience as sizeable balls dangled beneath.

Murmurs of approval floated across the crowd of villagers watching the spectacle. Sparrow felt a blush rise in her cheeks as she tore her gaze from the men to glance at Shea-Ann who stared, a satisfied smile on her lips.

"Now this is what I call entertainment," said the older woman.

"I think it's a disgrace," Sparrow muttered, yet she watched in fascination as another slave— female this time—joined the men. A beaded vest concealed her breasts, and she wore a short leather skirt. Her wrists were manacled, and she bore the brand of murderer on her left bicep. A long, blond braid dangled over her shoulder as she paused in front of the men. One of them approached her from behind. She leaned her back against his muscled chest as he unfastened the ties on her vest so her breasts popped free. He squeezed the globes and rolled the nipples between his fingers while the other man knelt in front of her and lifted her short skirt. He ran a tongue over his lips before covering her clit with his mouth. The woman moaned, arching backward, lost in the ecstasy of one man's mouth and the other's hands.

"I can't believe this." Sparrow's lip curled with disgust.

"How much for the pair of them?" bellowed a short, gray-haired woman standing close to the platform.

One of the bounty hunters laughed. "Probably more than you could afford!"

"Give us a quote!"

"Fifteen hundred silver pieces for both of them."

"What about just one?" the woman shouted.

"Sorry. They're being sold as a set."

A lithe redheaded woman whom Sparrow recognized as a fur trader waved her hand in the air. "How much for the woman?"

The bounty hunter laughed. "So that's your flavor, is it, Miss? I'll let you have her for two hundred gold pieces."

The fur trader narrowed her eyes. "One hundred."

"Come now! Look at her! She's built for strength and endurance."

Sparrow noted it certainly appeared that way. The blond slave stood between the men, writhing with passion, her hands roaming over the bulging shoulders of the slave lapping her pussy. She tilted her head, biting the earlobe of the man squeezing her breasts and rubbing her nipples with the pads of his thumbs.

"One fifty!" the redheaded fur trader called.

"One seventy five!" the bounty hunter argued.

"All right, one seventy five!"

To the crowd's disappointment, the bounty hunter motioned for the other guards to stop the slaves' love play as he stepped down to settle the bargain with the fur trader.

"What are they doing now?" Sparrow asked Shea-Ann.

Two bounty hunters dragged a tall, blond man to the platform and chained him between two thick, wooden posts.

"Damn," Shea-Ann said. "The punishments are beginning."

"Let's get out of here," Sparrow suggested, but the crowd closed in behind them, pushing them nearer the platform.

One guard stood behind the prisoner whose face tensed with terror. The guard raised his whip and snapped it, slicing the blond's flesh. He gritted his teeth in silence for one more blow, but on the third slice he bellowed with pain.

The bounty hunter in charge of the auction returned to his place on the platform and called out to the crowd, "This man is a horse thief, wanted in the kingdom of Upper Kenna. Unless anyone wishes to speak for him, he will be punished up to fifty lashes!"

The whip hissed and the prisoner screeched.

A woman behind Sparrow said, "I think I'll speak for him. He looks big enough for wood cutting but was screaming like a tortured cat before the third lash fell. He'll be simple to control."

The woman's voice rose to a bellow. "I speak for him! I offer ten silver pieces!"

"The Emperor of Upper Kenna will give us twelve!" the guard called back.

"You're going to quibble over two lousy silver pieces when you'll have to drag his arse back to the Kennas, feeding him along the way?"

"A silver piece is a silver piece!"

The whipping guard pulled back his weapon, but the bartering guard held up his hand, signaling a pause in the beating.

"Eleven silver pieces. No more," the woman stated.

"Sold for eleven silver pieces!" The guard shook his fist in the air. "Cut him down, tie him up, and deliver him wherever this woman would like. Bring up the next prisoner!"

A shorter, thicker man with curly red hair was fastened to the posts.

"This man is wanted for highway robbery in Zaltana. He tried to strangle the wagon driver."

Another guard tore the shirt down the prisoner's back. The lash whistled in the air as the bartering continued. "Twenty five lashes is his punishment! Twenty five and the mark of a thief burned on his chest!"

"I was only trying to feed my family!" the redhead screamed as the lashes fell in rapid succession.

"Ten gold pieces!" A middle-aged woman called out. "What's in his pants alone looks like it's worth it!"

"Sold for ten gold pieces!"

"She's right about that," Shea-Ann whispered to Sparrow. "Looks like he has a tree branch in those breeches."

Sparrow raised her eyes to the heavens. "This is the most disgusting display I've seen since my brother was king. I'm going."

"Me too, in another moment."

Ten more slaves were paraded across the scaffold. Most were sentenced to whippings, some were tortured with hot pincers, some branded, and others stretched on a rack set up behind the whipping posts. Many women bought the prisoners out of their punishments, glad for free workers or bed mates, even if they were condemned. Slaves required little more care than animals, and the women of Blue Hollow liked their personal freedom. Some of the prisoners suffered longer than others, particularly the unattractive ones. Some were courageous and refused to scream while others screeched before the first strike landed.

"With all those bloody backs and burned body parts, my business will be flowing," Shea-Ann remarked. "Still, I can't believe some of these men are being bought. There are a few who deserve death."

"I've had enough of this." Sparrow was about to turn away when the next prisoner caught her attention. Though chained and shackled, it still took ten guards to drag him up the steps and hitch him to the poles. Tall and barefoot, he wore only a loincloth. His limbs were long and muscled, his broad chest and back littered with old scars. A shaggy gray and brown beard sprouted from his face, and dark, kinky hair streaked with white dangled over his shoulders and back in matted tendrils. His eyes, the pale blue of bird's eggs, shot defiance and rage but held no hint of fear.

Sparrow heard several women murmur over the man's raw beauty, but no one spoke for him. Strangely, the guard didn't announce the man's punishment or ask for a bid.

A third guard stepped forward, carrying a scourge consisting of several strips of knotted leather. The crowd grew quiet as the punishment began. Sparrow counted twenty five blows before she whispered to Shea-Ann, "I wonder why they haven't asked for a price on him?"

The smaller woman chuckled. "No one's likely to pay it. If I'm right, that's the pirate Lock the White. He's a devil. Any woman would be a fool to bid for him."

Sparrow glanced at the pirate's slashed back. Blow after blow fell until blood dripped down what was left of his skin, darkening his trousers and staining his boots. Other than a blinking of pale blue eyes and a sheen of sweat on his face and chest, the pirate revealed no sign of pain. Sparrow had lost count of the strikes of the whip, but she knew most men would have shrieked already.

"How much for him?" she shouted, scarcely recognizing her own voice.

Shea-Ann grasped her arm and hissed, "Are you crazy!"

"We cannot take a bid yet," the guard told her.

"Why?"

"He's sentenced to death, but if we sell him, the punishment is reduced to torture until he faints."

Sparrow's brow furrowed as she stared at the pirate's upright posture and stoic expression. He didn't look ready to scream, let alone faint.

Several moments passed before the first signs of pain appeared in the form of blood dripping down the pirate's forearms as he strained against the manacles holding his hands above his head. A second guard joined the beating, his whip wrapping around the pirate's waist, leaving a bloody trail over his stomach and side. He staggered almost to his knees, his arms stretched to the limit above his head. He struggled to right himself amidst the storm of knotted leather, his chest heaving with each ragged breath.

Sparrow's hands balled into fists, her heart pounding in her throat. The guard claimed this man's punishment wasn't death, but if the pirate didn't lose consciousness soon, the severity of the beating would surely cause internal damage.

"If you don't let me bid on him, he's going to be useless!" Sparrow shouted to the guard.

"These orders come from Zaltana. You know how their ruler feels about his word being obeyed. In case you don't know, woman, this is Lock the White, pirate, murderer, thief, and I wouldn't doubt rapist and child molester too, though those crimes have never been mentioned."

The crowd murmured. Several woman turned away from the sight of the pirate's shredded back. Sparrow wondered how he'd managed to stand again beneath the violent onslaught.

"Come on, let's go." Shea-Ann grasped Sparrow's hand and tugged. She jerked away from her friend.

* * * * *

Lock wondered how much longer his legs would support him as he jerked himself upward, using the manacles as leverage. He'd lost count of the blows long ago, and though he was accustomed to pain, he'd never felt anything like this. The guards wielded their weapons well, managing to make their whips land directly in previous cuts until he felt as if the blows were slashing at his very skeleton. He'd meant it when he'd said he'd rather die than be a slave, but with each strike of knotted leather, the idea of being shackled to a mistress became more appealing. When he heard that his punishment would continue until he passed out, he knew he wouldn't live to see the sun set. Lock had never fainted in his life, though there had been more than one time in his childhood when he'd wished for oblivion.

He tried focusing on the horizon, tried separating his mind from his body. Though he felt hot enough to dissolve into the cracks in the bloody platform beneath him, he resisted the urge to shiver, the urge to shriek. If he'd been a praying man, he'd have prayed for unconsciousness.

The beating stopped suddenly, and he was released from the post. He fell forward, managing to catch himself with his hands, agony hotter than the sun shooting up his arms, seeping into his shoulders and what was left of his back. Tears of pain sprang into his eyes, His vision momentarily darkened, but it cleared too quickly. He pushed himself to his feet as guards half-dragged him across the platform toward the rack. Beneath the deadly device, coals were arranged for the fire. The thought of heat against his torn flesh instilled a fear in him he'd never experienced before. His strength returned in a blind rush, and he pulled hard on his bonds, dragging both guards to their knees.

Several more bounty hunters jumped on him, grasping his chains and hauling him to the rack.

From somewhere in the crowd, he heard a woman's voice bidding on him, and he nearly laughed, giddy from pain and the realization that his nightmare - the one which had inspired him to spend years conditioning himself to torture - had actually come true.

One of the guards approached with a heated blade and carved symbols around both of Lock's arms. To keep from crying out, he bit his lips until he tasted blood, the smell of burning flesh making bile rise in his throat. If he vomited while strapped to the rack, he'd choke to death. *What a humiliating way to die*, he thought.

"How much is Zaltana giving you for him?" the same woman's voice called again.

"More than you can afford, Missy!"

The coals were lit beneath the rack, and as the heat grew, Lock struggled against his bonds. He gasped until his throat felt raw, his heart threatening to explode before the flames actually reached his flesh. The whip fell across his abdomen and he mewled, sickened by the pathetic sound but unable to force it back down his throat. Another whip flicked at his chest, but his limbs were pulled so tightly he couldn't so much as flinch.

Why hadn't he drowned with the rest of his crew? *Because that's how my life has been from the first. . .*

* * * * *

Sparrow stared in horror at the spectacle on the platform. She wondered how the pirate was still conscious when she felt ready to faint herself. What more could they do, short of killing him? The coals grew hotter, and she saw the first flames springing to life.

"I'll pay for him with jewels from the royal family of RedHorne!" she shouted.

Shea-Ann's jaw dropped. "You can't do that! It's all you have left from. . ."

Sparrow shot her a look that would have stopped a charging war horse in its tracks.

"That family was unseated years ago. How did you come by such jewels?" The bartering guard sounded suspicious.

"She was a RedHorne Princess!" one of the villagers called to him.

"I want to see the jewels, then," the guard said.

"Stop damaging him first." Sparrow stepped forward. "As it is, I'm already paying for destroyed merchandise."

The guard motioned for the flames to be doused and the torture to stop.

Sparrow approached the scaffold, unfastening the pouch on her hip. Though crime was uncommon in Blue Hollow, she'd always feared a random thief and the loss of the only ties left to her family, so when she ventured out for the day, she kept her jewels with her.

As she climbed the steps to the scaffold, she caught the reek of blood and smoke and nearly gagged. She glanced at the pirate. His eyes were unfocused with pain, his body slick with blood and sweat. She knew he'd committed terrible acts, but couldn't help feeling pity for his suffering. If they'd wanted him to pay for his crimes, why couldn't they have simply killed him and gotten it over with?

Sparrow turned her attention to the guard, extending her hand, her mother's ruby and sapphire necklace resting across her palm.

The guard snatched the bauble and inspected it closely.

"Nice," he said. "Very nice. Zaltana is willing to pay two thousand gold pieces for him. As beautiful as these jewels are, they're not worth quite that much. Nearly, but not quite."

"If you don't bargain with me, you'll still have to travel to Zaltana to collect payment. That's quite a distance, and you know how dangerous it is for strangers to cross Zaltanian land."

The guard pondered her words then nodded, his gloved hand closing over the necklace. "He's yours. Where would you like us to take him?"

"My farm several miles north of here."

He glanced at the group of guards. "Do what she says."

The guards unchained the pirate from the rack and hauled him to his feet. Disoriented, he took two unsteady steps before one of the bounty hunters kicked him down the scaffold stairs, dispersing the crowd. Lock landed with a grunt on his stomach. He braced his hands against the packed dirt, the muscles in his big arms straining as he attempted to raise himself. A second guard approached with a pail of water that had been heating beside the coals. He threw it on the pirate's mutilated back. The shriek of agony that sprang from Lock the White's throat made Sparrow shiver.

"So he is human after all," the bartering guard muttered.

Sparrow flung the man a vicious look before walking from the scaffold. The guards dragged Lock to his feet, wary of the pirate though he was far too weak to fight them again. Beneath his dark skin, his face was as pale as the streaks in his hair and beard. His eyelids flickered rapidly, and she wondered if he was fighting for consciousness or oblivion.

"This is going to be a disaster," Shea-Ann said from beside Sparrow. The small woman folded her arms across her chest and shook her head. "I cannot believe what you've done."

"Don't tell me you didn't feel a little sorry for him."

"I feel sorry for the people he's hurt, too, but somehow I doubt he has any regrets. You, better than anyone, should know that."

Sparrow's chest tightened. Shea-Ann was right. Sparrow knew first hand the damage a man like the pirate could visit on decent people, such as herself. By rights she should have reveled in his pain and destruction, but her fury was reserved for one man alone. Lock the White had nothing to do with her - until the moment his stubborn strength had touched an unexplored part of her spirit and driven her to this unthinkable deed.

"One more thing, Missy." The guard Sparrow had paid approached her with a wicked smile. "You are aware of Empress Daryn's law?"

"What law?" Sparrow lifted an eyebrow. In truth, she'd always avoided the slave trade and knew nothing of the laws surrounding it.

"Anyone who purchases a prisoner wanted for murder agrees that should he escape, she will take his punishment for him."

"Death?" Sparrow felt a little sick.

The guard shook his head. "No. It would never be death. Empress Daryn isn't unnecessarily cruel. You must take his lesser punishment, the one used during bartering."

"Tortured until I faint?"

"That's the one, Missy." The guard smiled brightly. "Nice doing business with you."

The bounty hunters cleared the remainder of prisoners back to the wagons, but Sparrow remained planted at the bottom of the scaffold.

Shea-Ann clicked her tongue. "Now you've done it! That's what you get for having such a soft heart. Compassion has always been your worst fault."

"You should talk! You're the healer. I'm just a farmer."

"A farmer who has responsibility for Lock the White, the worst pirate to ever sail out of the Archipelago of SothSea!"

Enjoy the following excerpts from:
Ellora's Cavemen:
Dreams of the Oasis I
Featuring:
Myla Jackson, Liddy Midnight, Nicole Austin, Allyson James, Paige Cuccaro, Jory Strong

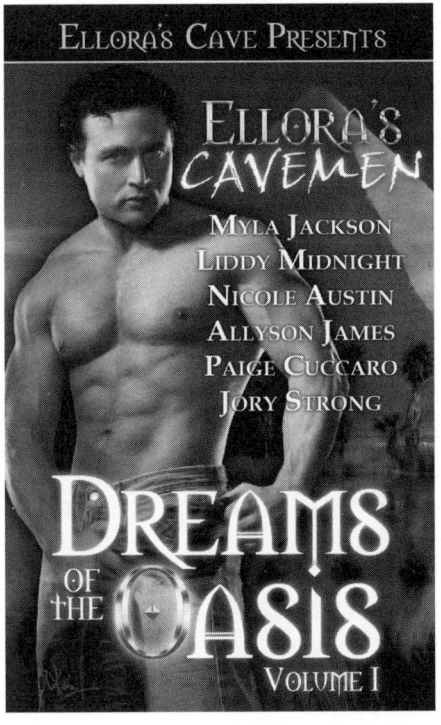

A special edition anthology of six sizzling stories from Ellora's Cave's Mistresses of Romantica. Edited by Raelene Gorlinsky

THE AMBASSADOR'S WIDOW
Copyright © MYLA JACKSON, 2006.
All Rights Reserved, Ellora's Cave Publishing, Inc.

"Okay, give me everything you've got." Andre settled in his seat on the small Lear jet blasting through the sky en route to Padel. Having showered at the hangar, he wore sweats and a T-shirt, preferring to make the transformation in clothing that didn't bind and had a little give.

Sean O'Banion leaned over Andre and pressed a button on the panel above him. A computer screen dropped down and blinked to life. "Here's all the footage we could muster on the man and we provided notes from one of our operatives on the inside."

"What about DNA?"

Melody handed him a jacket with several brown hairs scattered across the shoulders. "Try this. It was the jacket they found on him when he died."

Andre turned the jacket over. Armani. The guy had taste.

"No one saw him croak but our operative. We think we got him out in time, the press didn't get wind."

Andre knew how the agency worked. The less the press knew, the more easily a Chameleon blended in.

"For now." Melody sat in the leather seat next to Andre and crossed one leg over the other. "But we can only hold them off so long. When the ambassador doesn't show up for the meeting tomorrow morning, the media will be all over it."

"So how much time does that really buy us?" Andre's gaze remained on the screen.

"Since only our operatives know he's dead, we have until he doesn't show up in his room tonight."

"Why should that matter?"

"His wife will worry."

"Wait a minute. You guys didn't say anything about a wife." Andre leaned back in his chair and held up his hands.

Melody laid a hand on his arm. "Keep your shirt on, big guy. They're somewhat estranged."

"Somewhat?" Andre's eyebrows rose. "Define 'somewhat'."

"Insiders say they sleep in separate rooms and as far as anyone knows, they haven't made love in months."

Muscles knotting in his belly, Andre had a sudden feeling of being trapped. "You know how I feel about widows. I don't do widows. You can turn this plane around right now. I'm not doing it."

CALL ME BARBARIAN

Copyright © LIDDY MIDNIGHT, 2006.
All Rights Reserved, Ellora's Cave Publishing, Inc.

"Oh, look! The gladiators are up next! You should hear the buzz among the women, about the two brothers from Sudania. They are quite the swordsmen, if you know what I mean." Her arch expression made me look at her a little more closely.

"Really?"

Before I could pursue this line of inquiry, fighters entered the arena and I became distracted, too busy admiring their oiled muscles and strutting bodies to start up a gossip session. As a rule, I understand, gladiators are a vain and rutting lot, but oh, are they gorgeous!

The southern brothers led the second round. From the moment they stepped forward, they dominated the arena. They moved with confidence and a charismatic quality that kept all eyes on them. Their peers and opponents paled in comparison.

My pulse quickened and I could not tear my attention away, even when Tilda touched my elbow.

I could understand the excitement generated by their bouts in the ring, for they were in truly excellent shape. Not overdeveloped, as some bodies in the arena appear, but balanced and fluid in their movements. I admired their tanned skin and what looked to be strong profiles, although their faces were mostly hidden by their half-helmets.

Dark hair flowed down their backs, worn longer than is customary in the ring—especially as they favored trident and net as weapons. Those permit the wielder to capture his opponent's weapon and render it useless, then move in to grapple hand to hand. Close fighting can be dangerous with long hair, as it gives an opponent something to grip. Flexible as eels, the brothers eluded every attempt to hold them and won the ensuing wrestling matches in short order.

Flowers and coins showered into the arena as the crowd awarded them the victories. They had mastered what I call the "winning strut", the victory lap that every winner takes around the arena, to cheers and catcalls.

When they turned to acknowledge the Emperor and removed their helmets, my breath caught in my chest.

SPONTANEOUS COMBUSTION

Copyright © NICOLE AUSTIN, 2006.
All Rights Reserved, Ellora's Cave Publishing, Inc.

"Tell me your deepest, darkest fantasies."

The words were breathed in a husky, sultry tone against Maddy's ear. Warm breath caressed her neck, raising the fine hairs at her nape and sending chills coursing down her spine.

She didn't have to turn around, knowing instantly to whom that deep sexy baritone voice belonged. How she would love to provide explicit graphic details of her most intimate fantasies for him. Or better yet, maybe they could act them out.

"Come on. Tell me, babe. What is it? Being bound to the bed, or maybe oiled up on a Slip N' Slide? Do you dream of sweet lovemaking, or hard fucking? One lover or several?"

Icy shivers prickled along her skin. Just the sound of his voice, his erotic words, had her nipples puckered and pressing against the bodice of her little black dress. She had worn it in hopes of catching his eye. Not that he would ever notice Maddy as a woman. His buddy, sure. A woman, never. His words were all in jest as usual, right?

"How much have you had to drink tonight, Jake?" she questioned, then gasped as he licked a hot wet path along the ultrasensitive skin behind her ear.

"Stop it, Jake!" Maddy squealed in protest. Of course, stopping him was the last thing she wanted to do. But giving in meant risking both heart and soul. She couldn't stand the thought of being rejected by this man, the only one who really mattered.

Jake Cruise had been her best friend and neighbor since college. They had shared everything. Well, almost everything. She couldn't share her true desires with him, could she? As if he'd ever want to have sex with her. He was such a tease.

Maddy gave herself a mental shake. What was she thinking? Of course she couldn't. It would ruin their friendship. Probably freak him out to hear her dark, forbidden passions.

DRAGONMAGIC
Copyright © ALLYSON JAMES, 2006.
All Rights Reserved, Ellora's Cave Publishing, Inc.

Arys felt his dragon body turn inside out, then there was a bright light and he was standing, naked, on two human legs inside a cozy, one-room cottage.

"Damn witch," he growled at the voluptuous woman bent over the fire. "What do you want now?"

The witch Clymenestra stood up calmly, eyeing him with her usual smugness. Arys was tall, with bronze-colored skin over hard muscle, waist-length white-blond hair, and dragon silver eyes. Clymenestra looked him over like she owned him.

The bitch knew his true name and could call him from Dragonspace anytime she liked. *Not forever, darling*, he thought. *Not forever.*

"I need dragon's blood," she said, letting her gaze rove his body.

"Always blood. What is your spell this time?"

"Never you mind." She looked at him with dark, possessive eyes. "I hold you, dragon, and you'll give me your blood." She smiled. "I'm always willing to pay for it."

He knew her thighs were wet with her cream, her opening hot, anticipating. Arys' cock was already swollen and hard, standing straight out from his body. His long hair warmed his back, but his arms prickled with cold in the night air. Human skin was too damn thin.

Clymenestra had bound him to her with the magic of his name—but one day, one day, he'd be free. He knew the secret of his freedom, she didn't.

"So you called me all the way from Dragonspace for a drop of blood?" he growled. "I was deep in important business."

"Two drops. And you were lying on your back in the snow, sunning yourself. Silver dragons are the laziest things in creation."

Arys didn't deny this. In his dragon form, he lived to eat and hoard and mate as often as possible. He also worked his own kind of magic, which was lightning fast, like a fiery needle in his brain.

He loved dragon magic. Human magic was too much like work.

FALLEN FOR YOU

Copyright © PAIGE CUCCARO, 2006.
All Rights Reserved, Ellora's Cave Publishing, Inc.

"You think they'll try to kill me?"

"Yes." Zade wouldn't look at her. His gaze fixed on the streetlamp across from Isabel's bedroom window. The light's honey glow was a safer sight by far than the little witch drifting toward sleep behind him in the dark.

He was a Watcher, a once-mighty angel, and still this woman could bring him to his knees with a negligent sigh. Zade clenched his jaw, his hand fisting around the Roman coin he always carried in the pocket of his slacks.

Her soft, sleepy voice already had his cock as stiff as a Watcher's sword. And the scent of her sheath was only a wicked tease of how perfectly she'd fit his blade. His dick twitched at the thought, but he pushed the erotic image from his mind.

A rustle of covers, like the sound of a warm body rolling in bed, teased behind him. "Why now?" she said.

"Your skills have grown these past months. All those attuned to the ancient power will have felt your touch. You are a threat to the Oscurità as well as a temptation."

Her small snort was muffled in the pillows. "And here I was only hoping to tempt you."

Zade's nails dug into his palms, every muscle in his body coiling tight. He closed his eyes and reached soul deep for the strength to deny his need. He was here to ensure her safety and train her in the use of the ancient power—nothing more.

Isabel and her kind were the key to destroying the Oscurità, the prideful fallen angels. A mission he and his Watcher brothers had failed to achieve so long ago. For ten thousand years they'd suffered the punishment for their ill-fated complacency. Sentenced to an eternity linked in name and penalty with those they'd been sent to destroy.

She and her witch sisters were the Watcher's second chance and Zade would let nothing distract him this time.

THE JOINING

Copyright © JORY STRONG, 2006.
All Rights Reserved, Ellora's Cave Publishing, Inc.

Rumors abounded of women not only being taken to brothels or sold as slaves, but of ending up on the nearby planet of Adjara, where the men formed marriages with each other, and needed a woman only long enough to produce a child for them.

Siria shivered. Little was known about Adjara. It was primarily a desert planet, harsh, unforgiving, closed to outsiders. Few in their right mind would attempt to go there, though the dream of gaining riches beyond measure by exploring the small range of mountains for rich deposits of precious stone had lured many to their deaths.

Her mother had been fascinated by Adjara, making it a game in the evenings to search though whatever news reports could be captured using their ancient computer. Telling Siria that her ability to locate water would make her a princess in such a place.

Once her mother had even found a rare picture of an Adjaran without the trademark robes and face covering they wore even when they weren't in the desert. He'd been stripped to the waist, his body bronzed by the sun, lean and fit from life on a planet where the weak didn't survive, one arm covered from shoulder to hand with exotic tattoos. Siria closed her eyes, remembering that day.

"Here's a prince to your princess," her mother teased.

"And what about the rumors of women being used to produce a child and then being disposed of?"

"I'm not so quick to believe them," her mother answered with a shrug. "Look at the rumors that abound on Qumaar!"

"You win. Of course, what makes the rumors about Qumaar so frightening is that the truth is often more horrifying!"

"True. Now admit he's handsome at least," her mother pressed, running her finger over the computer screen.

Siria knew when she was beat. "I'll admit it. He's handsome."

"And if rumor is true, he comes with a second man."

"Mother!" Siria yipped, her face flaming, only to realize by the play of expressions on her mother's face that she hadn't intended it to be a sexual comment. But once she did realize how her comment had been interpreted, her mother's laughter filled the room, contagious and fun, irresistible, and they'd both ended up in tears, holding sides that ached from their amusement.

"Still," Siria said, when they finally stopped. "No one has ever heard of a woman going to Adjara and leaving again."

Her mother shrugged. "The same could be said, except in reverse, for Qumaar. No one who leaves here is ever heard from again."

Why an electronic book?

We live in the Information Age—an exciting time in the history of human civilization, in which technology rules supreme and continues to progress in leaps and bounds every minute of every day. For a multitude of reasons, more and more avid literary fans are opting to purchase e-books instead of paper books. The question from those not yet initiated into the world of electronic reading is simply: *Why?*

1. ***Price.*** An electronic title at Ellora's Cave Publishing and Cerridwen Press runs anywhere from 40% to 75% less than the cover price of the exact same title in paperback format. Why? Basic mathematics and cost. It is less expensive to publish an e-book (no paper and printing, no warehousing and shipping) than it is to publish a paperback, so the savings are passed along to the consumer.

2. ***Space.*** Running out of room in your house for your books? That is one worry you will never have with electronic books. For a low one-time c ost, you can purchase a handheld device specifically designed for e-reading. Many e-readers have large, convenient screens for viewing. Better yet, hundreds of titles can be stored within your new library—on a single microchip. There are a variety of e-readers from different manufacturers. You can also read e-books on your PC or laptop computer. (Please note that Ellora's Cave does not endorse any specific brands. You can check our websites at www.ellorascave.com or

www.cerridwenpress.com for information we make available to new consumers.)

3. *Mobility*. Because your new e-library consists of only a microchip within a small, easily transportable e-reader, your entire cache of books can be taken with you wherever you go.

4. ***Personal Viewing Preferences.*** Are the words you are currently reading too small? Too large? Too… ANNOYING? Paperback books cannot be modified according to personal preferences, but e-books can.

5. ***Instant Gratification.*** Is it the middle of the night and all the bookstores near you are closed? Are you tired of waiting days, sometimes weeks, for bookstores to ship the novels you bought? Ellora's Cave Publishing sells instantaneous downloads twenty-four hours a day, seven days a week, every day of the year. Our webstore is never closed. Our e-book delivery system is 100% automated, meaning your order is filled as soon as you pay for it.

Those are a few of the top reasons why electronic books are replacing paperbacks for many avid readers.

As always, Ellora's Cave and Cerridwen Press welcome your questions and comments. We invite you to email us at Comments@ellorascave.com or write to us directly at Ellora's Cave Publishing Inc., 1056 Home Avenue, Akron, OH 44310-3502.

THE
☥ ELLORA'S CAVE ☥
LIBRARY

Stay up to date with Ellora's Cave Titles in Print with our Quarterly Catalog.

TO RECIEVE A CATALOG,
SEND AN EMAIL WITH YOUR NAME
AND MAILING ADDRESS TO:

CATALOG@ELLORASCAVE.COM

OR SEND A LETTER OR POSTCARD
WITH YOUR MAILING ADDRESS TO:

CATALOG REQUEST
c/o ELLORA'S CAVE PUBLISHING, INC.
1056 HOME AVENUE
AKRON, OHIO 44310-3502

Make each day more *EXCITING* With our

Ellora's Cavemen Calendar

www.EllorasCave.com

Cerridwen, the Celtic Goddess of wisdom, was the muse who brought inspiration to storytellers and those in the creative arts. Cerridwen Press encompasses the best and most innovative stories in all genres of today's fiction. Visit our site and discover the newest titles by talented authors who still get inspired - much like the ancient storytellers did, once upon a time.

Cerrídwen Press
www.cerrídwenpress.com

Discover for yourself why readers can't get enough of the multiple award-winning publisher

Ellora's Cave.

Whether you prefer e-books or paperbacks,

be sure to visit EC on the web at
www.ellorascave.com

for an erotic reading experience that will leave you breathless.